Inception

By Steven F. Deslippe

This is a work of inspired pure fiction.

Names, characters, places, incidents, and remote possibilities, either are the product of the author's wild imagination or are used fictitiously, and any actual resemblance to persons, living, dead or existing in ethereal form, business establishments, events, or locales, is entirely coincidental.

© 2017

Edited By: Edit This One, LLC., Fairfax, IA.
www.editthisone.com

Published By: Edit This One, LLC d/b/a Wordy Gerty Publishing

Wordy Gerty Publishing

The original image used and modified for the cover of this novel was taken from the website www.pixabay.com whereas it has been released free of copyrights under Creative Commons CC0

ISBN 978-0-9981046-3-8

E-mail contact: sdeslippe@sympatico.ca

Acknowledgements

*** A special thanks to Tina Rosekrans (Edit This One, LLC) for taking the time to proof read, make suggestions and edit this novel. Without her help, this novel more than likely would never see the light of day and it would probably just stay on my computer for no one else to read. ***

*** I would also like to acknowledge those authors whose work I not only thoroughly enjoy reading, but have inspired me to work hard at this craft and put forth the best possible story I could — Steve Perry, Stephanie (S.D.) Perry, Nyx Smith, Diane Carey, William Shatner, Stieg Larsson, Sherrilyn Kenyon, Laura K. Hamilton, Kevin J. Anderson, Kristine Kathryn Rusch, David R. George III, Dayton Ward, Michael A. Martin, David Alan Mack, Una McCormack, Keith R.A. DeCandido, Jana Oliver, Kristen Beyer & Christopher L. Bennett. ***

About the Author

Steve F. Deslippe was born in Canada on September 24th, 1966. He grew up in a rural community, right next door to his Grandparent's farm, just outside of the town of Amherstburg, Ontario.

Farming wasn't of interest to him, but music was. Beginning in late 1987, and lasting for fifteen years, Steven worked as a disc jockey, playing music and emceeing weddings, parties, dance clubs, rock clubs and gentleman's clubs. It was during this time period where he discovered a passion for reading and writing — both of which he admittedly did not like, nor was very good at when he was younger. But as the years went on by, and the more he wrote, not only had his skills greatly improved, a self-confidence that had never been there before, had appeared.

The result of this new found belief and dedicated hard work, now forever captured in his very first novel.

How this story came to be...

The initial concept of this book came from my warped mind more than twenty-five years ago. To this day every so often, but especially during the early years of my adulthood, I would suffer with bouts of insomnia — and usually, this would take place over a period of several successive nights. During one of those three night episodes, I decided to dreamscape, in hopes that it would help me to focus my mind so that I could then relax and fall asleep. Unfortunately, it did not work. But by the end of night two, the story that I had created in my mind was too good to let fall into the abyss of untold tales. For that reason, I decided to try and document what I had created in my mind.

English, like a lot of school subjects, was not so easy for me to grasp — which is one of the reasons why I never felt confident enough to further my education. So when I began to write my first story, the initial draft was just a basic fifty page, he said, she said; he did, she did, type of script. And although I believed that the story had a lot of potential, I was smart enough to realize at that point it was nowhere near good enough to let someone read. So I just put it aside for awhile.

However, because I had written that story, I suddenly found myself wanting to pick up a book. And although the classic works of the past didn't really interest me, modern science fiction did. That was when I had decided to read my first novel (outside of the ones that I was forced to read in school), strictly for pleasure. That novel was William Shatner's Tek War. By the time I had completed the third book in the Tek War series, I felt that I was ready to attempt a re-write of my story.

Although I was happier with my expanded re-write and the new direction that the story took, I still knew that it was nowhere near good enough, so I again put it aside. Needless to say, it took about another two years and about twenty more novels read before I felt confident that a significant improvement to my story would come from a third re-write.

Once I had completed it, I decided that it was finally time to have someone else read what I had created. So I had asked a friend, whom I was working with at the time, to read my story. Not only was that friend nice enough to spend her free time reading what I had written, she graciously took the time necessary to make corrections and suggestions, followed then by her honest opinion of my story. For the most part, it had been positive. It felt good to hear someone say that your story was very interesting and had the potential to maybe one day, being great.

Without a doubt, I can definitively say that moment was the catalyst that motivated me to work much harder than I ever had before, both on my English skills and my ability to tell a good story.

The end result, consisting of many more re-writes, did not come easy to me. I am one of those individuals who cannot absorb something simply by seeing or hearing it one time — I learn by repetition. It is why this first novel of mine has taken as long as it has to complete, as I tend not to be satisfied, believing that it could always be just a bit better.

There are those who would probably say that continually having to re-write a novel as many times as I had (nearly twenty times), should have been enough of a disincentive to just give up instead of wasting a good portion of my life trying to get it right. To those who believe that, I say... you are wrong. What I have just accomplished is something that I can be very proud of; something that I would have never dreamt I would have ever been capable of when I was much younger.

Was this a lot of work? Definitely! Did I squander a good portion of my life doing this? I don't think so. In fact, I personally feel that by re-writing this first book as many times as I have, I've not only learned how to properly express myself; and not just when it comes to writing, but I have also, without a doubt, strengthened my knowledge and drastically improved my skills when it comes to the English language, as well as bettered myself as a human being.

I hope you the reader, enjoys the results of my many years of hard work. ~ Steven F. Deslippe

*** I have included this quote below, because I find these words to be a very fitting analogy pertaining to many of the characters, as well as the storyline, of this and all of the planned subsequent novels ***

"Every man's heart one day beats its final beat; his lungs breathe their final breath. And what that man did in his life makes the blood pulse though the body of others. It makes them bleed deeper in something larger than life. Then his essence, his spirit will be immortalized by the storytellers, by the loyalty; by the memory of those who honor him and make the running the man did live forever."

(Quote from James Hellwig, a.k.a., the Ultimate Warrior, spoken on April 07, 2014, one day before he passed away.)

Introduction

We only wish to live a long and prosperous life in a community in which we feel safe. For some of us, our career path is thus chosen because of that desire. Alas, that yearning to solidify our reasons for doing this could over time, end up evolving into an obsession; inadvertently shaped and influenced by extenuating circumstances. And when that happens, those clear cut lines between right and wrong suddenly become indistinguishable, leaving the possibility of understanding and escaping what they have allowed themselves to become a part of, nearly impossible to do.

Detroit, Michigan, for generations, has been plagued with a stigma — and rightfully so. Decades of political ineptitude, financial irresponsibility, and a documented history of violent crimes against its fellow citizens have given the city a reputation for being a very dangerous place to live, work, or even visit. All of it unfortunately, unintentionally supported by severe economic hardships, and media exposed melodrama.

However, at the very beginning of the twenty-first century, several predominant local business men stepped to the plate to try all on their own to revitalize the city that they loved. They began to invest in it by buying up abandoned landmarks, dilapidated properties, and even making the bold move of relocating their own offices to the downtown core. It was an inauspicious beginning for them, but one nevertheless that did not take too long for the public to support and rally behind. They praised these brave individuals for their desire to restore the luster of this once classic American city; a city which had for so long been left out in the back alley to rust like an old car, rot like a pile of garbage, and fade from memory like those afflicted with Alzheimer's.

There were many critics who believed that those business men were crazy to commit clear economic suicide by investing in what they all thought was a city beyond hope. But within a matter of only a handful of years, the gradual rebirth of it could easily be seen — and not just within its downtown core. Soon, more businesses followed on the coattails of these brave initial investors, and it wasn't very long before this city, that had not too long ago been written off, begun to show signs of a rebirth.

Although the violent crimes that the city had become famous for had not subsided as much as had hoped, its people, and others from outside, no longer shied away from visiting or working there. Finally, after feeling like an abandoned child for so long, the people of Detroit could begin to hold their heads high and proclaim who they were and where they lived without feeling one bit of shame.

For an officer of the law, the city's turnaround had done a lot to ease the biggest concern about their job — their own safety. However, like any city in the United States, they still had its typical issues to deal with. One such issue was the long-standing existence of the Detroit Underworld Organization (the D.U.O.). Unlike the mafia that exists in New York, New Jersey, Philadelphia, or Chicago, the Detroit Mob wasn't known for murder. It was known for smuggling, extortion, and various kinds of white-collar crimes, because its main objective was to get filthy rich while flying under the radar as much as was possible.

For twenty-five years, Vance Palmalino had run the organization. He was an eighth generational, whose grandfather Mario Palmalino had started the organization shortly after he had immigrated to the United States. Although it wasn't considered an actual mob back then, Mario had been the leader of the city's most notorious gang of thieves; a gang that had evolved from petty theft, to grand larceny and extortion. Mario's twenty-five year old son, Angelo took over the family business when Mario had unexpectedly died at the age of fifty-five. It was he who then took the group from being a feared gang of thieves, to a legitimate mob organization. Angelo had officially christened his organization the D.U.O. and then ran it until the age of seventy. He could have continued to effectively run the family business, but chose to step away and retire — his son Vance took over from that moment forward.

Unlike his father and grandfather, Vance never had a son; he only had a daughter, Madonna Palmalino, who disavowed herself from the family business the moment she turned eighteen and moved away, leaving Vance without a willing heir to one day take over the reins.

And it was because of this well known fact that Vance's closest, trusted associate, Antonio Marcone, began to hatch a plan.

Antonio knew that he would be the next in line to take over the D.U.O., if and when Vance Palmalino decided to retire or had unexpectedly passed away. Antonio had always been driven — that was how he had ascended through the ranks of the organization to begin with. An immense amount of patience however, was never something he ever had. Antonio did not want to wait to inherit what he felt rightfully was going to be his. He knew that it could be another twenty years; maybe even more, before the leadership of the organization was handed over to him, as Vance Palmalino had only just turned fifty and still had a lot of productive years ahead of him. So, Antonio Marcone took matters into his own hands and kicked the door open himself. It was a very risky move on his part, but it was the only logical course of action that he believed he could take — it was the only way for him to ensure that he got what he wanted.

It took a lot of careful planning, some luck, and the right people having their palms greased. It was calculating, cunning, and underhanded — and it worked flawlessly. Antonio Marcone had successfully made Vance Palmalino, his mentor disappear from existence.

1

*~ We all have a pre-determined destiny to fulfill. But on
occasion, something unforeseen will happen which will alter the path
that we were supposed to take, thus allowing our lives to take on a
much more important meaning than what it was originally supposed to
be. ~*

April 1st, 2007 — Holy Cross Cemetery

This was an unfortunate aspect of the job, burying one of their
own. When a person takes an oath to serve and protect, there is always
a possibility that they will lose their life in the line of duty. Though
the likelihood of this happening is a foregone conclusion, it is a finality
that any police officer hopes never happens to someone they know. It
not only emotionally scars that person's family, their friends, and their
fellow officers, but it ends up leaving a hole in their community that
may be impossible to patch — which is exactly what had happened
when Captain Maven Potter was shockingly found murdered in his
home.

Events such as these, continually remind everyone of the
reputation that the city of Detroit, for too many years, has had. Its
people, its businesses, even its media have worked tirelessly together
to try and erase from memory the perception that those who don't live
here, have. But whenever a situation like this occurs in which a
recognizable name is attached, there always tends to be someone who
makes it their mission to publicly remind everyone of the city's
reputation. They are the ones who continue to doubt and don't even
wish to give them the benefit of the doubt — even though the majority
of the rest of Detroit's citizens are doing the best that they can in order
to try and make a difference.

Although saying goodbye to Captain Potter was a difficult
thing to do, those whom he had worked with: on the job, within the

city offices, and within the community, were willing to pick up the broken pieces that were left behind from this tragedy. In their own way, each of them was going to honor his memory and do what they could to help achieve his dream of a city that the world would no longer be afraid of. No matter how trivial their part seemed to be, each knew that their combined efforts would help to make that happen.

Lieutenant Christopher White was a man of mixed ethnic heritage, who physically appeared to be in his late-twenties — but in actuality, he was only a few years shy of forty. He stood just over six foot tall and weighed pretty close to two hundred and twenty pounds. His hair was cut and parted in the typical style of the times, and his face was nicely accented with a trimmed, thin shaped goatee. In his left ear lobe, there was a very visible tiny hole where once, all throughout his youth, a gold loop earring had been — he permanently removed it the moment he joined the police academy.

After the service was over, he and several of his other fellow officers: Colin Ramirez, Joshua Brampton, Maxwell Banks, Denny James, Sharna Williams, Samuel Everett, Abdul Hassam, Aaron Thompson and Charles Blake, were on their way back to their vehicles when Christopher heard an unfamiliar voice behind him — he then felt a hand gently touch him on his shoulder. His first instinct was to reach for his gun, but he quickly remembered that he wasn't on the street. He turned around and was surprised to see who had come up behind him.

Although Christopher had only spoken to this man a few times in the past when Captain Potter had briefly left him in charge of the precinct, he was uncertain as to why the chief of police, Jacob Winslow, had gone out of his way to speak with him.

"I hope you don't mind everyone, but I'd like to speak with the lieutenant in private for a few moments."

None of the other officers objected, leaving Christopher and the chief standing alone in the middle of the cemetery at the front path of one of the site's garden mausoleums. "What can I do for you, sir?"

"You know... they say that someone's misfortune is someone else's window of opportunity. You've had an impeccable career, albeit a relatively short one so far. However, it is imperative that I find Captain Potter's replacement as soon as possible."

In that moment, Christopher knew exactly where this conversation was headed — and he was uncertain that he wanted, or even deserved what he could only assume was about to be offered to him.

"And that is why I have decided to promote you to captain."

As flattered as he was, Christopher promptly dismissed the offer. His reasons of course, were heavily influenced by his doubt. "Thank you for your confidence in me, sir, but I'm not too sure that I want, or do I think that I'm anywhere near ready for such a promotion."

"You are, Chris. I am fully confident that you can fill the big shoes that were left behind by Captain Potter."

Christopher was grateful that the chief held him in such high regard — but having to replace a legend within the police department scared the holy crap out of him. There would certainly be a large amount of scrutiny placed upon him the moment he took over, and he knew that failure to live up to Captain Potter's legacy would not be accepted. "Captain Potter was..."

"...was a man who thought highly of you, Chris. That is why he had trusted you to man the fort whenever he was unable to." The chief then placed both of his hands onto Christopher's shoulders and looked him directly in his eyes.

It became clear to Christopher right then and there that he needed to reevaluate his hasty decision and accept the offer; he could straightforwardly see just how much faith the chief had in him. He understood that a responsibility like no other was being handed over to him in which he had to find a way to excel. He could not let the chief down; he could not let his peers down. Christopher could not let the people of Detroit down — nor could he let Captain Potter down. It is what his predecessor would have wanted him to do: step up, take charge, and aspire to live up to the legacy that his friend and mentor had left behind. "Ok. I will accept."

The chief received Christopher's extended hand and sealed the deal. "Good. Now let's walk, as we have some things to discuss."

Instead of walking towards their parked cars, they walked in no particular direction across the grounds of the cemetery. By the time they had finished their conversation, the grounds were all but abandoned. Everyone who had come to pay their final respects to Maven Potter had left — other than the two attendants who were in the process of lowering the captain's casket into the ground.

"You understand what it is that I am asking of you, Chris?"

"Yes, sir. And I will make sure that we find and arrest Captain Potter's killer."

"I know you will."

They went their separate ways. No sooner had Christopher arrived at his car, the reality of what he was being asked, consumed him. This was going to be a monumental task; one that he knew he had to complete. But the only thing that really bothered him about what Jacob Winslow had asked was that he was going to have to place one of his fellow officers, one of his friends, in a position that potentially could cost him his life.

One week later...

He was still trying to arrange his personal effects the way he wanted them throughout his new office. Inside, a bit of him still felt guilty; he felt as if he was invading a private space that had belonged for so many years to his predecessor. But life had to go on, and Christopher knew it. He felt the toughest part of all of this, wasn't taking over the captaincy of the precinct, it was handling the dubious task of packing up all of Maven Potter's personal items so that his widow could have them — he had learned more about his ex-boss, his friend, during that task than he had learned during his nearly nine years under the man's command.

Deciding that he had wasted enough of his day putting things in their place, Christopher walked over to the office's threshold and called out to Officer Ramirez. He then walked back over to his desk and took up a seat behind it where he patiently waited for Colin to arrive. A few moments later, Officer Ramirez appeared, closed the door behind him, and then took up a seat in front of the desk. "Have you found anything yet that could lead us to who it was that killed Captain Potter?"

"Unfortunately, I have not. If I had, you know that I would have told you right away."

"I know. It's just that I would like my next progress report to the chief to be a bit more promising."

"You're worrying again about whether or not the chief will second guess his appointing of you as our new captain. He's not going to expect this case to be wrapped up in only a matter of a few days. He knows that this investigation you assigned to me is going to take some time... and he is well aware that we had absolutely no solid leads at all to begin with."

Christopher already knew all of this — he just wanted to give some sort of update to the chief. He had been instructed at the cemetery to do whatever he had felt was necessary to solve Captain Potter's murder, but up until now, Christopher was reluctant to do anything more than just having one officer; Officer Ramirez, checking leads and going over what little evidence was collected at the crime scene.

Christopher knew that it was his own fear of the unthinkable happening that was holding him back from making any difficult decisions. But now, he realized that it was time to cut his own restrictive ties; he had to give his officer all the necessary leeway that was possible and allow him to dig as deep as he could to find out who had killed Maven Potter. "Ok. From this moment forward, the only time I want to see you here in the precinct is when you are doing paperwork. Get out on the street, contact whomever you feel can help you gather the needed information, and find us a solid lead to work with. This is your case, so I am giving you free reign. Take whoever you need to help you and do what you think is necessary, short of breaking the law, to find out who killed Maven."

"Right now, I don't think that I'll need any help. But I will promise you that the next time you see me in here, I will at least have a solid lead of some kind to work with... hopefully even more. Then, I'll probably need that help."

Officer Ramirez got up from his seat and left Captain White's office. The door was left open, which allowed Christopher to follow his officer with his eyes, to his desk, and then out of the precinct. Once Colin was completely out of sight, Christopher leaned back in his chair and sank into deep thought. All different kinds of scenarios suddenly appeared within his mind — most of them had a negative conclusion. But that was just a byproduct of his uncertainty. He knew that Colin Ramirez was a damn good officer; one of the best this precinct had. His skills would not only protect him from the possibility of harm, they should allow him to acquire the information that was so desperately needed; a solid lead on a suspect, and possibly even a reason as to why someone felt the need to kill a very well respected, and genuinely liked man.

   The building itself wasn't much to look at from the front; it blended in seamlessly with a row of other similar storefronts on either side of it in the community of Corktown; a stone's throw away from where the soon-to-be demolished Tiger Stadium, stood. This place was the perfect location for the D.U.O., because those who would walk or drive by would not think twice about the building housing anything more than just the advertised pawn shop. In actuality, the D.U.O.'s headquarters was there, conspicuously hidden in the basement.

   The place was relatively small; a mere two thousand square feet, but it served its purpose. Antonio Marcone, the recently implemented head of the D.U.O., had a plan; a plan that would take him and the D.U.O. out of this basement and into a penthouse. He had taken that first step not too long ago — and it was why he was now the boss. But for him to be able to achieve his dream, a lot of hard work still needed to be done.

   Up until he had taken control of the D.U.O., the organization went about their business quietly and meticulously; everything they did, they did without trying to ruffle too many lawful feathers. And although that method of operation had been quite successful up until now, for Antonio, it wasn't near profitable enough. In order for his dreams of one day building and owning a hotel and casino to become a reality, he needed to pad the D.U.O's bank account at a much faster rate. He needed to push the envelope and involve the organization in the more profitable areas of crime, areas that would surely draw attention — both from the law and the media. Antonio understood the risks that came with wanting to do this, but he honestly believed that he had no other choice — there just wasn't another viable option for him to take.

An underground organization like the D.U.O. cannot operate without having trusted outside contacts — Vance Palmalino had had many. However, out of all of them, there was only one that Antonio felt would be able to help him to shift the D.U.O. into the direction that he envisioned it to go. James 'Jimbo' Lewis wasn't a man with any form of credentials, but he had smarts. He wasn't a crooked cop or an individual with a degree; he was just a man that lived out on the streets who over the past ten years had been providing the D.U.O. with credible information.

Jimbo was sincere, genuine, and trustworthy. He had no obvious agendas and he never once had sold them out to the highest bidder. That was why Antonio had liked the man — what you see is what you get. Anytime he had spoken to him, and had asked him to provide the D.U.O. with some information, Jimbo had scrupulously done so — and not once had his information been bad. If Antonio had been born an honest man, Jimbo was someone he'd want as his close friend. The man was as authentic as they come. However, he did believe that Jimbo had a deep, dark secret. What that was, he did not know. It was none of his business — even though it did gnaw at his curiosity. Antonio himself had many secrets that could ruin him, so for that reason, he had to respect the man for keeping certain things private. There was this time a few years ago however, where Antonio's curiosity had admittedly gotten the better of him and he asked a personal question that he quickly regretted. *"Why do you, Jimbo, choose to live out on the streets when you have clearly made enough money gathering and providing information for not only the D.U.O., but for whoever else might want it?"* He couldn't take back those words that had escaped his mouth — all that he could do was hope that his unnecessary prying would not be all the incentive that Jimbo needed to refuse ever helping the D.U.O. again in order to keep his skeletons locked tightly in the closet.

Antonio hadn't intended to invade the man's privacy, but after years of knowing him, he just could not fathom why Jimbo had chosen to live like this — he honestly just wanted him to have a better life.

Jimbo's reply to him that day was brief and meandering — he had simply made a huge mistake when he was eighteen in which he felt obliged to one day make amends. Antonio had to respect that, even though his curiousness now wanted to hear the man's entire story. It was not at all surprising to him however, that Jimbo did not willingly go on to elaborate. He could not fault the man for his scruples. He had made some difficult, some would say unethical choices himself in his day — including what he knew now had to be done so that the D.U.O. could begin to evolve into what he had envisioned it could become. And for that to even have the possibility of ever happening, Antonio needed Jimbo's help once again.

He honestly believed that what he was going to ask of the man was probably going to be beyond his talents of acquisition, but there was no one else that he could think of. He had the utmost faith in his own trusted, loyal associates — but in this instance, he just did not believe that they had the innate ability to find the necessary resources in order to make what he wanted done, a reality.

He was reaching for straws. But at the moment, it was the only option that Antonio felt he had.

He had never followed the rules, nor cared what his parents thought — he was a young man who didn't give a damn that what he was doing would one day lead him down a path with severe consequences that awaited him at the end. At thirteen, he drank, smoked, and did whatever drugs he could get his hands on. He was indestructible; he was untouchable — so he believed. Jimbo did whatever he wanted because he truly believed that it made him the coolest thirteen-year-old in his neighborhood.

It hadn't taken long for all of his peers to recognize that Jimbo had dramatically changed. Almost overnight, he went from being no one to someone. Not because puberty had changed his appearance, but because his personality had. No longer just a blip on the radar screen, he was now the most significant kid in school. And once everyone became aware of the reason behind his sudden transformation, they too wanted to be like him; they wanted to feel like he did, and experience things that they never imagined they could. Jimbo became an influential individual — he became the hook-up for everyone of his willing peers.

In a short amount of time, he had accomplished his goal — and he was going to milk it for all it was worth. Which is why Jimbo decided to start what he called 'Teen Excellent Experience Nights'; parties that would take place in either someone's basement when that person's parents were away or in an abandoned building that they were able to gain access to. For four years, Jimbo was the host of these private parties, providing all of the alcohol and hallucinogenic substances that the partygoers wanted to try. And not only did these parties quickly become an underground phenomenon; drawing hundreds, and on occasion, nearly a thousand teenagers, but Jimbo's wallet became very padded.

His evolution throughout high school, all due to his daily substance abuse, had also gotten him suspended multiple times. For some reason though, Jimbo had gotten lucky as the school had felt that none of the reasons behind his six suspensions warranted them having to involve the law. And because of that, he started to believe that he was in essence, a messiah, and that his fellow students were his devoted followers.

However, it was that erroneous belief that would eventually lead to his downfall. One night during one of his famous parties, on his own eighteenth birthday, he made a big mistake — it would end up being the one that would change his life forever.

He had never once thought or cared about the potential dangers that came along with the drugs and booze — that wasn't his problem. His only concern was making sure that he had the supply to cover the demand — and not just what was the current, trendy designer drug, but certain specific ones that his group of partygoers loved to combine; a resulted merging that Jimbo dubbed 'uniflying' where he would carefully mix XTC with OxyContin and a low grade batch of Cocaine.

That concoction affected people differently. For Jimbo, his birthday 'trip' had caused him to completely lose his moral judgment, and he ended up forcing himself upon a fifteen year old Asian girl.

She had attended the party that night with her older sister, but did not sample one bit of the buffet of substances like everyone else had. She had instead, only gone there for the music and to hang out with those whom she knew through her sister.

The following day, Jimbo was arrested and charged with statutory rape. His unabated assault had also resulted in him fathering a child. After he served five of the seven years he had been given for his crime in the state penitentiary, and completing a mandatory drug rehab program, Jimbo was released; his life now completely straightened out.

While he was in jail, like so many others, Jimbo had found God. It was the Almighty Lord whom he professed had placed him on the right path and had encouraged him to undertake a mission of personal restitution. That mission he chose had taken him directly to the streets, not to help those who lived there, but to join them and live out the remainder of his life alongside them. That decision would seem illogical to many, but to Jimbo, it was the only way he felt that he would be able to truly pay the necessary penance for the sins he had committed.

So it was there on the streets where he would spend his days helping those who wanted help, no matter who it was that would ask him for it. And every day, he would try to make whatever money he could, doing whatever tasks he could, not so that he could eventually find a place to live, but to make up for what he had done. Every single penny he made or had luckily found, he put in a college savings account for his daughter — his bastard child.

The door to his office opened and in walked the two men that Antonio had handpicked to be his trusted associates: Louie Mazotti and Salvadore Batiste — each had a specific skill set that Antonio appreciated, and each were on board with the new direction that he wanted to take the Detroit Underworld Organization in. "Take a seat, please. It is time that we take the next step and move this organization forward so that it will become the predominant entity that I believe it can be."

"Good. I'm tired of us being labeled as a second class mob organization."

"As am I," Sal affirmed — which was a rare occurrence whenever Louie would give his opinion. "What are your plans, boss?"

Antonio turned the monitor on his desk so that his two men could see what was on it — the screen displayed an architectural 3D rendering of an elaborate hotel and casino. "This is my dream... to one day build a hotel and casino that would not only rival those of Las Vegas, Atlantic City or Monte Carlo, but possibly even surpass it. And even if that doesn't happen, I would at least want my casino to bury one of the four already in the area; preferably the one across the river in Windsor."

"That should be easy, as it's a government run casino."

"Not anymore. Once the construction of the new tower and coliseum is complete, Caesars Entertainment will take it over... if they haven't already?"

"Damn!" Louie said, knowing that a corporate run casino would be much harder to compete against.

"It's bad enough that there are already three corporate run casinos here in Detroit. That's all we need is another one right across the river."

I agree, Sal. But that is not going to stop me from trying to grab a large slice of the profits they all make. However, before any of that can even begin to happen, this organization is going to have to get creative and drastically increase its current revenue. "We," Antonio made a circular motion with his right hand; implying that he was referring to himself, Louie and Sal, "I am certain, will not be granted any loans by any financial institution to build this. That means we will be left with no other option but to find a more profitable source of income than the one that we currently have."

"What do you have in mind," Louie asked.

"Guns!"

Sal and Louie each looked at their boss with uncertainty as to what the word 'guns' actually meant. "You want to get in the business of selling street weapons?"

"No, I want to steal military weapons and then sell them to any militant organization that wants them."

Antonio's idea was bold — they both had to admit that. But Sal and Louie were unsure if what their boss wanted to do was wise, as this would most certainly come with a lot of risk. "Are you sure that this is what you want? Stealing weapons from the United States Military is not going to be an easy thing to do."

"I am aware of that, Louie. That is why I want the both of you to try and find us a reliable source within the military that is willing to work covertly for us."

"You want us to find you a mole?"

"Not a mole, Louie. A well compensated subcontracted business associate."

"That may be easier said than done," Sal declared.

"I am aware that what I am asking of you both is a difficult, maybe even an impossible task. But I am confident that one of you will be able to find us someone whom we can trust to do this." After a few moments of silence passed by, Antonio gave Louie and Sal their instructions. He told Sal that he wanted him to make contact with Jimbo and have him look into the possibility of finding them someone who was willing to do what he wanted. And although Antonio was hopeful that Jimbo could find him the insider that he was looking for, he had to accept the possibility that the man could not. Therefore, he had to have another option on the table. Unfortunately, he just could not come up with one that he was confident in. The only thing he could think of was options that he was all but certain would fail — but he had to explore it nevertheless. So he asked Louie to head thirty-some miles north to the military community that surrounded Selfridge Air Force Base. It was there that he wanted Louie to go and visit some of the local military hangouts and discretely, try his best to recruit a willing participant.

After Louie and Sal left to carry out their assignments, Antonio sunk back into his well worn black leather chair; a chair that was held together in a few spots with duct tape, and thought. In order for the organization to prosper as quickly as was possible, Antonio was certain that his decision to take on this kind of risk was the right one. But he was also not too optimistic that his two associates would return with the right candidate to do his dirty work and supply him with the weapons that he needed to start up his new smuggling network of illegal military arms. If they both failed, then Antonio wasn't too sure what his next step would be. The pawnshop above was the only legitimate business that they had on the books, and it only made enough money to pay its employees and the building's utilities — it wouldn't solely fund a future hotel and casino. The organization's traditional way of making money wouldn't work either; they could only extort and bribe so many people — it would probably take them close to three generations to accumulate the money needed to accomplish it. This meant that Antonio's options would be down to one. It wasn't like he wouldn't resort to doing it, but he'd rather have a military man in his pocket instead of using the threat of harm against a family member of someone who served this country. But until that option was all that was left, Antonio decided that he didn't want to think about it. He'd rather think about the future, his dreams, and what he could do once he had achieved what he wanted. And when that day finally came, the first thing that he was going to buy for himself was the most expensive office chair he could find and throw the patchwork piece of junk that he was presently sitting on into the Detroit River.

2

The dark ominous clouds that hung overhead, made the day itself appear as if it was going to be a miserable one. Officer Colin Ramirez was thankful that, for the moment, the skies had refrained from opening up like they had the previous three days. He would be happier if the sun would find a crack in the clouds and at least give him a bit of natural light to brighten up this Monday, because six hours into it, Colin was beginning to get a little frustrated. The free reign that Captain White had given him, hadn't made a difference — he still had found nothing. Twice so far, he had crossed the proverbial line: first threatening to arrest one individual who had violated his parole — the man had innocuously walked out of a strip bar; a place that he was not supposed to be anywhere near. The second time, Colin had broken the nose of a piece of street scum; a drug dealing pimp who knew people who knew individuals that might kill a police officer for the right price.

Frustrated, Colin felt that he only had one other option left. He had to somehow find a man whom he had never met before, but who apparently had a reputation of being an accurate source of information and who supposedly lived somewhere on eight mile road. That area was by no means the safest part of the city, but it was an area that he at least, was very familiar with.

He exited his car; a black amethyst colored, 1988 Chevy Monte Carlo SS, and then promptly made his way into Blackstone Park. Off in the distance, Colin could see an African American man going about his own business. He appeared to be middle-aged, which was what his target was supposed to be, but he did not look at all as if he was down on his luck. The man that Colin was in search of, had been a convict, who ever since his release, was rumored to have lived only on the street; a life that should have taken a toll on the man's well being. Nevertheless, Officer Ramirez was certain that he had found who he had been looking for. The slim built man stood about five-foot seven, had a short and scraggly cropped haircut, a scruffy layer of facial hair that was mixed in with the odd strand of gray, and a very

14

visible tribal-like prison tattoo of thorns in the shape of a cross on his left forearm.

After a few seconds of shrewd observation from afar, Colin followed the man as he strolled through the park. Because he knew nothing, other than an assumed reputation, Colin chose not to announce himself because he was unsure if the presence of a police officer would spook the homeless man.

Apparently, the man was in his own world, as he just didn't seem to notice that he was no longer alone — but that still didn't put Colin's uncertainty at ease. Instead, Officer Ramirez continued his pursuit and quickly made up the distance that was between the two of them. When the homeless man stopped at a birdbath, Colin halted his forward progress as well. He stood where he was and curiously watched as the black man dipped his hands into the rainwater, and then splashed his face and head with it. Colin could not fault the man for what he had just done. The man lived without basic hygienic accessibility, so washing up in a park's birdbath only seemed logical.

As the man began drying his face on the front of his somewhat clean shirt, Colin continued on towards him. By the time the man had completely dried off, Colin had arrived at the man's side. "Are you James Lewis?"

The man didn't answer Colin right away. Instead, he ran his fingers through his hair in an attempt at combing his damp, disheveled locks. "I am... but my friends call me Jimbo. What can I do for you, officer?"

'Well... so much for assuming that an officer of the law might spook the man,' Colin thought. "I guess that there is no need for me to show you my badge, then."

"Nope!"

"I am in need of some help. And since I hear that you are very good at acquiring information, you seemed to be the logical person for me to approach."

Jimbo did not respond to Colin's declaration. He instead, just looked at the man inquisitively as he combed through his hair one final time and then clasped his hands down in front of him. A few seconds of awkward silence then commenced between them. It wasn't until Jimbo was positive that Officer Ramirez had realized his mistake did he reply. "I am more than adequately capable of acquiring the information that you need." He reached out his hand and accepted the fifty dollars that Colin had removed from his wallet.

"The police department has come to a wall in an investigation that we cannot seem to get past. I am sure that you are aware that the captain of one of our precincts, Maven Potter, was murdered in his home a few weeks ago."

"I do not subscribe to the newspaper, nor do I watch the news on the TV or use the Internet, as I can't afford any of it."

Other than stating the obvious, Colin wasn't sure if the man's declaration was meant as a sympathy ploy or if he was just trying to make him aware of the facts. Whatever the case may be, Colin didn't care — he was here now in Blackstone Park, hopeful that the rumors about Jimbo's information gathering skills were true. "I was hoping that you would be able to use your sources and find me a solid lead that will point me in the right direction. We are desperate to find the person who had the nerve to kill Captain Potter."

"I can try and do that for you, no problem. But I won't make you any promises that I know I can't honestly keep. Doing so would mean that I would be at the same level as a politician."

Colin cracked a smile at that comparison. "I appreciate your sincerity. I will meet you back here in a few days."

"I'll find you when I have the information that you seek. I will also find you if I reach a dead end."

"Ok. You can contact me at the downtown precinct."

"I already knew that. Just like I knew that you had been following me in your black Monte Carlo, three blocks back before you parked across the street over there," Jimbo pointed out Colin's car, "and then imprudently walked over to me."

"You are very intuitive."

"That, I am."

"Did you know that I was looking for you?"

"Yes... I did"

"How?"

"The same way that I knew that man over there," Jimbo motioned off to the left with his eyes, "was going to stop by today and pay me a visit." Jimbo promptly moved his attention away from Colin and focused it directly at a rather large man who was making his way towards him.

The approaching man looked evil with his long hair, his diamond inlaid gold earring, and the very visible tattoos on his arms — he looked as if he could kill someone without having to break a sweat.

When the man arrived, Jimbo immediately introduced him. "This is Salvadore Batiste. Sal, this is..," he hesitated for a moment, but not long enough for Sal's mind to question. He wasn't one to out a police officer, as he had no problem providing information for either side of the law. Instead, Jimbo decided to give Officer Ramirez a false name and an alibi, "this is an old friend of mine, Manual. Manual Velázquez."

Sal did not extend his hand in greeting. He instead, stayed still and sized up Jimbo's friend. "This... is your friend?"

"Yes, he is."

"I thought that you didn't have any friends?"

"I don't have any close friends. Manual's friendship with me is strictly a business one."

"A business friend?" Sal took a moment and scrutinized Colin. In the world he was a part of, Sal had to be cautious. He could not openly accept the word of someone, even if he completely trusted that person. However, Sal wasn't about to be rude towards an individual until his own curiosity was satisfied. "So, Manual... what do you do for a living?"

Before Colin could respond to Sal's question, Jimbo spoke up. "He's a private investigator. Sometimes he helps me when I am unable to use my own sources to procure the information that I am looking for."

"Really? Why do you help Jimbo?"

Colin realized that he had unwillingly just been placed in a situation in which he knew he should extricate himself. As soon as Sal was introduced to him, Officer Ramirez knew who the man was and whom he was affiliated with. But if Colin played his cards right, this impromptu meeting with a member of the D.U.O. could end up being what the Detroit Police Department needed.

Although he had come here strictly with the purpose of acquiring some possible information about Maven Potter's death,

Colin could not dismiss the opportunity he now had to gather some intelligence on Detroit's Mob. So he took a second, gathered his thoughts, and quickly fabricated a backstory. "Because he helped me once before to gather some information that was too sensitive for me to try and acquire on my own. Ever since then, we have helped each other whenever either one of us is placed in a position where we both need our anonymity kept."

Sal generally never really liked a lot of people, especially when he first met them. But there was something about this Manual Velázquez that continued to intrigue him. He hadn't come here to make a new contact; he had come here to ask Jimbo to do what he does best.

For the moment, Sal kept his attention on Jimbo. He removed his money clip from his front pocket and fanned through the bills. He then handed Jimbo two hundred dollars. "I have a huge favor to ask of you."

"Of course."

"Will you excuse us please, Manual?"

"Certainly." Colin walked about one hundred feet away from the two of them and stopped at the somewhat rusted jungle gym set. He could have just left the park, as that would have been the logical thing for him to do, but his gut was telling him to stick around, even though the potential was there for this to evolve into a dangerous situation. Yes, he knew that allowing a member of the Detroit Underworld Organization to become familiar with him might end up being hazardous to his health — but so were numerous other habits. If he were to allow a yellow streak to suddenly appear on his back, then he may as well just return to the precinct and turn in his gun and badge. Sal did not know his real name; he only knew a few fabricated details.

At that moment, Colin decided that he had to take advantage of the unexpected situation he found himself in and hope that it might lead to something that the police could possibly use — that is what a good officer is supposed to do.

It didn't happen all too often, but Colin's curiosity decided to start knocking on the door — he wished it would stop, as Jimbo's conversation with Sal was none of his business. Besides, he just needed to be patient because he had a strong feeling that as soon as their meeting was over; Sal would make his way over to him.

"Jimbo... we are looking for someone to work for the organization that is also a member of the United States Military and has access to the main armory depot."

As interested as he was to learn what it was that the D.U.O. was up to, Jimbo was just too smart to ask — they paid him handsomely and he wanted to keep that business arrangement with them alive and well. "I actually know someone; a guy that I went to middle school with... although he was a few years behind me. Needless to say, his parents literally forced him into joining the military to straighten his act out. The man has had no motivation and no desire to do anything with his life. That is why he has never been promoted beyond being that of a private. I'm sure if I dangle a carrot in front of his face, he will nibble — he's been looking for a reason to throw it all back in his parents' faces."

"Ok. Go ahead and dangle that carrot."

"I will. And I will let you know if he bites."

They both shook hands and then parted ways. Jimbo walked towards the far side of the park and Sal walked towards Colin, just like he had thought he would.

"Let's go for a walk, Manual. Your occupation certainly intrigues me... and I just might have a proposal for you after we get to know a little bit more about each other."

~ You can never rewind or erase a moment that you later on, wished had never happened. But you can certainly influence that occurrence so in the end, it works out in your favor. ~

Colin returned to the precinct without the information that he was looking for. Instead, he returned with something else he hadn't expected — a situation and an opportunity. He knew that his unexpected introduction to Salvadore Batiste should have ended at just that, but Officer Ramirez's police instincts had prevented him from walking away. And because he hadn't, he now found himself wrangling with a dilemma.

Though he had yet to commit to anything, Colin knew that his life was about to take a completely different path. If he were to keep to himself what had happened and pretend that his introduction to a member of the Detroit Underworld Organization had never taken place, he knew that a battle with his own conscience would continuously occur. If he informed Captain White about what had happened in the park, and the captain agreed with what he had been thinking about doing, then Colin's personal life would change and his family's continual safety would become a major concern.

He had his foot in the door; all that Colin had to do was step across a very dangerous threshold. And then once he did, he undoubtedly would become immersed in a lifestyle that he never expected he'd experience. He had a lot to think about, but he also knew that his decision could not be postponed for too long.

In what would be somewhat symbolic of the dilemma Officer Ramirez was wrestling with, once he crossed that threshold of his captain's office, it would essentially begin. That was why he went straight to his own desk first. He had a few messages to check, a few past reports that needed updating, and a few non-essential items to dillydally over while he made his decision.

That hadn't become any easier like he had hoped it would. In fact, the longer he sat at his desk, the more uncertain questions popped into Colin's head. But there was always going to be questions; answers were not always going to be as clear as he would like them to be — and on occasion, challenges would suddenly appear for which he would have to find a way to deal with. Some could easily be overcome, others could be adapted to, but some would end up being almost, if not impossible to conquer.

After a lengthy period of indecisiveness, his eyes unexpectedly directed him to of all things, the nameplate on his desk. What was on it was an obvious reminder of who he was — a Detroit police officer. He had become one so that he could do his part and help the city that he loved, become a better place to live — and he simply wasn't the kind of individual who backed out of something, just because the potential was there for it to end badly. So he got up from behind his desk and walked over to Captain White's office. Once there, he gingerly tapped on the door jam.

Without a word being said, Captain White motioned for him to enter. While he waited for his captain to finish his phone conversation, Colin took up a seat across from him and curiously, but not too obviously, surveyed the room. Yes, this office no longer belonged to Captain Potter, but it still felt a little odd being inside it with all of the personal changes that Christopher had made — he also knew that some rather drastic changes were soon going to be a part of his life. So he, like everyone else, just had to find a way to adapt.

"I hope that you have some good news for me?" Christopher said the moment he finished his call.

"Depends on how you are going to view what it is that I have to tell you."

That was a rather vague answer, and one that also grabbed his curiosity. Christopher tried to read between the lines and guess what it was that Officer Ramirez had walked into his office to say, but the possibilities were endless. The only thing he was certain of was that the news he wanted to hear was probably not what he was going to be given. "I'm thinking that what you are about to tell me is not what I want to hear."

"That, I do not know, but... Although I have yet to find out any pertinent information concerning who killed Captain Potter, I was able to actually make a friend today within the Detroit Underworld Organization."

Captain White almost spit out his coffee. "I'm sorry. What did you just say?"

Colin could not help but chuckle, as he figured that he was going to get a surprised reaction out of his boss — and he was also thankful his captain was able to refrain from giving him a morning shower of regurgitated caffeine. "Today, I went in search of a man who has had a reputation on the streets of being able to acquire just about any kind of information. Shortly after I was able to find him, another one of his 'clients' showed up. Salvadore Batiste, being that person."

"Shit! He didn't peg you as a cop, did he?"

"No. But we did have a long talk."

"About what?" Christopher was still in shock. No one had ever attempted to make contact with anyone from the D.U.O. before, and he was afraid that his officer; his friend, had just signed his own future death warrant. But from the self-assured smile he saw on Colin's face, Christopher had recognized that Officer Ramirez had learned something of value; something that had apparently been worth the risk he took.

The two of them then engaged in a conversation that neither one of them had ever imagined. The topic, then Colin's outrageous proposal that followed it, had left Christopher at a loss for words. What had just been suggested to him, in theory, would allow the police department to have their own ear inside an organization that he felt was on the brink of becoming more than just a thorn in the side of the city. However, with what Colin was willing to do, that also came with a lot of personal risk. Christopher had only been a police captain for a few weeks, and he was nowhere near ready to take on the responsibility of ordering, or even allowing one of the officers under his command, to infiltrate a criminal organization. Yet, this was part of the job that he had accepted — difficult decisions were going to be placed in his lap. They may not seem to be rational, or they may not even seem to be logical, but sometimes these complicated decisions just had to be made — whether or not they made any sense. In this instance, Christopher had no other choice but to acknowledge that a golden opportunity had just fallen into their lap; an opportunity that he knew was probably never going to come around again. They had to take advantage of the ignorance of the D.U.O. and gather all of the information that they could — for as long as they could. But before Christopher White gave his officer the ok to do what he had wanted, he said to him, "I need to run this by the chief before I consent to this idea of yours."

Understanding the position that he had just placed his captain in, Colin quietly left the office, shutting the door behind him, and leaving Captain White to the unenviable task of trying to convince Chief Jacob Winslow that inserting a mole inside Detroit's Underworld Organization was actually a good idea.

Ambition was something that he always had; an egocentric personality is what had driven that ambition. That is why Antonio Marcone had risen through the ranks as fast as he had, and that is why he had done what he had to place himself into a position to lead the

Detroit Underworld Organization — all that it took was a well thought out plan and Antonio had eliminated the only person that was in his way. He had no regrets about killing his boss, his mentor. He knew that it had to be done — otherwise, he would have been Vance Palmalino's lackey until the man's old age was his only reason for death.

Antonio sat back in his office chair, sipped on a rock glass of Canadian Club, and reviewed his past decisions — he had no regrets about any of them. He hoped that his vision of what the D.U.O. could become, was only a few short years away from taking place. And the only thing he felt could stop that from happening sooner, rather than later, was if Sal and Louie were unable to find him a patsy within the United States Military. If they had failed to do so, Antonio was uncertain what he was going to do next; what options he would need to explore in order to accomplish his goal. He didn't want to continue on with what the D.U.O. had always done because the world around him was ever evolving, and he knew that the organization had to do that as well in order to survive.

Patiently, he waited in his office for a report; one glass of whisky down and half of another gone before the first of his associates had returned. And Antonio knew, just by the disappointing look on Louie's face, that he had not been successful. "No luck, I take it?"

"I'm afraid not. Of the three places I went into, the club that was the closest to the air base seemed to have the most promise. Discretely, I had spoken to a handful of prospective personnel, and actually thought that I had found us the perfect mole, but just when I was about to close the deal, I realized that the entire bar was about to lynch me — I must have ruffled too many feathers while in there. Luckily, I was able to exit the bar before I got ripped apart by a group of angry soldiers." Louie paused for a moment, expecting Antonio to say something — he didn't, so Louie continued. "I honestly hope that you are not pissed at me for coming back here empty handed."

"No, I'm not pissed. And just so you know, I do have the utmost confidence in your abilities. I honestly figured that this was going to be a nearly impossible task for you to pull off. However, it was an option that had to be explored nonetheless. Hopefully, when Sal returns, he'll have brought back with him some encouraging news.

But if he has failed as well, we'll just have to figure out some other way of getting ourselves a person on the inside or a person with connections to help us with what we want to do."

"I doubt he'll come back with a mole for us. He's far from the brightest man in our organization."

"You don't need to be smart to have a needful purpose."

"But you need to have a bit of intelligence to understand what your purpose is... and Sal always seems to forget just where he stands within the organization."

"He's only behind you because I chose you to be my trusted number one. If this went by seniority, Sal would be my number one."

"And we'd be in a lot of trouble if that had taken place."

"I can't argue that point. But you need to give Sal a lot more credit than you do. He is smarter than you think he is."

"Then he must be using those smarts to play dumb, because he's got me fooled."

Much of their conversation, Antonio could not dispute — but he could also tell that a rivalry, even some animosity, was beginning to build between his men. He didn't know if the foundation of that was jealousy, or if there was a general dislike between the two. The only thing that Antonio knew for sure was that his two men needed to find a way to co-exist or his tenure as the head of the D.U.O. was going to be filled with daily migraines.

The office door opened up, and Sal walked through. His expression was different than what Louie's had been — it instantly gave Antonio some hope. "So... were you able to find us a mole?"

"Yes, I actually have. Jimbo apparently has an old friend of his from his school days who is currently in the military and whose career seems to be going nowhere."

"Is this somebody we can trust?"

"I hope so. Jimbo told me that this guy's parents forced him into joining the military because he wasn't motivated enough to straighten out his act or to do anything productive with his life. He was a burnout and had a major substance abuse problem when he was still in school. Because his whole family is in the military, they forced him to enlist, thinking that it would straighten him out. Instead, for the past five years, he has just existed there and done nothing to warrant an advancement of any kind. He is just complacent to live out his life as a lowly private, collect his pay, and maybe even a pension."

Louie wasn't happy that Sal had actually come through. But just because he had, didn't mean that Louie was going to change his opinion of the man.

"Sounds like our man," Antonio declared. "What's his name?"

"Casper."

Bewilderment suddenly consumed Antonio. "Casper? You're kidding, right?"

"I'm not. The man may not be motivated, but he's not stupid. He refused to allow Jimbo to tell us his real name."

Louie rolled his eyes and shook his head; Antonio's opinion was different — he actually understood the man's reluctance to reveal his real name. "So do we have to contact this 'Casper' through Jimbo?"

"No." Sal handed Antonio a piece of paper with a cell number on it. "Call him when you are ready, and he will arrange his own transfer to the east coast armories."

"How can he do that?"

"His father is a commanding officer in the personnel department."

Antonio was thrilled that Sal had come through for him. He walked over to his small liquor cabinet and poured three rock glasses of Canadian Club to celebrate. He returned to his desk, handed the two other glasses to Louie and Sal, and sat down in his office chair. "Well then... I think that we need to plan our first weapons heist and search out our first few clients."

"Agreed," both Louie and Sal said simultaneously. Sal then followed it by saying, "But I think that it should wait until after the meeting I have arranged."

"You've arranged a meeting with this... Casper?"

"No. Manual Velázquez."

Antonio's mood quickly shifted from happy to being perturbed. He was not pleased that his associate had taken it upon himself and arranged a business meeting with a man, a client, before they even had a mole in place. "You need to explain your actions, Sal."

Louie could not help but feel satisfied. It hadn't taken Sal long to go from being the hero to being the idiot who just didn't know how long the proverbial chain on his leash went.

"I realize that I may have overstepped my authority here, but during my visit with Jimbo, he introduced me to a man who is a business friend of his; a private investigator whom Jimbo assures doesn't have any ethical standards. He apparently does whatever is necessary to get whatever information he needs and he doesn't care whom he has to burn in the process."

"Why would Antonio want a meeting with this man?"

"Because Louie, I believe that he would be a good person to have in our back pocket. We need more outside assets other than just Jimbo."

Antonio was no longer as mad as he had been, but he still was not happy that Sal had assumed that this man could be a valuable individual to the organization. In hindsight however, Antonio could not dismiss this unexpected opportunity. He knew that smuggling weapons could not be his only means of making money. He needed to use some of the other lessons that he had learned under the tutelage of Vance Palmalino, such as extort and then acquire. If this Manual's skills and scruples were what had been proclaimed, then this man most certainly could help him acquire other assets much easier. No longer would they have to do all the dirty work themselves. "Ok. We'll meet with him."

"Good. I'll call him and tell him that he is picking up the dinner tab." Sal left the office to go and make his call; Louie stayed behind and voiced his opinion about what Sal had done. Antonio listened openly to what his right hand man had to say, but soon realized that all of Louie's negative points were merely stated because of his personal feelings towards Sal — a developing concern that Antonio knew he had to address at some point. But right now, he had more important things that needed his full attention — the groundwork needs to be laid so that the future of the D.U.O. could begin.

3

He wasn't sure why, but there was something inside of him that told him he needed to speak with the man who had essentially put him in the position he now found himself in. Thankfully, Colin didn't have to search the entire city to find Jimbo again as he was in the same place he had been the last time — Blackstone Park.

Although Jimbo was dressed in the same clothes, he felt as if there was something different about him. What that was, Colin was uncertain — but that didn't matter, as he only wanted a few minutes of his time. So he took a few steps towards Jimbo and knew almost immediately that his initial assessment had been correct. Something indeed wasn't right; something seemed very strange.

Jimbo was by the birdbath; he had just finished washing up. He shook the water off of his hands, wiped his face with his shirt, and then stepped off to the side. Immediately, Colin could see that there was another person there whose presence had been concealed behind where Jimbo had been.

This person, a man, was clearly much larger in size than what Jimbo was — why Colin had been unable to see him until Jimbo had moved, he did not know. Yet, even though this person's presence had been revealed, Colin found it difficult to clearly see what the man looked like.

The mystery man left the birdbath and he headed over towards the largest tree in the park; a one hundred year old maple — Jimbo followed right behind him. Once they arrived at the tree, the mystery man began pounding what appeared to be a large stick into the ground. This immediately drew Colin's curiosity. Wanting that satisfied, he called out to Jimbo — but he didn't answer him. Colin called out to him again — and again, he did not acknowledge him. It wasn't until he was about fifty feet away that Colin realized that it wasn't just a stick that the unknown person was pounding in the ground — it was a shovel, and that person had been using it to dig a hole.

The closer Colin got, the larger the hole seemed to be. For what little time that person had been digging, the hole should not have been as big as it was — but it was. One more time, he called out to Jimbo. This time, his presence was finally acknowledged. He smiled at Colin, but said nothing; the man doing the digging ignored his being nearby and kept on digging. Two more shovels of dirt later and the hole was now the size of a grave. The unknown man now seemed satisfied that he had accomplished what he had set out to do, so he set the tip the shovel's spade on the ground, used the shovel's handle to lean upon for support, and then motioned for Jimbo to come and stand next to the edge of the hole.

"Why did your friend dig that hole, Jimbo?"

Jimbo did not reply; the other person did. "Is it not obvious why?"

"Not really?"

"It should be... seeing that you weren't smart enough to walk away when you should have."

Colin was unclear as to what it was that this individual was talking about. Puzzles were never Colin's forte; he needed an obvious clue before he could begin to figure anything out. He was about to ask the unknown man to clarify what it was that he was trying to get him to understand when something happened — the laws of nature were suddenly broken. Right before his eyes, the man had morphed from the out of focus image he had been, into someone whom Colin immediately recognized. "What the hell?"

The man then took the shovel, turned it parallel to the ground, and with the butt end of it, rammed it into the small of Jimbo's back — Jimbo fell forward into the grave. Without thinking, Colin ran over to the hole, hoping that Jimbo was alright. Maybe it was shock; maybe it was uncertainty, or maybe this was just some weird and twisted alternate dimension that he had somehow found himself in. Whatever it was, Colin had forgotten to pay attention to the fact that the now revealed man, Salvadore Batiste, had just been given the opening he needed.

Sal had taken the shovel, brought it up and back behind him like a baseball bat and — he didn't hesitate. He swung it at Colin with all his might.

Colin saw it coming out of the corner of his eye, but he just didn't have enough time to get completely out of the way. The backside of the spade hit Colin square between the shoulder blades. The impact of it sent him straight towards the edge of the grave-size hole.

Although it wasn't quite enough to send Colin into the 'grave', it had knocked him face down on the ground, where he ended up close enough to the edge that Colin could see over it. Yes, his focus had been partly knocked out of whack by the impact of the shovel, but he was still able to realize that the hole should not have been that deep — but it was, as the bottom appeared to be endless. What Colin was now looking down at should be impossible.

He could lie there all day and try to understand this mystery, but that wasn't the only thing here that didn't make sense. Suddenly, a light turned on in Colin's head: the shovel in Sal's hand, the grave that he had dug, and the bottomless pit. He now understood what this was — it was a metaphor, a possible prequel to his pending future.

Yes, he should have just walked away from Sal after his initial introduction — but it was too late for that now. Instead, he had willingly allowed himself to step into a world that he now realized was going to be nearly impossible to ever escape from — and it was probably going to cost him his life. But this had been his decision. Colin had freely made it and he was going to follow through with what he had chosen to do — because he was a man who had unwavering principles.

Now understanding fully what was going on here, Colin was determined to get some answers before all of this came to an end. So he tried to push himself up off of the ground; he wanted to address Sal face to face. But before he was able to do so, Colin felt the end of the shovel handle up against his butt. He didn't have enough time to react as Sal promptly nudged him forward over the edge.

He didn't scream as he fell; he didn't hit the bottom either. There were however, the roots of the one hundred year old maple tree sticking out through the sides of the grave-size hole. Somehow, Colin had managed to grab a hold of one — the problem now was that he was dangling about twenty-feet from the top of the hole. Colin looked *down, hoping that the bottom would now be visible to him. It wasn't — he still could not see it.*

A single root from the old maple tree had saved his life. But in reality, he knew that he was totally fucked — no other roots that he saw above him looked strong enough to support his weight if he attempted to use them to climb out. As much as Colin hoped that he would be able to find a way out of this hole, recognition had quickly set in that an escape from his predicament was going to be impossible. So Colin did the only thing that he could do — he let go of the root and let whatever was going to happen next, happen.

Colin awoke from his dream, put his hands over his face, and shook his head. He had never been someone to believe that one's dreams were actually a glimpse into their possible future. But what he had just experienced was scary enough for him to almost change his views.

He walked into his bathroom, ran himself a cold shower, and did his best to contradict what his mind had just conjured up. He controlled his own fate; that was what he believed. His subconscious was not the same as a certified fortune teller's crystal ball; it did not have the ability to show him exactly what his future was going to be. In fact, he was going to make sure that what he had just dreamt about, did not take place.

After a quick breakfast, he said goodbye to his wife and two year old daughter, left his apartment, and headed to work; not to the precinct, but to his new office — the one that he had been given to use to help establish his cover.

Although Captain White thought that he could have continued to work out of the precinct, Chief Winslow agreed with Officer Ramirez's opinion that it would be a lot more convincing, and a lot less of a risk, if he had an established base of operations — a fake detective agency; a front to help convince the D.U.O. that he was who Jimbo had stated he was.

This new office would certainly give him the freedom to work at his own pace and not be disturbed with everything else that happened on a daily basis within the walls of a police station, but he unfortunately, was not being allowed to work completely alone. He was being given a secretary — or rather, someone within the police department to pose as one. Who that person was, Colin did not know. He only knew that she was currently working within the department's intelligence division.

An hour after he had arrived at his new office, she arrived. Her look said she was pure geek. She sported thick-framed glasses, had long dark hair that was braided into two ponytails, and she wore absolutely no makeup. Her name however, Lenora Lexington, immediately caused Colin to think that it suited more a porn star than her — that thought of his, he soon realized, was uncalled-for.

Before she had arrived, his mind had already been made up. And now that she was here, this woman, Colin honestly felt, did not look, nor could ever pass as being someone's secretary — even if she went through a complete physical and external makeover. He thought about calling Captain White and requesting that they send someone else, but then he saw Lenora removing her police revolver from her travel bag. His curiosity suddenly caused him to pause; he intently observed as her geeky mannerisms instantly changed with that gun in her hand. The way she treated it as if it was one with her own mind, told Colin everything that he needed to know. Yes, she certainly did not look the part, but contentment quickly set in once he realized that he had been assigned a very competent backup.

Lenora's looks were something that he would approach her with later on. What was more important at the moment however, he felt, was that there was still a lot of prep work that needed to be done before Colin could officially enter the world of the Detroit Underworld Organization. So he pulled up a chair next to Lenora's desk and they began.

By midday, Colin's mind had yet to dissolve the images of his dream; they were still disrupting his ability to think straight. This wasn't good, and he knew it. Later on this evening, Colin would know whether or not he would be accepted into the fold and he had to be on his game when the time came for him to meet with the head of the D.U.O., otherwise he was going to blow an opportunity that he knew the police department would never get again.

He had to find a way to settle down his unfounded thoughts, and the only way Colin felt he could do that was to leave his new office and go out and try to track down Jimbo. He knew that the man wasn't the reason he had dreamt what he had, but thought he may have been the catalyst that triggered Colin's internal need to know why Jimbo had manufactured a lie that had nudged him into the position he was now in.

He went straight to Blackstone Park; Jimbo wasn't there. Assuming that the man did not normally venture too far away from the park, Colin got back into his car and then drove up and down Eight Mile road, hoping to get lucky and spot him walking down the street somewhere. First, he drove three miles west. He did not see him. He then turned his car around and drove back east. Two miles past the park, Colin stopped again and turned back around. He drove back west a couple of blocks before pulling into the Bank of America parking lot. Frustrated, but not deterred, Colin sat there and tried to figure out what his next course of action was going to be.

Luck had to have been on Colin's side this day, as he did not have to rack his brain for long. He wasn't sure why the homeless man was coming out of the same bank that he was parked at, but there was Jimbo. What the man did with his money was his own business, but keeping it at a bank was something that Colin would have never suspected he did. For all intensive purposes, the man lived off the grid and leaving a financial paper trail would eventually alert some government official to his existence.

For now, Jimbo's secret seemed to be safe — he did not need to worry that Colin would investigate the man's finances, and then rat him out for not paying his taxes, as that was not why he was looking for him. Colin only wanted to understand the man's reasons why he had done what he had; why had he introduced Salvadore Batiste to him?

As Colin exited his car, Jimbo saw him immediately and walked over in his direction. "Officer Ramirez. I'm glad to see you. I could use a ride home. I don't feel like walking back to my park."

"You were expecting me again, weren't you?"

"Not today. But I did expect you to show up eventually. I am assuming that you have some questions regarding what I did."

"I do."

Jimbo got into Colin's car and off to Blackstone Park they went. When they arrived, they both exited the car and walked over towards a rather large maple tree. A sense of déjà-vu quickly consumed Colin — it was the exact same tree that he had seen in his dream. Instinctively, he looked down on the ground, thankful that there was not a grave-size hole or a shovel that was anywhere close by. He then turned around and quickly scanned the perimeter of the park — Sal was also nowhere to be found.

"I haven't yet found out anything pertaining to Captain Potter's murder."

"I'm sure you'll let me know when you do."

"I will." After a few moments of quiet between the two, Jimbo said, "I can only assume that you came looking for me today because you would like to know why I introduced you to Salvadore Batiste?"

Colin had been, and was still somewhat baffled at the man's intuitive nature. If only he had the same forewarning abilities as Jimbo, his pending venture into the underground world of the Detroit Mob wouldn't be so terrifying. "That is correct. Why did you tell him that lie about me?"

"Because, Officer Ramirez. I've been supplying information to the D.U.O. for the past ten years... and I've made a good living from it. I've tried to justify the information I acquire for them as being necessary for me to achieve my goal, but my deep spiritual beliefs are no longer allowing me any more leeway. I need to completely remove myself from their association so that what little time I have left on this earth can be spent repenting the remainder of my sins. That way, when my time is up, I will be forgiven and allowed an opportunity to solicit passage through the Pearly Gates."

"So, you seized the unexpected opportunity you had and pawned them off onto me."

"Yes. I'm sorry, but you are much more equipped than I when it comes to finding a way to deal with them. I believe that they are a threat to our city and they need to be stopped before it becomes too late to do so. I am a man with many unforgivable mistakes attached to his name. Since I have become a born again Christian, I have tried to help out all those who are in need. But I unfortunately am powerless to do

33

anything to impede the inevitable spread of the disease. Yes, I am guilty of contributing to it for many years, but I had a personal goal that had to be reached which was more important at the time than my moral values. I am now confident that I, in the near future, will be able to reach my goal, and therefore, I feel that it is time for me to wash my hands of any association I have to the Detroit Underworld Organization."

Not only did Jimbo sound like a man of conviction, albeit conflicted, he sounded like a Profit. Maybe he did have an extraordinary ability to foresee the future, or maybe his past had caught up with him and his mental stability was not what it appeared to be. But Jimbo was right. The D.U.O. had to be stopped before it was too late. With their existence currently at a manageable level, now was the time to infiltrate their organization and plant a 'virus' that would shut them down for good.

Satisfied with what he had heard from Jimbo, Colin left the park, got back into his car and drove home. He still had most of the day left of which he knew he should spend back at his new office. But since he was technically out on his own, he decided to scrap the remainder of his day until it was time for him to show up at his meeting — he had a wife and a two year old whom he knew were going to be starving for his attention. So before he became fully immersed in the underground world, he wanted to spend some quality time with those whom he loved the most.

What he was only moments away from doing was about as crazy as walking mindlessly through a rattlesnake pit barefoot because you firmly believed that you wouldn't get bit. That was literally what Officer Ramirez was about to do — walk himself into a dangerous situation without any form of assurance or backup whatsoever. He could not risk any police being spotted; he had to attend his first business meeting with the D.U.O. alone and hope that whoever was waiting for him inside would not suspect him of being an officer of the law.

As he sat in his car outside of Thibault's By The River, a place that he had been to several times over the years with his wife, Olivia, Colin could think of nothing but the what ifs. What if he were successful in convincing the D.U.O. that he was an asset that they could not ignore? What if he got himself in so deep that he just could not get out? What if he walked through that restaurant door and was unable to pull the wool over their eyes? Or worse, what if they saw right through his bull shit and pegged him for who he really was? They would surely kill him. What would his sudden death do to his family? Who would take care of his wife and daughter, Ana? There were just so many questions that Colin had in which an answer would do a lot to remove his uncertainty. Any bit of information pertaining to what was waiting for him on the other side of those restaurant doors would surely be welcomed — at least then, he would be able to put together a decent enough plan to help ensure his safety. However, with no psychic sitting in his passenger seat to confer with, all that Colin could do was hope that everything was going to work out all right.

Once he was as ready as he was going to get, he took one last relaxing deep breath, cleared his mind, and then exited his vehicle. He took a moment and looked at the restaurant. From the outside looking in, it appeared to be busy. This was a good thing, as it helped to give Colin a bit of the reassurance he had sought, because a busy restaurant meant that those whom he was meeting inside would strive to stay anonymous and not create a public scene if his true identity were to somehow be discovered.

When he walked inside, no one greeted him — but within a matter of only a few seconds he saw Sal sitting at the bar. The man didn't need to say anything, as Colin's heart immediately began racing — there was no backing out now.

Sal got up off of his barstool and began to walk towards the back corner of the restaurant; Colin followed him, doing his best with each step he took to slow his heart rate down and stay calm.

Sal, he expected to see. Antonio Marcone, he did as well. But Colin never expected that there was going to be a third member of the D.U.O. here with them. This unbalanced the odds even more than what Colin had anticipated. He had felt that at any time during this meeting if there was a possibility that he was not selling his purpose for being there, than having the odds of two against one were still somewhat in his favor if he needed to bail — he no longer felt that way.

"Mr. Velázquez. Please take a seat."

Colin complied with Antonio's request.

"Before we get started, I never conduct a business meeting without first having a stiff drink to stimulate the nerves." Antonio looked over at the bar and within a matter of only a few seconds; a waitress had arrived at their table with four rock glasses of Canadian Club.

Colin wasn't much of a drinker, but he didn't want to insult the head of the Detroit Mob so he took a sip of his drink; an unfounded fear suddenly consumed him. It could have already been known that he was a police officer and this drink that he had been served could have been laced with a poison of some kind. Chances were though that it wasn't — it was only Colin's paranoia and still unsettled heart rate that was allowing his mind to assume such a scenario before this meeting even began.

After he swallowed what was in his mouth, he took another moment and tried to calm his nerves. Once he felt that they were down to a manageable level, he looked at Antonio and said, "I appreciate the drink, Mr. Marcone. Thank you."

"You are welcome. Now let us get down to business. I am told that you are a private investigator who isn't afraid to exploit a client when there is a profit to be made in doing so."

Colin took another sip of his whiskey before he confirmed that statement. "That is something that I have always been willing to do."

"Then why, may I ask, is your office in a little shithole building in Hamtramck?"

Although he expected to be grilled until Antonio was satisfied with his disposition, he never expected that he would be asked to validate why his new 'office' was where it was — nor did he even expect that the D.U.O. would already know about it. Colin took another sip of his drink, pausing long enough to not only swallow it, but to create a reason. He then said, "It is my own money that I have to spend to operate my business. I find no valid reason to have a lavish office space that would be used less than a quarter of my entire workweek, nor do I need comfort when I am there. So long as the place is clean and not crawling with cockroaches, I am content."

Antonio could certainly appreciate the frugalness. The D.U.O., as it was, was in a basement under a pawnshop. Therefore, he felt no reason to dispute the man's answer. But he still had a few other questions that he wanted to ask before he would consider bringing this man into the fold. "That's fair enough. So... why is it then that you now wish to work for me?"

"Because... I wish to exploit your desires."

"Excuse me?" Antonio replied, almost spitting out his whiskey when he heard that answer.

"Although I don't know you or everything that your organization is about, I can easily assume that you are a driven man; a man who desires both wealth and power. Let's just say that I want to ride on your coattails of success. The more wealth and power you gain, the more money I will make."

Antonio now understood the man's answer — and he could certainly respect the man's gumption for wanting to latch on to his future success. "And how is it that you're going to help me?"

Colin had brought with him a business-sized envelope. He slid it across the table and instructed Antonio to open it up. "That is a five year business agreement between you and me. It states that I will provide you with any information you need on someone, a place of business, or a perspective event, in exchange for a commission; an amount where we will determine a certain percentage depending upon the difficulty of the pending transaction. I will also guarantee you that the information I will provide to you will be everything that you will need to acquire the asset you seek, or to put pressure on an individual to succumb to your demands. Then after this five year agreement is over, we will either renegotiate it or we will both go our separate ways."

Before this meeting had begun, Antonio was uncertain if this apparent unscrupulous man that Sal had found was going to be worth his time. He honestly assumed that the man was going to be in essence, all smoke and mirrors; a con artist, a used car salesman — a scheming narcissist. But as he continued to listen and observe, his initial opinion had disappeared. This Manual Velázquez had not only impressed him, but his sureness was an attribute that Antonio most definitely liked.

He ordered another round of drinks and then began to skim over the contract that Colin had presented to him. Signing an agreement such as this was something that had never been done before by anyone in the long history of the Detroit Underworld Organization. But in this unusual situation that was before him, Antonio recognized that this was something that needed to be done. This man brought with him a lot of possibilities to the table. And in order for Antonio to achieve his own goals, he needed to do things differently than what his organization had done in the past. Therefore, he felt that it was necessary to take this kind of risk and trust that this man would fulfill his end of the agreement — nor could Antonio fault the man for wanting to protect himself from becoming bound to the D.U.O. for the remainder of his life.

Antonio smiled, took a healthy sip of his freshly delivered whiskey, and savored it on his pallet. After borrowing the waitress' pen, he took a few moments to read over the contract before he signed it. Once he had done that, he passed it over to Sal and then Louie, asking them both to sign as witnesses to the agreement. When that was completed, Colin sealed the deal with Manual's signature.

During the duration of their meal, Antonio explained what it was that he was expecting from Colin and what his long-term plan was. As Manual Velázquez, he would be able to easily acquire and present the information that Antonio would ever want and need. But as Colin Ramirez, the police officer, having to step across that invisible line in order to accumulate evidence against the D.U.O., was going to be not only an ethical challenge, but an emotional one as well. There were going to be times when he knew that he would have to financially destroy some lives in order to get what he needed — a deed that was going to be a bitter pill for him to swallow. But it was something that he knew had to be done. He just had to get used to the idea of screwing over some people, preferably lowlifes, to get whatever it was that he needed in order to get the job done.

When their meeting had concluded, Colin had achieved what he had set out to do. He was now firmly planted on the other side of the law and had instantly become a part of the underworld, undercover and always in jeopardy. He just hoped that this world that he was now a part of did not follow him all the way to the front steps of his own home.

~ *It only takes a brief moment for your world to turn upside down. And there is no guarantee thereafter, no matter how much time you are willing to spend, that it will ever return back to the way it used to be.* ~

Right after his meeting had taken place, Colin returned to his new office. He immediately called Captain White and gave him his full report on everything that had happened. Out of respect for his captain, he should have gone straight to the precinct and done that. But there was still a bit of paranoia floating around in the back of his mind as the location of his new 'office' was already known — he didn't want to risk being seen walking into a police station by someone who was associated with the D.U.O.

After his call was completed, he wrote up his report and then had Lenora encrypt it for him. He wasn't that computer savvy; he only knew the basics when it came to a computer: E-mailing, searching the web for information, and creating documents. She was after all, his 'secretary'. But in all honesty, he hated having to have her perform such menial tasks as this. If he were at his desk back at the precinct, he would not have to worry about protecting his soon-to-be accumulating files. But he wasn't. There was a very good possibility that the D.U.O. would show up at his 'office' one day when neither he nor Lenora were around and help themselves to his files — simply out of curiosity or because of suspicion.

One week later...

It had been the easiest, stress-free week Colin had since he and his wife had gone on that Caribbean Cruise three years ago; the same cruise that their now two year old daughter was conceived. Though he welcomed the break from the everyday grind of being a police officer, he was beginning to wonder if what he had volunteered for was actually going to occur — he had yet to be contacted by the D.U.O. since their initial meeting.

Either they currently had no use for him, or were waiting for the right moment to come so that they could quietly get rid of him. Yes, he was being paranoid again, but this was now his life; no longer routine with guarantees. He could only speculate what each day was going to bring. And for as long as he was going to be undercover, Colin not only needed to take every cautionary measure he could, but had to find a way to adapt accordingly to whatever unexpected situations that were sent his way in order to ensure that he survived this assignment.

"I'm curious, Lenora. Do you know if any sort of lead has surfaced pertaining to Captain Potter's murder?"

"I'd prefer it if you called me Leni... and no. I just finished looking over the latest reports in the Detroit Police Department's database and nothing new has turned up. However, I did learn that Captain White has now assigned two other detectives, Maxwell Banks and Joshua Brampton, to the case. They apparently went out in search of that Jimbo guy you went to talk to last week, but after two full days of looking, they could not find him."

"Hum? I wonder why they could not find him. As far as I knew, he never left his neighborhood. Did they try the bank?"

"That I don't know, but..." The door to the office opened up and in walked a man whose presence demanded respect — Lenora promptly shut down her connection to the police database, replacing it with the pcmag.com website.

Dressed sharply in what was obviously an expensive suit, this tall, dark-haired man, walked right in without saying a word, brushed off the antique-ish looking wood seat that was in front of Colin's desk, and then sat down. "Could you ask your intern to leave, as we have something important to discuss?"

"She's not my intern, Mr. Mazotti. She's my secretary, Lenora. What you need to speak with me about can be said in front of her as she is well aware that your organization and I now have a working agreement."

After a few seconds of scrutinizing Lenora's appearance, and not personally being impressed, Louie said, "You could have done better when choosing a secretary; one that would be more 'serviceable' than just keeping notes, getting you coffee, and answering the phone."

She may have only been five foot four and weighed just over a buck ten, but twenty-seven years of defending herself from the wrath of four older athletic brothers had given her a very thick skin. Lenora never backed down from any asshole or bitch that desperately deserved an ass whooping — no matter how big, tall, fat, or old they were. However, if it wasn't for the fact that this man was associated with what they were investigating, Lenora would have seriously thought about walking right up to Louie and giving the man an unnecessary tracheotomy by ramming her shiny new Bic pen into the man's throat for his deliberate chauvinistic comment. Instead, she smiled, knowing that she had just been tested — she knew, from her years of training, that Louie had purposely tried to get a reaction out of her in order to assess what kind of person she was.

Although Colin hardly knew her, he could tell that Lenora was fuming inside. That smile she posed was obviously a fake one — but it also showed that she was not easily affected by a few words spoken from an insensitive asshole. "So... what can I do for you, Mr. Mazotti?"

"There's no need for you to be formal... although I do appreciate the courtesy, as we will be working closely together over the length of the agreement, so I see no reason for us to not be on a first name basis."

"Ok."

After a few more moments of scrutinizing Lenora, and finding her to be just a bit too plain for his liking, Louie said to Colin, "I am here because Antonio has decided that he is ready for you to begin living up to your end of our agreement."

Officer Ramirez was relieved that he and his fictitious skills were actually going to be used, as he really did not want to take it upon himself to go out and prove to Antonio that he was wasting his skills by being left on the sidelines. "So... what kind of information would he like for me to acquire?"

"Anything that you feel might be useful. Antonio wants to begin to accumulate some legitimate assets."

"Does he having anything specific in mind?"

41

"No. It will be your choice."

Colin didn't see that one coming. He was expecting detailed instructions from the head of the D.U.O., not a blank slate for him to work with. Whatever the reason was for this, Colin needed to make sure that he understood exactly what was being expected of him. "Can you clarify, Louie, what it is that Mr. Marcone is asking of me?"

"Antonio feels that it is necessary to begin assembling a portfolio of assets. Having these assets will add a much needed legitimacy to the future growth of the organization. So as of right now, it doesn't really matter to him what businesses you help him acquire, so long as they will make him money."

At first, Colin wasn't too sure why Antonio Marcone was entrusting him to make such a big decision, but after a few moments of thought, he realized why. This was a test; a test to see just how good his skills were, what kind of damaging information he could provide to him, and what kind of overall judgment he had. "Ok. But I hope that Mr. Marcone realizes that this assignment he has placed me on is one that will not happen overnight. In order to bring your boss the best opportunity to acquire an asset that has the potential to make him a worthwhile profit, he will need to be patient."

"He will be... to a point. He is giving you two weeks to get this done."

Two weeks was a lot of time — but it might not be enough time for Colin to figure out a way to accomplish this task without actually burning someone to do it. Unfortunately, he feared that he might have no other option but to do just that.

Satisfied that he had successfully delivered his message, Louie stood up from his seat, turned, and then headed for the office door. Lenora could no longer keep up the façade she had expertly erected. In fact, her eyes were immediately locked onto Louie's back as he was leaving — it looked to Colin as if she was trying to burn a hole right into the back of the man's skull. He could easily understand her contempt for Antonio's right-hand man, however, he needed to make sure that she did not accidentally ruffle any feathers, so he raised his right hand and mouthed the word 'relax' to her, as he needed her to dial down her emotions — at least until Louie had actually left.

As much as she didn't want to, she complied with Colin's request. Yes, Louie Mazotti was the enemy and she was an officer of the law who was also undercover. However, this was her first field assignment and her entire career up until this point had been behind four walls and in front of a computer. She needed to quickly remind herself what protocol was and remember that a police officer was suppose to comply with their superior officer's orders — in this instance, that was Officer Ramirez. Lenora had to stay smart, think before she acted, and not let her emotions interfere with her job. This was a very critical assignment, and if she became the reason that it failed, she just might not get another opportunity to go out in the field.

Once Louie was gone, Colin and Lenora documented the meeting. When that was done, he asked Officer Lexington to begin a general search for any businesses that might currently be on the law's radar. Colin needed a back-up plan just in case he could not figure out an alternative to having to bury an actual business owner.

4

Four days into the short window he had been given, Colin had been at a loss. He had spent a few hours brainstorming with Captain White, even had picked the brain of a few of his fellow officers, but could not figure out a way to create a believable prospective asset for Antonio to acquire — at least, not one large enough that would give them all the leverage they needed to shut down the D.U.O. for good. This left him with only one other avenue to pursuit; an option that he didn't really want to explore because once he did, he knew that this would be the only route that he would be able to take from that moment forward.

Surprisingly, Chief Winslow had given him the green light to do what he really didn't want to. It seemed unethical; morally wrong to burn someone. He kept trying to convince himself that the end result would be the same — it was after all, one wrong simply being swapped out for another. However, he had an uneasy feeling that when all was said and done, the accumulated amount of wrongs would never be corrected. And because of that probability, Colin feared that he may never be able to return to being what he was — an officer of the law.

But he had been left with no other viable option, and he knew it. This was his case and he had to do what he had to do in order to put himself and the police force in the best possible position to shut down the Detroit Underworld Organization — he just hoped that all of the assets that he was going to be sending Antonio's way would not in turn, make it more difficult when the time came to doing what he had signed up for.

In hindsight, Colin was thankful that the department had assigned Officer Lexington to him. His initial assessment of Lenora had been way off. She was actually very good at what she did; proven by all of the information that she had been able to gather. All that he had to do before he handed it over to Antonio Marcone was visit the

Old World Café & Restaurant and confirm that the information that she had collected for him was correct.

The Detroit Police Department and the Department of Immigration had been working together for months to confirm multiple reports of illegal immigrants working at that restaurant; not just as servers, bartenders, and kitchen staff, but there had been suspicions of a brothel being operated above the place. The rumor was that the owner of the restaurant would pay fifty thousand dollars to a 'broker', who would then arrange to smuggle workers into the country; workers who were kept locked up as prisoners. By day, these immigrants worked the restaurant and served the public. By night, they served high paying clientele until they each had earned the owner four times what he had originally paid for their services. This type of situation disgusted Colin to the point where he didn't care that he was about to burn this man; this cold-hearted bastard for what he was doing to these people.

That evening, Colin showed up at the restaurant, went to the back alley door like Lenora had instructed him to do, and then rang the doorbell. When the mail slot opened up a few seconds later, he placed four hundred dollars into it. A moment after that, another slot in the door opened and a set of eyes looked back at him. In a thick, heavy, but obviously fake European accent, the man behind the door said, "Password!"

"I'm hungry and I am in need of a late night snack," Colin replied.

The slot on the alley door shut and the actual door opened up. The man who had been behind it was no longer there — he had disappeared as fast as Colin's four hundred dollars had.

The hallway was dark, lit only by a few black lights. There was nowhere for Colin to go but up or back out to the alley — he went up. He got to the top of the first floor and the only door that accessed that level had a sign on it that read, 'Mexican'. The second floor access door sign read, 'Asian'. The third and final level had 'Eastern European' on it.

Colin opened up the door on the top floor and immediately stepped into the anteroom — what he saw, proved what the law had suspected. Twelve women and three men sat there dressed in outfits that any self respecting stripper wouldn't be caught dead in, as what they had on didn't leave much to the imagination. They all stood up (yes, even the three men did) and did their best to sell themselves to Colin, knowing that the sooner they paid off their debts, the sooner they would be free to leave.

However, before things got out of hand, Colin just smiled, politely said no thank you, and left. Once he was outside the building, he knew that this place needed to be shut down. Ideally, the law should do it, but this was exactly what Colin needed to solidify his cover as a corrupt private investigator.

The next morning, he called Louie and told him that he had what Antonio was looking for. An hour later, Louie had swung by Colin's office, picked him up, and brought him to the headquarters of the organization. Needless to say, by the time Colin had finished passing along his information, what little trepidation that had been there, was no longer as Antonio now seemed very happy; very content that he had chosen to sign that deal with 'Manual'.

This time, it was Sal that had driven him back to his office. However, before he drove away, Sal said, "You will know if this doesn't work out because we will be back to in essence, void our contract. If it works out, then you'll have earned Antonio's trust and you will have no reason to ever worry about your life. Go out and have a beer and enjoy the rest of your day."

Colin knew that the information that he had supplied to Antonio was solid enough for him to extort the restaurant and the entire building from its owner. But that still didn't prevent a seed of doubt from being planted in his mind. He would not be able to sleep this evening until he knew whether or not he was going to live or die. He could only exist until he knew for sure what the future held for him.

The Old World Café & Restaurant was just the first of many assets that Antonio Marcone was able to acquire, all due to the information that Colin was able to supply him. In total, he had helped the D.U.O. procure seven businesses during his first year undercover. Manual Velázquez was becoming a key asset; Colin Ramirez was becoming more conflicted about who he was. There had been a lot of days, a lot of situations in which Colin had completely forgotten about what was right and what was wrong. Sometimes, he didn't care about what he was doing; sometimes he did. When that little devil would unexpectedly appear on his shoulder, he wouldn't always swat it off. That was why on occasion, Lenora had to step in and remind him of why he went undercover in the first place and that they still had a lot of work to do because the evidence that had been accumulated, just wasn't quite enough yet to shut down the rapidly growing Detroit Underworld Organization.

Thankfully so far, no one had been unnecessarily killed during the extortion process. Two restaurants, a theater, two nightclubs, and two strip clubs, were each now assets of the D.U.O. because of Colin's collected information. Surprisingly, no one within the police department had voiced a concern that one of their own was helping a criminal remove other criminal elements from their city. Still, it bothered Colin that he had not made enough headway with this case. He needed to go much deeper than he had first anticipated; he needed to become more than just a tool of acquisition, he needed to become a trusted associate of Antonio Marcone — and the only way he felt he could do that was to fabricate a lie that would cause Antonio to pause and reassess his business practices. But before Colin could implement his idea, he needed to get permission from Captain White — because what he now wanted to do, would involve him.

He thought about going directly to the precinct, but then thought better of it. Over the last year, he had only been there three times — and each time he went, in the back of his mind, he was certain that he was going to be followed. And although Colin had now earned Antonio's complete trust, there was still a small part of him that refused to allow him to let his guard down. He could have simply called or e-mailed Captain White in order to inform him of what he needed to know, but the man deserved to hear what Colin's crazy idea was in person. However, a secure place first needed to be found in order for that to happen; a place where the risk of his one on one conversation being witnessed or overheard, was minimal.

Feeling somewhat uncertain, of many things, he walked up to the ninth hole at the Detroit Golf and Country Club in Highland Michigan, paying close attention to his surroundings the entire time. Needless to say, his surprise appearance caused Christopher White's

47

tee shot to slice severely off to the right — it hit a tree, ricocheted off of it, and then nearly hit another golfer who had been walking on the adjacent fairway. "I apologize for coming here to see you on your day off, sir, but I figured that being out here in the open might be safer than meeting at the precinct."

"You could have called, Colin."

"Yeah... I know. But I'm glad that I didn't because what I want to speak with you about also concerns the chief. And since I see that he is part of your foursome today, you won't have to relay our conversation afterwards."

"What is so important, Officer Ramirez, that you felt it necessary to speak with us out here in public."

After Chief Winslow hit his tee shot, Colin walked with them down the fairway and explained what it was that he wanted to do. He honestly thought that his idea was probably going to be shot down, but he didn't know what else to do. He needed to push Antonio's button and force the man into doing something significant in order to obtain that damaging piece of evidence.

And just like Colin had thought; there was an objection — but not from the person whom he thought it would be. The chief was completely against it; Captain White was not. "We've been patiently gathering evidence for more than a year but have yet to get our hands on that smoking gun. If what Colin wants to do will finally give us that, then I am willing to let him do it."

"It's too risky, Chris."

"That's what we signed up for, Jacob, when we chose to become police officers. Sometimes we have to willingly put our own lives on the line in order to get done what needs to get done."

It was bad enough that Officer Ramirez's own life, and even Officer Lenora Lexington's life, had been in jeopardy over the past year. Colin preferred not to have to put the life of any other officer in harm's way if there was another option. But the existence of the D.U.O. has gone on for way too many years and Jacob Winslow was fully aware that conventional means had yet to provide them with any sort of results. It was time for them to think outside of the box — that was why Officer Ramirez had suggested what he had.

The group arrived at the one ball that was still the furthest from the hole — it belonged to Chief Winslow. The chief took his next shot and then put his club back into his bag. As they walked over to where Captain White's ball lied, the chief turned to Colin and said, "Ok. You have my permission."

No longer did he have to be escorted to the D.U.O. headquarters. Because of the trust he had earned, Colin had been allowed to come and go as he pleased — so long as he used discretion.

Today was a day in which Colin was confident that his status within the D.U.O. would change. With what he had planned on divulging to Antonio, it would either draw him fully into a world that would surely consume, and more than likely change him forever, or the information would be so unsettling, he would be kept on the outside looking in for awhile longer until not only proof was found, but the situation that the D.U.O. found themselves in was dealt with.

Colin's plan, he hoped, would allow him an opportunity to finally find out first hand everything that went on within Antonio's organization. And if he were finally brought completely into it, he knew at that point that he would be able to acquire the evidence that was needed to finally shut down the city's biggest growing threat.

As he entered Antonio's office, both Louie and Sal were there sitting side by side in front of the desk. It had appeared that the three of them were in the middle of an important discussion. What the topic was, Colin wasn't about to guess or inquire about — at least, not until he was certain where his status was. That was why he had come here today, as he wanted to see just how much trust he had actually earned. "I hope that I'm not interrupting?"

"Well... you are," Sal stated, with a not too impressed tone to his voice.

"It's not his fault. Manual has been given an open invitation to come here whenever he wants," Louie felt the need to state the obvious. He then wanted to follow it up and make his opinion be known that he believed those who were not officially a part of the family should not be allowed to invite themselves to the table whenever they wanted, but he knew that Antonio would not be too impressed with him, questioning a decision already made.

"He should have at least called first."

"It doesn't matter, Sal." Antonio raised his hand to signal for his associate to drop the subject before it became an unnecessary topic of debate. "Manual is an integral part of this organization and has earned my trust."

"I'm glad that is how you feel, Mr. Marcone. It is why I have come here today, as I wish to speak with you about my position."

"What's wrong?"

"Nothing's wrong. I just think that I am being underutilized. I now feel that I can offer the organization more than just being an outsourced employee."

"You want completely in?"

"Yes, Louie. I want to become a full fledged member of the D.U.O."

"I vote no. He's not Italian!"

"You don't get a vote, Sal." Antonio got up from his desk and walked over to where there was a fresh pot of coffee sitting. He poured himself a cup; it was too early in the day for whiskey. After returning to his desk and savoring his first sip, he said, "I had a feeling that you were going to ask me this one day. This is however, something that I will have to think long and hard about before I say yes or no. As you have shown us the dedication that any of my loyal associates must, bringing you completely into the fold is a risk that I need to guarantee is worth taking. Everyone within this organization is of Italian decent, and I'm not sure that allowing it to become a melting pot is the correct thing to do."

"I can understand that, Mr. Marcone. All that I can say is that Jackie Robinson broke the color barrier — and now that the game has incorporated the talents of individuals of many ethnic backgrounds, it is better and stronger than it has ever been."

"I can't argue that point. I will let you know what my decision is within the next few days."

Colin's cell phone rang; right on cue. Lenora had called him, just like he had asked. Now it was time to plant the seed of suspicion and see what kind of reaction he'd get from the three that were in the room with him. "What's up, Leni?" Colin purposely placed his phone on speaker so that those in the room could hear the rehearsed conversation they were about to have.

"Well... I was checking my on-line blogs like I do every week and came across an apparent leaked report that claims an F.B.I. agent, name not mentioned of course, recently had a meeting with a Detroit police captain."

"That happens all the time, Leni."

"I know. But this captain, Christopher White, has supposedly gathered enough circumstantial evidence to point the finger at the D.U.O. for the plane crash that took the life of Vance Palmalino just over a year ago."

Colin glanced around the room as discreetly as he could, hoping to see a surprised reaction on someone's face; there wasn't one on any of them. This fabricated accusation was meant to strike a nerve and force Antonio to do something retaliatory against Captain White to silence him. They needed a reason to arrest him and shut the organization down — Colin's idea had apparently just fizzled out. "You said, circumstantial?"

"Yes!"

"Then this captain has no proof; only his own suspicions."

"That is correct. But his 'evidence' has given the F.B.I. a reason to look into the possibility of it actually being true."

Colin thanked Lenora and then disconnected his call. Antonio sank back into his office chair, took another healthy sip of his coffee, and said, "I can't believe that the Feds never suspected me of this before and that it took an overzealous local pig to get them to consider me as a suspect in that plane crash."

"And they'll never prove that you did arrange it," Louie said, "As they have yet to find anything other than a few pieces of luggage floating around in the Bermuda Triangle."

"I never did get a thank you for that," Sal pointed out.

This sudden burst of table talk had caused perplexity to suddenly seep into Colin's brain.

"You're right, Sal," Antonio acknowledged. "I do owe you a belated thank you. The bomb that I had asked you to plant was most certainly powerful enough to blow that plane to smithereens."

Colin never expected that it would be he in this room that was shocked. They had only fabricated the allegation to get Antonio to do something to prevent an investigation from taking place, knowing that any kind of attention drawn to him by the law would not be wanted — he just never expected to walk into this room and confirm their fictitious accusation. "Are you going to do anything to stop this from being investigated?"

"No, Manual. That is what I have you for. I want you to keep tabs on the investigation. And when it gets to the point that they have actually found some hard evidence against me, I will then do something about it. Until that happens, there is no need to tip the boat over before the sharks get here."

Colin was at an impasse. He now had firsthand knowledge that Antonio Marcone had arranged the death of Vance Palmalino. But his awareness of the facts would still not be near enough for the law to shut down the D.U.O. — at least, not yet anyway. He just had to document this conversation and place it with the rest of the accumulated evidence he had and hope that Antonio Marcone would accept his request to become a full fledge member of his organization. If that didn't happen, then Colin was beginning to believe that he was never going to be able to build an airtight case from the outside looking in.

Antonio had made his decision; Colin wasn't happy with it, but in all honesty, he couldn't blame the man for it. He was after all, the head of Detroit's Mob and he had to ensure that any decisions he made would not come back to bite him in the ass. So for now, Colin Ramirez was denied a membership into the organization. But that was ok; he still had Antonio's trust and respect. And because he had that trust, a day was going to come where he was going to inadvertently let his guard down. When that happened, Colin was going to use everything he had accumulated and bury the man.

Over the following year, Colin was able to assembly quite a bit of evidence against the D.U.O., but like he had been doing since the beginning, all that he could do was put it with the rest — the dagger that would ultimately destroy Detroit's Mob had yet to find a way into the palm of Colin's hand. Still, he was hoping that everything he had already gathered just might be enough.

With Lenora tailing behind him in a separate car to keep a watchful eye on the surroundings, Colin brought all of the evidence he had, including his documented account of Antonio's admittance that he had killed his predecessor, to the Detroit Public Safety Headquarters when he met up with Captain White and Chief Winslow. Once they had thoroughly reviewed everything that Colin had accumulated, and after quite a bit of discussion amongst themselves, they all came to the same conclusion — they just did not have enough evidence. Theoretically, they could arrest Antonio Marcone and charge him with the premeditated murder of Vance Palmalino, but there was no guarantee that the charges would stick because their evidence was based on hearsay. And knowing Antonio like Colin did, the man undoubtedly had a very good lawyer at his disposal; one that would probably be able to easily convince a judge that the evidence had been clearly fabricated so that a supposed murder could be pinned on his client.

Because of that distinct possibility, Chief Winslow and Captain White decided that it was best to just keep accumulating more evidence to their pile; a pile that to Colin, seemed to be gathering layers upon layers of dust instead of the needed hard facts.

Two months following that meeting, no more evidence had been gathered. Colin's daily routine became repetitive, boring, and unproductive — not by choice, but because Antonio Marcone had chosen not to contact him. Colin had actually thought that he finally had been kicked to the curb, essentially ending any more opportunities to find that smoking gun. But that hadn't been the case at all. Apparently, Antonio had been working on a rather large deal, which had forced him to dedicate nearly all of his valuable time to it, a now completed deal that had apparently netted him a large sum of cash.

When Antonio finally contacted him a month later, Colin felt relief — he also felt disappointed at the same time. Yes, he was happy that the proverbial door had not been slammed in his face and locked, but he also was secretly hoping that he no longer was going to be associated with the criminal world. In fact, Captain White had just given him a one-week notification — if by the end of it, he had not been contacted, he was going to be pulled out.

After apologizing to Colin for keeping him in the dark for as long as he had, Antonio let him know that he was ready to continue expanding his empire. But unlike the past when Colin had been given free rein to choose what businesses to target, this time Antonio had chosen it for him — he wanted the recently renovated Weston Book Cadillac Hotel.

This was a request, which Colin knew he could not fulfill, as this was not a business that was being monitored by the law. This was instead, a very well respected historic hotel in the downtown core. Why did Antonio want it? Why did he even think that it would be possible to take possession of this away from the rather large corporation that owned it? Those were baffling questions that Colin could not even begin to speculate on. However, after just a bit of deductive reasoning, he assembled what he believed might be the answer. The hotel just happened to be located somewhat central to most of the businesses that Antonio had already acquired through him. Logistically, and financially, it made sense for Antonio to want to own the famous hotel because it, unlike any of the other businesses he had acquired, was the perfect showcase piece to have in the portfolio of his ever-growing corporation.

He felt like he was stuck in a pad of drying cement. He really didn't know what he was going to do. Colin just wasn't sure if he would even be able to supply Antonio with any pertinent information — whether it was real or fabricated. And although he still wanted to continue to impress the man with his 'work' so that he could stay undercover, he really didn't want to go any further across that proverbial line than he already had. If he did, Colin feared that slipping seamlessly back to his old life was going to be a rather monumental challenge — going back to being just a regular old police officer afterwards however, he was all but certain was going to be impossible. When this was finally all over, his life was going to be forever changed.

After an hour of internal debate, Colin had made a decision; one that could make his undercover status become more difficult to continue in — nevertheless, he felt that this was what he had to do.

Although he knew that what he was about to get himself involved in was going to test his code of ethics, Colin felt obliged to continue on with what he had volunteered to do. But before he committed to the task that Antonio had asked him to perform, he was going to try his best to make the man understand that what was being asked of him was going to take a lot of time and effort and just may not be worth it in the end. If he could somehow get Antonio to see that a hostile takeover of the Weston Book Cadillac Hotel would be a waste of his time and money, then Colin would simply be able to resume what he had been doing all along. If for some reason he was unable to talk Antonio out of what he wanted, then Colin knew that he would be left with only one other option — he would comply. But that didn't mean that he was going to throw away his life and fully commit to the 'dark side', he simply would just have to approach his task in a completely different manner. Somehow, he would have to find a way to drag out his gathering of the desired information on the hotel for as long as he could and buy some time until the last card he had up his sleeve could be played — that being whatever other evidence he might gather along with the twenty plus months of accumulated hard work that was just waiting to be revealed.

The next day, with a game plan in hand, Colin met Antonio in private — for the first time ever, neither Louie nor Sal was present. He was unsure why no one else was there in the room with them, but he could only assume the reason for this was that Antonio just did not want to hear any objections from his close associates — they after all, had a tendency to bitch and complain for no real reason other than to simply annoy each other. This unexpected occurrence could very well mean that Antonio was having second thoughts about his request to obtain the Weston Book Cadillac Hotel and wanted Colin's honest opinion on the subject before he committed himself to such a rather large undertaking. Then again, this could be the day that he had been waiting for. Today might be that day in which he finally became a full-fledged member of the Detroit Underworld Organization. And if that was what was about to happen, then Colin was as ready as he was ever going to be to take that first step onto a path that he was all but certain was going to lead him on a very treacherous, life altering journey.

When their meeting was complete, it had been exactly what his initial suspicions had been. Antonio had listened to and agreed with Colin's assessment and opinion. And although Antonio really wanted to gain ownership of the hotel, he understood just how enormous of a task this was going to be. For that reason, he was willing to be more patient than he had ever been before. He had all the faith in the world that Colin would acquire the needed information for him however, until that came to fruition, Antonio also wanted him to continue on with what he had been doing all along — find other perspective businesses for him to acquire so that he could continue to expand his ever growing empire.

By the end of the second year, Colin had forwarded the information to Antonio that had allowed him to acquire four more additional businesses: another restaurant, a sporting goods store, a rather large tattoo parlor, and one of the city's most popular nightclubs. But as far as the Weston Book Cadillac Hotel was concerned, he informed Antonio that he had made very little progress. Unfortunately (on purpose) he had been unable to find anything damaging for Antonio to use against the corporate entity that owned it — other than a tax discrepancy from a few years back.

Antonio was now beginning to get impatient. However, he was still willing to wait just a little while longer and allow 'Manual' some more time — but not much more, as he was getting pretty tired of running his organization out of a pawnshop basement.

With the window nearly closed when it came to Colin obtaining the required information that Antonio so desperately wanted, a disappointing realization was now starting to become inevitable. For the first time in his life, he felt as if he had failed, as he no longer believed that he was ever going to acquire that one all important piece of damaging evidence. He admittedly, had been one step over that proverbial line for quite a long time, and he knew that all he had to do was keep going further beyond it to get what he needed — but he just could not do it. Therefore, with his conscience not allowing him to do that, Colin knew that the time had come for him to get out and leave the life of Manual Velázquez behind for good.

Had it all been worth it? Yes, as the good guys now had more intimate knowledge than ever before pertaining to the inner workings of the D.U.O. The downside to his being on the inside was that his 'employment' with them had actually helped to evolve them into something more than just a fly-by-night operation. The Detroit Underworld Organization had become a rather large corporate entity and had grown larger, faster, and stronger, than what anyone could have foreseen. Therefore, in order for the Detroit Police Department to even have a chance of permanently shutting them down, Colin felt that it was time to go back to the drawing board and come up with a new plan. In his opinion, the current playbook had to be tossed out the window and an unexpected Hail Mary executed so that the game being played would officially come to an end.

When he had informed Lenora about what he wanted to do, she quickly voiced her opinion; accusing him of being yellow for wanting to detach himself from everything that he had accomplished, and being for afraid of getting his hands even dirtier than they already were. Colin had a few women in his younger days berate his manhood, but never had anyone reprimanded him and challenged his willingness to do whatever was necessary to get the job done. "But this case is at a standstill, Lenora. Without officially being accepted into the organization, I fear that I won't be able to find what we need to permanently shut them down."

"So then fabricate something and see what kind of reaction they have."

"I tried that already, remember? It didn't work. They all but laughed at the accusation."

"It's been more than a year. It won't hurt to try again."

"I'm not even sure if I would be able to conjure up the kind of allegations that would not only shock them, but cause them to get nervous."

"Correct me if I am wrong, but did this undercover assignment of yours not start shortly after you went looking for information on who killed Maven Potter and then got unexpectedly introduced to Salvadore Batiste?"

"Yes. And to this day, the department still does not have any viable leads regarding who killed our former captain."

Lenora didn't need to say anything else. She just sat behind her desk and allowed Colin's brain to accept the subtle suggestion she had just given to him. He felt stupid for not thinking of this sooner. The ultimate insinuation had been there all along for him to serve to Antonio on a silver platter, and Colin had unintentionally left it on the counter. If he had only used his brain, he could have possibly avoided the majority of the double life he had led. But there was nothing that he could do about that now — the past is the past. What Colin needed to do instead, was be grateful that his wish was soon to be granted because the Hail Mary that he was looking for was just handed to him.

Like the last time, presenting Antonio with some new fabricated evidence pertaining to Captain Potter's murder, was going to be a huge risk. In fact, Colin knew that such an allegation as this could actually get him killed on the spot if he wasn't careful. But every attempt to acquire that one bit of damaging evidence needed to assure the complete dismantling of the D.U.O. had so far, failed. This was going to be Colin's last shot at victory. But before he walked right over to their headquarters to present his accusation, Colin Ramirez needed to prepare himself; he needed to be brought up to speed regarding every bit of information that there was about Maven Potter's murder.

He admittedly, found himself in a position that he didn't really want to be in. But he had never quit on anyone or at anything before — even though the temptation was certainly there for Colin to walk away. He desperately wanted his old life back — and not just because he had missed a lot of what was important to him, but because he suddenly was getting that same uneasy feeling that he had right at the beginning of this whole thing. For the first time ever, he felt scared, felt as if he had been all but forced to draw the invisible short straw and sacrifice himself. What Lenora had accused him of being, was inaccurate. He was not yellow and he was not afraid of getting his hands dirty — he was just afraid of the potential end result being the reason why the lives of those whom he loved the most, were changed in such a manner that a burden beyond all imagination would be unfairly placed upon their shoulders.

5

~ Even though the light at the end of the tunnel can be seen, there's no guarantee that its terminus can actually be reached ~

For the first time in nearly six months, Colin walked through the front doors of the precinct. There were two reasons for his visit this day: the first was that his now four year old daughter had been begging him for a very long time to bring her there so that she could see it. The second reason was that Colin had to let his captain know exactly what he needed and what it was that he wanted to do. How Christopher was going to react to his request however; was anyone's guess.

The moment he walked through the doors of a police station, a slight bit of Jamais Vu enveloped him. As familiar as the place was, it strangely felt somewhat foreign to him. The people inside, Colin knew most of them well — but it was as if he was a stranger in a strange land. Nevertheless, he smiled, shook some hands, and took a moment and said hello to every one of his police brethren.

It didn't take him that long to catch up with his fellow officers — and it didn't take him long to feel like he was back where he belonged. But he wasn't there to renew old friendships, as he had an important issue that needed to be discussed — but not until he took a few moments and showed his wide-eyed daughter around the place.

After her tour was complete, Colin took his daughter to the only place left that she wanted to see — her daddy's boss's office. Colin tapped on the doorjamb; Captain White waved him in and warmly smiled when he saw what his officer held by his hand. "Your daughter is getting big, Colin."

"That she is. It's too bad that I've been forced to miss a lot of important moments in her life during the last two years."

Ana surprisingly let go of her father's hand and walked over to Captain White. Without any hesitation, she went behind his desk and climbed up onto Christopher's lap. That surprised Colin, as he distinctly remembered that his daughter had always been shy around those whom she didn't know — her new found confidence must have been one of those things that Colin had missed seeing develop.

He thought about going over to his daughter and taking her off of his boss's lap, but then he realized why she had done it. Something on the captain's desk had grabbed her curiosity — and it was now in her tiny little hands. She quickly slipped into her own curious world and played with the captain's prized autographed Al Kaline baseball that had been sitting on a display stand at the right side edge of Christopher's desk.

Although he had no children of his own, the fatherly instincts in him kicked in and Christopher held her steady on his knee while she played. He smiled at her; she didn't notice. Christopher surprisingly became content with having this child perched up on his knee. And soon afterwards, a moment of wonder enveloped him; a moment where he finally had a glimpse of what he had been missing in his life. No, it wasn't too late for him to become a father, but he wasn't sure if a family was in the cards as his wife was just as busy as he was with her career in commercial real estate.

With Ana now captivated with what she possessed, Colin began an informative conversation with his captain; one that brought him up to date on everything that had taken place since the last time they had met face to face — including his recent desire to want to back out of his undercover assignment.

Christopher could fully understand why Colin would want to do that — and he couldn't fault the man for it. None of them ever imagined that the D.U.O. would evolve like it had. And everyone had agreed that commandeering assets from many unscrupulous individuals in order to become a trusted asset to the D.U.O. was the logical thing to do. But they never would have fathomed how strong of an entity the D.U.O. would become from it — and they never expected that after two years, their mole would still be kept on the outside, looking in.

Nevertheless, Colin's foot was still firmly planted on the welcome mat. It just didn't make sense to pull him out and attempt to replace him with someone else. Too much was at stake here. The city of Detroit was changing, and it was only going to be a matter of time before Antonio Marcone's greediness put him in a position to claim at least partial ownership of the city; just like he had gained ownership of so many other businesses with relative ease.

For the first time since he had taken over the captaincy of the precinct, Christopher actually thought that he'd have to pull rank, fully expecting Officer Ramirez to submit an official request to be removed for the assignment. But he didn't have to; Colin instead threw him a surprising curveball. "I understand that I am in a position that will be impossible for someone else to seamlessly transition into. And as much as I want out of this, I do realize that now is not the right time to bail."

"I agree."

"However, things have changed and the clock I am working against is counting down fast. If I don't get Antonio the information he is seeking to take over ownership of the Weston Book Cadillac Hotel, then I can only speculate what will happen to me."

"So... are you telling me that you think that the time has come for us to just arrest the man and then hope that the evidence we have will be enough to get a conviction?"

"Up until yesterday, I honestly thought that was what I was going to ask you to do... but not now."

"What has changed, Colin?"

"Lenora reminded me that we still have one game piece left to play; one that I completely forgot we had."

"Which is?"

"Captain Maven Potter."

Captain White sat there quiet for a moment scratching his head. He couldn't quite understand how Colin thought that their former captain's murder tied into all of this. "I'm not sure I follow?"

"It's simple, really. In order for us to nail the coffin completely shut, we first need to drive a stake through the vampire's heart."

Captain White hated it when people chose to use metaphors instead of just getting to the point. "Ok. What is it exactly that you have planned, Colin?"

"I want to do the same thing we did last time. Accuse Antonio."

"If I remember correctly, it didn't really work, as the man admitted right to your face that he had done it and then basically laughed it off." It was at that moment when Christopher White clued in what his officer was talking about. Colin didn't want to revisit his previous accusation; he wanted to accuse the man of a different murder. "You know… that just might work. We have never been able to find any substantial leads pertaining to Captain Potter's murder, so I don't see any problem with accusing Antonio Marcone of the crime.

Colin smiled, knowing that he now had the support of his commanding officer. "We just need to hope that he'll take the bait. And if that doesn't work, then I'm sorry, but I will want out."

Although Christopher had the authority to deny such a request, as the man's long-time friend, he simply could not stand in the way of what he knew was the right thing to do. "Ok, Colin."

Colin got up from his seat, walked over to his boss's desk, and then took back his daughter — Ana placed the ball back where she had found it, and without her father having to tell her, she said thank you to Christopher.

After taking with him a copy of what little file information had been accumulated regarding Maven Potter's murder, Colin went home. He then dropped off his daughter, kissed his wife, who he knew was anxious for him to return to a more normal life, and then left to go to his office — he had some information to assimilate and a plan to construct before he presented his new accusation to the head of the Detroit Underworld Organization.

Antonio wasn't too happy that he had fallen for one of the oldest maneuvers in the book. He had allowed himself to openly trust when instead, he should have kept his guard up. Because he hadn't, he ended up getting the wool pulled over his eyes. Never before had he been made a fool of like this — and never, he swore, would it happen to him again. Of course, he only had himself to blame for allowing his own greed to blind him; it had erroneously caused him to believe that someone who was not part of the 'family' would freely bestow themselves to the cause. However, Antonio was far from being a closed-minded individual. One day, he believed, a non-Italian would be accepted into the family. However, he was not going to actively look outside of his lineage.

Before all of this unsettling news came to his attention, he had been actively scouting a man from China to possibly become their overseas liaison. The reason for his doing this was simple — the Asian market was ever growing and he wanted a slice of the pie. Yes, he could easily just send Louie over there to take care of that end for him, but Antonio felt that someone of Asian heritage to oversee the operation, made more sense to him. Now however, he was unsure if he was going to go through with his plan — it all depended upon how the rest of this day unfolded.

Today was a big day, and he wasn't about to let his anger ruin it. Later on this evening, everything that he had diligently worked on was finally going to happen, as his first major gun shipment was scheduled to take place. Casper had done a great job up until this point at arranging several minor gun shipments; a series of limited risk test runs over the last few years to see if stealing weapons unnoticed from underneath the nose of the U.S. Military was even possible. Two dozen carefully planned small thefts and shipments later, and they had satisfactorily worked out all the kinks of such a sensitive operation. Now, it was time to up their game and ship out a transport truck full of weaponry to a group of Serbian Nationalists. But before they could do this, there was one small piece of personal business that needed to be taken care of. Honestly, Antonio never thought that he would have to do this, but things change and he knew that he had no other choice — it was a byproduct of the business he ran. Thankfully, he didn't have to send Louie or Sal out to look for Manual Velázquez; he had called Antonio earlier and told him that he was on his way with some very important information — little did he know that there was something very important waiting at the D.U.O. headquarters for him.

"Is everything in order for tonight, Sal?"

"Yes, boss. Louie is at the warehouse right now overseeing the packing of the weapons into their crates. Once that is done, he will make sure that the shipping containers get loaded and delivered to the docks."

"Excellent... although I'd feel much more comfortable if you were there with him."

"Honestly, I'd rather be here. The less I am around Louie, the better."

"Why don't you and Louie like each other?"

"Basically, he's oil and I am water."

'*It's more like one is gasoline and the other is a match,*' Antonio thought. "I really don't care what your differences are. You both really need to find a way to coexist."

'*I doubt that will ever happen,*' Sal said to himself. "I'll try, but there is no guarantee that he will."

The door opened up and in walked Colin. "Hey, what's going on?"

"A lot. Grab a seat and I'll explain."

Colin did. He was never one to be nosy, but his eyes immediately locked onto some notes in a ledger that was on Antonio's desk. He scanned the upside down writing quickly, doing his best not to become too obvious.

"A year ago, you asked me to bring you completely into the family."

"I did."

"Well, I'm glad that I didn't."

That declaration was all that it took for Colin's confidence to immediately disappear. Something had changed; Antonio's demeanor seemed different than usual, and the overall relaxing vibe that generally existed in the basement office, also no longer was present. "Why is that?"

"Because… I no longer trust you."

Colin was dumbfounded. He had come here today to accuse Antonio of a crime that he hoped would end up causing him to make that one crucial mistake the Detroit Police Department needed in order to finally be able to assemble an airtight case against him. However, he did not like where this conversation was going, because it now appeared to him that the tables were about to be turned. "You can trust me. I've done nothing to cause you to think otherwise. In fact, I've come here today with some information that I'm certain will prove that I can still be trusted."

"And what would that be?"

"I was able to find out that the local police have finally made headway in the murder from two years ago of Police Captain, Maven Potter. They now believe that you are behind it and they have apparently accumulated enough evidence to have you arrested."

Sal just sat there and laughed; Antonio grinned in victory. Colin instantly went from being dumbfounded to completely confused. Just like before, he didn't understand why this information did not cause either one of them to panic. It was as if they both were knowingly spitting in the face of the law — again. "Are you not at all scared that the law is about to come knocking on your door?"

"No, because..."

The door to Antonio's office opened up and in walked a woman that Colin knew all too well. And she was the last person that he ever imagined would make an unannounced appearance in the office of the D.U.O.

"...I know, without a shadow of a doubt, that the law is not going to come knocking on my door. Isn't that right, Leni?"

"That's right... boss!"

Colin's jaw literally hit the floor.

"You see, Officer Ramirez. Yes, I do know who you really are. I was the one who provided Lenora with that little bit of information about Captain Potter. And for the record, I did have him killed. He knew about Vance Palmalino and, although he only had enough circumstantial evidence to make my existence as the new head of the D.U.O. a very difficult one, I could not allow him to have me investigated and possibly charged with my predecessor's murder."

Colin still could not believe that Officer Lenora Lexington had been lured over to the other side. She had accumulated a lot of invaluable information for him with her researching skills over the past two years. And if it weren't for her, Colin would not have been able to accomplish what he had. "Why, Lenora? Why?"

"Simple. It all comes down to appreciation and recognition. In all the years that I worked for the intelligence division, I was never fully respected for my talents. Working with you these past two years was even worse."

"How so?"

"You took all the glory for my hard work."

Jealousy — that is what made her do it. Colin could not believe that someone as talented as she was, felt the need to have her work recognized — she wanted full credit and she wanted to be in the spotlight. "I never figured you to be a glory hound."

"I'm not. But I feel that my talents are better served here with an organization that is rapidly on the rise instead of one that is stuck in a quagmire of outdated rules, regulations, and procedures."

The next thing Colin knew, he was being forcefully yanked out of his seat. Sal slammed him onto the ground and then quickly bound his hands and feet together. He then lifted his vulnerable body upright and held onto him so that Antonio could say a few final words. "I really do appreciate the work that you have done for this organization, as it couldn't have grown as much as it has without your help. And I'm sure it pained you to bend the law so that you could protect your own cover. But when you started to delay with getting me the information that I wanted to take over the Weston Book Cadillac Hotel, that little man with the red horns began to whisper some really good advice into my ears. And I am glad that I listened to him. Goodbye, Officer Ramirez, it's been… fun."

Lenora opened up the office door and Sal dragged Colin out, down the hallway, and up the back stairs to his awaiting car out into the back alley. Lenora opened up the trunk and then Sal unceremoniously tossed Colin inside.

The trunk wasn't empty; there was barely enough room in it for his bound body. Immediately, Colin realized why that was — he wasn't the only person in the trunk. Jimbo was in it as well.

At the time, Colin had thought that it would be worth it in the end, his making a personal sacrifice for the greater good of the city that he lived in and loved. But now, he was facing the consequences that came with the risk that he had been willing to take — his life undoubtedly, was going to come to an inauspicious end. In hindsight, Colin should not have stayed undercover for as long as he had. But he had allowed himself to become complacent. He had allowed Antonio's well-earned trust to influence his decision to stay. And now, his wife and daughter were going to have to emotionally suffer because of the bad decision he had made.

Never in a million years did Colin ever believe that an officer of the law; an officer that he had worked closely with for the last two years, would throw him under the bus. Yet, as he watched Sal close the trunk on him and Jimbo, Colin saw exactly why Lenora had done what she had done. Standing behind her, arms wrapped around her waist, was Antonio. For the first time that Colin could remember since he had known Lenora, she actually smiled; a smile that had probably been coerced — a smile that he was certain also had a lot of self-righteousness behind it.

Yes, he should have walked away — but it was way too late for that. Besides, it's not that easy to suddenly step off of the path that you've agreed to walk. Colin knew this, but he still wished that he had allowed his principles to override at least one of his rash decisions. All of the fears that had haunted him from the beginning had returned. This time however, Colin knew that they were about to come true. Wherever Sal was taking them, it would be the last place that he and Jimbo would ever see alive.

Instinctively, he tried to reach into his front pocket for his cell phone, but he remembered that Lenora had taken it from him when Sal was in the process of tying him up; his gun and his back-up weapon had also been taken. There was no use in trying to fish through an unconscious Jimbo's pocket, as he doubted that a man who lived on the streets would even own a cell phone. They were both at the mercy of the car ride they were taking.

About fifteen minutes into the most uncomfortable trip Colin had ever taken, they stopped. Sal opened up the trunk and roughly hauled him out. Across the way, he could see that the sun was going down — so did he, as Sal unexpectedly backhanded him, sending him face first straight into the ground. By the time he was able to right himself, Sal had removed Jimbo from the trunk. Then, with Colin's gun in Sal's left hand and Jimbo slung over his right shoulder, he ordered him to walk.

Soon, his surroundings became familiar — *'this is a bit ironic',* he thought, realizing then that they were both back where this whole thing had started — this was going to end in Blackstone Park.

Sal marched Colin over to the one hundred year old maple. Immediately, his mind replayed his two-year-old dream; the one that he had brushed off as being just a trivial manifestation of his amalgamated troubled thoughts. Instinctively, Colin looked around and felt a small sense of relief that he did not see an already dug grave — but he did recognize that the old tree had been the key item in his dream. This was where he was going to die. If by some miracle he were to survive this, he swore right then and there that he was going to pay much closer attention to his dreams and acknowledge that they were indeed an allegorical glimpse into the future.

Sal dumped Jimbo off of his shoulder, and then propped him up against the tree. He then removed a bottle of water from the inner pocket of his spring jacket and dumped it over the man's head. "Wake up, Jimbo!"

His eyes opened. A few seconds later, he had gathered his bearings. At that point, Sal didn't have to say any other words to him, as Jimbo already knew what was going to happen. He didn't try to beg or even attempt to get up and run, he just sat there and looked content to accept his fate.

"Stand up, Jimbo!"

He did.

"I always liked you and you always provided us with some solid information. But you do realize what your mistake was?"

"I do... and I don't care. I made a lot of stupid decisions in my youth for which I had decided to spend the rest of my life making restitution."

"And living on the streets was your penance."

"Yes, Sal. By doing so, I was able to save every penny that I have ever made so that my biggest regret would be taken care of. Now that I have accomplished my goal, I have a favor to ask of you before you do what you feel you must."

"This man is going to kill you, Jimbo, and you are asking him for a favor?"

"I now know that I have reached the end of the path that God wanted me to walk. Not the path that he had originally placed me on, because I had deviated from that one when I was much younger, but the one that he reassigned to me when I finally allowed him to become a part of my life."

"You don't deserve to die, Jimbo."

"It is my time, Officer Ramirez."

This was a part of the life Sal lived that he always looked forward to. Yet this time, he was finding it somewhat difficult to do what he knew had to be done. Jimbo was a good man and had done a lot to help the D.U.O. evolve from what it was to what it has become. However, just like he had stated, it was time for Jimbo's life to end. And as his friend, Sal felt honored to be the one to do it. "Out of respect for you and what you have done for the D.U.O. over the years, I will do one last favor for you, Jimbo."

"Thank you, Sal. Could you please go to locker 426 at the Amtrak station?" Though both of his hands were tied together, Jimbo was able to reach into his front pants pocket. He then removed a key and flicked it towards Sal. "Inside the locker there is an envelope containing a name, an address, and all the money I have ever saved. It is to be given to my daughter so that she can go to college. Please ensure that she gets it."

"Ok. I can do that for you."

"Thank you, Sal." Jimbo turned around and faced the tree. And although he wasn't Jewish, he decided that it was appropriate to quote a line from the book of Job. *"Therefore I reprehend myself, and do penance in dust and ashes."*

Those were the last words that Jimbo said right before his body slumped to the ground. With a silencer attached to his gun, Sal had put two 9mm bullets in the back of his head. "Sorry old friend, but you know that it had to be done." He then walked over to Colin and, using a six-inch pocketknife, cut away the binds from Colin's hands. "Move him over out of the way."

"What?"

"I said, move him now!"

Colin walked over and grabbed Jimbo by the back of his shirt and belt and moved him away from the base of the tree.

"Now stand right where Jimbo was."

Reluctantly, Colin did what he was told to do. As he stood facing the tree, a million things went through his mind; not one of them was about him, as they were all about his family. He was about to die and his family was about to be heartbroken.

"Just so you know you are not going to be the first cop that I've killed."

"It was you who killed Maven Potter, wasn't it?"

"Yes. It was Antonio's wish."

"Hey! What the hell is going on over there?"

Colin turned his head and saw on the outer edge of the park, silhouetted by the sunset, two police officers that had been walking their beat. *'Maybe I'm not going to die tonight after all,'* he thought. That was until he felt pain in his back; it immediately burned. The stability he had in his legs all but disappeared. He fell unceremoniously to the ground, landing a mere few inches away from where Jimbo's body lay.

Officer Ramirez closed his eyes and waited for his life to end. In that moment, he wished that religion had been more a part of his life — but God had never been incorporated in his upbringing. Yet, as he lay there with holes in his back, Colin prayed that it was not his time; he hoped that the root of all life would reach out and provide him with a lifeline. And if it did, he hoped that his continued existence wouldn't end up like it had in his dream. He didn't want to feel helpless as if he was hanging in the middle of that bottomless grave. He would rather fall into nothingness and have it be all over.

Whatever happened next, Colin was all but certain that things would never be the same. In one callous moment, liked he feared, his family's existence had changed forever.

He had caused his family pain; more pain than he would have ever wished upon them. It was his fault entirely — all because of his sense of duty, his responsibility as a police officer. Yes, there was even a bit of pride that had driven his decision to go undercover and gather as much information as he could so that the city he lived in would not eventually become overwhelmed by a corrupt organization. However, two unforeseen things had caused him to fail; an assumption that he would be able to walk away at any point, and a betrayal. Never in a million years did he ever expect to be stabbed in the back — everything

that was important to him had been instantly taken away from him because of that self-interested choice.

As he stood off to the far edge of the graveyard, Colin Ramirez watched as his family and his friends paid their last respects to him. Although he was only an apparition of who he once was, his emotions were getting the best of him. He had failed as a police officer, he had failed as a husband, and he had failed as a father. He just wished that he could correct his failures and touch the ones who meant the most to him one more time — or at least, enter their thoughts if it was at all possible so that his wife and young daughter understood just how sorry he was for causing them so much pain.

But he couldn't do that; he couldn't do anything anymore. He was no longer alive and only moments away from letting go of that root he clung onto. And when that happened, once he was officially gone from this world, his family would be left with scars so deep, they may never be able to fully heal.

He opened up his eyes and for a moment, was confused. This most certainly didn't look like a place that one would see when they entered the afterlife — it looked to Colin more like a hospital. Sure enough, that was where he was. He hadn't died. Somehow, he had survived. He tried to get up, but his body would not move. He tried to speak, but couldn't as he soon realized that something was down his throat. He began to panic, but that went away when he felt a delicate hand touch his arm. He turned his head and would have smiled if it were at all possible. Seeing his wife at his bedside in that moment had done wonders to ease his emotional burden — but what heavy burdens she would soon have to deal with, had yet to be determined.

Two days later...

Captain White walked into Colin's room and saw, what to him, was a miracle. His officer looked like hell, but he was alive — that was the important thing. The breathing tube had been removed, but he was still lying flat on his back. "How are you doing?"

71

"I'm... ok, considering."

"The doctor said that he is lucky to even be alive," Colin's wife, Olivia stated. "I thank the Lord that he is."

"What did the doctor say his prognosis was?"

Olivia hesitated to answer; Christopher could see it in his officer's eye that his doctor had not given him good news.

"I'm never going to walk again. One of the bullets severed my spinal cord."

Christopher didn't know what to say. This was the first time that a police officer under his watch had been shot. It is something that a commanding officer hopes they never have to deal with — but at some point, they all know that time will come. "I'm sorry this happened to you, Colin. I should have never allowed you to go back in after you let me know that you were mulling over the idea of having me pull you from your undercover assignment."

"I contemplated for a long time on whether or not I should walk away. But I honestly thought that we finally had a good chance of putting Antonio in a position where he would do something irrational to protect his own skin. I mean..."

Christopher sat there by Colin's bed, patiently waiting and expecting him to validate his reasons for not requesting to be removed from his assignment — but that didn't occur. What Colin told him next came as a complete shock. Never in a million years did Christopher expect to hear that Antonio Marcone had ordered Maven Potter's murder. But just like his admission to Colin that he was responsible for Vance Palmalino's disappearance, without any hard evidence, Officer Ramirez's version of what he had been told might not be enough to convict Antonio Marcone. Still, Christopher knew that they had to try. They had been sitting on all of the information they had, waiting for that smoking gun. Not only did they know of four murders that could be tied to Antonio Marcone: Vance Palmalino's and his pilot, James 'Jimbo' Lewis & Maven Potter, but they also had the attempted murder of Officer Ramirez, as well as the extortions which culminated in the acquisitions of numerous businesses.

Christopher felt that it was now time they charged the bastard. And seeing that his officer; his friend, was lying paralyzed in a hospital bed, only fueled his desire to do it. Still, it wasn't his call. It was up to his superiors. However, Christopher was going to do everything in his power to convince them that it was time they arrested Antonio Marcone and his associates. "Don't worry, Colin. I promise that what has happened to you will be avenged."

"Good. Then after you arrest those three assholes; feel free to lynch the bitch who sold me out."

Christopher excused himself and then left the hospital. Vengeance was on his mind, but his sense of duty was doing a good job of keeping him from doing something stupid.

After stopping to pick up a much needed coffee, Christopher turned on his cell phone, called Chief Winslow, and asked him for a favor. He didn't tell him anything pertaining to what he had just learned from Officer Ramirez, he just asked him to make sure that the state prosecutor was there when he arrived at Jacob's office.

The mood in the precinct was somber. That was to be expected as one of their own had lost his battle against the enemy. Everyone liked Officer Ramirez and would have volunteered to take that bullet for him if they had the opportunity to do so. But none of them had been there; none of them could change what had happened. They could only hope that they would be the ones called upon by their captain and chosen to go out and arrest those who were responsible.

Anticipation grew as Captain White returned to the precinct — but he didn't stop to address the room. He instead, went straight into his office and shut the door behind him. That, right there, only added more to the uncertainty that had already been present and caused the idle chatter that had been going on throughout to instantly die down to a level that only a dog could hear, leaving each officer that was there to his / her own uncertain thoughts.

The officers under his command had clearly expected him to state what they were going to do next, but Christopher just wasn't ready to speak. Disappointment had enveloped him, as his meeting with Chief Winslow and the state prosecutor did not go well. And even though he felt that they had enough evidence to have a judge issue an arrest warrant for both Antonio Marcone and Salvadore Batiste, the chief and the state prosecutor felt it was best to hold off from doing so. Christopher did not agree with their position, but he understood the reasoning behind why. The arrest of those two men would not put an end to the Detroit Underworld Organization, as Louie Mazotti would still be there to run the operation. Not until they could find some irrefutable evidence against him as well, would the state finally agree to pursue charges — they wanted to remove all three of the D.U.O.'s major players at the same time.

Never before in his life had he had such a headache. Christopher never suffered from migraines and never got them due to sinus pressure. He only on occasion, would get a headache due to stress or a lack of nutrition. This one he had, he wanted to attribute it to the irrational logic of the state prosecutor, Carl Calabrese, and his ability to sway Chief Winslow to his side. In his opinion, the man was resolutely blinded by his tenuous belief that they still had not collected enough hard evidence to petition the courts to issue them an arrest warrant. The chief, although just as anxious as Christopher was to start removing the ever growing cancer from the city of Detroit, reluctantly decided to support the state prosecutor's position — but only because he did agree that there was a strong chance Louie would promptly conduct some form of retaliation against them.

Feeling defeated, Christopher just wanted to leave, go somewhere secretly, and pretend that this rather large problem did not exist. Belize, Fiji, Indonesia, or maybe somewhere in the Virgin Islands — he didn't care where, he just wanted to leave it all behind and disappear. But he was never one to run away from his problems; problems were meant to be faced head on and then solved — that was what he knew he had to do. So he walked over to his coffee maker and poured himself a cup. Yes, it was late in the afternoon, but he didn't care. He needed to calm his nerves before he did what he knew had to be done — place two more of his men on an assignment that had the potential to end the same way it had for Officer Ramirez.

Once he had squeezed every last drop out of his coffee cup, he got up from his desk, walked over to his office door, and opened it. He couldn't hesitate any longer; it was time for him to assign the most important case this precinct has ever had to his two remaining best men. "Banks! Brampton! I need to see you in my office."

Yes, he had been able to turn the tables before any serious damage had occurred, but if it hadn't been for the unexpected revelation that had been voluntarily handed to him on a platter, Antonio was certain that his organization would have eventually been shut down.

He had never found a reason to ever suspect that Colin Ramirez was actually a Detroit Police Officer. But that little voice in his head would on occasion, surface and urge him to be suspicious. Normally, Antonio would just brush that aside whenever that happened, but when 'Manual' continued to delay in acquiring for him the damaging information that he had requested about the Weston Book Cadillac Hotel, he could no longer dismiss those doubts. Still, no evidence of his betrayal had been there. However, Antonio needed to be one hundred percent certain that he was not being played, so he dipped into his personal Swiss bank account and withdrew a quarter of a million dollars. Little did he suspect at the time that Colin's 'secretary', Lenora Lexington, was also a police officer, nor did he expect that she would be willing to throw the man under the bus for money.

When the truth was finally revealed, Antonio became pissed; pissed that he had been played, and pissed at himself for allowing that to happen. Never before had someone been able to fool him like that. Antonio was the boss of the Detroit Mob, and no one but he was going to control the game — he was never going to let anyone do that to him again.

To learn the truth had cost him quite a bit of money — but it had been worth every penny he had spent. Lenora Lexington had not only provided Antonio with the cold hard facts, but she had provided him with every copy of all of the two plus years of information that had been gathered on him and his organization. Needless to say, that evidence, as damaging as it was, would help Antonio's lawyer to create a solid defense if the day ever came that the police decided to arrest him.

But that wasn't the only thing that Lenora provided. For Antonio, it was an unexpected bonus — and one that he was happy to accept. No, she wasn't even close to being a supermodel, but she was also far from being a woman in which you would need to be loaded up with alcohol in order to touch. Other than her breasts, which he thought were near perfect, her body did have a few forgivable imperfections. Her face was ok — even without makeup, and her dark purple-framed glasses were actually kind of sexy. Overall, Antonio would rate Lenora's appearance as being seven and a half out of ten — but he quickly reassessed his rating when he discovered something unexpected. She had made up for her flaws the moment she hit the sheets, prompting Antonio to give her another point and a half because the woman had a talent like none that he had ever experienced before. Lenora Lexington was a sex-pert.

Admittedly, he had been with quite a few tens in his day — he'd also been with some that were a lot worse looking than Lenora. But those occasions had been a result of desperate times — and only because he had wanted to break out of a slump. It had been difficult to lower his standards for them. However, all that Antonio had to do was remember what his Uncle Benito had once said to him when he was sixteen, *"all women feel the same when they are facing down"*, then Antonio was all in — a disparaging belief of his uncle's, but one that helped him once he had committed himself to bed someone who he would usually pass on.

Lenora had this innate ability to satisfy every one of those male urges — a skill that not always was properly taught. Her talents had exceeded way beyond Antonio's initial expectation. And because of this discovery, he had to admit that her usefulness needed to go way beyond that of just helping him to set up Officer Ramirez. In fact, Antonio had decided that he was going to take back in trade, every bit of the two hundred and fifty thousand dollars he had paid her. And then, once he had gotten his money's worth, he'd know for certain whether or not he would issue an invitation for her to officially join his team — only then, would he make a decision regarding what kind of relationship the two of them would actually have.

6

Six months later...

All of God's creatures were unsuccessfully looking for the smallest bit of shade, though in a concrete jungle, finding it this day was nearly impossible. With the noon sun positioned perfectly perpendicular to the six lanes of historical Woodward Avenue in downtown Detroit, the aligning buildings naturally absorbed, then reflected the heat that only intensified the already unbearable day which to some, felt almost hot enough to boil mercury.

Unfortunately for both police officers, Maxwell Banks and Joshua Brampton, they had no other option but to sit in their car and suffer through the blistering heat, right along with everything and everyone else. Their assignment this day was to stake out the Davis Brothers Warehouse. From a semi-concealed area that was partially down a junk laden side alleyway between a vacant office building and a recently boarded up, fire charred nightclub, they patiently sat in Maxwell's brand new dark burgundy limited edition Dodge Charger, and astutely observed.

Trying to cope with these unbearable conditions was near impossible, yet the both of them had experienced these types of circumstances many times before during their careers — a small detail that each knew any undercover police officer would have to deal with on occasion.

Knowing that their anonymity was of the utmost importance, they took every precaution that they could to ensure that they stayed out of sight. That meant they were forced to stay inside the car with the windows up and engine off — no running car equals no running air conditioning. And of course, rolling down the extra-dark tinted windows, even just a small crack to get a flow of fresh air, was not an option — they had to stay all the way up in order to provide them with the cover that they had to keep. A sunroof in this instance, would have at least allowed the stuffiness to escape, but Maxwell's new car did not come with one — nor did he want one, as he felt that they were tacky and had the potential to leak. This left the both of them with really no other way of keeping cool other than trying to stay hydrated with bottles upon bottles of cold water or Gatorade.

The uncomfortable conditions inside the car were starting to affect Joshua the most. He just couldn't sit still for more than a few seconds at a time because the overbearing heat was causing his skivvies to uniformly adhere to his manhood. He was trying not to be too obvious, yet he couldn't help but continuously adjust his nether region — even though he knew that his partner was fully aware of what he had been doing.

Under normal everyday circumstances, Maxwell would have slapped any other guy on the back of his head that had knowingly been doing what his partner was doing in plain sight of him. However, it really didn't bother Maxwell too much, seeing that he was also experiencing those same uncomfortable conditions inside the car.

Dealing with the unbearable heat was one thing, but what really bothered Maxwell more, and made him very uneasy, was being isolated and unable to fully be aware of all of his surroundings. But this was where there had chosen to sit and keep watch; tucked back in a secluded alleyway in a section of Woodward Avenue that was known not to be one of the safest areas of the twenty-one mile stretch of the city street. It certainly was not an ideal situation for them to be in, but such unnerving circumstances had a way of testing ones resolve — even for someone who was as experienced as they were. Unfortunately, they knew that no better option had been there for them as not another unobstructed spot within the surrounding area of the warehouse that they had to keep watch over would give them a better line of sight than what they now had. It also helped that the shadows casted by the surrounding alleyway buildings, blanketed them — a natural occurrence that essentially cloaked their presence in the neighborhood.

Although he would not let it be known, sitting in the darkness where he was really made Maxwell nervous. He didn't like being vulnerable or in a position where an approaching adversary would have the upper hand. Because they were basically cornered, he felt almost like a yellow duck at a traveling carnival's shooting gallery, waiting there inanimate for some crazy motherfucker to come along and unload a few rounds at them.

Every day for the past half year, Maxwell and his partner had basically been working on their assigned case; a case, which admittedly was beginning to consume both of their lives — just as it had done to Colin Ramirez. The only difference was that they had not been asked to infiltrate the D.U.O. It was an assignment that, although Colin had been successful at and had been able to gather up all kinds of incriminating evidence, he should not have taken on alone. But the Detroit Police Department didn't know then what it does now — nor did they expect that not only would the enemy grow as fast as it has, but that one of their own had decided to spit on their fraternity and jump on over to the dark side.

The mistakes that had been made were costly. Fortunately, Colin did not die from being shot twice in the back. However, he was going to have to live the rest of his life confined to a wheel chair. Now, every bit of evidence that they continued to accumulate was important. No longer was the D.U.O. classified as a low-level criminal organization — they had elevated themselves to the top of the state's most wanted list.

Even though it had not been said to either of them, Maxwell and Joshua both knew that the pressure was on them to succeed. Each was not at all surprised when Captain White had called them into his office to hand them this assignment. And although the vote of confidence that each had received from their captain was appreciated, they suddenly felt an immense weight being placed upon their shoulders — not because they didn't believe in their own abilities as police officers, but because they had not so long ago, failed at their most important case to date.

After being handed the responsibility of taking over the investigation into Maven Potter's murder, both Maxwell and Joshua felt confident that they would find their former captain's killer. Six months later, they still had no suspects; the case was thus considered cold. And although that failure took place eighteen months ago, it was, and is still, the only asterisk on the impeccable records of both officers. However, that blemish was not enough of an excuse for Maxwell and

Joshua to withdraw their names — even though the temptation was there to do so. Their boss had unequivocally placed faith in them, and it was up to them both to step up and do everything in their power to ensure the cancer that was spreading throughout the city of Detroit, was eradicated.

It didn't help their confidence however, that up until now, dead end after dead end was all they had found. No matter how close they got, they always kept running into that damn proverbial brick wall. They were both mentally drained. They each wanted this to end so that they could reclaim their normal lives, as they both wanted to spend more time with their families. That was why they were willing to suffer this day inside the sauna of Maxwell's new car. It was after all, a small price for them to pay in order to hopefully restore the balance in their lives and the normalcy back to the city. Still, there was a small part of them that honestly believed this was just going to end up being another day in which their valuable time was being wasted; that this very well could be another one of those 'almosts'. Maxwell was sick of that being the case. In fact, his unintentional negative thoughts were trying to convince him that one more missed opportunity just might be the catalyst behind their eventual residency at a place that had white padded walls and a stainless steel table with leather straps, in which a daily cocktail of designer antipsychotic drugs was on the menu.

"You know, Max. I'm starting to get this funny feeling that your informant has finally gone and screwed us over."

"I know you really don't care much for Chevy's unique, yet sometimes eccentric personality, but you do have to admit it, Josh, that his info is usually pretty accurate. Besides, I really can't think of a reason why he would screw us over."

It wasn't so much that Joshua didn't believe that Chevy's information wasn't any good. He knew that he was the most accurate and trustworthy informant that they had. Joshua just found it very hard to look past all of Chevy's idiosyncrasies and accept the man the way he was. "Yeah... I suppose that you're right, Max. Other than his inability to find us a credible lead on Maven's killer, Chevy has never failed to acquire the information that we ask him to get."

"Then why, after all this time, do you not like him?"

"I just… I find it very hard to accept someone into my inner circle of friends who insists that it is his invisible best friend who actually acquires the information for us."

"He's harmless. And he's a nice guy."

"He's not stable. And he needs professional help."

Maxwell understood his partner's reservations about Chevy. In fact, there were times over the years that he himself had questioned his informant's sanity. However, he and Chevy had this personal connection, and he never once had been given a reason to doubt his 'odd' friend.

Both Maxwell and Joshua sat there dormant for what seemed to them like forever, staring straight through the car's windshield at the oblivious citizens that moved along the early evening streets. Neither one of them were willing to be the first to break the unnerving silence that had encompassed them both. Focused, is what they knew they had to be; yet both of their minds would occasionally begin to wander.

Realizing that he had to snap out of his mental miasma, Maxwell took a very big and somewhat excruciating drink of his ice cold Gatorade. He knew that he had to regain his focus because at any moment, his skills would be called upon. He had to be ready so that any sort of possible distraction or hesitation would not be the reason why they again, failed in their assignment. *'I knew that I should have brought some Red Bull with me,'* he thought.

After he quenched his thirst, Maxwell's focus began to return; Joshua's had not. Instead, he suddenly felt the urge to revert back to his past juvenile ways — he had after all, eaten three-bean burritos from Taco Bell at lunchtime.

Nonchalantly, he looked over at Maxwell to see if he was paying any attention to him. He wasn't, so Joshua quickly returned his eyes back to a straight-ahead stare; a stare that now accompanied a slightly twisted, devilish, guilty grin on his face. Joshua then set off his silent assassin. Within only a few seconds, the stagnant, hot air of the car became polluted by Joshua's expunging of his internal gas.

Maxwell's head quickly snapped towards his partner; he immediately sent him a piercing look. Joshua started to laugh, but quickly stopped after he realized that his decision to break wind inside a sealed hot car had been a mistake — his partner's expression was all that he needed to see for him to realize that Maxwell was not happy that what breathable air there had been left inside their vehicular sauna had now become contaminated.

With the fun he wanted to have no longer there, Joshua nonchalantly, and against departmental policy, cracked open his window a few inches to release the trapped fumes.

"Close your damn window, Josh! You know that it's against procedure."

"Yeah! Yeah, I know," Joshua empathized. "I thought it was time that we get a bit of… fresh air. Things were beginning to get a bit ripe in here." After quickly inhaling some fresh air from outside, Joshua rolled his window back up.

Time couldn't have passed by any slower, as each had someplace that they wanted to be. Joshua wanted to get to the Detroit Opera House before the box office closed so that he could pick up a pair of tickets for the upcoming Sarah McLachlan concert — an anniversary gift that he wanted to surprise his wife with. Maxwell just wanted to get home and spend some time with his wife and newborn son. But unfortunately, they each knew that what they wanted to do would have to wait. They just had to stay patient, keep focused, continually review their situation, and mentally map out the area encompassing the warehouse so that no mistakes were made when the time finally came for them to do what they came here to do.

"By the way, I've been meaning to ask you about your wife and your son. How are they doing?"

"They are both doing quite well," Maxwell replied. The still somewhat plastered pissed off look that had stayed on his face, suddenly changed to that of one where pride was now showing. "It's hard to believe that my son will be two months old tomorrow. You should see him. He's looking more and more like me every single day."

"You named him Sabastian, right?"

"Yes, we did. My wife wanted to name him that because it is a traditional French name. However, since she likes to be different, she insisted we use the old Greek spelling of it."

Joshua sunk back in his seat. Since his partner no longer appeared to be pissed off at the juvenile prank he pulled, he decided to take a harmless jab at him. "Sabastian Banks? That's a good name. At least your wife was smart enough not to forever scar your son by naming him after you."

Maxwell rolled his eyes at his partner's attempt at an insult; but he did have to concede his point — his poor son would probably have hated him his whole entire life if he had to continuously answer to the name, Max Jr., Max II, Max 2.0, Mini Max, or some hybrid of his name made up by his school peers in order to make fun of him.

Maxwell was about to return his full attention back to watching the warehouse, when a realization hit him; his partner was actually beginning to struggle with the heat. Yes, regulations stated that they were at all times, expected to remain concealed during a stakeout. But Maxwell could no longer ignore Joshua and his struggles, as he was starting to look like a marathon runner who was very close to collapsing just a few miles short of the finish line.

He watched as his partner kept on trying, and failing miserably, at removing all of the beads of sweat that continuously streamed on down his face. Staying hydrated only did so much. No matter how many bottles of water or Gatorade his partner drank, he could see that Joshua was beginning to lose the battle against the overwhelming heat.

This was after all, Maxwell's sting operation; Captain White had placed the responsibility of it on his shoulders. And yes, the temptation was certainly there for him to disregard protocol and allow himself and his partner to get some much needed relief — but that would certainly increase the risk of blowing their near perfect cover. They were oh so close to finally shutting down the D.U.O. and he just did not want to risk anything that could cause them to screw this up.

Maxwell took one more thorough scan of the warehouse and the surrounding property, saw that there was still nothing of interest going on over there, and then made a decision. He was going to take that risk — he needed to take a leak after all and the idea of using one of the empty Gatorade bottles to empty his kidneys inside his new car was not what he really wanted to do.

His bathroom break would have to wait, however, as Joshua reached over and tapped him on the arm. His partner then pointed at some unusual activity he had just noticed happening on the north back side of the warehouse.

Maxwell immediately pulled out a pair of binoculars from underneath his seat and promptly took a look at the activity by the warehouse. He then smiled and said, "Well, what do you know. It's Louie 'Piece of Crap' Mazotti!"

No other words needed to be said at that moment, as Maxwell and Joshua both knew that the presence of Antonio's right hand man at the warehouse was the last piece of the puzzle that had been missing. Once this sting operation was completed, and Louie's hand was caught in the proverbial cookie jar, the Detroit Police Department would finally have all that they needed to officially shut down the D.U.O. for good.

Firmly believing that victory was soon to be theirs, and with a renewed sense of purpose, he looked over at his partner. Without exchanging a word, Maxwell understood exactly what Joshua was thinking. This, what the department had been waiting a long time to get, was now here. And soon, the son-of-a-bitch behind all of the madness was going to get what was coming to him — not only for putting a bullet into the back of their fellow officer, but for the senseless murder of their former captain.

Joshua reached half way down to the center console of the car and grabbed a hold of the police radio. "This is primary unit calling all backups. The mouse has entered the trap. I repeat… the mouse has entered the trap. Move your vehicles into your assigned positions and then wait for further instructions. Over!"

The structure that Maxwell and Joshua had been watching was small compared to a typical industrial warehouse, yet it was still large enough to hold an enormous amount of any kind of illegal merchandise — in this case, stolen military arms and hardware.

Inside, the nervousness had begun to show amongst the ensemble of low-life rejects and scumbags. If it were not for the cocky, arrogant man named Terrance Burelli calling the shots, the entire operation would probably be in complete disarray. He was a proto-typical young military man; it ran in his blood — as far back as six generations on his family tree, there had been at least one of his ancestors who had served this great nation in some capacity.

In spite of his highly trained skills, Terrance's physical appearance alone was very intimidating. He was in his early twenties, stood six foot four, and weighed just slightly less than two hundred and sixty pounds. His muscles were admirably cut and his face appeared to be chiseled from a stone. He wasn't ugly by any stretch of the imagination, but he did have a few imperfections that simply added to his threatening look. When he walked, he purposely flaunted his two unsightly, yet visibly distinctive four-inch scars that lay almost parallel across his right forearm. This old injury had occurred when he was just a young teen. His childhood friend, while both were walking along the edge of a farmer's field, jokingly nudged Terrance towards a barbed wire fence. He should have easily been able to keep his balance from the nudging, but he had unknowingly stepped on a fair-sized rock at the same moment. It caused him to stumble and lose his balance — he fell right into the fence. Needless to say, his mother was not at all happy with his friend.

Terrance had become involved with the D.U.O. because he just happened to be at a point in his life where things weren't so clear-cut. Although he had already been enlisted for a few years, he still wasn't sure if a career in the military was for him — nor was he sure if his enlistment had been an obligation or a want. Just because his family had a long history of being a part of the military, didn't mean that he had to follow in their footsteps. It did however, mean that Terrance needed to figure everything out before he did something to tarnish the Burelli name; a well-respected military name.

One day, while on a brief two-week leave from the military, a friend of his took him to Detroit for the first time to see a football game between the Lions and his favorite team, the Browns. At half time, he met a man in the public restrooms who immediately identified him as being a U.S. Military Officer. The man then unexpectedly, presented him with an offer, an option — something other than a career in the military. Terrance didn't commit to the man's surprising offer right away, because in the back of his mind, he still was wrestling with the idea of a military career. So instead, he made an unconventional deal with the man.

Three minor transactions later, and Terrance had made up his mind — he wanted out of the military and he wanted to become a part of the Detroit Underworld Organization. But for his status within the organization to be solidified, he had to make sure this current assignment he had been given, was completed without any problems; major or minor. And once that happened, he felt all but certain that an olive branch would be extended and he would officially be invited to join the organization. At that point, Terrance would take the necessary steps to get honorably discharged from the military.

Terrance Burelli's military background was limited to only a few years of active service however, he felt confident that his first hand experiences would be invaluable if he had to make any sort of hasty decisions while overseeing this assignment — and he didn't have a problem using his personal experiences of being drilled by the toughest military instructors the United States of America had, to intimidate those whom he had been put in charge of. "Come on you guys! Get your lazy asses moving! We ain't got all fuckin' day to get this goddamn truck loaded! Hurry up! Let's go, let's go, let's go!" Terrance steadfastly walked behind his men, projecting his authority as he continuously motioned with his shoulder harnessed military assault rifle for the men loading the truck to keep on working. Intentional or not, he positioned himself close enough to those workers to not only instill the fear that he wanted, but he got close enough to them to literally see the wax and hairs in each of their ears.

"You need to seriously ease up a bit there, Terrance!"

Upon hearing the subordinate voice that resonated from behind him, Terrance immediately pivoted around and saw a pompous, well-dressed man who radiated of class, walking in his direction — the man's gait alone told everyone in the warehouse that he was someone of utmost importance.

This man appeared to be in his early to mid-thirties — although no one really knew for sure just exactly how old he was. He was clean-shaven and smoothly tanned. He had shoulder length dark brown hair with a few strands of grey blended unnoticeably throughout, and he had it neatly styled back. He wore various gold rings on the majority of his fingers and he was dressed in a dark gray pinstripe suit with tiny gold cuff links. He wore a blue/gray silk, metallic looking dress shirt, and a complimentary silk tie that was attached to the shirt with an engraved gold pin. Rounding out his expensive wardrobe, he wore on his feet a pair of patent leather boots that were uniquely accented by a tiny gold chain, draped across each foot. "You keep pushing those men like that, Terrance, and they'll all go on strike. If that happens, then guess what? You'll have to move your well trained military ass and load the rest of this damn truck all by yourself."

Terrance slowly moved towards the man of power; not intimidated whatsoever by his importance. He didn't care that this was the same man who had recruited him only a few short weeks ago, because he didn't appreciate being berated in front of everyone inside the warehouse — especially from the likes of someone whom he knew he could easily tear apart if he chose to.

Using all the restraint that he could find, he held his anger back, moved up close to within a few inches of his superior's nose, and then looked him right in the eye. He erected his right index finger, pointed it sharply, and taunted him with it as he spoke, progressively raising his voice. "I know what I'm doing here, Louie. So just move your pampered little ass over to the sidelines and let me complete what you recruited me to do!"

Louie was blown away that this arrogant 'probie' actually had the balls to argue with him. Then again, Louie knew the moment that he had seen him at Ford Field walking through the stands that he had 'it'; had the characteristics it took to become a valued asset to their organization — that was why he had followed him that day to the public washroom.

Terrance had been Louie's first recruit. And yes, just like Sal's first recruit, he wasn't Italian. But just because his blood wasn't the same as those who were a part of the D.U.O. family, didn't mean that Terrance Burelli couldn't be useful to them. Louie just needed to ensure that this man didn't end up screwing them over like Colin Ramirez had.

Right after that had happened; Antonio swore that he was never going to go down that road again. But once Louie had explained what Terrance's credentials were, Antonio had no choice in that moment but to reassess his position. Besides, he already had one military man on his payroll and so far, Casper had done a good job for him. With Terrance, the only issue there appeared to be up until now, was that he was having a problem understanding where exactly he stood on the food chain.

Being stabbed in the back by Colin Ramirez had hurt Antonio more than he would have thought — he really had liked the man. Had Sal completed his assigned task, the pain left behind from his betrayal would have immediately subsided. However, the bastard cop was forever stuck in a wheelchair. For a man whose mission it had been to ultimately ruin him, Antonio was content with the end result. Sometimes, a life of suffering is a more appropriate punishment than death itself.

That one mistake could not be the reason that the door would never open up to any non-Italians. In order for the organization to continue to grow and reach its goal of becoming a global entity, Antonio had to change the 'rules'. Now, six months later, he was ready and willing to allow contributions to come from people of any ethnic background. Anyone who could be of value to the D.U.O., he would openly consider. However, so that he never got screwed over again, Antonio decided that he needed to create a new rule when it came to recruiting; one that he dubbed the 'Manual' rule — working agreements and close associations with non-Italians were permitted, but the amalgamation of them into the family would not be. However, since this was Antonio's new rule, he, and he alone, had the ability to make an exception to it — but that would only ever happen if he found someone whom he felt had the ability to make his organization much stronger than it already was.

Like all new recruits, Louie knew that it was going to take a lot of time and patience to properly train Terrance. He admittedly admired the man's drive to succeed, but his attitude and arrogance needed to seriously be adjusted — something that he was unsure would even be possible. "You need to relax and shut your damn mouth for a moment, Terry, and listen to what I have to say!" Louie brushed away the man's finger from in front of his face and continued, "Mr. Mar…"

"I told you when we first met that I don't like to be called Terry. My name is Terrance." Two slow, deep methodical breaths taken and Terrance was once again able to keep his temper in check.

He knew that he was just a hired gun and considered dispensable until such time came that he had earned his keep — and although he assumed that he was very close to firmly planting his roots within the organization, he was fully aware that at any time, he could be removed from the picture without just cause.

Louie turned his back to Terrance and took a few short steps away. He then removed a cigarette pack from the inside pocket of his jacket, pulled out a strange looking type of cigarette, and lit it. After a few tension releasing puffs of the clove-flavored nic-stick, he turned back around and faced Terrance, starring sternly straight into his eyes. He then purposely blew some scented smoke into the man's face, just to see how he'd react. It was bad enough that Louie already had one hot-head within the D.U.O. that he had to put up with everyday — another insubordinate testing his resolve would surely cause him to consider killing one of the two.

Terrance didn't react to the smoke in his face like Louie had expected. This was good; his temper had apparently been reeled in and it showed that Terrance might actually be trainable after all. The question that Louie now had was how would Terrance react when he informed him that the boss was due to arrive at the warehouse within the next few minutes?

As expected, the military man didn't take the news very well that the head of the D.U.O. was planning on making an appearance — it forced him into taking a few relaxing breaths in order to attempt to stay calm. It didn't seem logical — it was just too risky for Antonio Marcone to come down to the transfer site and observe. Terrance knew that the man was an extremely intelligent individual who had to know that operations like this one had the potential to turn into a dangerous situation. For that reason, he felt that he had an obligation to remind Louie of all the obvious reasons that he could think of why his boss should not show his face.

"He understands the risk he is taking, Terrance. But this is the most important shipment that we have ever had. His vision for the future of the D.U.O. depends upon this being completed on time and without any unforeseen issues. Besides, Terrance, just because you have a future interest in the organization, does not mean that our worries are yet yours. Just do the job that you were hired to do, and all will be well." Louie didn't bother telling the man in that moment that his boss's other reason for making an appearance was so that he could see firsthand what kind of an asset Terrance Burelli just might actually be. That's all he wanted was to have a man with anger issues having one other unnecessary thing to worry about.

"Well, you should have told me before we started this that Antonio was planning on coming down here!" Terrance took a quick glance over his shoulder to make sure that his workers were still doing their jobs. Once he was satisfied that they were, he took another moment and carefully went over in his head what he was going to say to Louie, knowing that he was already trying the man's patience. "If I was your boss's right hand man, I would have done everything in my power to ensure that he stays away from here. As you can see, everything here is under control and everything will be on time. Therefore, I suggest that you call him and tell him to…"

One of the workers loading the truck stuck his head out the back of it and yelled over to Terrance. "Hey! I think we have company?" Both Louie and Terrance turned and looked through the dust caked window at the side of the warehouse and saw that there was a limousine approaching.

This customized Lincoln Continental was completely bulletproof, painted in an arsenic grey color, and had all of its windows darkly tinted. Wherever there would normally be chrome trim, the vehicle was instead accented in gold plating. The car also sported a solid gold, six inch rotating hood ornament of a nearly naked, goddess like woman, and the license plate read 'NTRPRENR' (Entrepreneur).

A few moments after the limousine had stopped, a man and then a woman exited. The man was clearly an astute looking individual. He appeared to be in his mid to late thirties, stood roughly five foot, nine inches tall, and weighed slightly less than two hundred pounds. He had short dark hair, cut to the style of the times, and he sported a thick, but neatly trimmed dark moustache. The man also came dressed in style. He was decked out in an expensive European tailored black suit with an off white silk shirt, a complimenting tie, and matching patent shoes. His only accessory was a small leather satchel; a murse, or man-purse that he had in his left hand.

The woman who accompanied this man was almost as tall as he (but that was only because she was wearing platform shoes with five-inch heals). Her appearance really didn't draw your attention; physically or in an intimidating manner — she definitely wasn't eye candy. But there was a confident aura about her that one could easily determine — which was more than likely why this man, Antonio Marcone, had decided to keep Lenora Lexington, the ex-intelligence officer for the police department, around.

Between the limousine and the warehouse, Lenora cautiously surveyed their surroundings. Although Antonio looked calm and cool, just as if it were another day at the office, Lenora was acting almost as if she was uncertain of their surroundings. More than likely, her past training and years of experience of being a police officer was telling her not to take this short walk to the warehouse for granted — they were now out in the open; they could easily be under surveillance.

As they arrived at the entrance to the warehouse, Lenora placed her hand onto Antonio's arm. They both paused for a moment as Lenora scoped the surrounding area one last time. Although she still seemed uncertain, she gave Antonio the ok. He entered the warehouse by himself and Lenora took up a position guarding the door.

Across the street, both Maxwell and Joshua began to feel a bit antsy. Six months of hard work, six months of stress, six months of dead ends and disappointments for them; all of it was only moments away from finally ending — or so they hoped. Police officers were not suppose to let their cases affect them personally — both Maxwell and Joshua knew what could happen if that occurred, as they saw firsthand what it had done to Colin Ramirez. Thankfully, they had not allowed themselves to become emotionally attached to their case. However, there admittedly was still an open wound that had yet to be attended to that overtly exposed the inadequacies within the Detroit Police Department.

Both Maxwell and Joshua refused to be baited. In their eyes, what Antonio Marcone has been doing since day one is patiently wait for that one crucial mistake to be made. Only then, did they assume he would take that next evolutionary step. As things stood now, the two of them firmly believed that the game had not yet tilted in the enemy's favor. And as much as they wanted to just spring out of their car, rush toward the warehouse, and steal the presumed win away from him, they knew that they had to hold off until the right moment. Just like a professional card player, patience was needed from them until it was time to reveal the ace they had tucked in their sleeve.

"I can't begin to imagine what good deeds we've done to deserve this unexpected visit from Antonio Marcone," Maxwell said. "This is going to taste just as good as the two freshly baked paczkis that I had this morning for breakfast."

"Well... at least you won't have to go to the gym afterwards. I'm sure you've already sweated off the eight-hundred calories from those just by sitting in this car."

Maxwell could not help but crack a smile at his partner's comment. In fact, he was certain that he had sweated off more than just his breakfast. "Is it just me, or doesn't that woman who came here with Antonio look to be just a little bit nervous?"

Joshua had grabbed the binoculars that Maxwell had used earlier and took a closer look at the woman. In that moment, he didn't know if he should celebrate or be pissed off, as he immediately recognized who she was. "You mean, Lenora Lexington? Yes, she should be just as nervous as Antonio."

Satisfaction suddenly consumed Maxwell. The reason that Colin Ramirez got two bullets put in his back was right there in front of them. And now, they had an opportunity to kill two birds with one stone. It was just too bad that their former fellow officer could not be here with them at this moment, as Maxwell was certain that Colin would want the opportunity to get his revenge against the bitch that sold him out. However, as a favor to his friend, Maxwell was more than willing to be the proxy and get that for him. "Are you ready, partner?"

As stereotypical as it was, Joshua said what was on his mind anyway. "I am ready to put that Italian bastard into a pair of concrete shoes and unceremoniously drop him in the Detroit River."

Maxwell reached across and picked up the police radio. He proceeded to inform all of their backup units of Antonio Marcone's unexpected arrival, and then quickly reviewed what everyone's assignment was. Once that was done, they exited their car to take care of business.

———————————————— ♋ ————————————————

Since he had taken over control of the D.U.O., Antonio Marcone has all but ignored the existence of the law. To him, they were nothing but an unwanted nuisance. Occasionally, for his own amusement, he would toy with the police and allow them to feel a sense of optimism, when in actuality, he was just stringing them along because he knew that their egos would one day cause them to make a crucial mistake — little did he suspect that the mistake being made today was from him.

As soon as he entered the warehouse, Antonio took a quick survey of the surroundings. Seeing that the truck was nearly loaded, he produced a satisfying grin. He then walked in the direction of his right hand man, greeting Louie with only his eyes, a look that showed his satisfaction. Antonio then leaned in close to him and whispered something that was only meant for his associate to hear. The smile that immediately appeared on Louie's face was all that it took to understand that his boss had just acknowledged him for a job well done.

"Mr. Marcone, what a pleasant surprise it is to see you here. Would... my 'paycheck' happen to be inside that satchel you are carrying?"

Antonio gave Terrance a look that immediately answered his question, a look that told Terrance that not only had he offended him, but that assumption of his had also been erroneous. He immediately apologized for his transgression and then left the area to make sure that those under his watch were still doing their jobs. After that quick check was completed, and seeing that the loading of the truck was near complete, Terrance pulled aside four of his men and sent them outside to ensure that the perimeter was secure — he wanted to make sure that Antonio Marcone saw that he could be more than just a hired gun.

Antonio was not too impressed that Louie's recruit had the nerve to inquire about his pay before the job was even done. The one thing that he hated more than anything was impatience — and this scab, though obviously useful, had one too many irritating qualities.

Yes, he had successfully completed a handful of previous assignments. But in Antonio's opinion, Terrance had yet to even come close to proving his worth. Still, the potential was there for the man to be a huge asset for his organization. But then again, his arrogance was more than enough to sway Antonio into reassessing his worth. This military man had an upside he could not deny, but he also had the potential to be an extremely large pain in the ass.

He took a moment and thought, trying to sift through all of the positives and negatives. Unfortunately, he just could not find enough positives. Terrance, he felt, could not be trusted enough to be an asset. Lenora Lexington and Casper were not Italian and they both had turned out to be trustworthy individuals — but then again, they might just end up being the rare exception when it came to the 'Manual' rule.

Although he was not the kind of man who made any sort of rash decisions, especially those that were based upon emotion, Antonio was beginning to lean heavily in one direction. It seemed a shame to cut ties with a man who had the potential to become something special, but he was really considering ending his brief association with Terrance Burelli after the conclusion of the shipment.

Antonio was never one to procrastinate when it came to difficult decisions that had to be made — even ones where a bullet in the back of someone's head was the only way to end an association. Sometimes, he knew, it just had to be done.

As Antonio observed the workers loading the last few crates onto the truck, he made a decision concerning the few what ifs that he still had. To him, it just wasn't worth the potential headache. "Louie… as much of an upside as Terrance has, I have not seen enough from him to convince me that he can become a valuable asset to our organization. I have a feeling that his precariousness would eventually cause a lot of internal problems."

"I hate to admit it, but I agree with you."

"I was willing to give him all the opportunity in the world to prove his worth, but I am uncomfortable with a man whose behavior on occasion, can be somewhat irrational and volatile. Therefore, I've decided that Terrance's employment with us needs to be terminated after this shipment is complete."

"Ok. How would you like for me to do it?"

"Not you. Have Sal take care of it."

"I'm sure he'd be glad to do it. Hopefully, he won't fuck it up this time."

Without warning, gunfire echoed outside. Hysteria quickly erupted as bullets ripped through the windows of the warehouse, cutting through the stale air. All within a matter of moments, pandemonium ensued.

Lenora Lexington flew through the large, dust caked front window of the building — glass went everywhere. She landed unceremoniously a few feet in front of Antonio; her tiny body bloodied from massive gunshot wounds that had nearly ripped away her right thigh and left shoulder. Her face also had a large gash just below the left eye socket; a horrific wound caused when her body was launched through the pane of the warehouse window.

Antonio did not know what to do. Lenora was badly wounded and he was pinned down by a bevy of led mosquitoes. If he got up from where he was and tried to run, he was certain that he would end up like Lenora. Instead, he crawled over to her and checked for any signs of life. There was none — she was dead. Sadness enveloped him. In what little time she had been a part of his life, Antonio had never been happier. All of his needs and desires had been well taken care of by her. He closed his eyes and said a silent prayer for Lenora — although he doubted that any God would listen to him. But he felt that she deserved that nonetheless.

Fragments from the warehouse walls, glass and bullets continued to fly by. Antonio stayed where he was, beside Lenora and tried to make his body as small as he could. He hoped that by doing so, he would reduce his chances of being hit by gunfire. He was in a no win situation, and all that he cared about at that moment, was surviving.

In a final gesture of appreciation for what she had done, Antonio leaned over Lenora, and in the only spot that had yet to be covered in blood, gave her a parting kiss on her exposed left shoulder. "Goodbye, Leni. You will be dearly missed."

Antonio was on his own now; neither Louie nor Terrance were anywhere to be seen. He had no idea where they were or if anything had happened to them. All that he could do was assume they had somehow escaped. For him however, the only thing left was to wait for what was to come next.

The police barnstormed the building a few minutes later, and launched several canisters of tear gas through the broken windows. A few seconds later, those who were still inside had quickly succumbed to the effects of the gas. Antonio covered his mouth in an attempt to avoid inhaling it, but his effort for survival quickly became futile. It was over, and he knew it.

Antonio scanned the smoke covered warehouse through watery eyes and saw a pair of ghostly silhouettes advancing toward him. He knew that these 'things' where not angels sent from heaven to take Lenora to her eternal resting place. If any otherworldly beings were to make an appearance here, Antonio knew that it would be the Grim Reaper coming to take him away. These corporeal-like 'ghosts' instead, were more like a representation of the epitome of his ego. It was time that he paid the piper. He had finally been defeated. He had no choice at that point but to accept his unexpected defeat and surrender.

Everyone who had been inside the warehouse had been arrested — except for Louie and Terrance. Fortunately for them, during all of the commotion, they had somehow managed to elude apprehension. Not so much that they had been lucky enough to have escaped, but neither had been stupid enough to stay behind and fight — they both had high-tailed it out of the warehouse the moment that first gunshot had been heard. For the police, it was a victory that was long overdue. But it was also one that was bittersweet. No one on the right side of the law was dancing a celebratory jig. People had died here today, including someone who used to be one of them. And even though she had made her bed and had chosen to lie in it, it was still sad that a former police officer had lost her way; and then lost her life — but then again, this was just karma coming back to take a big chunk out of her ass. And although they were able to stop the massive stolen military arms shipment from leaving the warehouse, Maxwell and Joshua still felt disappointed — whom they had also hoped to arrest, was nowhere to be found. Just because the head of the D.U.O. was now going to jail, didn't mean that the man's empire would collapse.

Had Louie Mazotti been here, that just might have happened. But instead, its foundation had only received a bit of damage.

Undoubtedly, the D.U.O. was going to restructure itself. That meant that Maxwell and Joshua's assignment was far from over — they still had a lot of work ahead of them before they could ever attempt another strike against the city's number one criminal organization. But when they do, they both were pretty confident that the Detroit Underworld Organization was going to become nothing more than just another one of those forgettable memories from this city's not-too-proud recent past.

7

Antonio was fully aware of the consequences that came with the life he had chosen to live. Since the day he committed himself to the D.U.O. until now, seventeen years in all, he had continuously pushed lady luck all the way to the edge, only to survive each time earning the respect and confidence of his boss.

His ambition and fearlessness is what helped Antonio rise quickly through the ranks of the organization. He was lucky and he knew it. By being smart and purposefully stepping on the toes of those in his way, he had strategically placed himself in line to take on a position of influence. And when that time had finally come, Antonio already had a plan in place to eliminate the only person that stood in the way of his complete and full control of the Detroit Underworld Organization.

Through many channels, several greased palms, and a willing associate, he was able to ensure that the organization's private plane that carried Vance Palmalino, crashed into the ocean shortly after it had taken off from the Dominican Republic on its way back to the mainland. He then made sure that the only individual who suspected him of doing that, stayed quiet. Maven Potter's murder had been necessary — just like the bomb that was planted on the airplane. Both of those acts were purposely committed by Sal, per his orders.

For the next three years following, Antonio had been on top of the world, living his life the way he had envisioned it, and he was running the organization that he had helped to build. But now, his life had apparently come full circle. His luck had run out. Antonio had to pay for his crimes. And as much as he wasn't looking forward to being locked away, he could not deny all that he had done.

It may seem odd, but right before his day in court, a slightly warped perspective of his pending future had consumed his thoughts — that was when he realized there was actually a silver lining to his arrest. No longer would he have any expectations to live up to, no longer did he have any responsibilities, and no longer would he be consumed by stress — the burden of all of that would now lie on the shoulders of both of his associates. However, in no way shape or form did it mean that Antonio was going to hand over complete control of his empire to them. Just because he was facing a long-term sentence, didn't mean that he was going to allow himself to be kept in the dark.

It made sense to him to use his pending long-term incarceration to relax, refocus his objective for the organization, and construct a plan; one that he would put in place sometime in the distant future. Nevertheless, there was one thing that Antonio wanted first — a bit of revenge. Yes, he had always been a relatively patient man, but in this instance, he wasn't willing to wait. The ones who were responsible for his arrest, he wanted to make suffer. And then once his associates arranged for that to happen, Antonio knew that not only would he have peace of mind throughout the upcoming years, but what hardships he may endure during his time in prison will be nothing compared to the emotional suffering that those individuals responsible for putting him in prison, will have to bear.

At the conclusion of his trial, Antonio had been convicted on four counts: possession of stolen government property with the intent to sell, extortion, conspiracy, and being an accessory to the attempted murder of a police officer. He had also been charged with the murders of Maven Potter, Vance Palmalino, and Vance's pilot. But a not guilty verdict was read, as the jury was uncertain if Officer Ramirez's first-hand accounts of the confessions were completely accurate or embellished so that a murder conviction against the defendant was assured.

As he was being escorted from the courtroom, Antonio turned and stared callously at Maxwell; a stare that froze the man with utter confusion. After a few tense moments of silence, Antonio spoke, keeping his eyes locked in on Maxwell's fossilized face — while at the same time, ignoring his partner, who had been standing a mere few feet away. "You won't know when, but a day will come when you will feel immeasurable pain; pain that will slowly eat away at your soul and scar you for the remainder of your pathetic life."

Maxwell had been chastised at the conclusion of a trial before and nothing had ever happened to him. He would usually just brush it off, believing that every threat that had been sent his way was empty.

But never before had words like those that came from Antonio, felt so prophetic — it promptly caused Maxwell to believe that what had been said, was something more than just a bunch of spiteful words. An unnerving chill settled in his veins. Antonio's declaration had forced Maxwell into suddenly carrying an unwanted burden of worry on his shoulders.

The next morning, Maxwell and Joshua had learned that Chief Winslow had graciously made arrangements to send them and their wives on a three week sabbatical — this was done in order to help ease the stresses that had accumulated during their long investigation and subsequent trial. The chief was well aware of just how emotional the entire ordeal had been for them — as well as the threat that Antonio had made. For that reason, he thought that it would be best to give both officers some well deserved time off — not just because of the hard work that they put in, but because their objectivity needed a chance to return to a normal state.

At first, Maxwell and Joshua didn't want to take the offered vacation because they both knew that there was still a lot of work to do. From the moment they arrested Antonio Marcone, till the end of his trial, they had yet to make any other significant progress in tracking down the remaining high ranking members of the D.U.O. — both, it appeared, had gone into hiding. So as far as Maxwell and Joshua were concerned, that was their first priority — not time off. They both knew that the longer it took for them to find and arrest Louie Mazotti and Salvadore Batiste, the greater the chances were that the D.U.O. would have time to restructure and start back up their daily business practices again. But Jacob Winslow insisted that they take the vacation. His reasoning was simple — Detroit needed its best two detectives at the top of their game when the time came to smash another corner or two out of the foundation of the Detroit Underworld Organization.

Three weeks later...

Upon their return home from their obligatory vacation, both Maxwell and Joshua went directly back to work, feeling exactly as the chief of police had hoped they'd feel. However, the moment they stepped foot back into their precinct, a wave of reality hit them both — they were back in their everyday lives and the D.U.O. was again priority number one. They both had hoped that their first day back would be nothing short of easy, because each had quickly gotten used to doing absolutely nothing and enjoying every bit of that kind of lazy lifestyle. In fact, the prospect of early retirement had actually crossed each of their minds the more they spent time with their wives and enjoyed what was to them, a taste of the good life.

Neither of them really felt like doing much once they made it to their desks. They were just content to relax and savor their morning coffee — that was, until Maxwell's phone rang. "It figures. I haven't even been back to work for more than two minutes and my damn phone has to ring. All that I wanted today was to sit back, relax, and attempt to enjoy this free tar that they try to pass off as coffee. Instead, reality has to slam me hard in the face and remind me of the job I have and the responsibility that goes with it."

"Well, I see that your time away from here did not help one bit when it came to retrieving the sanity you had lost. You're still a mess. Maybe you should see a doctor and have him put you on stress leave before you have a complete nervous breakdown."

Max took a sip of his 'coffee', made an indescribable face as he swallowed it. He then said to his partner, "Maybe I should just file a complaint with health and safety about this crap that I'm drinking."

Joshua humored his partner and let out a small chuckle.

"I wouldn't be such a miserable prick half the time if what little amenities they gave us were of a higher quality."

"I agree. But what would it take for you to not be a complete jerk-off the other half of the time?" Joshua just sat there with a cruel grin on his face; a few of the other officer's in the precinct, whose desks were within conversation range, concurrently expelled a chortle that filled their area of the room.

Maxwell just sat there perturbed; he chose to keep quiet in that moment and not respond to the good-natured ribbing, even though he knew that he was much better at the insult game than his partner.

"So, Max. Are you going to answer your phone or are you going to just wait until the ringing stops all on its own?" Joshua asked.

Conceding that his call might be from someone with something important to say, Maxwell finally answered it. Curiosity then encompassed Joshua as he listened intently to Maxwell's conversation. At first, he wasn't exactly sure who it was that his partner was talking to. But by the end of the conversation, Joshua had a pretty good idea whom it had been. "So... What did Chevy want?"

Maxwell leaned back in his chair and placed his right hand on his stomach. The two cups of coffee that he had on the red-eye flight home had been good; the cup he had here at the station was causing his stomach to churn. It felt to him as if his insides had been used as a beaker in a high school science lab in which some idiotic student decided to conduct an experiment that went horribly wrong.

He slightly moaned and bent himself forward, hoping to relieve the discomfort. After indiscreetly passing a good healthy bit of gas, Maxwell grabbed his cell phone off the top of his desk, motioned for his partner to follow, then headed for the precinct exit. However, they hadn't even taken two steps away from their desks when a piercing voice barked at them from across the room, causing them both to freeze. Without even having to turn around to see where that shrill had come from, they both knew right away that their day was about to get much worse than the free coffee.

Standing at the threshold of his office was Captain White; he was fidgeting with the twisted, cross like figure that always hung around his neck — the family treasured heirloom was made from ivory and was thinly trimmed in gold. It was definitely an unintentional habit, but it was also a warning to those who knew Christopher well, because whenever he would start aimlessly playing with that cross, it was understood that he was angry about something.

"Shit! Now there's a voice that could make the milk in your morning coffee curdle," Maxwell said. His words were only loud enough for his partner to hear.

"Are you insinuating that the captain is responsible for your bad cup of coffee?" Joshua replied.

"No!"

Christopher White stood at his office doorway and spoke in a tone loud enough to ensure that his two best officers were centered out,

"Where the hell do you two think you are going? You guys just got back from your vacation."

Maxwell stood there trying desperately to think of a good explanation as to why they were leaving so soon after just coming back to work. He never really liked telling his captain what he was up to, no matter how important it was, until he had some solid information to give. So he plastered on his face the best 'innocent' expression, hoping that it would help him to sell his soon to be fabricated lie. "Umm… We meant to stop on the way into work this morning and pick up some fresh coffee and doughnuts for everyone, but we were running late. We felt bad for not doing this, so we were just going to step out for a few minutes and go and get everyone in the precinct some. What would you like in your coffee, sir?"

Captain White stood unmoving with a plainly obvious 'not too impressed' look on his face. He then sternly looked across the room at Maxwell and said, "I'm not really in the mood for any bullshit this morning. Both of you get your lazy, overly sunburned asses into my office right now!"

From the moment that Maxwell and Joshua had entered Christopher's office, they could feel the immense tension in the room. Cautiously, they sat down in front of the captain's new, rather large, dark oak desk, and waited for him to speak.

Only a few seconds had actually ticked by, but today it felt like many long and agonizing minutes. And even though they both had known Christopher for years before he became their captain, he had developed a knack for making them feel uneasy and nervous. "So… do I have to insist or is someone going to willingly tell me what it is that you two are keeping from me?"

"I knew you let your damn phone ring way too long," Joshua whispered, as he gently tapped the back leg of his partner's chair with his foot.

"I swear the captain has my desk bugged," Maxwell replied softly, while turning to his partner and slightly rolling his eyes upward.

The captain just sat still, not removing his 'I want to know now' stare from both of his officers. He clearly had heard what they quietly had said to each other, but as usual, he just ignored it knowing full well that these two officers liked to test his resolve for some unknown reason. "Did neither one of you hear the question that I asked?"

Even though he had, Maxwell chose the route of being stupid. He apologized to his captain and then he asked him to repeat it.

"Where in the hell were you two guys going to in such a hurry?" The captain reiterated, with enough force in his voice for it to be clearly heard right through his office walls.

"We already told you, sir. We were just going out to get everybody some fresh coffee."

"Don't bullshit me, Josh!" Although Christopher White had a high tolerance for almost anything, childish bantering was not one of them — and today definitely wasn't the day for it. He was quickly beginning to lose his patience with both of his detectives. Just because they were his best men, and he had known them each for years, didn't mean that they could meaninglessly try to kick him around like a hacky sack ball.

Captain White got up out of his chair and started to pace behind it. He did this with his back turned away from both of his officers so that they could not see that he was trying to vent off some of his built up frustration. "You two don't really think I'm that stupid, do you?"

'No, but sometimes I wish you were,' Maxwell thought.

With no real reason behind it, Captain White reached up and snatched a hard cover book from the shelf that was directly in front of him. He stared at the back of the book momentarily and then in one motion, he pivoted and slammed it down hard on his desk. This caused both Maxwell and Joshua to literally jump out of their seats.

Now that he had their attention, Christopher looked sternly at both of his officers and said, "I saw you out there talking on your damn phone, Maxwell. And do you want to know the reason why I just happen to see you talking on your damn phone? Well, let me tell you how I know. I saw you talking on your damn phone because while I was reading an important E-mail from Chief Winslow, I kept hearing it ring. It must have rung at least forty fucking times before you finally answered it. Either you were intentionally trying to see if I would come out of my office, or you were just trying to irritate the fuck out of me. Either way, I don't appreciate it when my work gets interrupted for no goddamn reason."

Captain White took a moment and composed himself. The last thing that he wanted was to cause a rift between himself and his officers — his friends. "Now are you two going to come clean and tell me what the hell you're really up to, or are you going to force me to have to place the two of you on an un-paid extension of your recent vacation?"

Maxwell paused for a moment as he placed both of his hands up to his face. He began to rub the bridge of his nose with his fingers and tried to contemplate whether or not to stop their intentional pissing off of their old friend. After a few seconds had passed, Maxwell decided that it was best that he and his partner cease their childish behavior, act like the adults that they were, and inform their captain of what was really going on — or at least, tell him some of what was going on. "First of, my phone only rang like ten times... I think. Which I know is irrelevant, but... It was my snitch that called. He said that he has acquired some new information that I would definitely be interested in."

The captain plastered a sarcastic look onto his face and said, "There... was that so hard? So what kind of information are we talking about here?"

"I'm not sure yet? Maxwell replied. My snitch never gives me any details over the phone. But he did confirm what we all knew was probably going to happen. He said that the D.U.O. did not fold when Antonio got convicted. Louie Mazotti and Salvadore Batiste had only temporarily gone into hiding, resurfacing only a few days ago when they were certain that it was safe to begin restructuring the organization."

Joshua nudged Maxwell and then showed him his watch. Maxwell acknowledged that their time was rapidly evaporating, so he asked Captain White if they could be excused as their contact was expecting them within the next fifteen minutes. They did not wish to be late because Maxwell's contact, though he had never done it before, might change his mind and leave before they actually got there. He also wanted to get the hell out of Christopher's office, knowing that if he and his partner stayed there to halfheartedly answer more questions, they each would more than likely get the other half of their asses chewed off.

"Fine! You may both leave and go to your damn meeting. But I will expect a detailed report as soon as you get back… and I mean, everything that you have learned. No matter how trivial you may think it is."

Both Maxwell and Joshua promptly got up out of their chairs, left their captain's office, and headed directly for their meeting. As soon as they had gone, Christopher sunk deep into his chair. He wasn't exhausted; he was frustrated. He just could not understand why Maxwell and Joshua felt the need to routinely push his buttons. The ever present premature graying he had, he felt was entirely their fault. Maybe it had something to do with the fact that it had been less than three years earlier that he had been their equal and that they still felt comfortable enough to rib him, just like they had before he became their superior.

Whatever the reason, Christopher needed to find a way to make them understand that at work, he was not their friend; he was their boss and they needed to treat him as such. However, disciplining them for their unprofessionalism was something that he had been trying to avoid. But if things didn't change soon, he knew that he would have no other choice but to do just that. And when that time came, their friendship outside of work, would change as well — it would probably be no more.

Looking at the book he had slammed on his desk, Christopher reached out and firmly picked it up; his intent was to put it directly back on the shelf — but he didn't. He instead, flipped it over and for a moment, he imagined that it was Maxwell's neck in his hands. Symbolically, he just wanted to strangle him for his behavior. But he quickly realized that he could not, even if he wanted to — it was only his emotions that were driving those unabated thoughts.

He stood up from his chair, and then his eyes curiously clued in to what the title of the book was. In his hands was an odd bit of irony. This book, which had been a gift from his wife on their first anniversary, never once had been looked at. It was entitled, *"Fifty Simple Ways to Help Relieve Work Related Stress."*

Dumbfounded, he gazed at the cover for a moment. But instead of placing it back where it belonged on his bookcase, he sat back down into his office chair and began to skim through the pages. He honestly didn't think that he'd find anything in there to help him deal with his officer's juvenile behavior, but he was certain that an hour immersed in something other than what was already occupying his thoughts, would be just what he needed to relax and forget about the pending bull shit that he knew he would soon have to deal with once Maxwell and Joshua returned from their meeting.

Three weeks had gone by since Antonio Marcone was handed a sentence of thirty years in prison without any eligibility whatsoever of parole. It was then decided by the judge that his prison term was to be served at the maximum security state penitentiary in Jackson, Michigan — there, was where a good portion of the remainder of his life will be lived.

Visiting him at the prison this day, the first one that Antonio has had was a man of Sicilian/Croatian decent. This individual, although not that tall at five foot, ten inches and weighing roughly two hundred and forty pounds, had a rather intimidating presence about him. His hair was dark brown, somewhat long and wavy, with just a few noticeable strands of grey intertwined. In his left ear he had a tiny ruby earring, and his left forearm was completely covered by a tattoo of a mutated scorpion like creature that sat atop of a banner — inside that banner was written one simple word, 'Omertà'.

Normally, Sal would keep his tattoo covered. But today he wanted the guards to notice it. Not everyone would know what the word 'Omertà' meant, but those who did would certainly let it be known amongst their peers that it was a simple, unspoken warning not to test him while he was visiting. "It's good to see you again, Antonio. We've missed you at the office."

Sal sat down in the chair in which the prison guard had directed him to. He then waited patiently for the man to take up his watch position by the entrance of the visiting room before doing what he had come here to do — discuss some important business with his boss. "So… it appears that prison life has already done you some good. It looks to me like you've already lost a bit of weight?"

"Can the crap, Sal. I'm really not in the mood for your brand of humor."

"Sorry, boss. I was just trying to break the ice. Anyway, the reason that I came here today is to tell you that I have found out that our two friends have finally returned from their long vacation."

Antonio had thought about carrying out his revenge while Maxwell and Joshua were on their vacation. With the connections that Antonio's organization had, it didn't take them long to find out that his two enemies had gone to Jamaica. It would have been easy to have the bodies disposed of there without anyone being aware, but it hadn't taken much thought before he decided that he wanted to enact his revenge right here at home. "Well it's about fuckin' time that they got back." Now feeling a little more at ease, Antonio sat back in his seat, took a few relaxing breaths, and looked at his trusted associate with an eager smile. He then said the only two words that were needed to be spoken, "Permission granted."

Sal took a nonchalant look over at the prison guard, just to see if he was paying any attention to them before he continued his conversation with Antonio. He then reassured his boss that everything was set and ready to go, the word had already been put out on the street, and that they should be seeing some results very soon. He also informed Antonio that, while he was making all of the necessary arrangements, he had found out something of interest about one of their adversaries that they could use; something that would be the equivalent to an actual dagger through the heart — if he decided that they should go that route in case things didn't quite go according to plan.

"You and Louie are the only ones that I trust to not only do what I ask, but to keep the organization running while I'm locked up in here. However, before the organization can even begin to evolve and move forward with our long-term plan, those two cops need to be dealt with. As you can see, they've forced me to alter my plans and have turned my expertly manipulated life into a monotonous hell. And because of them, I am now stuck here in this damn prison for the next thirty years. Therefore, I feel that it is only fair that they experience a bit of what hell on earth is really like." After a few moments of unspoken understanding had taken place, Antonio continued, "Just promise me that you will make those two pigs squeal?"

"Oh, I promise you that will happen. You can count on me to carry out your wishes." The prison guard left his position next to the door and walked over towards Sal. He didn't have to say a word; Sal knew that his brief visitation was over.

He got up from his chair, reassured Antonio that there were no reasons for him to worry, and then promised that he would keep him up to date on all that had happened concerning the family. While Sal was leaving the visiting area, he began to quietly whistle that old dance song from the nineteen-eighties, *"You dropped a bomb on me."* The guard was young; only in his early twenties, which was probably why he did not recognize the song — nor did Sal think that the man would be bright enough to put two and two together. Antonio however, recognized the song — and it brought a smile to his face.

As he was heading back to his cell, satisfaction consumed him. His desires would soon be fulfilled, his dreams could begin to develop, and his wants would one day become a reality. Unfortunately, he wasn't going to get to see any of it come to fruition until his prison sentence was over.

The morning was almost half over and Chevy, full name, Chevy Roy Leigh, was waiting in what used to be an office inside of an old canning factory. He was a scrawny young chap who looked to be in his early twenties, yet nobody really knew for sure exactly how old he was. His face was freckled and very ashen, which was accented by his long, thick, scraggly, straw-like, strawberry red hair. He had his hair haphazardly braided into a ponytail that draped almost all the way down to the tip of his tailbone. He also had multiple piercings: both of his ears, his nose, above his left eyebrow, one of his nipples, his tongue, and his lip. But what made the young man think that he was more unique than what his appearance would suggest, was that he firmly believed he not only was a reincarnated descendant of the man who founded the Roman Empire, but he believed he possessed the man's ancient soul — and that was why he had the man's name,

Augustus, tattooed in Latin across his throat, just underneath his Adam's apple.

Chevy's posture was rather diminutive, for he probably weighed just over a buck and a half, soaking wet. The jeans he wore were ripped at both knees and he had on a white stained T-shirt that displayed a three dimensional-looking animated green hand, flipping you the bird, with a caption that read *"COOL, CRISP and CLEAR! Get the picture?"* Obviously, his attire was less than desirable for someone who insisted that he was at one time a Roman Emperor — but at least he took some pride in himself, as he obviously understood what the concept of personal hygiene was.

As Chevy waited patiently, he had begun to get an unusual sensation that something wasn't quite right. His looks would never make the cover of G.Q., but he had this uncanny and unique ability to foresee trouble; a sixth and seventh sense combined — an inherent gift he believed came from his ancient soul.

Uneasiness began to show, but Chevy knew that he had to pull it all together. He could never let his friend Maxwell down — he owed him his life. All of a sudden, something had made him hastily whirl. He quickly glanced over his shoulder and looked through the broken, dust layered window that was next to the front door of the factory. He saw something coming his way; a car that he did not recognize that was kicking up stones and speeding toward the building that he occupied.

As the black muscle car got closer, restlessness began to hit Chevy. His first instinct was to bolt across the factory for the back door — but he didn't. He stayed right where he was and watched the vehicle get closer. When it finally stopped, the expected panic did not automatically consume him. Instead, it was his curiosity that came to the forefront — it caused him to carefully study the stationary vehicle that was now parked only a short distance away from the building.

Although it was close, it still wasn't close enough for Chevy to see who owned it — that was the only thing that he seemed to be uncomfortable with. He never liked to be caught in the middle of a situation that he had no control over — it was a lesson that he had learned all too well when he was younger. It wasn't so much his size that made him throw up the caution sign, but he just wasn't the kind of person who could physically defend himself.

His conscience started to push aside his curiosity — it was again telling him to run for the back door. But for some reason, his feet weren't listening to what his mind was saying. Instead, he chose to scrutinize the two important, astute looking individuals that had just exited the parked vehicle.

One of them stood lofty, weighed close to two hundred and thirty pounds, and his body appeared to be nothing but solid mass. He had short dark hair, a neatly trimmed moustache, and he walked with a haughtiness that few could actually back up. The other one stood a few inches taller but weighed slightly less. Unlike his counterpart, this man had a body that was cut; an individual that obviously took pride in being fit. He also had light brown hair, which hung down just above his shoulders, a neatly trimmed goatee, and was tanned. Confidence also seemed to follow him.

Both of these men left the area of their vehicle and leisurely made their way towards the old factory. Again, Chevy's conscience was desperately trying to get him to leave, but then it finally realized that he had never been in danger — the coward, that for the most part dominated his personality, had been wrong as these two men who were approaching the factory were in fact, Chevy's friends; Maxwell Banks and Joshua Brampton.

For a moment, he felt stupid for even contemplating what he had. But as he replayed in his mind what had just taken place, a possible reason for his doubts, quickly popped into his head. *'Maybe it is time that I look into getting a pair of glasses, seeing that I almost didn't recognize my friends.'* Then again, that could be just a convenient excuse for him to use so that he didn't have to admit to himself just how paranoid of an individual he actually was.

"You guys are late," Chevy said, while standing at the threshold of the factory door entrance. "Another couple of minutes and I would not have been here." Chevy stepped back from the door and then walked away from it, stopping once he arrived almost in the middle of the rather large room.

Maxwell shut the door once he and his partner were inside. He then instinctively took a quick look through the broken window to make sure that no one was hanging around outside and being curious. "Give me a break. You weren't going anywhere. Besides, this is almost like a second home to you."

Chevy snickered to himself, realizing that his friend knew him better than he sometimes did. "You're right, Max. I wasn't going to go anywhere. Though René was starting to get pretty agitated."

Joshua always kept an open mind, but he wanted nothing to do with this charade that always happened every time they met up with Chevy. He could never understand why his partner would continuously humor the man and all but acknowledge that Chevy's invisible friend 'René', actually existed. He probably did exist in the man's eccentric mind, but it didn't mean that Joshua had to play along in order to get whatever information they needed.

Unwilling to sit through another one of these 'sessions', Joshua had made a selfish, some would say even a childish decision on the way to the factory — today was going to be the day that he permanently put an end to this unnecessary bullshit before it even got started.

However, knowing his partner as well as he did, Maxwell swiftly put an end to what he sensed his partner was about to do — and he did it just by looking at him. Once that understanding had been made with Joshua, Maxwell moved himself away from the desk that he had been leaning up against and strolled over toward a different broken window. After a few moments, his curiosity was satisfied, so he dragged an old steel stool towards himself and placed his right foot on it. As he brushed off the dust that had instantly clung to his shoe from the stool, he asked Chevy the obvious question. "So... What do you have for me?"

"You don't actually think that I'm gonna spill my guts for nothing, do you?" Chevy looked over at Maxwell and, as per their ritual, held out his hand.

Smiling, Maxwell reached into his front right pocket and pulled out his money clip. He fanned through it and removed two hundred dollars.

For the first time since he had known Maxwell, Chevy felt insulted. "Hang on there a minute. I don't think that you realize what we had to go through to get you this information!" He then held up his other hand and showed Maxwell four fingers.

"Four hundred?" Maxwell uttered, as he inquisitively looked at his snitch. "Ok. I have no problem with paying a little extra for some good information." Maxwell then thumbed out another fifty from his money clip.

"Two fifty?" Chevy turned his back to his friend and took a few tantrum-esque steps away. After a few seconds of attempting to sell his disappointment, he turned back around and then presented his counteroffer by insisting that he be paid no less than three hundred and fifty dollars. Then right after that, Chevy tried his best to make his friend feel guilty by reminding him that he needed the cash to buy food for not one, but two people — he and his friend René.

Chevy had a track record; one that Maxwell could not dispute. No other informant that Maxwell had used had ever been this reliable. The only other one that Maxwell had known of who had a reputation of reliability had been Jimbo Lewis. But unfortunately, he was no longer alive.

Knowing he could trust that whatever information Chevy had was going to be well worth the cost, Maxwell placed the two hundred and fifty back into his clip and returned it into his right front pocket. He then removed his wallet from his back pocket and removed the three crisp, new, one hundred dollar bills he had — this was his 'emergency' money. He held it up enticingly for Chevy to see, and then he threw it down on the desk off to his right side — where it landed, it somewhat divided the two of them.

Chevy took a moment and mulled over the offer that was lying on the desk. He soon realized that three hundred dollars was more than what his friend had ever offered him before. So, without having to think about it any longer, Chevy picked up the money, blew off the thin layer of dust that had clung to it, and then extended his hand in appreciation of Maxwell's generosity, sealing the deal.

"Now that that's settled," Maxwell stated, "how about you tell me what you know?"

"I don't know anything, but René said he does. At least, he told me that he does." Chevy turned about face and walked about thirty feet across the floor to an empty chair — he then slightly leaned over in a manner in which it appeared that he were in conversation with his invisible friend.

"Here we go. This should be real good," Joshua whispered cynically. Unwilling to subject himself to this farce, he promptly informed his partner that he was going out for some fresh air and would wait outside until Maxwell was finished. But as Joshua was leaving the factory, he just couldn't resist being the bully — the childishness that still occasionally resided inside of him, came to the surface. Deliberately, he passed right alongside the chair that René was supposedly sitting in and then mockingly went through the motions of patting him on the back, as if he was trying to apologize to him.

This immediately upset Maxwell. He didn't however, have to say a word, as his partner could plainly see just how pissed he had become. Joshua wasn't about to apologize; not in front of Chevy — he didn't feel that he needed to. Yes, he had acted insensitively towards their informant, but he believed that the man shouldn't be treated with kid gloves. If he were to ever earn Joshua's respect, then he'd have to first address the delusions he had. Until then, Chevy would only be considered a good source of information — nothing more than that in his eyes.

He again looked over at his partner and could see that Maxwell was still not happy. At that moment, he decided it would be best that he just leave the canning factory and let his partner deal with Chevy all on his own — so Joshua walked out the front door.

About three minutes after Maxwell's partner had left, Chevy had concluded his 'conversation' with the empty chair. He returned to where he had been a few minutes earlier and began to explain to Maxwell everything that he had supposedly learned from his invisible friend.

Disappointment immediately showed on Maxwell's face. Chevy had confirmed what they feared was going to happen — both Louie Mazotti and Salvadore Batiste had officially been handed the responsibilities of running the D.U.O. while Antonio was locked up. Maxwell had unrealistically hoped that the organization would either go into a long hibernation or just dissolve without Antonio Marcone there to run the show. But now that he had the apparent verification, the normal lives that he and his partner had hoped to return to, was going to have to be put on the back burned for a while longer.

The Detroit Underworld Organization, to Maxwell, was just like that Greek mythological creature, the three-headed Lernaean Hydra — they had essentially beheaded the one in the middle, but the other two were still alive and kicking. Eventually, like that creature, the missing head will re-grow and it will return to being just as powerful as it had been before.

What was more important at that moment was what had promptly invaded Maxwell's thoughts? Not only was the D.U.O. going to continue on with all of its illegal activities, but he was certain that the elimination of both he and Joshua was going to be their first priority. That meant that they needed to be on their game from this moment forward, and approach things in a completely different way than what they usually did. It didn't mean that they would no longer be aggressive, but it did mean that new subsections would have to be added to their book of unwritten rules.

Maxwell took a deep breath and gathered his thoughts. An important question suddenly came to his mind, but it was one that he doubted Chevy had an answer for. *'Are they planning on killing us?'* Instead, he asked him one that he hoped would at least give him an idea as to what was going to happen next. "Do you know what their plans are?"

"Yes," Chevy replied. He then informed Maxwell that René had told him that the previous arms shipment bust was basically a write-off for them — a minor setback. The D.U.O. actually had many other larger and more valuable shipments already in the works of which they now plan on completing over the upcoming few weeks.

"Damn it!" This visibly upset Maxwell as he slammed his fist on top of the dust covered desk. "I was hoping we had dealt them a bigger blow than that. It's as if we just stuck out our foot and accidently tripped them. I can't believe that they've already gotten back up?" From where he stood, Maxwell looked out through the broken window, and took a few more deep breaths. He then turned back around, looked at his informant, and fired away his next question. "Do you know exactly when their next shipment is going to be?"

"I do." Chevy proceeded to inform his friend that René wasn't one hundred percent positive, but he had heard that it was supposed to take place around midnight this evening. He then told Maxwell that he believed it was scheduled to take place on the east side of the city at the old abandoned Tuckerman's warehouse, and that he was under the impression that this was going to be a shipment that was supposedly twice the size of the last one.

Chevy then reached into his back pants pocket and pulled out a piece of paper. He handed it over to Maxwell and explained to him that he had made a list of the guns that he was aware of that the D.U.O. were planning on smuggling out of the country.

Maxwell took the piece of paper from Chevy, unfolded it, and carefully read it to himself.

400 - Smith & Wesson 22 Match Heavy Barrel M-41's
400 - Master Model 52 Auto's (a.k.a. 38 special)
300 - Remington's
200 - XP-100 Bolt Action Pistols
400 - Winchester 70A Magnum Rifles
200 - Beretta Model 76 Auto Pistols
300 - Beretta BL O/U Shotguns

He then took a moment and tried to understand why the D.U.O. would suddenly decide to run normal street weapons instead of hi-end military ones like they had been. To him, this seemed just a bit strange, but never the less, very interesting.

As with every meeting that took place with Chevy, one of their unwritten rules was that a time limit of fifteen minutes would be imposed. That was so any chance of Chevy attempting to convince Maxwell to stay for an extended, personal visit, would be greatly reduced — seeing that he was probably the only person who could 'understand' him. And so that request didn't happen, Joshua re-entered the factory exactly when he was supposed to, and walked over to Maxwell. He then informed his partner that his cell phone had rung and it had been his wife who had called with an emergency — which of course, the forgetting of his cell phone in the car was a lie. She never really called — it was just the excuse that Joshua had decided to use this time to drag Maxwell away from his meeting with Chevy.

He nodded his head in acknowledgement of his partner's information, and then apologized to Chevy about having to hastily leave — even though he had previously promised to him, and quickly regretted ever doing so, that the next time they had gotten together for a meeting that they would spend some quality time together afterwards and possibly go and have some lunch.

Although Chevy was crushed, he said that he understood. Maxwell admittedly felt like a piece of crap for doing what he had, but his personal feelings for this young man were not as important as what he and his partner had to do — they needed to get back to the precinct, as the information they had just acquired, wasn't something that they could keep to themselves for a rainy day.

8

Once they returned to the precinct, Maxwell and Joshua went straight into Captain White's office and informed him of everything they had learned. Upon hearing what his two detectives had found out, Christopher sunk deep into his office chair. The look on his face was easy to read; he was visibly annoyed that the conviction of Antonio Marcone had not caused a much larger disruption in the operations of the Detroit Underworld Organization than just them being on a three week hiatus. He couldn't blame his officers for not doing their jobs well enough — he instead, blamed himself for not doing everything within his power to make sure that the D.U.O. was put out of business for good.

The accumulated evidence had been sufficient to convict Antonio Marcone — but what little they had that connected Louie Mazotti to any sort of criminal activity was only circumstantial. Salvadore Batiste on the other hand, had murdered James 'Jimbo' Lewis and attempted to do the same to Colin Ramirez — but the bastard had immediately fallen off the grid the moment Antonio had been arrested.

Christopher knew that both Louie and Sal should be behind bars right now; he just could not understand why the state prosecutor had felt that they had not established their guilt enough to have them charged even though the meticulously kept files that documented Colin's time undercover stated otherwise. The belief was there — Sal had planted the bomb that killed Vance Palmalino, and Louie was the one entrusted to orchestrate all of the weapons deals.

After nearly three years, Captain White still felt as if they were two steps behind. For every bit of momentum that would come their way, something would put a halt to it and promptly drag them back even further. If a way wasn't found for them to barrel right through whatever roadblocks would appear, then the much needed evidence to put Antonio's associates in the same cell block as he, would probably never be acquired.

At that moment, Christopher felt as if he was being relegated to his own chair. He had to make sure that the next step they took was the correct one, the one that put an end to it all. Otherwise, the entire city of Detroit would become their playground to do with as they please.

Ideally, Captain White had wanted to take his time, pool together all of the resources that he could, construct a fool proof plan, and then send a team of well prepared officers after the remaining ranking members of the Detroit Underworld Organization. Unfortunately, there just wasn't much time on their side — but then again, they only had themselves to blame for that. Captain White and Chief Winslow had decided that with Antonio Marcone safely out of the way, there would be no need to unnecessarily risk the lives of any of their officers and hastily go right after the rest of the Detroit Underworld Organization in an attempt to permanently shut them down without first having that smoking gun in hand. However, they both now had to admit that they had underestimated their adversary. Maxwell and Joshua had been right — they should not have been forced to go on a vacation; they should have been allowed to stay in Detroit and finish the job first. And because they had not done that, the D.U.O. was allowed to regroup and continue on right where they had left off.

After a few moments of unnerving silence, Captain White gulped back the remainder of his two-hour-old coffee. He then got up from his desk and called out from the threshold of his office door to his next six best officers to join him, Maxwell, and Joshua, in the precinct's conference room. Once everyone was inside the room and had found a seat, Captain White shut the door and then began to gather ideas from each of his officers. Their first priority was to stop this evening's scheduled arms shipment. Afterwards, if they did not happen to luckily arrest Louie Mazotti and Salvadore Batiste, then a closed-door meeting would be needed with not only himself and his team of handpicked officers, but with Chief Winslow as well because a way to eliminate the unwanted existence of the D.U.O. had to be found as soon as possible.

Everyone in the conference room knew that what they had been asked to do this evening came with a lot of risk — and none of them even thought for one moment about requesting to be excused from this assignment. They all understood the immense pressure that Captain White was under to stop the city's cancer from continuing to spread, and each one of them were determined to work together as a team to do all that they could to make that happen.

While all of this was going on, there was another impromptu meeting that was taking place. This one was in the basement of the pawnshop in Corktown. With Antonio away in prison, that left Louie and Sal to run things by proxy. He wouldn't admit it, but that made Antonio very uneasy, knowing that both Louie and Sal were like cats and dogs — they generally didn't play nice with each other.

Louie, having been Antonio's right hand man ever since he had taken over full control of the D.U.O., automatically assumed that he was going to be placed in the interim position of leader — but that had not yet officially been bestowed upon him. It was no secret that Louie really didn't like Sal. He fully believed that the only reason Sal had the kind of organizational power that he did was because he really enjoyed siphoning the crap that came out of Antonio's ass. Yes, the man had his usefulness, but his greatest talent seemed to be his ability to get under Louie's skin.

Admittedly, Sal had trouble pushing aside his personal animosity toward Louie — he just could not find one thing about the man that he liked. Yes, the man had a great understanding for the business side of the organization, but he had a superiority complex that made Sal want to knock him right off his high horse.

But that wasn't the only reason why he loathed the man. Sal had earned his rapid ascent up the ladder, and in his opinion, Louie had not — yet the man had somehow vaulted himself to the head of the class. And even though Sal was technically only one position below Louie in the organizational ranks, he believed that with Antonio now locked away in jail, that he should at least have equal say in all matters concerning the D.U.O. because he had been in the 'family' longer than Louie and had known Antonio ever since he was a teenager.

"Jesus Christ, Sal! Can't you close that damn door gently like a normal person?"

"Nope! Because I know that you don't think that I'm even close to being somewhat normal. Therefore it only makes logical sense for me to act in a manner in which you perceive me to be." Sal was smart enough to realize that he had to pick his spots carefully from this moment forward to irritate Louie. He knew that he had a huge responsibility over the next thirty years while Antonio was incarcerated and that he had to swallow his pride and do what was best for the organization by trying hard to suppress his dislike for Louie and get along with him — although he wasn't sure if such a miracle was even possible.

Having very little patience to begin with this day, Louie hoped that whatever it was that Sal was in 'his' new office for would be worth the rash of irritation that he could now feel growing where the sun didn't shine. "Well... since you're here now, how about telling me what your reason is for disturbing my peace?"

Immediately, Sal realized that Louie had just handed him an opportunity to rip off a nasty wisecrack about Louie not having his 'piece' disturbed. But once again, he knew that he had to restrain himself — this just was not the time, nor the place to really piss off his fellow associate.

Sal moved over to the vacant chair in front of the desk where he calmly sat himself down and then stared his cohort straight into his eyes. As difficult as it was, he brushed aside his ever-growing malicious thoughts — but only because he quickly realized that he had unintentionally placed himself within arm's reach of his advisory. It also didn't help that Sal could plainly see that Louie was fidgeting with a gold plated letter opener in his right hand — the man had used a weapon much smaller than that before to leave a indelible mark on a man who once screwed him over. "I... I just came by to let you know that everyone has been briefed on their assignments and they are ready. Oh, and I also just got off the phone with Vladi. He's still extremely pissed at us because of what happened three months ago."

"I can certainly understand why he is pissed, Sal. Did you try to explain to him what had happened to his shipment and why it wasn't our fault?"

Sal sat back in his chair and lit a cigar; he exhaled the first few rings of smoke from it just above Louie's head. "I did, but he still didn't care. In fact, he told me that he'll never, ever do business with such an amateurish organization like ours again."

Louie leaned forward across the desk and snatched the cigar out of Sal's hand — he then crushed it in his own. "You get back on that damn phone right now and you use whatever it is you have up there that passes itself off as a brain and you try everything that you can think of to explain to Vladi that the pests that infested and ruined our last shipment, will be exterminated tonight. Use whatever means necessary to get him to agree to order more weapons from us. And tell him that I'll personally guarantee anything that he orders and ship it to him without any delay. Got it?"

Sal then stood up and pulled out another cigar. He lit it and again blew the smoke towards Louie — this time directly at his face. "Yeah... Just remember that the boss's chair," he pointed to it," and this office," he encircled the room with his right hand, "isn't yours yet. It still belongs to Antonio and he still calls the shots around here. And as much as I don't want to, I will do my part and try to get along with you. So long as Antonio has a heartbeat, he is my boss. Not you! So don't even think that you can order me around. It won't happen!" As Sal turned to leave the office, he thought to himself. *'I should have grabbed that letter opener and shoved it right through his Adams apple when I had the chance.'* He then purposely slammed the door on his way out.

"Sal, you damn fuckin' grease-ball!" Louie screamed.

Evening was rapidly approaching and Maxwell was sitting outside on the steps of his back porch. He was sipping on some Chai tea, absorbing the peaceful surroundings, and reflecting on all of the good times that he and his wife, Sylvia, have had. Soon after reaching a state of tranquility, induced by joyous memories and the delicious tea, Maxwell's cell phone rang which snapped him out of his trance and caused him to slightly spill some of his tea — Captain White was calling him so that he could quickly go over the details for the evening's sting operation.

After his brief call was over, Maxwell deeply inhaled the cool, early fall evening air, and then he slowly moseyed back inside the house. He then made his way into the kitchen to place his empty tea cup into the dishwasher when he felt a dainty, soft pair of hands begin to massage his tense shoulders.

"Was that Captain White whom you were just talking to on your cell outside?" Maxwell's wife asked.

"Yes, it was. You don't miss a thing, do you dear?"

"You should know by now that I am a pretty perceptive individual. That is why I came over here to help put at ease whatever it is that might be bothering you."

Maxwell loved his wife, but he hated telling her things that he knew would make her worry. Tonight, for the first time in a very long time, he was uncertain about his assignment, as he hadn't the faintest idea what he and the rest of the assigned task force were about to face. And because of this unknown, Maxwell wasn't about to tell his wife what it was that he was about to do, knowing that she would do nothing but worry. He knew that he had to tell her something, and even if he held back all of the details of his assignment, his perceptive wife would still be able to figure out, just by looking at her husband, that he was about to be a part of something that could be very dangerous. "Don't wait up for me tonight, dear. I have a feeling that I will be pulling an all-nighter tonight. Hopefully though, we'll be able to finally close the file on one of our longest standing, and most important cases."

"Maxwell. You don't usually work late unless something big is going down. You know that I worry a lot about you when you have to work these kinds of shifts."

Maxwell turned around to face his wife and then slipped his hands around her slender waist. He leaned forward and placed a soothing, gentle kiss on her forehead. He didn't want to break away from that moment. There hadn't ever been a day when his wife didn't smell good, and this day was no exception.

Sylvia could only assume that her husband was soon to be involved in what was surely going to be a dangerous situation — it was an aspect of Maxwell's job that she long ago accepted. That however, didn't mean she was at ease with it, so she purposely made an effort to tap into his senses and use her womanly magic to awaken his hormones. She knew that it would probably be a futile effort on her part, but she tried anyway to convince her husband to call in sick and stay at home, as it was the only thing that she could think of to ensure her husband's safety.

Maxwell looked into her desperate eyes and got locked in her attention. Like staring at Medusa, he was frozen in the moment — and he found it extremely difficult to break away from her powers. He allowed himself to lower his lips to meet his wife's, and then gave her a tender, re-assuring kiss. However, before things got past the point of no return, Maxwell summoned all of his inner strength, broke the seal he had made, and returned to reality. Then, with a soft and reassuring voice, he once again reminded his wife what she already knew in her heart.

Acknowledging her husband's words, Sylvia responded, "I accepted long ago everything that came with being a police officer's wife. But I don't know, Max. For some strange reason, I'm really scared. I've got this bad feeling that something horrible is going to happen tonight."

Maxwell gave his wife a long loving embrace. He then released her, walked to the bedroom, and headed straight for the closet. He reached inside it and pulled out his lucky black steel toe shoes, sat down on the edge of the bed, and put them on as his wife entered the room — she sat next to him. "I have to get going, dear. Joshua will be calling me if I don't pick him up soon. I'm guessing that I'll be home around three o'clock in the morning. Hopefully, it will be sooner. Call me on my cell phone if you need me for anything."

"You most certainly can expect to hear from me tonight," his wife forewarned. "I'll feel much more at ease when I can hear your voice and know that you're all right."

"It may be a good idea if you turn in early tonight and get some rest. I'll be home before you know it."

Right after they left the bedroom together, they stopped in front of their son's nursery. Quietly, Maxwell walked up to Sabastian's crib, kissed him on his forehead, and whispered to him that he loved him. After spending a few more seconds in loving thought, he took his wife's hand and led her to the front door. There, he wrapped his arms around his beautiful wife once again and gave her an extra long kiss. He knew there wasn't much that he could do at that moment to put his wife at ease, but he had hoped that his kiss would help to reassure her that he was going to stay safe and that everything was gonna be all right.

Not a lot of time had passed since their stakeout had begun —
it was only ten minutes to midnight, and it felt like the hands on
Maxwell's watch had been super glued in place. This sting operation
wasn't supposed to go down until sometime after twelve, but Maxwell
had honestly hoped that it would happen sooner rather than later. He
really didn't feel like being where he was; he wanted to be with his
family. And it didn't help that his wife continued to call him, because
the more she did, the more he wanted to be at home, nestled up next to
her in their bed. But he knew that he had a job to do and he
continuously had to reassure his wife every time she called that
everything was going to be just fine. He hated being the asshole, but it
got to the point where Maxwell literally had to order her to stop calling
him and to just go to bed and get some sleep.

As time continued to slowly pass by, Maxwell had begun to
second guess himself on the validity of Chevy's information. He truly
thought that the day would never come in which he would not be able
to trust Chevy — now, for some reason, he wasn't so sure. He
searched his memory for the day that he had met him. On that day, he
had a strong feeling about the young man; a feeling that Chevy was the
most honest and trustworthy person that he would ever know.

Maxwell sat back and allowed his thoughts to wander down
memory lane, remembering every detail that happened on the day that
Chevy's calamitous path, crossed his.

*At the time, Maxwell was an R.C.M.P. Officer on loan in a
joint investigation with the F.B.I. and the local Detroit Police
Department to try and stop a well-established drug smuggling
operation of Cocaine, L.S.D. and Heroine, along with almost every
new designer drug out there today. Somehow, someway, it was all
consistently finding its way across the heavily secured United States /
Canadian border. Yet for some unknown reason, local law
enforcement on both sides continued to fail at stopping the flow of it.
The F.B.I. had known for a long time that Detroit was the city that the
drugs were shipped to from all parts of Mexico and South America.
What they didn't know was who was behind the operation and exactly
how these drugs were being smuggled across into Canada.*

Maxwell's specialty was not in drug enforcement; it was in investigating and locating criminals who were very good at covering their tracks. Therefore, his skills were the reason that he came highly recommended when the F.B.I. had asked the R.C.M.P. for some assistance in cracking this case.

Since Detroit was obviously a foreign city to him, Maxwell had been assigned a liaison from the Detroit Police Department's drug task force. According to his temporary 'partner', the best way to get any inside information on all of the local drug activities that happened in, around, and throughout the city, was to go to this rundown eight square block area that was known as 'The Dead Zone'. It was a part of the city that was appropriately named — and not just because of the constant threat within that area of being shot or stabbed. It was because those individual who lived in or hung out there, either knew a lot, had a lot to hide, just didn't want to be found, were plain ruthless, vicious, had no morals, were wanted by the law or another criminal, were unstable, or were just plain nuts. And the majority of the time, anyone who was stupid enough to venture into 'The Dead Zone', disappeared forever. If they somehow were lucky enough to leave it, it was usually in a body bag.

The residences of 'The Dead Zone' were sort of like chameleons. They tended to take up an invisible sanctuary in and around the dilapidated buildings. You knew that they were there, because it was never completely quiet. Numerous chilling and overlapping sounds continually reverberated throughout the area: sounds of unseen individuals walking, garbage being stepped on or kicked around, alley cats and stray dogs hissing, growling, and fighting each other, or echoing screams for which an obvious conclusion could be drawn. But no matter how hard you looked, any visual proof that some sort of existence was indeed there, was nearly impossible to find without sticking your nose where it didn't belong. It's no wonder that any normal person stayed far away from that enigmatic part of the city.

Most of Detroit's police officers didn't like to go anywhere near that area unless they were heavily armed, and it was deemed absolutely necessary. Maxwell's assigned liaison refused to go there and search it with him. He felt that it wasn't necessary to enter the

'Dead Zone' and risk his life — they weren't looking for a local supplier; they were only looking for information that could lead them to who the main players were behind the smuggling.

Maxwell didn't agree, but this wasn't his town. However, he wasn't about to let the possibility of any good lead go by the wayside because his assigned 'partner' was just too cowardly to go and find it. So that left Maxwell in a position that he didn't like — alone and in a city that was completely foreign to him. But he wasn't about to abandon the oath he had taken; he was going to do what he had been sent here to do. So with no other choice, he headed into the 'Dead Zone' all by himself to acquire the information that he sought.

He hadn't a clue where to start his search, so he figured that his best bet would be to just walk around the area and try to act like he belonged there. He had no idea who lived there or how they would even react to him. But he was real sure that he would eventually attract someone's attention — he just hoped that he didn't attract the attention of some nut-bag willing to gut him on the spot, just for shits and giggles.

Maxwell hadn't even been in the 'Dead Zone' for more than five minutes before he had heard a gunshot coming from what sounded like only a few blocks ahead. And of course, curiosity got the best of him, so he cautiously moved toward where he believed that the shot had come from. As Maxwell moved closer, he heard someone mercilessly screaming, followed shortly thereafter by another gunshot. As he continued to where he had believed both of those gunshots and the cry for mercy had come from, a third gunshot rang out.

For Maxwell, that third gunshot happened way too close for his liking. It caused him to instinctively take cover at the side of a building, halfway down the garbage filled, putrid smelling alleyway.

After catching his breath and restoring his focus, Maxwell gripped his police revolver and cautiously peered through a small hole in the wall, where obviously an exhaust vent had once been, in order to get some kind of idea as to what was going on inside the building. Sure enough, this was the place where the gunshots and scream had come from.

Inside the place, there was a young man who looked to be in his early to mid teens, tied to a chair, and covered in his own blood.

He had been shot in both of his legs and also his left shoulder. It didn't take much for Maxwell to determine that the teen had been severely worked over by two rather large bikers, both sporting the colors of The Disciple Riders.

These bikers were a steadily growing, cult type of gang, considered to be a very mentally unstable and vicious group. They truly believed that slowly taking the life of a young adult in a painful and torturous manner would strengthen their souls and increase their powers over all lesser of beings. Of course, Maxwell didn't know this about The Disciple Riders at the time when he decided to interrupt their ritual.

After Maxwell had saved Chevy's life that day, he had taken him to a local hospital where he had his wounds attended to. After spending four days there, Chevy was released — and it was at that moment when he had made it known to Maxwell that he was forever in his debt for saving his life; a debt that he honestly doubted he could ever repay. He did however, pledge to help him in any way he could, whenever he needed him.

Chevy had contacted Maxwell two days after that, letting him know that he had taken it upon himself to acquire the information that Maxwell had come to Detroit in search of. Surprised, but thankful nonetheless, Maxwell forwarded that information to the F.B.I.; crucial information that had not only allowed them to shut down the massive drug smuggling operation, but locate the main players that were behind it.

Because of his efforts and willingness to do whatever was necessary to get the job done, Maxwell was handed an open invitation by the then chief of police to join the Detroit Police Department's investigative unit, if he was ever looking for a change of scenery — an offer that he took up six months later.

Maxwell returned from his memories, still unsure. He'd never gotten like this before a sting, but for some reason, this just didn't feel right. Some bewilderment began to surface. It was now past midnight and there hadn't yet been any sort of stirring going on whatsoever at the warehouse, which only added to the doubt that swam through his mind; doubt that Maxwell knew he had to expunge before his duty was called upon.

Joshua was the type of person who normally had no fear — he was solid as a rock when it came to facing the unknown. But for some reason tonight, he also began to show signs of having some uneasiness. He did his best to put aside his trepidation, but found it difficult to keep his mind clear. Like Maxwell, he too was thinking more about what was most important to him; his wife Carol, and not on what they had come here this evening to do.

A cool light rain had started rhythmically pelting their vehicle. Listening to it fall was like hearing a meditative nature recording being played softly in the background. Subconsciously hypnotized by nature, an unresisting form of pure relaxation, the tranquil repetitive sound of the rain had caused each of them to intermittently dose off.

After a few moments had passed, the pace of the rain started to quicken. Still, it was gentle enough to lure Joshua and Maxwell into a deep comatose like sleep. Each of their thoughts became very pleasant — even romantic at times. Cheap fantasies quickly over took their minds. They could easily get caught up in the perfect illusions. For a few blissful moments, this wondrous escape through one's own imagination had the potential to envelope them wholly and keep them away from reality for hours upon hours, if they chose to let it happen.

Abruptly, Maxwell awoke from his unintended nap. As he was beginning to sort out his thoughts, he noticed that his partner had done what he had. And knowing that they would both be in some serious shit if either one of them were to be caught sleeping on the job, Maxwell leaned across and flicked his partner's left ear. "Josh! Wake up!"

"Ouch! What the hell was that for?"

"You fell asleep, man."

"I did not!"

Maxwell knew that his partner had, but he wasn't about to waste his time trying to convince him of the truth. Instead, he resumed what they were supposed to have been doing all along — watching the warehouse. Like before, nothing had been going on. So Maxwell decided to check out what the situation was like with one of the other staked out police units that was with them — he hoped that there was something of interest taking place where they were positioned. "This is primary unit calling secondary unit. Can you give me a status report on what's happening your way? Over!"

"Absolutely fuck all is happening here," Officer Charles Blake relied. "It's just as quiet here as Aaron's sex life is at home."

"Come on now. We all know that Officer Thompson's sex life at home is not that quiet. Think about it? Just because it blows up, doesn't mean that a sound is not made while it is being loved." Joshua instantly burst out into a severe hysteria of laughter; Maxwell cracked a devilish grin. Yes, it was cruel to rip on someone who was single and going through a rather long dry spell, but their target of ridicule was someone whom they knew would do the same to them if they had an opening to do so.

"Hey! That shit ain't too fuckin' funny!" Aaron emphatically protested over the open airwaves.

Joshua could hardly talk because he was still howling. However, that instantly changed as soon as he saw what he and Maxwell had been waiting for. Their fun had immediately ended and a rush of adrenalin filled their veins in anticipation. Without hesitation, Maxwell spoke into the police radio and informed all of the backup units of the developing situation, and then he ordered them all to hold their position until he gave them the official word to move on in.

Sylvia Banks had been through evenings like this before — that didn't mean however, that tonight was going to be like those others. All night, she was feeling very uneasy — her mind was completely out of sync with her body. She tried to watch some television, hoping that it would help to calm down her anxiety. She chatted on the phone for a while with Joshua's wife, spent some time browsing the on-line catalogue for Macy's, and even stepped out onto the back porch and lit a cigarette; something that she hadn't done since Maxwell had asked her to quit the day that they had officially started to date. None of those things had worked. And even though she believed that a hot bubble bath would not help her to relax, she took one anyway right before she called it a night.

With the lights turned down and some dragon's blood incense filling the room, she slipped into the tub, sipped on some chamomile tea, and immersed herself in not only the soothing feeling of the bubbles, but in the music she had playing — her favorite artist, Kitaro. Tonight, it was his Grammy Award winning CD, 'Thinking of you' that she was listening to — she hoped that all of it would help her finally balance her mind with her body.

It had, somewhat — but the fear that had been in her thoughts since her husband had left the house, was still present. She had called Maxwell numerous times, hoping that by just hearing his voice, she would feel a bit more at ease. And after she had finished her third phone call to her husband, she decided — well, she was all but ordered by Maxwell to call it a night and go to bed. Reluctantly, she slipped under the cold covers and as much as she tried to organize her thoughts and create a pleasant dreamscape, she struggled to form any relaxing images — her mind just would not erase her trepidation.

She almost got up out of the bed to call her husband again, but decided against it, knowing that Maxwell would be really upset with her. Instead, she took a healthy drink of water out of the glass that she always had on the nightstand next to her side of the bed, hoping that it would help her to fall asleep — it hadn't.

After about twenty more minutes of tossing and turning, Sylvia had finally begun to slip into that state of bodily rest, only to be pulled away from it a moment later and into an unwanted awakening. "Maxwell? Is that you dear?" Sylvia rubbed her eyes and tried to focus on the silhouette that was standing in the dimness of her bedroom doorway. "You're back earlier than…"

The bedroom lights came on and Sylvia froze. She knew right away that it was not her husband standing at the entrance to the bedroom. But her mouth just could not synchronize with what her brain was telling it to do — scream. By the time she was able to react, the intruder was already standing at the foot of her bed — she began to uncontrollably shake. "Who..? Who in the hell are you?" She yanked the covers up to her neck while at the same time, trying to reach for the phone on the nightstand that was opposite her side of the bed. "Get the hell out of my house now before I call the police!"

The intruder just stood there with a confident, maybe even an arrogant smile on his face. "Go right ahead and try to call the police, Sylvia — but that won't do you any good because you see, it will be impossible for you to make that call." The intruder then showed her what was in his hand; it was her cell phone. Two seconds later, he whipped it across the room. It whizzed by just inches above her head and smashed against one of the two sconces that hung on the wall behind the bed.

"What do you want?" Sylvia asked. "And… How in the hell do you know my name?"

The intruder took a few steps around to the left side of the bed and he leaned forward towards her. He then spoke in a soft, yet intimidating tone of voice, explaining to her that he knew what her name was because he was good at what he did, and he assured her that there would be absolutely no reason for her to ever know who he was. He then straightened himself up and gave Sylvia an icy cold stare into her baby blue eyes — one that Jack Frost would've been proud of.

Sylvia tried to compose herself, but again found her body lacking behind what her brain was trying to get her to do. She knew though that she could not let the intruder see how scared she really was. She even tried to remember everything that her husband had once told her to do in case something such as this was to ever happen to her. But her heart was racing so fast that she just couldn't focus enough to remember any of it.

After a few moments of tense silence, the intruder, who seemingly had Sylvia under his control, switched his gun to his left hand and lowered his right. He then placed his free hand on top of the burgundy silk bed sheets; it rested a mere few inches away from Sylvia's still trembling body. After a few seconds of silence, he removed his hand from the bed sheets, stepped around to the foot of the bed, and placed it back in contact with the silk sheet. He then slowly began to trace the outline of Sylvia's two feet.

She took a deep breath and tried again to focus. This man's touch was sending eerie chills up her spine. Her instinct was to pull her feet up toward her body so that the intruder could no longer touch them, but she was afraid that if she did this, the intruder just might get angry with her. At the moment, the man seemed to be relatively calm, and Sylvia knew that she needed to keep him that way if she even had a chance of surviving this. However, she also knew that she could not let this man dictate what was going to happen next. She needed to do something to try and take control of the situation, but the only thing that she could think of was to try and reason with him. "If you leave now, I will just forget that you were ever here. And I promise that I won't call the police."

The intruder just stood there looking at Sylvia, scathingly laughing under his breath. It was at that instant she realized that reasoning with this man was not going to work, so she took a moment and mustered up all the courage she could. In as stern of a voice as she could project, Sylvia informed the intruder that if he didn't leave her house immediately that she was going to scream bloody murder.

"Bloody murder?" The intruder raised his gun and pointed it right at Sylvia's head. He then moved away from the foot of the bed and stepped back around over to the left side. With his right hand still in contact with Sylvia's covered, trembling body, he began to trace the outer lines of it with his free hand — he traced the entire length of her body as he made his way to the head of the bed. Once he got there, he cocked his muzzled gun and brought it to within a foot of Sylvia's face. "You know, one should never draw a conclusion based upon what you see. I, for the record, have no plans on making any kind of mess."

Tears began to freely flow down both sides of Sylvia's face as she desperately tried to plead for her life. "I'll do anything you want me to do. Just please, I beg you not to hurt my son."

"Your son? Oh, I wasn't planning on hurting him. So... what did you say his name was?" While his hand continued to trace Sylvia's body, he kept his focus on her face because he wanted to see how her expression changed with each area of her body his hand had gone to explore: her stomach, up in between her breasts, around them, down to her pelvic region — her reaction to being touched in those places surprisingly had not changed.

After a few moments of having his fun trying to gage just how scared Sylvia was, he removed his hand from her groin area, and leaned forward as if his intention was to give her an apologetic kiss. But instead of doing that, the intruder grabbed her by the throat with his right hand and in one effortless motion, yanked her out of the bed — he then unceremoniously slammed her body onto the hardwood floor.

A surprised, yet pleasant smile came to the intruder's face as he realized then that she was nearly completely naked — except for the tiniest transparent red and black-laced teddy that she was wearing. What he now saw with his eyes, all but confirmed what he had imagined Sylvia had looked like by the simple touching of her covered body with his hand. He was also astonished at just how good she looked, considering that she was only a few months removed from giving birth.

The intruder paused for a moment as many pleasurable things flooded his mind; things that he badly wanted to do to her; wanted to experience. Without a doubt, this woman would satisfy all of the needs that he had — it had been way too long for him to even remember the last time he had tasted the wonders of a woman.

In front of him now, was a once in a lifetime opportunity. So he knelt down beside her on one knee and again gently touched her stomach with his right hand — instantly, more enjoyable things entered his mind. But then the real person that was somewhere inside the mind of the intruder began to take over. Those unabated animalistic thoughts that had consumed him should have been easier to control. Yet, for some unknown reason, they had pushed their way forward and dominated his thoughts. The intruder was an outlaw, a mercenary, and a hired gun, whose training had prepared him to block out his emotions and suppress all urges. Distractions such as this could easily get in the way of completing his mission. Yet, Sylvia was an amazingly beautiful young woman, and the feeling of silk and lace against his hand, combined with the heat that radiated from her body, was what had unleashed those long ago suppressed urges.

He had never before been this close to a woman as stunning as Sylvia was. So he slowly moved his right hand down her stomach and laid it to rest on her inner right thigh; only a few inches away from where he wanted to begin. Once again, the real person that he was started to overrule his animalistic urges. He stopped what he was doing — he wasn't a rapist. He was a lot of things, but a monster he wasn't. He had only entered Sylvia's bedroom for one reason and that was to complete the job that he was being paid to do.

After a moment of gathered thought, he finally regained control, stood back up, and he looked down at Sylvia with an almost apologetic look on his face. "You know… you are a very beautiful young woman who obviously would be hard for any man in his right mind to resist. As much as I'd enjoy exploring every inch of you for hours upon end, I have decided not to. I may be a lot of things, but a rapist I am not."

Sylvia felt a moment of gratefulness now that the intruder seemed to be having second thoughts. However, that didn't mean that she was no longer scared. Just by the way he was looking at her, made her believe that he was still going to hurt her in some other way — and she was right.

"It's a shame that I have to do what I am going to do to you. But I'm sorry, as I have no choice in the matter. I'm being paid rather handsomely and I intend to complete the task that I was hired to do." He raised his muzzled gun and pointed it directly at Sylvia's forehead. Once again, he demanded that she inform him what her son's name was.

Fearing for her and her son's life, she answered the intruder, hoping, but honestly not believing, that he would just leave once she told him. "It's… It's…"

At ten minutes past midnight, a charcoal gray colored Lincoln Navigator limousine had arrived at the old Tuckerman's warehouse; a white Dodge extended cube van followed closely behind it. Both vehicles pulled up to a large door at the far end of the building, waited a brief moment for the door to fully open up, then they drove inside.

Once the vehicles had disappeared into the warehouse and its large door had closed, Joshua reached for the radio and called the other police units. "This is primary unit. We've got movement at the backend of the north side lot. Hold your positions and wait for our signal. Over!" Joshua placed the radio back where it belonged, looked over at Maxwell, and then gave him the 'I'm ready when you are, partner' look.

"Any chance I can sit this one out?" Maxwell asked, somewhat jokingly.

"Um… No! You signed up for this, bud. Remember what the captain said to us. Be cautious and stay on alert for anything that looks suspicious. So I suggest that you quit thinking about your wife and son because your lack of focus is what is going to get us both killed. Besides... Nobody can pull off a sting better than we can."

Maxwell took a few slow, methodical, soothing deep breaths, and then looked over at his partner. "I'm ready for my job to have a lot less stress, and a life that is somewhat normal. Let's go and put the D.U.O. out of business for good."

After waiting a few more unnerving moments, the same amount of time needed for the evening rain to nearly stop, Joshua radioed the rest of their team and then both he and his partner proceeded to their position at the front of the warehouse. Once they arrived there, Maxwell noticed that the front door was not locked — but it was tightly swollen shut. With a little unresisting persuasion, Maxwell cautiously opened it — although not as quietly has he intended.

"That was no different than sending the enemy a text message, letting them know that we're outside waiting to come in. Thanks for spoiling the surprise, Max."

"I'm sorry. Next time, I'll bring the WD40 and leave my gun at home — I do have a lighter in my pocket after all. I mean, it doesn't get any more intimidating than to stand there and tell the enemy to freeze with a makeshift flamethrower in my hand." Maxwell decided at that moment a good natured jab of his own had to be sent Joshua's way in retaliation, "Besides, it's not my fault that the old door creaked almost as loud as that bed in the cheap motel you stayed at during your honeymoon." There was no need to wait and see the reaction that was to come from his partner — Maxwell knew that he was going to be irritated. Instead, he turned his attention to what they had come here to do; he cautiously stuck his head through the door. After seeing that the coast was clear inside the warehouse, he opened up the door all the way and quickly scanned the interior.

He took only a few steps inside before he motioned to his partner to look over at the far side of the warehouse. There, sat the same white cube van that they had seen enter the warehouse just a few minutes earlier. However, the car that came in ahead of it was nowhere to be found.

Joshua paused for a moment, trying to analyze what he was seeing — he knew that there was more to this than just the apparent abandoned cube van. *'I'm not at all liking this,'* he said to himself.

"They've got to be in here somewhere, Josh. This is a rather large building with multiple wings attached, so I can only assume that they and the car are somewhere else inside here."

"Let's hope, partner."

"While we apparently have this section of the warehouse to ourselves, I'm going to take a look around and see what I can find. You go check out the cube van and see if there is anything in it that we can use as evidence."

"No problem." Ignoring the old cliché, 'throwing caution to the wind', they both went on their way. Joshua headed over to the truck and Maxwell headed approximately one hundred feet over to the far side of the warehouse's main section.

After only a few moments of searching, Maxwell had spotted something other than the missing car that had snagged his curiosity. He noticed that there were four wooden crates at the south back corner against the backside of a hip-high cinder block wall. *'This is odd,'* he thought. *'I wonder why these crates are here, considering that this warehouse has been vacant for more than ten years.'* His instincts immediately told him that this wasn't an insignificant detail, so Maxwell made his way over to the crates to examine them. *'If these were intentionally left behind by the last owner of the warehouse, then they should at least have a thin layer of dust on them.'* They didn't.

After removing the unsecured lid from the closest one, Maxwell began to sift through the foam packaging. A few seconds after that, he unexpectedly became startled; it caused him to whack his knee against the side of the crate. Underneath his breath, he verbalized a few expletives.

He was in pain, but that was quickly canceled out by his anger when he heard the unsympathetic chuckling that was freely resonating right behind him — it had been Officer Aaron Thompson who had caused him his unnecessary moment of suffering.

Not at all happy that his fellow officer had chosen that moment to screw around, Maxwell shot the man the dirtiest of looks while at the same time, trying to massage away the pain that was still in his knee.

"Sorry, Max," Aaron apologized. "I only meant to get a little bit of revenge for that wise crack about my sex life."

"You could have picked a better time instead of right in the middle of a sting operation."

"I know. So have you found anything yet?"

"No. Not really." Maxwell took his eyes away from his fellow officer and looked back down inside the crate that he had been sifting through — he immediately began to remove some of the foam packaging that was covering whatever was buried beneath it.

Not wanting to feel useless, Officer Thompson's partner, Charles Blake, decided to open up one of the other crates. While his focus was on that task, Aaron asked Maxwell where Joshua was, for which came the reply that he was over investigating the cube van.

At that moment, Maxwell briefly stopped what he was doing; his partner's well being had come to his thoughts, so he quickly took a look over toward where the cube van was. He saw that Joshua was approaching the backside of the van with a long metal bar in his right hand — he could only assume then that his partner had taken a few moments and searched around the warehouse in order to find what was now in his hand, and that his intent was to break the lock on the rear door of the cube van.

Satisfied that his partner was all right, Maxwell returned to rummaging through the crate. A few seconds later, after he had removed the last of the foam packaging, something immediately caught his eye. He looked deep into the crate, pausing to try and process in his mind everything that he was looking at.

While looking over Maxwell's shoulder, Officer Thompson asked curiously, "Did you just find what I think you just found inside this crate?"

"If you're referring to the candle wax, the empty Vaseline container, isopropyl, canola oil, clear gelatin containers, and the flower residue on the bottom in the corner of the crate, then my answer is… Yes. If the recollection of my high school chemistry is correct, then I think what we have here are the ingredients needed to make an explosive — a crude version of C4."

Officer Blake removed his head from inside of the crate that he had been looking through and reported that he had found nothing odd inside. Maxwell then encouraged him to go ahead and open up the other crate that was directly across from the one he had just finished looking in. "Be careful when you open it," he warned.

Charles cautiously removed the lid from the other crate. After a few seconds of scanning its contents, he informed Maxwell that the crate contained a large pile of various types of computers that all appeared to have been pillaged for parts. Along with that information, he stated that there were also two-dozen empty cell phone boxes and a small pile of electronic wire, of various gauges and different lengths.

Maxwell paused. He was uncertain, but something had turned on a switch in his head. *'Bombs? The D.U.O. is supposed to be involved with selling illegal firearms, not making bombs. Explosives are not something that they have been known to be associated with?'* The illogical aspect of all of this was easy for him to figure out. It was highly unlikely that the D.U.O. was making bombs for their own use. Other than what Salvadore Batiste had allegedly used to crash Vance Palmalino's plane, they had never been linked to that kind of violence. However, he could not dismiss what he was seeing. This left his mind to assume that there was only one other possibility — they had to be making them with the sole purpose of selling the devices.

After that conclusion, an unspeakable thought unexpectedly came to him. Anxiety promptly consumed Maxwell as his mind began to race. *'How stupid they had been,'* he said to himself. Everything had come together all too easily and now they were standing in the middle of a death trap; a situation that Maxwell's wife had all but predicted.

Officers Thompson and Blake both saw Maxwell's face and each knew exactly what was going on in his head. Without hesitation they both hi-tailed it to the warehouse exit. Maxwell didn't hastily follow his fellow officers; he instead started to run toward the parked cube van, screaming his partner's name.

9

It had been a few days since the horrific explosion at the old abandoned Tuckerman's Warehouse, and all sense of normality had yet to completely return. For everyone who was personally affected by the tragic event, it had been difficult to accept that a small lapse in judgment, driven by an eagerness to put an end to an ever-threatening institution, had drastically changed the lives of everyone involved, and for those who also knew the victims.

The entire department was still in shock, but thankful nonetheless that five of the eight officers assigned to the sting operation that night had somehow survived — though not all uninjured. It wasn't just one big massive explosion that had taken place, but a cascading series of detonations that had originated at the back, water facing side of the warehouse.

The two officers who had been stationed outside of the warehouse at the east street side exit, officer's Sharna Williams and Samuel Everett, were the lucky ones. They were able to escape with only a few minor abrasions. The two officers that had been guarding the back water side exit where the explosions had begun; Denny James and Abdul Hassam, were sent straight backwards more than fifty feet and somehow, cleared the sixty year old wooden docks — they landed just past it safely in the river. However, both of those men sustained multiply lacerations, severe burns, bruises, a few broken bones, and several ounces of the not-so-clean Detroit River down their throats.

Unfortunately, three of the four officers who were inside the warehouse at the time of the explosion did not survive. Officers Blake and Thompson; both had tried to run toward the exit once they realized that they had been set up, but in doing so, had unknowingly headed in the same direction as the initial explosions — they didn't have a chance. And neither did Joshua, as he had been in the back of the truck and did not hear his partner shouting his name. By the time he had realized that something was going on, it was too late — the truck had been rigged to blow just like the warehouse.

Was it just his good fortune, or was some higher power watching over Maxwell? Somehow, he had been able to live through it — but barely, as he ended up suffering multiple injuries: fractures, second and third degree burns over many different areas of his body, and a massive concussion. His miraculous survival was the only thing positive to come out of this tragedy.

What had happened on that night was one of those historic moments that everyone would like to forget. Once again, a superfluous black eye has been placed on the city of Detroit. For decades, it has desperately tried to clean up its act and earn back its respect. But now, it all seems for naught; the wind that had filled its sails and allowed it to keep moving forward has all but disappeared.

As deflating as this setback may be, those who enforce the law knew that they were the ones who had to soldier on. It was up to them to continue performing their jobs to the best of their abilities, pool together its resources, and focus on the only thing that really mattered — find and arrest the evil sons-of-bitches that were behind this cowardly and heinous act. Only then, would any sense of normalcy and pride return to the city.

Ever since Christopher had taken over for Captain Potter, his main focus has been to shut down the D.U.O. — two and a half years later that had not happened. As much as he had butted heads with Maxwell and Joshua, Captain White knew that they were the best possible choice that he could have made to take on the task of shutting down the city's biggest threat. But so far, Christopher's tenure as captain had been one big failure — at least, that was the way he felt. And even though it had been filled with a lot of other smaller successes, including being responsible for removing the majority of the seedy individuals that had called the 'Dead Zone' their home, the inability of finding a way to shut down the D.U.O. was beginning to take its toll on his confidence. After all, one officer under his watch was now confined to a wheel chair, and three more had just died. Yes, the D.U.O. was to blame for all of this, but Christopher had to shoulder just as much of the responsibility. Charles Blake, Aaron Thompson, and Joshua Brampton, had not been just officers under his command, they had been his friends. And because of this, their deaths hurt

Christopher more than he would ever openly admit; ever willingly let show.

When someone makes a decision to become a police officer, they are entirely aware that their own death is a possibility — it is an unfortunate byproduct of choosing such a career. For Christopher White, being a captain also meant that he had to make decisions that were sometimes unwanted or unfair, but had to be made nonetheless. And because of this, his decisions meant that any sort of blame could not be deflected towards those who had failed — that was his cross to bear, whether or not he deserved it.

The pending consequences from what had happened were the least of his concerns. All that Christopher could think of was that this unnecessary tragedy was going to affect him not only as a police officer, but also as a person, a tragedy that without a doubt was going to scar him for the rest of his life.

It was extremely tough for Captain White to go to the hospital. He just did not want to see firsthand the condition that Maxwell was in. Yet, he knew that he had to. His friend, that tough son-of-a-bitch, somehow had survived being dropped into Hell and then unceremoniously, ripped right back out of it.

Christopher knew that it was going to be a long road ahead for Maxwell before he got back on his feet, and he also knew that his old friend was going to need his help along the way. So he gathered up all the courage that he could find and walked through the main entrance to Detroit Receiving Hospital, to the elevators, and then up to the burn ward. As he exited the elevator, he heard an unfamiliar voice address him. The captain turned to his left and saw that a middle-aged doctor was walking up towards him. "Oh. Hello. Are you Maxwell's doctor?"

"Yes. I'm Dr. Fuller. If you'd like, you can call me Greg. It's unfortunate that we have to meet under such circumstances, Captain."

Christopher reached out his right hand and greeted the doctor, while simultaneously asking him about Maxwell's condition.

Dr. Fuller replied to Christopher's inquiry by informing him that Maxwell was currently listed in temporary serious condition; he was still unconscious, and the burns that he had sustained, would need continual monitoring and treatment for at least another few weeks. He also informed the captain that there was a possibility Maxwell would end up needing a few skin grafts if his burns did not sufficiently heal.

"So then, he is going to be all right?"

"Physically, I'd say yes. Emotionally... Well that's another story in itself." Dr. Fuller encouraged the captain to walk along with him towards Maxwell's room — they stopped once along the way to pick up another patient's chart from the nurse's station. When they had arrived at Maxwell's room, Dr. Fuller placed his hand on the captain's shoulder and he extended his condolences to the police department and to the families of those who did not survive. The doctor then excused himself, informing Christopher that he had to check up on a young boy who had been attacked the day before by a stray pit bull.

As Christopher entered his old friend's room, a sick and uneasy feeling came over him the moment he saw Maxwell lying in the bed. He couldn't believe how nauseating he looked. *'Oh my God, Max. You look like a living piece of shit,'* he thought to himself, as he slowly made his way over to the bedside chair. *'If I were in your shoes, I would never want to wake up and have to face all of the anguish that's ahead of you. Although the one thing that I do know about you, Max, is that you are one of the strongest willed men I have ever known. If anyone can get through the physical and emotional pain, you most certainly can.'*

Christopher sat in the chair next to Maxwell's bed and looked at the far wall. He really didn't want to look at him, because then he would instantly begin to feel guilty. He knew that he was not actually responsible for this, but his friend was lying in a hospital bed. Someone had to pay, and unfortunately, Christopher was the logical choice to fall on the sword — even though it was the D.U.O. who was guilty.

He has been a police officer for more than twenty years, and his experience should have been enough to prevent him from letting his desires dictate his actions. Instead, Christopher's, his superior's, and his officer's anxiousness to bring down the D.U.O., had seemed like all the reason they needed to blindly leap at the opportunity they thought they had. He knew better than to do that; he knew that he should have been much more cautious and sought more proof instead of just relying on the word of a usually credible street snitch. But because they had failed to pursue the remaining members of the D.U.O. right after the arrest of Antonio Marcone, Christopher felt a personal responsibility to make up for his and Chief Winslow's earlier error in judgment — not just the error that caused this tragedy to happen, but also the error of thinking that all of the collected evidence during Colin Ramirez's two years of undercover work, was just not enough. Had they dug a little deeper then, things just might be a little different now.

"Aaaaa… Mmmmmm… Uuuuhhh," Maxwell uttered.

The captain turned his head and placed his left hand on Maxwell's non-burned shoulder. "Max! Are you awake?"

"Uuuuhhh…" Maxwell opened up his eyes and saw a familiar face sitting beside him. "I guess that I'll never be the one that clinches the Stanley Cup for his team with a game-winning goal in triple overtime. And I guess that I don't get the free trip to Disney World after all, do I?"

Christopher couldn't believe his ears. *'After what the man had just been through, he woke up cracking jokes. Then again, that's Maxwell Banks for you… always saying the unexpected.'* "It's good to see that you still have your stupid sense of humor."

"We screwed this one up big-time, didn't we, sir? I should have seen this coming."

Christopher removed his hand from his friend's shoulder. And even though he wasn't ready to admit anything — he did. "Max, this wasn't your fault. It's mine."

"Bullshit it is!"

"It's my fault because I should not have placed the responsibility of taking down the D.U.O. on just yours and Joshua's shoulders. This would not have happened if I…"

"You ain't too fuckin' old as of yet to be second guessing yourself… so don't! You made a decision, which you felt at that time, made sense; a decision that both Joshua and I agreed with. And now, we just have to accept the shitty hand that has been dealt to us. Don't even think of shouldering the blame for this all on your own. We are as much at fault for this mess as you are."

144

In his heart, Captain White knew this to be the truth — but he just could not allow Maxwell to accept any of the blame. For as long as he had known the man, he knew that this pig-headed friend of his was the kind of man who would not think twice about stepping on a landmine to save those whom he held in high regard — which was what his apparent intentions were.

Christopher took a moment and settled down his thoughts. He didn't come to the hospital to discuss which one of them was going to take the fall, he came because he had a lot of important things to discuss with Maxwell and he wanted to be sure that he remembered what they all were.

Before he started what he knew he had to do, Christopher took a moment and informed Maxwell of what his long list of injuries were. He then made sure that Dr. Fuller's assessment was fully understood by Maxwell and that he acknowledged and accepted that it was going to take quite a bit of time for him to completely recover. Once that was out of the way, Captain White formally placed his officer on medical leave. He knew that Maxwell was going to immediately protest his doing this, but he didn't care. Objection after objection would simply fall on deaf ears — as far as he was concerned, the only thing that his friend had to do, was getting better.

Just like he foresaw, his old friend had tried his damndest to get him to change his mind, but Christopher wouldn't budge. Finally, Maxwell conceded — but only after he realized that his boss was steadfast in his position. Giving in wasn't what he wanted to do, as he had never freely admitted defeat before — there had been a few times in the past however, where he reluctantly had waved a white flag. He was after all, pretty messed up and in no position whatsoever to help his fellow officers with the investigation.

Once Maxwell had accepted his situation, Captain White took a few moments and organized his thoughts. He knew that Maxwell was probably going to be angry with him because of what he had decided to do, but Christopher felt that it was necessary — he also felt that out of respect, Maxwell should at least be told why he did what he did. "I had two officers pick up your snitch this morning."

"Why? Chevy would never screw me over."

"Are you sure? Come on now, Max. Think back. Does this entire thing not seem to be just a bit too timely? I mean... first of all, Antonio Marcone is convicted and sentenced to thirty years in prison. And then the moment that the two of you get back from your vacation, you immediate get a phone call from your snitch. The next thing you know, you're conducting a sting operation. I know that you trust Chevy but... he gave you no viable proof."

Maxwell took a moment and thought about what his captain had just said. All the evidence, albeit circumstantial, did point to the possibility that Chevy could have set them up. Yet, as much as Maxwell didn't want to believe it, he had to acknowledge the fact that he just may have. "You believe that he played us?"

"Yes. That is why we brought him in. We have no other choice but to work under the assumption that he knows a lot more about the supposed arms shipment than what he told you. I mean, there weren't even any arms in the warehouse to begin with."

This wasn't really the right time. Nevertheless, Maxwell's inner child suddenly surfaced and he felt the urge to mess with his captain — even though he knew that he shouldn't. "While you are at it then, I suggest that you also track down and bring in Chevy's best friend, René, for questioning." A priceless, befuddled look is what Maxwell saw appear on his captain's face. That exact reaction was all that he would normally have needed to work a rib for all it was worth, but this was not the time or place to string along his captain until he got close to blowing a gasket. For once in his life, Maxwell had to push aside his gregariousness and treat this whole situation with the seriousness that it deserved.

After promptly apologizing to his captain, he explained to him who René supposedly was. Surprisingly, Christopher just sat there next to the bed with his arms crossed. That look, he had seen before — his boss was impatiently waiting for more bullshit to finish spilling out of his mouth. He tried not to let that happen. Nevertheless, Maxwell just could not resist interjecting bits of his infantile brand of humor throughout the story as he told it. When he was done, he immediately regretted everything unnecessary that he had said. Instead of just telling his boss that Chevy honestly believed that he had an invisible friend who helped him to gather information, Maxwell had

146

decided to create an elaborate narrative that Disney could easily take and turn into one of their fairy tales.

Christopher had no problem with some good-natured ribbing, but today really wasn't the day for it. Had it been anyone else, Christopher probably would have written them up for unprofessional conduct. His personal relationship with Maxwell had started long before he was put in a position of influence, and he had never really made an effort to change things from the way they were to the way they should be. In hindsight, that had been a mistake. He just let his friend be who he was; knowing that there was never anything malicious behind his words or actions.

As peeved as he knew he should be, he just wasn't. His heart had made him realize that a little deserved leeway was in order. His friend after all, should be lying in a coffin and not a hospital bed.

Unexpectedly, Maxwell closed his eyes and slouched forward. At first, Christopher had thought that he had slipped back into unconsciousness — that was until he thought he noticed a slight cheeky grin briefly appear on his face. This time, he could not hold back his annoyance. The captain hastily reached out and shoved Maxwell on his good shoulder. "Open your eyes you fuckin' bastard and stop..!"

Maxwell re-opened his eyes, and said, "Stop what? I just felt a little woozy and needed to close my eyes for a moment."

Captain White got up from his chair and walked away from Maxwell's bed, frustrated. "I thought you were fuckin' around with me again."

"I wasn't. Sorry for disappointing you."

Christopher rolled his eyes and shook his head. One day, he and Maxwell needed to have a long talk — his old friend simply had to get it through his thick head that his unnecessary crap was no longer going to be tolerated. Until then, the captain took a moment and gathered his thoughts, as there were a few important things that Maxwell needed to hear from him. And as much as he wanted to put off having to divulge what he knew, his old friend had a right to know. However, Christopher was suddenly finding it very hard to come clean.

"I can see that something is bothering you, Chris. Is there something that you want to talk about?"

"No. But there is something that I need to tell you." Captain White stood at the window across from Maxwell's bed, and stared aimlessly out into the city. Christopher always dreaded the day that he would have to do what he knew had to be done, but never in a million years did he think that he would have to tell someone whom he knew so well, the sort of news that they honestly would never expect to hear in their lifetime. "Listen Maxwell, I uh… I don't know how to say this?"

Maxwell struggled to lift himself up into a comfortable sitting position and stared in bewilderment at his old friend.

After a few more unnerving moments had passed, Captain White left his spot from in front of the window and started to pace the hospital room until he was able to compose himself, somewhat. He then turned and faced Maxwell. "I don't even know where to begin. This is so hard for me to say but… Officers Thompson and Blake didn't make it. And neither did Joshua."

As was expected, this news hit Maxwell hard, harder than a Randy Johnson fastball to the face at ten feet away. Officers Thompson and Blake had both become good friends with Maxwell. Joshua however, had become his partner within just a few days of his moving to Detroit. And even though Maxwell did have one biological brother of his own, Joshua had quickly become his other.

The effects of his concussion made it hard to concentrate. It forced Maxwell to take a few extra seconds to process what he had just been told. He looked at his captain and tried to understand how this could have happened. As best as possible, he tried to recall and organize in his mind what fragmented pieces there were of that horrible evening — even the ones that seemed to be irrelevant.

He remembered taking off toward the truck, then stopping in his tracks two steps later when the first explosion occurred from underneath it. Joshua had been in the back of the truck and there was nothing at that point that Maxwell could do for him. Then, he heard another explosion beside him; that caused him to immediately turn in its direction. As he did so, he became momentarily frozen as a series of sequential cascading structural explosions continued from that point and went right around the entire warehouse.

What he was seeing had honestly caused him to believe that his life was over; that his chance of survival would be impossible. So with nothing to lose, Maxwell took a gamble and made the only logical decision that he felt he had left. Instead of trying to make it to the warehouse exit, he ran back to where those wooden crates were behind that half cinderblock wall and took cover.

"Fortunately for us, Max, your decision to barricade yourself inside that crate of spare computer parts was what saved your life. It's a God forsaken miracle that you survived." Captain White returned to the window, where he again tried to gather his thoughts, knowing that he still had even more bad news to tell his friend — news that undoubtedly was going to destroy him.

He summoned up the courage that he needed and looked directly at Maxwell, letting him know what his opinion was. He believed what had taken place that night had two distinctive purposes. The first reason, Christopher felt, was strictly for revenge against the police department. The second reason, he was all but certain, was to send a message that just could not be ignored.

"Killing three officers', Chris, is sending one hell of a message. That just tells me that they are not the kind of people who give two shits about the law."

"The message I am talking about isn't for us. It was meant strictly for you."

"I don't need a message from them to have a pretty good idea what the D.U.O. is capable of. I am, after all, lying in this damn hospital bed because of them."

"I believe that was their intention." Once again, Christopher turned his attention back to what was on the other side of the hospital window.

This time, Maxwell knew that Christopher had not turned his back to him because he again wanted to double-check the weather outside. His old friend, he could easily tell, had some more bad news. "Don't let it consume you, Chris. What's wrong?"

Captain White did not move from his spot, nor did he contemplate responding to the question. He had clearly heard what was asked, but he was finding it extremely difficult to do what he knew he had to — he honestly didn't want to reveal what he knew was going to shatter Maxwell's world.

Silence encompassed the room. The only noises that could be heard were the faint ones that came from the monitoring machines that were attached to Maxwell's body. Christopher's lack of answers, he didn't want to accept. However, the hospital room really wasn't an ideal place for him do what he would normally do — use something that he knew as leverage in order to get what he wanted. Therefore, the only option he had left was to guess what the secrets were that his captain was keeping to himself. At first, Maxwell's train of thought led him right back to the Detroit Underworld Organization. But he quickly dismissed that notion, because Maxwell knew that anything that had to do with the city's biggest pain in the ass, his captain would certainly share it with him. Now Maxwell had to think outside the box. There were plenty of other possibilities, but nothing he could think of that would cause his old friend to stay bottled up. It wasn't until Christopher turned back around to face him that he noticed a single tear trickle down the side of his captain's face — the unthinkable suddenly appeared in his thoughts. "Sylvia? Sabastian?"

Captain White had to quickly return to Maxwell's side so that he wouldn't try to jump out of his bed. "I'm sorry, but... your wife is dead. I know that this is horrible, but you must stay calm and listen to me. It will do you no good to get all pissed off right now. You have to try to stay calm and stay in control."

"Calm! How the hell can you expect me to stay calm?" Maxwell tried to wiggle free of Christopher's grip on his arms so that he could leave his bed, but he was unable to do so — his injuries more so than the captain's efforts at restraining him, was what kept him where he was. Frustrated, he let out a long vibrato toned, ear shattering scream — a blast of sound that caused Captain White's facial features to slightly oscillate.

A few seconds later, with his anger exorcised, Maxwell looked up at his old friend and in as calm of a voice as he could muster, asked him, "Where is my son?"

Captain White didn't have a definitive answer to give.

Although words were not exchanged at that moment, Maxwell knew what was implied.

"I'm so sorry, Max. The captain then handed him the only bit of evidence that they were able to find; a note that was discovered lying next to his wife's body."

Maxwell took it and read it to himself.

"You've chosen my fate; I've done the same for you...
I've taken your family, because that's the logical thing to do.
I now live an unhappy life, here locked away...
So it's only fair you experience that, each and every day.
I'm sure that revenge will stay on your mind...
Until the day comes that we put our quarrel behind.
Thirty years is a long time; by then you'll be insane...
Due to all the anger that has flooded your brain.
So have a nice life, consumed by depression...
That will be brought on by an unhealthy obsession.
However...
We will meet again one day, and I know that you'll be brave...
But your foolishness will get you killed, and I will dance on
your grave."

When Maxwell was finished reading the note; the poem, he placed it over his face for a brief few moments and nearly wept underneath. At that moment, time stood still. He felt like he no longer existed. His whole world had been ripped away from him. Everything that meant something to him was gone. For a man like himself who radiated of strength, confidence, and control, he had instantly been reduced to a being of nonentity. What reason did he have to go on? The only thing that he had left was his rising anger.

Not thinking, he crumpled up the note; the prophecy according to Antonio Marcone, and threw it towards the window. Luckily the hospital windows were fixed shut. "This can't be real," he said in a rather serious, yet slightly trembling tone. "Please tell me, Chris, that this has been nothing but a very bad dream."

"I wish it were, Max." Captain White went over to the window to pick up that crumpled note. He held it up for his old friend to see, and then reminded him that the note was actually a crucial piece of evidence of which he had just attempted to throw out the window.

151

Maxwell struggled, again trying to pull himself into a seated position on his bed. He gazed across the room for a moment, then tilted back his head and stared randomly at the tiny pinholes in the ceiling tiles. Over the next few moments, Maxwell was able to calm himself down enough to actually think somewhat rationally. He reached up to his face with his hands and rubbed it while at the same time saying to his captain, "If Antonio Marcone thinks that he is going to control my life, he has another thing coming. Thirty years is a long time to wait, but I swear… there will come a day, either during or after my lifetime, one way or another, Antonio Marcone and all of those who are associated with the D.U.O., will pay dearly for their crimes."

"I wouldn't expect anything less from you, Max. However, there isn't a goddamn thing that you can do about it right now. Not until you at least get yourself better. I know that it's going to be extremely tough, but you are going to have to lay here dormant for quite a while and do absolutely nothing until your doctor says otherwise. Let us do the legwork and you just concentrate on getting better. That's an order!"

"Yeah, I know. You're right as always." After attempting to relax with a couple of short therapeutic breaths, Maxwell glanced back up at the ceiling for a brief moment, trying to hold back the tears he felt forming, and hoping to see a sign or something, telling him what he should do next. After unsuccessfully finding what he was searching for, Maxwell looked back over at his captain and asked him to please explain in detail exactly how his wife had died.

Reluctantly, he told Maxwell everything that he knew, including the fact that his wife had been shot once in the heart. "Whoever it was that pulled the trigger, knew exactly what they were doing to kill her with only one bullet."

It took all the strength that Maxwell had to not explode — and although Christopher wouldn't blame him if he lost it, it was easy to assume that his old friend was doing everything he could to hold back the flood of emotions that was ready to burst out of him.

Maxwell took a moment, looked within himself, and found what he needed to suppress his rising fury. Once he was certain that it was under control, he asked his old friend for a favor. "I wish to see Joshua's wife, Carol. That is, if she is up to it. I have to make sure that she understands just how sorry I am for what has happened. And I have to know that she is going to be all right."

"I'll see what I can do, but I don't know if that will be possible." Christopher had actually spoken to Joshua's wife right before he had come to the hospital and she had informed him that she had made the decision to go back to England right after Joshua's funeral was over. Her reasoning for this was simple; her mother's health had not been that great over the last year, and it made sense to Carol to go back to her home country to be with the rest of her family.

"That's enough visiting for now," Dr. Fuller said as he entered the room. "Lord knows this man here is in dire need of some serious beauty sleep."

"I was just about to leave anyway." Before the captain left however, he took a moment and reassured Maxwell that he was going to do everything in his power to arrest those responsible.

After a quick examination and conversation, Dr. Fuller left Maxwell alone in his room. No sooner had he closed the door, the floodgates opened up and Maxwell's emotions took over. Overwhelming emotions can break down any strong willed man — and that was exactly what had happened to Maxwell. For the first time in his life, he cried like a baby.

Unable to get out of his bed due to the injuries that he had, was probably a blessing in disguise. If he had been able to get up, then Maxwell would have probably destroyed the entire floor of the hospital. But smashing things would not bring back his wife, his partner, his fellow officers, or help him to find his missing son. Never before had Maxwell felt so helpless. He did not know what to do. He was a prisoner in his bed and a prisoner to his own tortured thoughts. The only thing that he could do was just lie there, let his tears flow free, and then try to figure out what his life was going to be like from this day forward without those who were the most important part of his very own existence.

───────────────── ◯◯ ─────────────────

Today was going to be Sal's day. Louie was in Chicago for reasons that he had erroneously assumed would never be known — but they were. Sal admittedly, could be a bastard, but he was also smarter than what he had ever been perceived to be. That was why he had chosen to keep the knowledge he had of his associate's secret endeavors to himself for a rainy day. Eventually, Louie was going to give him all the reason that he needed to let the cat out of the bag. And when that happened, he was just going to sit back and enjoy watching Antonio rip his right-hand man a new one for conducting his own side business deals.

With the entire police force now in shambles and his boss safely locked away in jail, Sal felt happier than he had in a very long time. No stress was there and no habitual asshole was around to irritate him. That meant that today, he was finally going to get the opportunity to do what he had always dreamed about doing. Yes, it was only going to be a temporary thing, but Sal was ready to get a little taste of what it was like to play 'Boss Man' for a while. So Sal opened up Antonio's office door, let himself in, and then plopped his overworked ass in Antonio's well-used leather executive office chair. After a few moments of imagining what it would be like to order people around, especially Louie, Sal decided that he deserved to treat himself for a job well done.

Using Antonio's computer, he tried for about an hour to access one of the organizations several secured overseas bank accounts. *'Why spend my money? I deserve a healthy bonus for everything that I have done for this organization,'* he thought. Unfortunately, Sal failed in his attempt — he just could not figure out what Antonio's password was. He had hoped that he would be able to withdraw enough money so that he could go out and enjoy those things he liked the most: food, wine, and very young, beautiful woman.

When these few opportunities of having free time on his hands came around, Sal wished that he were still living in his homeland of Sicily. He liked his woman as young as the law allowed and there, the age of consent was fourteen. But unfortunately, that wasn't where he was. He was in Michigan and would have to settle for someone who was a little bit older, as sixteen was the current state law.

Most people would consider Sal's sexual preferences to be immoral. Maybe it was, but no one has the right to claim it as being just that when the written law takes precedence over someone's beliefs. To be judged by those types of individuals who strongly feel the way they do, in Sal's eyes, they are the ones who more than likely have many more skeletons in their closet than he. Yes, Sal knew that hell was in his future, but he wasn't going there because of his penchant for young women, as everything else that he did was the reason he was headed to that domain for all eternity — and he was content with his pending fate. When it came to the age of consent laws however, Sal wasn't about to push his luck. As much as he hated those age restrictions, he was smart enough not to ignore, bend, or break them. Just because he lived a life on the edge, didn't mean that he had to give the law any more ammunition to use against him than they already had.

Determined to go out and have a good time tonight, Sal was left with no other option but to take a different approach at securing himself some cash. Covering his tracks was going to be a much more difficult task for him to accomplish, but one that he knew he would be able to successfully do. He may not be that business savvy like Louie, but Sal knew a thing or two about computers and how to erase his electronic footprint.

After easily dipping into the organization's corporate funds, money that had been made by the numerous legal businesses that they owned and had acquired over the years, Sal withdraw four thousand dollars. And so as not to draw any attention to himself, he had masterfully re-routed the amount that he took through one of Louie's side business accounts — something that he would not have ever considered doing if Louie wasn't such a prick to him.

With this stellar rouse of his completed, Sal proceeded to order himself up a couple of escorts from the only legal, on-line escort service in the state that offered sixteen year olds. Once that was done, he quickly made the necessary arrangements for his planned evening: limousine, champagne, roses, and restaurant and hotel reservations. This left him with only one thing left to do — figure out what it was that he was going to wear as he wasn't about to go out in the same three piece suit that he'd been wearing all day.

No sooner had he picked up the phone to call for the organization's driver to come and pick him up so that he could go to his apartment and change, the phone rang. "Shit! Who the hell could that be? Hello? Antonio, ah... Um... hey boss. How is your new place?"

"Shut the fuck up, Sal!"

Sal knew that he had just put his foot in his mouth — and it was so far down, there was no extracting it either. The smartest thing for Sal to do would be to just sit there quietly and take the verbal ass-ripping that was sure to come his way for his unnecessary comment. But that surprisingly did not happen. Instead, it was a threat that came his way. And although he felt that his boss wouldn't actually follow through on it, Antonio had made it clear that he had no problem arranging for him his own jail space and then personally introducing Sal to two rather large, hairy black men whom he recently met, that were eagerly looking for a white man to be the filling for their Oreo cookie.

"Please don't do that, Antonio. I promise you that I won't say anything stupid like that ever again."

"Good! Now where is Louie? I only have a few minutes of phone time, and I want to maximize my use of it."

Sal then carefully explained to Antonio that Louie currently was not in the office and that he had gone out of town for the day, leaving him in charge.

This wasn't turning out to be the kind of phone conversation that Antonio had expected. He was not too happy at all to hear that Louie wasn't around. That meant that he was either out tending to family matters, or he was out of town doing something he should not be doing — the latter, Antonio suspected was the case.

He had warned Louie before that the family was priority and nothing else mattered — it was what he had signed up for all those years ago. If only he wasn't where he was, he was certain that Louie would not be tempted to stray. The next time he talked to his right-hand man, if he didn't come clean, he would have to get Sal to find out for him if what he thinks might be taking place, was. "Well, since Louie has chosen to push aside his obligations, I guess that you're just gonna have to give me a quick summary of what had happened the other day?"

Sal took his time and explained in complete detail to Antonio, everything that went down. "Man, I wish that you could have been there at the warehouse when it blew up. The explosion was so spectacular that it kind of reminded me of a Shakespearian play — a little hard to fully watch, yet beautiful, romantic, and deadly all at the same time."

Antonio was furious. His men were instructed to make sure that Maxwell Banks did not die, yet it sounded to him as if Louie and Sal didn't really even care. Death to his enemy, although that prospect would all but assured that nothing again got in their way, was not Antonio's plan — he instead, wanted Maxwell to live and emotionally suffer for the remainder of his life.

Sal knew that they had been lucky. Neither he nor Louie was an explosive experts and the crude version of C4 that they made turned out to be much more unpredictable than what either had expected. Yes, he personally didn't care if Maxwell had died or not in the explosion, but in hindsight, he was glad that the man had somehow survived because he knew that Antonio would have strung him upside down by his manhood and left him hanging in the middle of the Florida Everglades for the alligators to feast upon.

Hearing that anger in his boss's voice, Sal quickly explained to him that Maxwell had actually survived the explosion and that he was currently recovering in the intensive care unit at Detroit Receiving Hospital — a place where Maxwell would be at for almost a month before he would be well enough to be released. "I tell you boss, Maxwell is so messed up."

"You and Louie are so fuckin' lucky that he's still alive. Now just give me the details about…"

Sal didn't get a chance to tell Antonio that three of the cops who were also inside the warehouse with Maxwell hadn't survived, or that the man's wife and child had been taken care of, because their phone connection had gotten severed.

After the odd moment had passed, and knowing that there was no chance that Antonio would be calling back anytime soon, Sal dialed the number to their driver and asked him to meet him out back of the pawn shop in five minutes. He then shut the door to Antonio's office, took a few steps toward the back alley exit, and then stopped in the middle of the empty hallway. There, his mind started to second guess the plans he had made earlier. He suddenly no longer wanted to go back to his apartment to change — he instead, wanted to go shopping for a new suit. His reasoning for this was simple — tonight was going to be a very special night and he wanted to look really good while out on the town with the three young 'ladies of the evening' that he had earlier chosen to accompany him.

After more than three weeks, frustration could easily be seen on Captain White's face. He had every single detective at the precinct working around the clock, trying to put together a case against the Detroit Underworld Organization. Every tip and every second guess had turned up nothing substantial — even his questioning of Chevy had given him little to go on. It had gotten to the point where Captain White was beginning to think that even if he had a limitless supply of resources and an ample amount of money, they still wouldn't be able to find a credible source that could supply them with the information they needed. But just because their investigation had stalled, that didn't give Captain White the excuse that he was looking for to avoid the inevitable. He had to bite the bullet again and accept the blame for the lack of any progress. And although no official word as of yet had crossed his desk, he fully expected a reprimand, a demotion, or possibly even the loss of his job because of the accumulation of mistakes that have been made since he had accepted the responsibility of dismantling the D.U.O.

Christopher's mind was a mess. He could not think straight. Nothing seemed to be going his way. It felt to him almost as if he was cursed right from the start, seeing that he all but had his arm twisted into accepting his promotion at Maven Potter's funeral — even though he honestly believed at the time that he was nowhere near ready for it. But Chief Winslow believed in him; those whom he knew and would be under his command would undoubtedly support him. That was why Christopher White had accepted the promotion and had become, at the time, the youngest person in the history of the Detroit Police Department to ever hold the rank of captain. Even now, knowing that he still had the endorsement of those who mattered, Christopher was still feeling as if he had made a mistake. Unfortunately, he could not go back in time and refuse the offer. This left him with only two other options — quit or fight.

Christopher had never before walked away when the going got tough — even if what he was facing seemed insurmountable to overcome. Yes, nothing had really gone his way since he had accepted the captaincy, but the exit light at the end of the long hallway can't stay burned out forever. Eventually, it will be changed — and that had to be done by him before he could officially leave it all behind. Still, it didn't make him feel any better that Chief Winslow had personally reviewed all of the available information concerning the incidents which had led up to this tragedy, and had concluded that Captain White should not be held fully responsible. But he also warned Christopher that a full inquiry into the incident would take place soon and that he would eventually be asked to appear before a review board. But until that time came, the chief had instructed Captain White to continue on with the investigation and not to worry about what may or may not happen.

To the best of his abilities, that was what he was going to do. He had to stay positive and not allow another misstep to drop him down another rung or two on the ladder — instead, he had to get a tight grip on it and ensure that he methodically headed upwards. But before he could do that, he had to finish his less-than-positive verbal report to his commanding officer. "Yes, sir! I have every available officer working double duty... including the eight on loan from the 16th precinct. I have them double checking all leads no matter how insignificant they may appear to be, but unfortunately, we just can't seem to find a trace of anything anywhere: no trails, no evidence, and no sightings. I don't know how, but they've somehow figured out how to make it appear as if the evidence that we know is there, no longer exist. It's as if we, the good guys, are just destined to continually stay two steps behind the enemy."

An unexpected, yet welcomed knock rattled Captain White's office door. *'Perfect timing,'* he thought. "Hold on a second there, sir." He could not tell who was standing on the other side of the frosted glass, but that didn't matter — Christopher invited them in anyway, knowing that his uninvited guest was the perfect excuse that he needed to cut short his report to Chief Winslow.

The office door opened up and a rather frail looking individual stood just beyond the threshold. "Hello, Captain. It's just me."

Captain White sat there in his office chair with a surprised and slightly shocked look on his face. He could not believe that the somewhat withered looking man that was now facing him was his friend. It had only been twenty-five days since the tragedy, but Maxwell now no longer looked like the same man he had known and worked with for all those years. "Hold on a second there, Max. I'm on the phone with the chief."

After promising to call his boss back, Christopher ended his conversation with him and then warmly smiled. For the first time ever, he didn't mind that Maxwell had interrupted him while he was in the middle of something important. "When did you get released?"

"Oh, about two hours ago," Maxwell answered, as he gingerly walked into the captain's office using the support of a cane. "So is it true that the chief's wife gave birth to a new baby girl a few days ago?"

"Yes she did, Max," the captain replied. "They named her Sylvia, in memory of your wife."

A sense of pride filled Maxwell as a slight chill went down his spine. He never expected anyone to do something like that, let alone someone whom he really didn't know that well. "The next time you talk to the chief, please extend my congratulations to him on his new daughter, and make sure to thank him for the kind gesture. I really appreciate that he and his wife would name their daughter in my wife's honor."

"I will," the Captain promised. "So… how are you feeling? I know that the hospital wouldn't let you attend your wife's funeral." Captain White got up from his chair and proceeded to get them both some fresh coffee.

"I went by her gravesite as soon as I left the hospital. For the most part, I have been able to keep my emotions in check ever since it happened, but then when I saw her headstone, it finally hit me just how real it all was — I immediately broke down and wept. I must have wept there for at least an hour or so. Damn, I miss her so much."

The captain handed Maxwell his coffee, then encouraged him to take the empty seat across from his desk; Christopher promptly returned to his seat on the other side.

After taking a few sips of his fresh coffee, Maxwell inquired about the ongoing search for his son. This was a topic that Captain White knew he couldn't avoid discussing, even though he felt like hiding his face in his hands instead of facing his friend. How can someone be expected to deliver even more disappointing news to a person, a friend who has already suffered through a very emotional and traumatic period in his life? It wasn't fair that the bearer of bad news seemed only to fall on his shoulders. But after a few moments, Christopher accepted what he had been anointed to do and drew the strength that he needed to complete his responsibility. "The only thing that we know so far is the bullet that killed your wife came from a military issued handgun. Other than that, our forensics team could not find anything of importance at the crime scene. There weren't any fingerprints on that note left beside your wife or on the smashed cell phone. There were no hair follicles, skin fragments, or blood traces left behind that wasn't yours or your wife's. The only thing that we found, which we are certain did not come from any personal item that either you or your wife own, were a few black fibers which the lab has identified as coming from a pair of Blackhawk cut resistance gloves."

"The same kind of gloves that the police and the military use?"

"Yes. And unfortunately, without any kind of DNA evidence left behind with those fibers, it would be useless for us to search the police database or petition the courts to gain access to U.S. military records in order to learn who did this."

"Well… since you know the gun that killed my wife was military, I would assume that the glove fibers came from someone who once had, or is currently serving."

"It would appear that way, Max. But you know as well as I do, what something appears to be, may not be that at all."

"I know. Is there any news about my son?"

"Again, I'm sorry. We have hit a brick wall."

Maxwell could see the regret in his old friend's eyes. It wasn't his fault that no progress had yet to be made — and he wasn't about to blame Christopher for it. He knew that his boss had done everything that he could up until this point to acquire a solid lead, but he just wished that a ray of hope would have been present this day, because Maxwell knew that by the end of his visit, more disappointment was going to be handed to his old friend.

"This entire case has been the most frustrating one that I have ever been involved with, Max. We have found absolutely nothing concrete that could tell us where Sabastian might be. Even after forensics spent a week combing through what was left of the warehouse, they could not find any evidence that could link the D.U.O. to this whole thing. I mean, we both know who is responsible, but we just can't prove a damn thing right now. I wish there was something more positive that I could tell you, Max. But unfortunately right now, there isn't."

"I fully understand your frustration, sir. I know that everyone is trying real hard to put the D.U.O. out of business. All that you can do is keep at it and something is bound to turn up."

Christopher took a healthy sip of his coffee; he nearly finished it off. He then asked, "Is there anything that I can do for you, Max?"

"Yes. There is one thing that you could do." Maxwell finished off the remainder of his coffee, set the cup onto the edge of Christopher's desk, stood up, reached into his back pocket and then took out his badge. He removed his gun from its holster next and then handed them both to Captain White.

He should have been more shocked than he was at that moment, but he had a rather strong suspicion that this was going to happen — even though he had hoped that it wouldn't. For a brief moment, Christopher thought about trying to convince his old friend to hold off on his sudden resignation and just take all the time that he needed to fully recover from his injuries before he made such a life-changing decision. But deep down inside, he knew that Maxwell had not been influenced to do what he had just done by everything that had happened — it was just time for him to move on.

With a heavy heart, Christopher accepted Maxwell's gun and badge. "Are you certain that this is what you want to do this, Max? I mean... You're one of the best damn cops that this city has ever had. Hell, you're the best damn cop that I have ever worked with."

Maxwell could not fault his now ex-captain's passive attempt to change his mind. He had spent every waking minute in the hospital thinking about his deceased wife and all that had taken place. And the more he thought about it, the more he began to second guess everything: his decisions, his life, and his future. Two weeks — that was all it had taken before he had made the decision to quit being a police officer. "I should have trusted my instincts more. And I should have listened to my wife. If I had done so, then none of this would have ever happened."

"You don't know that. And you also know very well that you can't dwell on the what ifs."

"I know. And I know that I can't change what has happened, Chris. I've accepted that." Out of respect for their friendship, Maxwell felt that Christopher deserved an explanation for his decision. His reasons may not seem logical, but Maxwell honestly felt that he needed to build himself a new life. And the only way that he honestly felt he could do that was for him to move far away from any reminder of what had happened.

San Antonio, Texas — that is where Maxwell had decided he was going to go. Not because the lifestyle there was completely different than Detroit, but because that was where his younger brother, Sydney lived. And it seemed like as good a time as any to go for a visit, considering that he had only seen his brother once since he had moved down there from Ottawa — and not because of a job offer, but because of a woman whom Sydney had met on-line. That relationship didn't work out, but Maxwell's brother ended up staying there anyway as he had found the Texas lifestyle more to his liking than the one he had long been accustomed to back home in Ottawa. "Who knows, Chris? If I like it there, I just may stay behind and open up my own detective agency."

Maxwell opened up his wallet and took out his, now useless business card, flipped it over and wrote on the back — he then handed it to Captain White. "Here is my brother's address and phone number in case you come across any new leads about Sabastian. I've really enjoyed working for you and you've been a good friend. Au revoir, mon ami."

"I hope things work out for you, Max." The Captain then reached out his hand and in a firm, good luck grip, shook the hand of his friend and wished him well.

The next day, former detective Maxwell Banks boarded an airplane for San Antonio. Two months after his arrival in Texas, Maxwell Banks did what he said he might do. He set up his own detective agency. He did this initially so that he could use it as a base for finding his missing son, but once he got started, he realized that he still had that hunger; that drive for being out on the street and helping people in need, hunting down fugitives, and putting away all of the low-life scumbags and dregs of society.

Over the years, Maxwell kept in contact with Christopher White, and he followed diligently any leads that his former boss would send his way — which unfortunately, always seemed to lead to another dead end. But Maxwell never gave up hope. He never quit, nor did he ever lose faith that he'd one day find his son — that was the promise he had made to himself the day he had gone to the gravesite to visit his wife.

Every day, he looked at the only picture he had of himself, his wife, and their newborn son. That photo was all the motivation he ever needed to continue on with his personal quest — and his love was the driving force behind his determination to never give up.

10

Twenty five years later...

They say that time will heal all wounds. But that is just a saying, as some wounds just won't stop bleeding. Scars will fade some over time, but those that run beyond the surface tend to stay forever lodged in our memories. For Maxwell Banks, it didn't matter how many years had actually passed since his world was drastically altered, because each and every day, the hurt continually flowed throughout his veins like a perilous river. He refused however, to let it show to those who were close to him.

Today was Maxwell's birthday and like all previous ones, he really had no reason to celebrate it. The things in this world that mattered to him the most had never been there. It had taken him quite a long time before he was able to actually get on with his life — but even to this day he still found it hard to accept the lack of finality. Was his son dead, or was he still alive? The longer those questions stayed unanswered, the chances grew slimmer that Maxwell would see his son again. But until the day he died, he would not give up hope that he and Sabastian would one day be reunited.

The last time he had seen his son alive he had been just short of two months old. Although it was unlikely, he could have passed him on the street and not even known it. And even if he were to somehow miraculously find his son, there was no guarantee that Sabastian would want to be a part of his life. And although such an outcome would devastate Maxwell, he would still love him with all his heart.

Today was like every other day for Maxwell, as he had arrived at his agency at eight in the morning, fully prepared for another day of work. Yet, today wasn't just another day in the life of Maxwell Banks. In his eyes, he officially became 'OLD' — and man was he ever feeling like it.

When Maxwell approached his agency, he pulled out his keys to unlock the door. Uncharacteristically, he fumbled with them as they fell meaninglessly to the floor, landing between his feet and slightly behind him. As he bent over to pick them up he paused for a moment, falsely sensing what felt like a ghostly presence brushing up against him. But no, it had to have been his imagination. He 'was' getting old — and just because the mind tends to be the first thing to go, didn't mean that it was already beginning to happen to him. He refused to let it. In theory, he should have at least another twenty years or so before any signs of senility started to show.

Maxwell picked up his keys, stood up, and then quickly scanned the hallway to see if any ethereal presence was indeed there watching him. As he suspected, there wasn't, so he inserted the key into the lock of his agency door. He opened it up and was immediately surprised. There wasn't a ghost waiting for him on the other side of the door, but what was there Maxwell wished hadn't been. He stood there slightly startled, but more perturbed than anything as his brother Sydney and his secretary, Savanna Rivard, were standing in the middle of the sparsely decorated reception area, celebrating what was to them, a joyous occasion.

Displeased as he was, Maxwell just stood there and let them finish singing happy birthday — even though he had previously told them on many occasions throughout the years, not to waste their time on something as trivial as the anniversary of his birth. "Like I've said to you both before, this is really not necessary." Maxwell walked right passed them and headed straight over to his own private office, entered it, and then placed his briefcase on his desk.

"Come on now, Max!" Sydney shouted, from where he had been standing in the main lobby area. "You're my 'older' brother and it's my job to make you feel old and useless." Sydney then made his way over to Maxwell's office and entered it. He had a plan this day that he was going to follow through with; a plan that would remind his brother just how old he was getting, so Sydney stood at the edge of his brother's desk and handed him a digital musical card that wished him a happy fifty-fifth birthday.

Reluctantly, Maxwell accepted the card. "You do realize brother that you're only a few years behind me and are as well, nearing the age of fossilization." He then gave Sydney a 'cease this old crap right now' type of look, walked out from behind his desk, passed by his brother, and left his office. Maxwell then walked over toward the sim-caf machine at the back kitchen nook, and poured himself a healthy mug of freshly brewed simulated coffee.

As per his daily routine, he then walked back into his office, passed his bemused brother again, and took up a seat behind his desk. Sydney continued to linger near the edge of it; Maxwell ignored him and gingerly sipped on his sim-caf while he stared and reminisced at the only family picture that had ever been taken of himself, his wife, Sylvia, and his newborn son. Looking at that picture was one of the few things in his repetitive day in which Maxwell felt a bit of sadness — it was also the only thing that he had which continually reminded him of the personal promise he made all those years ago. And until he could fulfill it, he felt that he could never truly be happy again.

Lost in his own damaged world during those few moments, his thoughts this day had taken him back to the place in time where he and his wife had spent a quiet weekend getaway up at Mackinac Island — and it was during this trip that Maxwell's wife had sprung the surprising news upon him that she was pregnant with their first child.

Savanna knocked on the doorjamb of the open office door; that brought Maxwell back to reality. Indiscreetly, he put down the picture he had in his hand and directed his attention to his secretary. "What can I do for you, Savanna?"

She took a few steps into her boss's office, stood just behind Sydney, and spoke. She wanted to apologize, as she felt really bad for springing their unwanted surprise and ruining Maxwell's birthday.

He wasn't mad at his secretary; it was impossible to be mad at someone who cared deeply about him — she was after all, just trying to show how much. Maxwell cared deeply for her also, but he always found it difficult to reciprocate his true feelings. He knew it was stupid, but he still had trouble for some unknown reason, even after all this time, of letting go of the past and living in the present.

Knowing Maxwell as long as she had, Savanna was well aware that he wasn't the most affectionate person on the planet. But she also knew that he cared for her deeply, as she did for him. Although blood did not tie them together, she could certainly read him like a book.

Today wasn't going to be an easy day for him — his, Sylvia's, and Sabastian's birthdays, never were — nor were he and his wife's anniversary. That was why she had tried to put a smile on his face with a surprise as he walked through the door. Unfortunately, she had failed. But that didn't mean that she wouldn't try later on to cheer her boss up. Still, she was concerned about the mental state that Maxwell currently appeared to be in — he looked more depressed than he usually did during these certain days. "Um… Are you ok there, Max?"

"Yeah, I'm fine," he replied. "I just had something on my mind that's all. Thanks again, Sylv… I mean, Savanna."

It never failed that her boss would choose to submerse himself in his own little depressive world and ignore everyone else around him. And even though she knew that drowning in one's own self-pity was not a healthy thing for Maxwell to do, she was thankful that these occasional episodes generally lasted for only a day — once it had come and gone, her boss would then again be his normal self.

Recognizing that Maxwell just simply wanted to be left alone, Savanna tugged on the back of Sydney's shirt. Even though he somewhat objected to what his brother's secretary was trying to get him to do, he could see it in her eyes that he should comply with her wishes and leave his brother's office with her.

Next to a fresh cup of sim-caf, another part of Maxwell's morning ritual was to fire up his computer. Before his day could start, he always checked his E-mail and V-mail for any kind of news — good or bad. *'It's been twenty-five years, and I can still get depressed when I look at that picture of my wife and son. What the hell is wrong with me?'*

While his computer was booting up, he tried to think of something else instead of the past. As much as those moments of reminiscing could make him happy, they could also easily make him angry. With today being his birthday, he didn't want to be angry. So he closed his eyes, took another healthy sip of his morning sim-caf, and forced himself to think of something other than his family.

As soon as his computer was ready to use, he typed in his password and then he entered in his security access code. *'I don't know what it is about today, but for some strange reason, I just can't seem to concentrate on anything else but them.'* When Maxwell saw that he had an awaiting Vid-message that had been sent to him by his old friend, Christopher White, now the current Governor of Michigan, he hesitated — it was just one of those days, and he wasn't even sure that he wanted to see it. Another message containing nothing but bad news wasn't what he wanted to hear. But then again, it could be good news for a change. He just did not know.

Over the years, Maxwell had spoken with, and received many leads from his friend and former boss about his son. Yet, with each glimmer of hope that came his way, came a harder pill to swallow when that information turned out to be just another in a series of dead end roads and disappointments.

Maxwell got up from behind his desk, walked away from it, and then went over to his wall of achievements. He just stood there and reminisced, looking at all the awards and accommodations that he had received during his years as a police officer. After a few moments, he turned his attention to the framed newspaper clippings that hung on the wall next to his accolades. Those articles forever reminded him of that horrible night — one stupid mistake he made in an otherwise nearly impeccable career. If anything, those clippings should be kept in a box, but Maxwell had purposely put them on display. Like the family photo on his desk, those were also reminders of his promise to never give up hope that he will one day find his missing son.

Within only a few minutes of recalling that night, a few tears begin to inch down Maxwell's face. "I'm a fifty-five year old, strong willed man. I can't let anyone see me like this." Hastily deciding at that moment that he no longer wanted to have any reminder of that day displayed out in the open for him to see, Maxwell reached up and removed all those framed news clippings. He then brought them over to his desk, and along with the picture of himself, his wife and son, placed them all on top of the filing cabinet that was next to it. He knew by doing this that it wouldn't stop the hurt he was feeling — but at that moment, it was the only thing he could think of doing. "I have to pull myself together here... And I guess that I should stop talking to myself as well, for everyone truly might start to think that I have indeed gone senile."

Maxwell sat back down at his desk, finished off the remainder of his sim-caf, and then began trying to predict what this video message from his ex-boss could be all about. The way that his mind was working this morning, his assumptions were probably going to be way off. So instead of sitting there and wasting his morning speculating what the video message was all about, Maxwell just played it — a pop-up dialog box immediately appeared on the screen.

'Warning! Encrypted security file. Finger print scan is required to continue.'

That surprised Maxwell. Only once before had Christopher White sent him a message that had been encrypted. And whatever the reason was for this, Maxwell knew that it had to be really important to be protected from accidental or curious eyes.

So after successfully completing his digital fingerprint scan, he sat back in his chair and stared obtusely at his computer screen. Was this to be the news that he had been waiting all these years to hear? He did not know. He only knew that by the time he was done listening to what his friend had to say, his day was going to change — he just hoped that it was for the better.

It wasn't. After letting the contents of the message sink in, Maxwell sat frozen in his chair. To him, it felt as if the whole planet was only seconds away from imploding in on itself. The room stayed silent. First, a bit of shock gradually appeared on his face, and then his rage began to build up. This was not what he had expected to hear — at least, not for another five years. His day hadn't just changed; but his life had again — and just as drastically as it had all those years ago following the warehouse explosion.

Maxwell tried, but failed. He just couldn't hold in his anger any longer and he let out an unmerciful, profanity-laden scream that filled the entire agency. Sydney and Savanna jumped out of their seats and went rushing towards Maxwell's office. Sydney reefed open the door and abrasively asked, "What the hell is going on, Max? Is everything all right?"

Maxwell couldn't reign in the fury that consumed him. By the time his brother and secretary had crossed the threshold into his office, he had retrieved the framed news clippings from atop of the filing cabinet and had whipped them against the wall where they had for decades, hung — glass flew everywhere as the frames smashed against his police awards and accommodations. He then stomped over to that same wall and slammed his fist into it, unintentionally hitting his police medal of valor in the process, and slicing the knuckle on his right ring finger wide open.

That act alone however, did not alleviate his anger. He then pivoted away from the wall, took one step, and kicked the waste paper basket that sat beside his filing cabinet — it went clear across the room and it narrowly missed his brother's head as it sailed out through Maxwell's open office door.

"What the hell is wrong?" Savanna inquired.

Although he still wasn't completely himself, the rabid animal that had taken control of him had begun to relinquish its hold. A few unsettling moments later, Maxwell was able to compose himself enough where he could again exist in reality. "I can't believe that this is fuckin' happening?" His eyes drifted toward his hand and he finally noticed that he had sliced his knuckle up pretty good. But that, he didn't care about at that moment, as his whole world had just become even more messed up than it already was. "What a fuckin' birthday present this is!"

Sydney walked back into Maxwell's office after retrieving the garbage pail, as it had sailed clear across the lobby and had landed only a few feet from the front door. He set the now dented pail back down where it belonged, and then bravely placed his hand onto his brother's shoulder, looked at him with an easily readable concern on his face, and said, "Why don't you just take a moment, gather your thoughts, and then tell us both what the hell caused you to blow a gasket?"

Acknowledging that his brother was right, Maxwell bent over and picked up the smashed picture frames while at the same time, trying to settle his nerves. Once he had all of the damaged frames in his hands, he went back over to his desk, placed them onto the edge of it, and then sat down in his office chair. Next, he forced himself to take some long, deep, slow, methodical breaths. It helped, but he still wasn't ready to explain what had set him off. So he reached for his sim-caf and took a sip; he realized immediately that his cup was empty. His first thought was to throw the empty cup in annoyance, but instead, he set the cup back down on his desk, placed his hands over his face, and took a few more moments to compose himself.

Although he wasn't completely ready, he knew that he could not delay any longer because those who were in the room with him would surely know that something, other than an unwanted birthday celebration, was going on inside his head.

He invited Sydney and Savanna to take a seat in front of his desk. He then calmly began to explain to his brother and his secretary what had caused him to lose control. And by the time he was finished, they both understood why he had nearly destroyed his office.

"I can't believe that they're letting that bastard out of jail in three days? I thought Antonio Marcone's sentence wasn't up for another five years?"

"It's not, Sydney. He's not supposed to be eligible for parole at all."

"Couldn't your governor friend pull some strings to keep him incarcerated?" Savanna asked.

With his already knowing the answer to that question, Maxwell proceeded to explain to his brother and secretary that Christopher White had already attempted everything that he legally could to prevent Antonio Marcone's premature release from happening. But the man had gone and hired himself this young, hot shot lawyer; the same lawyer who was somehow able to persuade a jury, just a few years earlier, to find a well known politician not guilty of a love triangle double homicide.

"Somehow, Antonio Marcone's new lawyer, Howard 'Howie' Swindle, had been able to find and interpret, in a manner that was completely different than it was initially written to be comprehended, a small provision in the federal law. He used this to argue that during the initial trial, his client received bias, unfair, and unjust treatment from the authorities. He also made it clear that the national media had consistently embellished the facts — so much so, that their repeated slandering of his client had given Antonio an undeserved reputation before the trial even had a chance to begin. The last aspect of his

172

lawyer's argument, the one that all but solidified it, was it had never been disclosed that the daughter of a man, who once owned a business that Antonio had 'purchased', had sat on the jury. And because she had, the woman should have been disqualified from the responsibility due to the assumed animosity she more than likely had towards his client.

So, after the Michigan Supreme Court had heard Mr. Swindle's convincing argument, they had no other choice but to concede and grant Antonio Marcone his unconditional release. "The only reason that this bastard is not out of prison right now is because the governor has used every bit of his political power to delay that from happening. However, he won't legally be able to keep his imminent release from taking place unless he can find a loophole himself."

"But he doesn't think that he will be able to find one, does he?"

"No, Sydney, he doesn't."

Savanna got up out of her chair, left Maxwell's office, returning a few moments later with a first aid kit so that she could treat Maxwell's still bleeding knuckle. "Please tell me that you're not gonna do anything stupid? I really hope that you'll just forget about all of this."

Maxwell didn't answer his secretary; he just let her finish administering first aid to his hand. As soon as she was finished, he leaned back into his chair and placed his feet up onto his desk. At that moment, he wished that he still had some of his morning sim-caf left, as he really did not want to get out of his chair and go and get some more — and even though he was sure that Savanna would refill his cup for him if he asked her to, he wasn't about to impose his want on her. "I'm not quite sure what or if I'm going to do anything yet." He paused for a few moments, recognizing that a regrettable decision could easily be made with the state that his mind was still in — that was something that he knew he could not make.

Knowing now that he had a lot of thinking to do, he kindly asked Savanna and Sydney if they could leave his office. As much as he valued their opinion, this, he felt, was something that he had to figure out all on his own.

About an hour later, with his mind made up, Maxwell came out of his office. He then walked over to his brother and asked him to go to the storage room and retrieve all of the boxes that contained his old files on Antonio Marcone.

"What for? You're just gonna waste your time." For a moment, Sydney felt obligated to remind his brother that he had been over and over those files hundreds of thousands of times throughout the years. And even though he thought it would be worth it to try and get his brother to realize that he was just wasting his time, Sydney thought better of it. If this was what his brother wanted to do, then Sydney was going to let him. Like so many times before, he knew that Maxwell was not going to find anything new. He'd eventually get frustrated, and then quit. It was a vicious cycle that Sydney wholeheartedly believed would one day be the death of Maxwell. Hopefully though, before that happened, he prayed that his brother would finally see the immovable wall that was in front of him and just walk away from it forever.

Like Sydney, Savanna also knew that her boss was one day, going to attempt to take another stroll on down that well-travelled, yet precarious path. And as difficult as this was for her, she had long ago decided that she was never going to get in Maxwell's way. She was going to support him until whatever outcome there was, came from it — but that didn't mean that she was never going to keep her opinion about this mission of his, to herself.

"I know what everyone is thinking. And you're all probably right." Maxwell walked over to the sim-caf machine to finally refill his cup. "I haven't looked at these files in a few years. Maybe I am wasting my time, but maybe I will finally find that one clue that I have somehow, mindlessly overlooked."

With his fresh cup of sim-caf in hand, Maxwell returned to his office; a few minutes later, Sydney entered carrying three boxes of files — Savanna was directly behind him with two more boxes in her hands. They set them all down next to Maxwell's desk; each being tempted to say something at that moment that would be deemed discouraging — but neither decided to.

"While I'm going over all these files, I would like for you," Maxwell looked directly at Savanna, "to try to get me as much current information as you possibly can on all of the D.U.O.'s activities in which either Louie Mazotti and or Salvadore Batiste are involved in or connected to?"

"Sure, I can do that. But do you honestly think that will help you?"

"I don't know? But I'm hoping that maybe I can find some kind of pattern, similarity, or any microscopic trace linking the past to the present. Hell, it could just be some dumb luck. I don't care what it is. I'm just looking for the one thing that will lead me to where my son is or at least put that low-life asshole and his organization out of business for good."

Although it officially hadn't been said yet, Sydney was beginning to think that his older brother was actually preparing himself to once again, pursue Antonio Marcone — and if that were indeed the case, he would have a problem with it. Sydney's earlier decision had suddenly changed, as he no longer was going to support what he now believed his brother wanted to do. "Max! This obsession of yours is gonna get you killed... and I refuse to contribute to that happening." Sydney promptly turned about face and stormed out of his brother's office, slamming the oak-framed, smoked glass door behind him in the process.

It immediately became clear to Maxwell that his brother had an issue. In fact, he wasn't even sure if there was a way that he could convince him that this was what he needed to do — but he had to try nevertheless. He immediately followed his brother out of his office and, just before Sydney got to the front door, he said, "Syd! I thought you understood a long time ago why I do this every once in a while. You know very well that I essentially died twenty-five years ago and that I can't honestly begin to truly live until I am able to solve the mystery that surrounds my wife's death and my son's disappearance."

Maxwell was unaware, but Savanna had followed him and was now standing right by his side. She gently placed her left hand against Maxwell's arm and said, "I may not agree either with what it is that you now want to do, but I will do everything that I can to help you with this."

Some of Maxwell's burden instantly became lifted, now knowing that what believed he soon was going to do, would not be done all alone. But he wanted Sydney's help and support as well — he was after all, the only family that he had left. Unfortunately, he could see it in his brother's eyes that was not going to happen. Still, Maxwell knew that he had to try. "So what do you say, bro? Are you going to stay and help also? I really need you by my side on this one."

Although Sydney was totally against what his brother wanted to do, he knew deep down inside that this was more important to Maxwell than anything else could ever be. He knew that his brother really didn't care if he died fighting Antonio Marcone, and he understood that his brother could only exist in this world until his own brand of justice was served. All that he had to do was to be there to the end. Yet, he found it impossible to agree with what Maxwell clearly intended to do.

Sydney looked at his older brother, and being as honest as he had ever been, told him exactly how he felt. "You've searched everywhere and done everything that you possibly can to find Sabastian. I've come to terms with the fact that I'll never see my nephew again. And until you do, you'll only be a shell of a man whose desire for vengeance will consume what life you have left. I'm sorry, Max, but I cannot in good conscience, contribute to your obsession." Sydney then turned his back to his brother and promptly left the agency.

Maxwell stood there and watched his brother leave, cross the hall, and then enter the awaiting elevator. For a moment, he thought about going after him, but he decided against it. He just could not force his want on his brother — it was up to him to make that decision to help him on his own.

Working pretty much around the clock over the last seven days had taken its toll on Maxwell. His renewed enthusiasm to satisfy his personal want for revenge began to evaporate into the thin air of hopelessness as each day passed on by. *'Sydney was right,'* he thought. *'It doesn't matter how many times I look over these damn files or how many hours I spend on the phone or my computer following up on a trifling lead. I'm not going to ever find that one definitive clue that I so desperately need.'*

Maxwell put down what had been in his hand; a copy of classified documents that had been given to him by his former captain which detailed Colin Ramirez's time undercover. He then got up from his chair, walked over to the lone window in his office, and looked out at the city of San Antonio; his home for the last quarter century.

Though his complete view of it was somewhat obstructed by several tall office buildings, the brightly lit, early evening moon helped to enhance the already lit streets and made it easier for him to see deeper into its heart. And while he really liked this metropolis and had lived here longer than he had anywhere else, Detroit still felt like home — and he missed it. But home would never again be that place until what needed to be done, had been — and what had been missing, had been found. Only then, did Maxwell believe that he would be able to go back to the Motor City and live out the rest of his days the way he honestly felt he was supposed to.

He looked up at stars, then beyond them to the heavens. After a series of low-spoken, heartfelt apologetic words to his wife, he made a decision. Maxwell had enough. After holding out hope for all of these years, it was finally time he threw in the towel — there was no other option left for him but to surrender and admit defeat. *'That's it. There's no reason for me to keep stressing out like this. If I don't stop now, I'm going to lose what little dignity and self-respect that I have left. It's time for me to live out the rest of my life as best as I possibly can.'*

Maxwell went back over to his desk and hastily shut off his computer. He then went over to the threshold of his office, shut off the light, left his office door open, and informed Savanna as he was walking towards her that he was done — for good.

Relief enveloped her; although she wasn't about to let it show on her face. In all honesty, she had expected that Maxwell would eventually come to the realization that his latest crusade was just like all the others — but she also felt bad that she had not been able to help him find anything substantial during this latest round of searching for that all important, elusive clue.

Yes, he was tired, but Maxwell stayed behind anyway and waited for Savanna to shut everything off that needed to be: the sim-caf machine, her computer, and the rest of the agency's lights. He then picked up her purse from on top of her desk, handed it to her, and then they left together.

Maxwell was just about to put his key in the door to lock it when Savanna's vid-phone started beeping. "No need to wait for me. I'll go back in and answer this call and then lock up afterwards." If this call had come a minute later, they probably would have been in the elevator and halfway down to the ground floor. Instead, Savanna went back inside the agency to answer the call — Maxwell stayed behind in the hallway and waited for her. It wasn't as if she had never locked up by herself before, but Maxwell was a gentleman, and that is what a gentleman is supposed to do — wait for the lady to finish up what she was doing and then escort her either to her car or to her home.

Maxwell hadn't had to wait in the hallway for too long. Upon the conclusion of Savanna's conversation, with a slightly perplexed look that was prevalent on her face, she walked towards the agency door and unexpectedly, stopped just before the threshold. "Um... Maxwell. I think that you'd better come back inside. There is a guy on the phone who says that it's very important that he talk to you."

"Who is it?"

"Someone named, Chevy."

All of a sudden, a rush of energy consumed Maxwell as he bolted back into his agency faster than what a fifty-five year old body should be able to move — somehow, he had made it right passed Savanna without even bumping her.

Had the door to his office been closed, there would have been no way that Maxwell would have been able to do what he had just done. Like someone would do in the movies when they needed to get to the other side of the car in a hurry, he jumped and slid his ass across his L-shaped desk (the side without the computer on it); nearly pulling off a perfect landing right in his chair. However, if it were not for the fact that he had knocked over the majority of the disorderly piled mound of printed files about Antonio Marcone that he had left haphazardly stacked on either side of it, what he had done, had he been recording it, most certainly would have become the next viral video sensation.

By the time Maxwell had gained control of his swiveling chair, Savanna had transferred his old snitch to his vid-phone; to Maxwell's surprise however, the video portion of Chevy's call was blacked out. "It's about time that you finally located your balls and called me after twenty-five fuckin' years."

Savanna always respected Maxwell's privacy, except when the call that he was getting was just too good for her to ignore. However, under the circumstances, she understood that this call was different than the usual ones, so she decided that she should just mind her own business for once. Besides, she knew that she would hear all about the whole conversation shortly afterwards.

She quietly walked over to Maxwell's office and closed his door to give him some privacy. The moment she did, she got a funny feeling that her boss was about to get into a very heated, and intense thrashing of this Chevy person — that was also something she really did not want to be a witness to.

While she waited for Maxwell to finish, she took what was left of her now cold and really stale sim-caf that she had left on her desk and placed it in the micro-regenerator to re-heat and revive it. She was too tired to make a fresh pot, even though she knew that it would probably be a while before Maxwell would exit his office. To her surprise, Maxwell had completed his conversation in only ten minutes; much less time than what Savanna had anticipated.

Maxwell opened up his office door and invited his secretary to come inside. As soon as she had entered his office, she could immediately see a change in her boss's eyes — almost a radiant glow of excitement now filled them. "I don't ever seem to recall you mentioning anything to me before about someone you once knew named Chevy?"

"He was just another part of my past life that I wanted to keep buried. You know, deep down inside, I always believed that he had nothing to do with what had happened, but I also had to accept the fact that there was the possibility that he did."

"Um… then why during your conversation with him, did you accuse him of selling you out?" At that moment, Savanna realized that she had just admitted to her boss that she had been listening to his conversation, albeit unintentionally. The walls that separated his office from the lobby area were rather thin, and any loud conversations that took place were pretty easy to hear on either side.

"This was the first opportunity that I have had, since the day my whole life changed, to feel him out and see whether or not he had set me up."

"Did he?"

"Well… Seeing that I am a bit out of practice when it comes to getting people to divulge the information that I want, I had to wing it. Thankfully, after only a few minutes, my talent for doing that came right back to me. I pushed every button that I could think of. I went up one side of him and back down the other; led him in one direction and hoped that he'd bring me into another. Yet, he seemed to have an acceptable answer for each and every one of my questions."

"So why did he call you?"

Maxwell opened up his top desk drawer and took out a small box. He opened it up and removed a 'real' Cuban cigar from it. He then briefly held it up to his nose, enjoying its pleasurable scent. "Chevy said that he had never forgotten what had happened to me. And even though twenty-five years have since passed, he said that he still owed me. He knew that I would one day want revenge, even after having to wait all of these years for an opportunity to get it. He said that he had spent all of these years trying to collect whatever information that he could for me; information of which he hoped I could one day use against Antonio Marcone. But unfortunately, he said throughout most of that period of time, he was unable to accumulate anything really substantial — until now.

Now, with Antonio Marcone no longer being in jail, it was easy for him to assume, what I also assumed — Antonio immediately took back full control of his organization and has already started the process of expanding the D.U.O. beyond all imagination. And because of a long ago planned expansion now finally moving forward, Chevy said that he was able to acquire the information that I have been looking for that will allow me to take down the entire Detroit Underworld Organization."

"So what information does he have?"

"I don't know? Chevy has never divulged anything to me over the phone. But that is ok. I'm sure that I'll find out what he knows soon enough." Maxwell was happy that a victory, albeit a small and unconfirmed one, had finally come his way. And even though this new battle with Antonio Marcone had yet to begin, he felt like celebrating. So he removed the antique Zippo lighter from his top desk drawer, the one that his father and grandfather had both owned, and prematurely lit his victory cigar.

Sydney had only caught bits of Maxwell and Savanna's conversation, as he had just entered the agency a few moments earlier. After a lot of soul searching, Sydney had decided that he needed to apologize and make peace with his brother. "Did this Chevy person happen to say if he found out anything about your son?"

"Yes he did." Maxwell then proceeded to explain to everyone that Chevy had informed him that he was pretty sure that Sabastian was alive and that Antonio Marcone has known exactly where Sabastian has been all this time.

"Are you sure that you can trust this guy, Max?"

"Yes, well... Well, I think so." Maxwell looked over at his younger brother with an optimistic look on his face. "That doesn't matter now. All that matters is that I may finally have a chance to locate my son. No matter how dangerous it might get, I have to do this."

As much as Sydney wanted his brother to find his son, deep down inside he had an uneasy feeling about all that had just taken place. He realized his earlier mistake by not supporting his brother and not being there for him over the past week. Yet, he still wanted to throw caution to the wind, so he made certain that his opinion concerning this whole situation was known because Sydney honestly believed this sudden golden opportunity that had just conveniently fallen into his brother's lap, sounded more to him like another well planned trap than a long awaited miracle.

Maxwell walked over to his brother and placed his left arm across his shoulder. "You're probably right. I love you, Sydney, but... I hope that you understand why I now have to take this chance, and why I have to pursue this, no matter what the risk?"

Maxwell removed his arm from his brother's shoulder, walked back over to his desk, and picked up the cracked picture frame of himself, his wife and his son. Embracing the renewed purpose he suddenly felt, he handed the picture over to Savanna, asked her to get a new frame for the photo, and then left his office to go and face whatever it was that would be waiting for him — he just hoped, as he crossed the threshold of his office, that this would not be the last time that he would ever see Savanna and Sydney.

11

Although it was physically there, it almost seemed as if it no longer was. Over time, what had been a thriving haven for sports, entertainment, the arts, industry, and populace, slowly progressed into a mere representation of a city that admittedly had allowed dust and cobwebs to accumulate on its mantle. And even though what is now there has for the most part, existed for generations, those who have always looked on from afar, still tended to make fun of it due to their own misinformed opinion. For the ones who have been born and raised within its boundaries however, they are never ashamed to announce where they were from — and that is why they collectively display on that same mantel, the abundance of successes that have been achieved.

There was a time when an honest attempt was made to remove that dust and those cobwebs, but something unwanted had gotten in the way of that ever being completed. Now, a gradual decrease in the metropolis' residency seems unable to be halted. The city certainly is not dead by any means, but it has now become nothing more than just a place where you work or have fun in.

Similar to Las Vegas, the district of New Woodward never closes up shop — not even on a holiday. Most of the businesses that operate there either are funded, supported, or fully owned and operated by the Detroit Underworld Organization — a corporate enterprise that began with a vision, driven by the greediness that Antonio Marcone insists is nothing more than just he doing his part to help to change the city for the better.

Shortly after he had first taken control of the D.U.O., Antonio began to execute his plan — it was long term, but within a few years, it had begun to take shape. Business after business in the downtown core became his via many unethical methods; methods that he had first learned to use courtesy of Colin Ramirez — that damn disingenuous cop.

Antonio's arrest and thirty year sentence should have prevented him from achieving his dream — but it didn't. In fact, his conglomerate had grown enormously during his years behind bars, all thanks to two of his closest associates who had been tasked with running the daily operations of the D.U.O. for him by proxy.

It could not be denied what Antonio had achieved, as he had been able to change the entire landscape of the city of Detroit from his prison cell. And because he had, not only had the financial incursion into the city that followed more than tripled what it had been just ten years prior, but the long ago earned stigma that it had; one that its citizens so desperately wanted to erase from existence, had finally begun to show signs that it just might actually disappear. However, there was still a good portion of the city that had not changed. Those areas still suffered from the same issues that it always had: abandoned buildings, poverty, drug usage and dealings, and excessive crime. Nevertheless, for the first time in at least six mayoral terms, the city was comfortably in the black. There wasn't an abundant surplus, but the financial future of the city finally seemed to be headed in the right direction. That meant, so long as no one fucked it up, within the next decade, the city would finally be able to step up and start addressing all of its visible issues without someone like Antonio Marcone having to again, do it for them.

Those who were in political positions or positions of influence: the mayor, city council, and the chief of police, didn't want to admit it, but they had Antonio Marcone to thank. His New Woodward district had become a pillar of success. The area was inundated with nightclubs, restaurants, concert halls, casinos and mega movie theaters. Not only that, day or night, those who went there never had to worry about their own safety.

Still, there were businesses within the area that were less than desirable for some. For others, it was the only reason that they went to the area, as it was the closest thing that there was to a Red Light District on this side of the pond. The sex industry was well represented — and it was usually fairly cheap: strip bars, peep shows, massage parlors, live sex clubs, private swingers' clubs, bordellos, and even the world's first, near life-like, holographic adult simulator.

Of course, right smack dab in the middle of all of that, was the spectacular, fully renovated, and recently expanded, New Book Cadillac Hotel and Casino. Not only had Antonio finally gotten his hands on what he had long ago wanted, but it had also become the centerpiece to Antonio's little empire. And although the hotel itself had been a main part of the organizations enterprises for years, the D.U.O. didn't move its operations to the top floor until its renovation was completed just a few short weeks ago.

Today, all of the accredited members of the organization were scheduled to gather there for an official welcome home party for their leader. But before everyone's scheduled arrival, Antonio had called an impromptu meeting.

"Let me be the first one to officially welcome you back home."

"Why, thank you, Sal. Now, get the hell out of my damn chair! I may have been incarcerated for a quarter of a century, but that didn't mean that you had earned the right to claim the command chair. I still ran this organization from that hellhole, and now look what this city has become. If I were you, I'd make sure I never allow that kind of false sense of security to enter into your absent mind again. Do you understand me?"

"Yes sir, Mr. Marcone." Although Sal didn't think he deserved to be ridiculed and chastised like that, he slightly lowered his head to make it appear as if he was indeed sorry for what he had done.

Louie snickered to himself, yet loud enough for Sal to also hear it.

For the most part, Sal and Louie had gotten along fairly well during their shared, long term responsibilities of running the daily operations of the organization. But there had been plenty of times over the years when Sal just wanted to quietly arrange for Louie's disappearance so that he alone could be in charge. But he smartly refrained from letting his emotions dictate his actions, as his own long term ambitions required that he use his common sense in order to one day achieve what he wanted. However, with a lot less responsibility now weighing on his shoulders, Sal's years of frustrations had quickly begun to surface. It took all that he had at that moment to suppress how he truly felt about Louie's constant personal attacks on him. Yes, he wanted to freely express exactly what was going on in his mind, but

Sal wasn't sure if Antonio had built up any more of a tolerance towards his and Louie's rivalry. Instead, he decided that he should just play it safe for the moment and send Louie a simple, clear warning, by shooting him a look that could not be misinterpreted.

Seeing that the animosity between his two associates was still there after all these years, Antonio quickly interjected. "I'm going to warn you two right now. I don't want to hear, nor bear witness to any of your petty bickering. That was the only good thing about being locked away for as long as I was; I never had to be subjected to the two of you going at each other's throats. I would have assumed by now, that after all of this time, you both would have been able to find a way to work out your differences and learned to get along."

With that now off of his chest, Antonio took a seat for the first time in his new office, in his brand new chair. It felt great to no longer be forced to sit on the edge of a prison cot, but instead a finely crafted, European synth-leather chair. "Now... we've got some important matters that need to..."

There was a knock at the door; it caused Antonio to stop in mid-sentence. Louie got up from where he had been sitting and went to see who was there. He didn't act surprised to the unexpected presence of their visitor — it was as if he had fully expected the arrival of the man now standing at the threshold to Antonio's office. "Roy!" Louie extended his hand. "Come on in."

Antonio was not at all impressed that Louie had invited this stranger to his office; a man whom he absolutely did not know, nor was even sure that he wanted to. "Who in the fuck is this scrawny, odd little prick, Louie?"

"Antonio. Let me introduce you to Mr. Roy Chevalier. He has been an invaluable asset to this organization; a man who has surreptitiously been our eyes and our ears in this great city, and has been a vital part of helping us to expand our empire to what it has become today."

Roy extended his hand to greet Antonio, but coldly, he didn't receive one back. "Um... It's a pleasure to finally meet you, sir. I mean... after working for you for all these years."

'Huh?' Antonio sat there confused, as he had absolutely no idea what this man was talking about. 'Invaluable asset to this *organization — surreptitiously been our eyes and ears,'* he thought to himself, as he leaned back in his chair, trying to understand what was going on. He really didn't know what to think other than Louie had apparently been keeping more secrets from him, secrets that seem to appear to be very questionable.

Without openly showing his displeasure, he looked at Louie with a 'please explain now' glare; a glare that instantly made Louie realize he had better have a damn good reason as to why he had decided to 'employ' this person without first getting the ok.

Antonio sank back even further into his chair and listened to Louie as he explained his reasons for the recruitment. First, he began by explaining that Roy had actually approached him on the street shortly after Antonio's arrest, volunteering his services to help the organization in any way that he could. When that happened, Louie had just ignored the offer. But then during the initial planning stages of that now famous explosion, he had come to realize that he needed to intentionally leak some information out on the street. A few days later, Louie was luckily able to locate Roy and had asked him to do a small favor for the organization — a test run that Mr. Chevalier had executed perfectly. And because he had done exactly what had been asked of him, Louie's uncertainty of the man's worthiness had seemingly changed.

Over time, Roy had proven himself to the organization; he had become someone whom Louie felt was an invaluable asset. The man's innate ability to acquire or distribute information was something that Louie felt few have ever had the ability to do. The only one he knew of who even came close to him, had been Jimbo — unlike their old 'business associate' however, Roy had never sold them out.

But Louie's opinion of the man didn't mean anything. It was up to him to make sure that Antonio saw what he saw, so he did his best to make sure that it was understood that not only had Mr. Chevalier been loyal to the organization, but has always completed whatever task he had been asked to perform without ever once questioning why he was being asked to do what he was.

Even Sal felt the need to throw in his two-cent's worth; he surprisingly backed Louie's endorsement — that alone, caused Antonio to have to reassess his initial opinion. "Is this true?" Antonio leaned forward in his chair and looked straight into the eyes of Roy Chevalier.

"Yes it is, sir. And I personally hope that your lack of awareness about the working agreement I have with your organization will not affect the possibility of any future endeavors together. I would very much be content to continue to assist you and your organization whenever, or whatever it may be that you would require me to do."

Quietly in thought, Antonio continued to stare at Roy, trying to figure out this enigmatic man. Although he was still pissed off and unsure of what he should do, he was smart enough not to hastily dismiss the backing of his associates. Yes, he was not at all impressed that neither Louie nor Sal had ever bothered to mention to him that this man would occasionally help his organization, but in hindsight, it may have been for the best that Antonio did not know about Roy, as he more than likely would have drawn an erroneous assumption based not only upon the way the man looked, but because of the fact that the wool had once before, been pulled over his eyes.

After a moment of thought, Antonio decided to take another chance — he just hoped that what his associates were claiming, was indeed true and that this was not going to end up biting him in the ass like the 'Manual' situation had.

He got up from behind his desk and walked over to the safe that was located in the corner of his office. He opened it up and took out an antique cigar box. Antonio then opened up the box and removed a rather large Cuban cigar. After lighting the cigar, he proceeded to place inside the box an A.I.M. (Antonio Ignatius Marcone) Enterprises V.I.P. Membership Card.

"Mr. Chevalier," Antonio said as he closed the lid on the cigar box and slid it over to him. "I placed inside this box a small token of appreciation in recognition of your past services — a gold A.I.M. V.I.P. scan card with which you may use at all of my fine establishments. Show this card to the manager and you'll be taken care of. There is also an insurance policy inside this box that I trust you will use if you are ever in a situation in which you need to protect the knowledge that you have accumulated over the years concerning us and our business practices."

"Of course, sir. I always protect what I know and whom I work for. That is why your associates have continually trusted me over the years."

"I have to assume then, that you have been well compensated for all of your contributions to the organization?"

"Yes... I have been well taken care of. And please let me take this opportunity, Mr. Marcone, to thank you again for your kind generosity."

Antonio smiled. He then let Roy know that he and his talents were going to be needed again in the very near future, and that Louie would be in contact with him as soon as the details of his task had been worked out.

Unsure if he should say anything or not, but believing that it was necessary to share what he knew, Roy informed Antonio that he had already been asked by Louie, several days before his release from prison, to leak the word out on the street, that he was going to be getting out early. "I'm sure that by now, the last surviving cop that was responsible for putting you in jail is already aware of your release and is probably on his way here."

Again, Antonio looked in the direction of Louie. This time, it was obvious to everyone in the room that he was not going to let his number one associate off the hook for his impetuousness. "What the hell are you trying to do... make it look like I am no longer capable of making the correct decisions?"

"Not at all, boss. I just figured that this was the first thing that you would want to do when you got out. So I just sped along the process a little bit."

"It was but... If you ever overstep your authority again, I may have to reassess my decision from long ago." Antonio looked over at Sal for only a brief second, but that was long enough for him to understand what he was thinking — and he quietly hoped in that moment that his boss would actually flip-flop he and Louie in the organizational chain of command. "Just remember, this organization does not yet belong to you, Louie. I still make all of the decisions around here." Antonio sunk back down in his chair and then waited a moment to make sure that no other surprises came his way before he said to both of his associates, "You may now start making all the necessary arrangements that are needed for Banks' demise. I, on the other hand, am going to get some lunch before the rest of our guests arrive. Mr. Chevalier, would you please stay and partake in my official welcome home party this afternoon? I would like to introduce you to the rest of the family."

"Thank you for extending me the invitation, Mr. Marcone. But I regretfully will have to ask for a rain check this time. I have a previous engagement that I cannot miss."

"Another time perhaps, Mr. Chevalier." This time, Antonio reached out across his desk and shook Roy's hand. "I'm sure that Louie will be in touch with you soon."

Roy then left the office.

While all of this was going on, Sal had just sat back and kept to himself, observing and patiently waiting for Roy to leave. "I'm not too sure if I like him or not, boss. He is an odd fellow who tends to come off as being a bit too smooth. Although he has never once screwed us over, I still really don't trust him that much."

"I'm not too sure if I trust him either, Sal, but he so far has shown me the respect that I deserve. And even though I do not know the man at all, I have a feeling that he is not the type of individual who would crack an unnecessary joke in order to break the ice."

Louie just sat there, chuckling under his breath, knowing that Antonio was referring to his associate's reputation for putting his foot in his mouth.

Sal turned and looked at Louie, trying his best not to explode. For all of the verbal abuse he has had to put up with over the years, he so wanted to lunge forward at that moment and shove his fist down the man's throat. But like he had always done, he regretfully restrained himself from doing so.

"Relax, Sal." With everything seemingly now in order, Antonio requested that both of his associates leave his office. Before everything that was planned for this evening took place, he wanted to enjoy a bit of peace and quiet — especially considering that he was going to have to mingle with all of the members of the D.U.O.; some who he hardly knew, and others whom he has not seen or spoken with in two and a half decades.

From the moment he had stepped onto the plane until the moment it had landed, Maxwell had trouble controlling his nerves. Never in his entire life had he been this much of a mess. He was literally the rock of Gibraltar during the birth of his son compared to the wreck that he was now, as he had spent half of the three hour flight locked inside the latrine, and the other half of it drinking sim-caf. He was an admitted disaster. He had even felt sorry for, and continuously apologized to the stewardess who had to put up with his sudden bout of ADD.

As soon as his flight had landed in Detroit, Maxwell hastily moved to the front of the plane, barely waiting for the exit door to open. Literally, he flew through the airport terminal and quickly picked up his bags; hoping in the process that he had grabbed the right ones.

Once he had his luggage, he hastily made his way to the nearest car rental counter. It had dawned on him just before his flight landed in Detroit that he had all but forgotten to have Savanna book him a rental car. So, using his internal radar, he quickly spotted the shortest line and hoped that they had something left that wasn't embarrassing for him to be seen in.

Normally, Maxwell was a very patient individual — but not today. Indiscreetly, he knifed his way through the awaiting renters, as he just wanted to get on the road as soon as he could — but in doing what he had, had unintentionally knocked over one of the two Nuns that were about to step up to the counter. "I'm really sorry Sisters, but I really need to rent a car, fast. It's a life and death emergency," he lied. "If you can find it in your blessed hearts, please forgive me and say as many Hail Mary's as you can. Lord knows that I will probably need them."

Before the holy women could decide whether or not to allow his cutting in front of them, Maxwell had stepped right up to the counter. He then rented himself a new tenth anniversary, Chevrolet Firebird; a car that started out decades earlier as a fantasy concept hybrid Firebird / Camero — a car that only went into production because of the enormous amount of public pressure the manufacturer was receiving to actually build it.

Maxwell's rental was painted cobalt black and had a slightly lighter black colored, holographic like silhouette of the famous 'Screaming Chicken' decal on the hood. It wasn't his intent to stick out like a sore thumb, but Maxwell just wanted to get where he needed to go as fast as he could.

From the airport, he headed straight to the State Capital Building in Lansing, Michigan, so that he could meet up with the Governor — his old friend. An hour and twenty minutes later, he arrived and the unsettled nerves that he had since his trip began, had all but disappeared. Still, he was admittedly quite a bit apprehensive about seeing his ex-boss again — it had been way too many years and he wasn't even sure what he would say to him.

In all the time that Maxwell had lived and worked in the State of Michigan, he had never been to the State Capitol Building — he was as anxious as any regular citizen would be to see the inside of it. And even though he personally knew the governor, he still felt completely out of place.

After a few minutes of confusion and some guide map deciphering, Maxwell found where he needed to go. He entered the main anteroom and immediately was stopped in his tracks — not by any security but by the most stunningly beautiful young woman he had seen in a number of years. Her face was near porcelain pure with only the faintest of freckles scattered sporadically across her profile. Her red brown hair was unevenly cut and styled; yet it perfectly accented her features — but it was her sea green eyes that gave her that irresistible and exotic look.

The pace of Maxwell's heart instantly quickened, his face became a bit flush, and his breathing grew slightly erratic. Those juvenile desires of years gone by had unexpectedly resurfaced, igniting his dormant hormones. However, his brain took over a few moments later, allowing him to realize just how big of an age gap there was between him and this woman. He shook his head; ashamed of himself for thinking like a teenage boy with a one-track mind. He was old enough to be that young woman's father and he certainly did not want to unintentionally submit his application for membership into the club for 'Dirty Old Men'.

Suddenly feeling as if he should be guilty of 'almost' committing a crime against the majority societal view, he quickly gathered himself and cleared his unabated thoughts before he approached the young lady with a respected, business-like veneer. "Hello, there. I've come to see the Governor. Would it be possible for me..?"

"Excuse me!" The receptionist stated, with an obviously intended attitude behind her words. "How in the hell did you get passed our security?"

"I, uh..." Maxwell didn't have an answer to that question. So he took a moment and quickly reviewed his memory, realizing that not one security guard in this government building even looked at him in a suspicious manner the entire way up to the governor's office. *'That's real odd,'* he thought to himself. "I'm sorry if I happen to have caused a problem. But I have traveled a long way to get here and I only wish to see the governor for a few minutes." Maxwell then tried his best, unsuccessfully at that, to convince this young lady that the governor was an old friend of his and that they had known each other for more than thirty years.

"Yes, I'm sure that you two are old friends. Did you know that being the governor's personal secretary has allowed me the opportunity to meet some very distinguished people? For example, the First Lady and I have become pretty close friends. In fact, at least once a month we'll shoot either a round of golf or play a few games of tennis together whenever the president and the governor get together for meetings. And I'll bet that you also didn't know that I actually just got back from England and had the privilege of having lunch with King William and Queen Kate."

"Oh... I didn't know that the First..." Maxwell paused, for he realized in mid reply that this young woman was feeding him a bunch of bullshit. There was no First Lady currently in the White House because the President of the United States was a woman. "You know... You didn't have to insult my intelligence like that."

"Listen, Mister. I don't know how in the hell you got in here without running into our security, but you aren't going to see the governor without first making an appointment. I get at least a dozen people a week trying to get in to see the governor claiming to be old chums of his. He's a very busy man and he's got no time to see just anybody off the street with some stupid complaint. So you might as well just turn right around and go back through the door from which you came through before I have you physically removed from the entire premises."

A distinguished, familiar voice echoed from a man as he turned the corner at the end of the hall and walked in the direction of the lobby area; a voice that instantly brought back many memories for Maxwell: memories of trust, respect, admiration, loyalty, friendship — and memories of having a lot of fun. "Sylvia, could you please get me..?"

The man stopped in mid question and stood aghast. What he saw just a few feet in front of him was someone that he wasn't sure he'd ever see again. He just stared at Maxwell and smiled, instantly collapsing inward all of the time that had passed. He could tell that the years had not been too kind to his old friend, yet he could still see that dynamic presence that he always radiated. "I had a feeling that a day was going to come when you uninvitingly showed up here."

Maxwell could not help but crack a smile. "I just wanted to see if I could get under your, now old and wrinkled skin, one more time."

The governor stood there with a disgruntled look on his face. He knew that Maxwell was just razzing him, but those memories of every headache he had that was caused by Maxwell's and Joshua's childishness, to this day, still irritated him.

"Come on, Chris. You miss our old bonding sessions, don't you?"

The governor's secretary kept quiet — even though she wanted to chime in with a comment. For once, someone who claimed to be an old friend to her boss had apparently been telling the truth. So she just kept to herself and watched with interest as two people renewed an old friendship, and wondering just how many interesting stories were shared between them.

Maxwell glanced over at Christopher's secretary and could tell that her opinion of him had immediately changed — no longer did she appear to be against him. This now meant that he could possibly influence her to join him on his side of the merry-go-round. So, with a

194

slight scheming tone to his voice, Maxwell said to her, "You know, if you ever feel the urge to piss off the captain… uh, I mean the governor, just let your phone ring over and over and over again. Then, when he comes out of his office all pissed off, just offer to go out and get him some fresh sim-caf and a bran muffin. Keep doing it every other day and eventually you'll have him trained. And then once you have that preverbal leash around his neck, you'll be able to get anything you want, whenever you want it. Ain't that right, sir?"

The governor walked up towards Maxwell, shook his hand and then lightly embraced him. "Unlike you, my old friend, I have a secretary who respects me and hasn't an evil, mischievous bone in her body."

"Maybe not yet, but now that your secretary and I have met, I can begin her training in the fine art of 'understanding how to expertly annoy the living hell out of your boss — and still keep his respect of you'." Maxwell looked at his ex-boss and cracked a slightly twisted, devilish grin — just like he used to.

"I appreciate your willingness, Mr. Banks. Right now however, I'll pass. But if things do happen to change around here, then I may take you up on your offer."

The governor looked at his secretary with a slight bit of surprise on his face. He wasn't sure how to take those unexpected words that just came out of her mouth. Since she had started working for him just over a year ago, she had never given him any indication whatsoever of having a malicious bone in her body. So after only a few moments of deductive thought, the governor just assumed that she was only trying to add a little humor to the moment.

He shrugged it off and then officially introduced Maxwell to his secretary, Sylvia Winslow, the daughter of their old chief of police, Jacob Winslow. Instantly, Maxwell's brain began to rip though the cobwebs that had encased his mind as he began to put together the pieces. He remembered the day he went to the precinct to resign his commission. That was when he had been informed by the man now standing in front of him, that the chief and his wife had named their new born baby girl in memory of his deceased wife. That had also been the last moment that Maxwell could remember feeling any sort of pride, any kind of joy.

A smile appeared on Maxwell's face; a genuine one that hadn't been there in decades, as emotions of his contentment now gleamed in his eyes. He went around uninvited to the other side of Sylvia's desk and he gingerly took her by the hand while placing a traditional French greeting upon both of her cheeks. "It is a pleasure and an honor to finally meet you, Sylvia… Miss Winslow."

After that Kodak moment was over, the governor escorted Maxwell down the hallway to his office so that they could privately catch up on old times. As soon as Maxwell entered the governor's office, his attention was immediately drawn to an old oil painting hanging up on the wall right behind Christopher's desk. This intrigued Maxwell, so he strolled up to it and studied it.

It was a vibrant rendition of what the city of Detroit had once looked like at the beginning of the twenty-first century. This brought Maxwell back in time and made him instantly feel as if the missing two and a half decade gap that was part of his existence had been abruptly closed. A flood of memories suddenly returned to him; some good and some bad. He missed those days; missed his partner and all his quirks. He missed the people in the inner city, even though back then it had a reputation of not being one of the safest places to live in — yet, he would argue that there was a driving spirit within its citizens that surpassed those who lived in more reputable metropolises. He had always felt proud to call himself a Detroiter, even though he had been born in Canada. But then came that day that he would never forget, the day that had changed everything. Yet, even with all the time that had passed, coming back to the State of Michigan; coming back home had been harder than what he had thought it would be.

After his few moments of reflection had passed, he returned to reality and moved his eyes away from the painting. If he had continued to look at it any longer, he was certain that more unpleasant memories of the past would begin to resurface — that's not why he had come back here.

He shuffled his body a few paces to the left. There he stood and stared out of the adjacent window, comprehensively dissecting the city below. "I can't believe how times have changed since we were enforcing the law. Things are so much easier for the police now. You rarely see a patrol car around unless there is a bust or something going down. And that only occurs because most major cities are now wired for sound. No one can even fart without the law knowing. I mean, where is the fairness in that?"

"I don't know, Max? But we all know that life isn't fair. So.., I guess you can blame me for some of that."

"Blame you?" Maxwell turned about face and looked bewildered at his former boss. "What the hell are you talking about, Chris?"

The governor sat down at his desk and encouraged Maxwell to take up a seat directly in front of him. "About eleven or so years ago, when I was the chief of police, just before the D.U.O. began to amalgamate the whole damn city at will, things in Detroit had started to get severely out of control. It was my suggestion to the then Mayor, Janet Ackerman, that her city be one of the first three to volunteer for the federal government's experimental **C-4** (**C**entralizing and **C**ontrolling **C**itywide **C**rime) project."

For a crime-ridden city like Detroit, this was the perfect tool that had long-since been needed, a state-of-the-art surveillance system that claimed to be able to 'blow away' crime. From Telegraph Road to Grosse Point Park to Eight Mile Road, the entire city was blanketed with wireless micro-digital cameras; cameras that came with military grade, nighttime image capabilities, and were discretely positioned at nearly every intersection. And the sound quality that came with them was just as precise as the digital images they took. In fact, the microphones were so sensitive that you could actually, if you were bored, listen to a rat scurrying around in the underground sewers below. But the biggest advantage to those cameras was that every one of them, at any time, was available upon demand to every police cruiser.

In some of the more dodgy areas of the city, like the area once known as the 'Dead Zone', robotic micro-isolate taggers were placed right beside those cameras. It gave the authorities an advantage, allowing them to be able to shoot a dangerous suspect with a micro-tracking tag so that they not only didn't lose them, but didn't have to put themselves in harm's way because once someone was tagged, they could safely track them until the right moment presented itself for the suspect to be apprehended. But that was not the only thing that the C-4

197

network was capable of. It also allowed every vital area within the city to be assured that it was fully protected from any type of terrorist threat: the airports, every government building, sporting complexes, and every public gathering venue had also been secured with the addition of chemical sniffers, and infrared and digital facial scanners. To the majority of the residence of the City, the C-4 network had finally given them piece of mind — to others, mainly those who were chartered members of the handful of known activist organizations, they felt that the security network infringed on everyone's right of privacy and freedom. Because of this, there had been a few instances; during an investigation and during an organized protest, where the police had to be extra careful to ensure that nobody's human rights were ever violated.

Maxwell sat there silent for a moment, looking at his old friend. He could tell by the offset smile on Christopher's face that his suspicions had been confirmed. Now knowing everything that he did about the C-4 network, it became obvious to him that his ex-boss had known long before he had shown up on his doorstep that he was coming to visit. And he was pretty sure that it was also why he was able to walk right into the State Capitol Building as easily as he had — Governor White had been alerted of Maxwell's pending arrival via that same C-4 network.

"So yes, before you even ask, I knew the moment you landed at the airport that you were coming, Max. When I had sent you the video message about Antonio's parole, I figured that you would eventually show up here. So I used my clout as governor and had homeland security flag your name and image for any incoming flights. The thing is… Antonio Marcone probably knows that you are here as well."

"How would he know?"

"No matter how high tech the city gets, we still can't seem to shut down anything that the D.U.O. is doing. They are always one step ahead of everything and everyone. I mean… it has yet to be confirmed, but we do believe that they have a former N.S.A. computer tech on their payroll who has successfully hacked into the C-4 system."

'Well.., that's gonna make things a bit more difficult for me,' Maxwell thought.

Christopher didn't need the C-4 system to find out why Maxwell had come back to Detroit; he already knew that he had returned here for one specific reason. And in all honesty, he didn't know how he felt about it. "I know why you are here, Max. And I can identify with the desire that you have to seek your revenge against Antonio Marcone. But as your friend, I'd really wish that you'd reconsider your intentions."

"You know as well as I do that this is long over do."

Christopher could not deny that. He wanted revenge as much as Maxwell did, but the position he currently held meant that his hands were tied together tighter than a military knot could be. "That's not the point, Max. You have no idea what you are getting yourself into. And you can almost guarantee that you'll be watched like a hawk — by the law and the enemy. You'll never be able to get away with it."

"Do you really think I care about that, Chris? I don't! I've waited twenty-five years to get justice, and that is what I am going to get."

"Sorry, Max. But I, as governor of this state, cannot condone what you came here to do. And as your long time friend, I really wish that you would reconsider."

Maxwell leaned forward in his chair and looked into his old friend's eyes. "Listen, Chris. I never came here to ask you for permission or your help. You knew the day would come that I was going to seek my revenge. And that is why I came here first, to ask you as my friend, to do one last favor for me. We both made mistakes that have haunted us to this day; mistakes that must be corrected."

That was also something that Christopher White could not dispute. But he just wasn't sure that his heart was willing to let him push aside his obligations in order to have all those past wrongs, righted.

"Not only is this personal for me, but there are still four families out there who have yet to gain any sort of closure. They, like I, deserve justice. Colin's paralyses should not be ignored; Aaron's, Charles' and Joshua's deaths should not be ignored, as none of these crimes have been paid for.

"I know, but…"

"But what? You know as well as I do that this can no longer go on. And I personally, really don't care if this turns out to be a suicide mission… so long as I take out that bastard and his two stooges with me."

The governor got up from his chair, turned his back to Maxwell, and then looked at the painting of the old city of Detroit. He really didn't look at it for any particular reason, but like Maxwell, he began to think back to a time when the city actually meant something to him. He tried to put in perspective just what it was that he was feeling at that moment — but he still wasn't sure.

Like the situation that he was faced with, his mind had trouble differentiating between what he should do with what he wanted to do. He closed his eyes, took a few moments of unremitting thought, and tried to understand why his friend suddenly had a death wish, and why he found it so difficult to allow that to occur.

Still unsure of how he felt, Christopher turned to face his old friend and looked at him with complete confusion. "Max. I'm the Governor of Michigan. I have a responsibility to uphold the law, just like when I was a police officer. As much as I agree that Antonio Marcone and the D.U.O. have to be permanently shut down, and that they need to pay for what they have done, I'm finding it difficult to understand how it is that you can expect me to help you all but put the rope around your neck?"

"I might get skinned, but I doubt that I will get lynched."

Christopher closed his eyes and just shook his head. Even after all these years, Maxwell still felt the need to insert a little levity when something serious was being discussed. Not wanting to reprimand his old friend for comments that he felt were unnecessary, Christopher turned away from Maxwell and walked across the room over to his personal wet bar. Once he got there, he poured himself a healthy shot of Wolfhead premium whiskey. "You've put me in a difficult position, Max. I'm not sure that I can help you, knowing that you intend to go and kill someone in cold blood; and knowing that you don't care if you die instead of the enemy."

"Oh boy, here we go. You haven't been my boss for... how many years? Yet, at this very moment, you still don't think that I know what I'm doing... or even believe in me. All that I'm asking for is a small favor. Besides, I seem to recall that you still owe me one."

"Excuse me?" replied the governor, as he quickly polished off his snifter of whiskey. "I don't recall ever owing you a favor."

"Sure you do, Chris. It has been a long time though. That dye job of yours must have seeped through to your brain and severely affected your memory, so I can understand why you don't remember owing me this favor."

Irritated, the governor reached up to the bridge of his nose and rubbed it with his right thumb and index finger. He wasn't going to win this time, and he knew it. Only because he had the utmost respect for Maxwell did Christopher decide to recant his position and give in to his request — he just hoped that he wasn't adding another mistake to the list of the ones that were already on his résumé.

Maxwell was happy. His old friend had given him his word that he would do everything that he possibly could to keep the law off of his back — too bad their wasn't a way to prevent the D.U.O. from knowing that he was here and was coming for them. He even willingly accepted Christopher's unwavering position that followed his agreement, where he declared that this was going to be the very last time that he would ever ignore his obligations in order to do what Maxwell asked of him — he did this only because he honestly believed that this was going to be the last time that he was ever going to see his old friend alive.

"Oh... and I will not pull your ass out of the pile of shit that I am all but certain you will get buried in.

"I seem to remember, Chris, you once said to me that I had already accumulated a mound that was almost as tall as the Renaissance Center. What's wrong with me adding a little more to my world record? Besides, it'll be over with before you know it. And I promise that my mess will be bagged and disposed of like it's supposed to be."

"Why don't I believe that?" The governor replied, knowing full well that every time Maxwell did something, it not only became front page news, the entire country knew about it.

Maxwell extended his hand; Christopher reciprocated. In that moment, the handshake meant more to him than it typically should, as it not only was a gesture that forever sealed a very unique friendship, it was a forever goodbye. "Listen Chris, I never told you this before, but out of every one of us that ever worked together, you were the only one I felt would one day make a great captain. I just never expected that it would have occurred so soon in your career."

"Neither did I. Take care, Max. It's been great to see you again after all these years. And please be careful." The governor meant every word that he had just said, even though his heart was telling him that he and his old friend were never going to cross paths again.

Content, Maxwell walked out of the governor's office. However, before he left the State Capitol Building to go to his next appointment, he made sure to stop at Sylvia's desk to say goodbye — it was a shame that he was not going to ever get a chance to get to know his wife's namesake better. But Maxwell had made his decision, and he was happy inside knowing that by proxy, a small part of his wife would live on.

After watching his old friend walk down the hall toward the exit, the governor returned to his desk and paperwork. Too himself, he then said as he sat, *'Owe him a favor? Where the hell does he get off thinking that I still owe him any kind of favor?'*

It was approaching mid-afternoon and for once in his life, Maxwell had arrived at the meeting place first. He wanted to make sure that it was he who had the upper hand when he met Chevy at the abandoned Marathon gas station on Michigan Ave. The place was boarded up and it looked and smelt like it had caught fire not too long ago.

While waiting, his mind once again began to challenge his belief of Chevy's loyalty. Since the day he had first met him, he never had any reason to doubt the man as being anything but a trustworthy friend. Yet, with everything that had happened, and with all the time that had passed, Maxwell's mind began to manufacture artificial memories. Sifting through all those false recollections and dismissing them had become an even harder task to accomplish the longer the actual facts stayed undisclosed. And even though he knew that he had to approach this meeting with an open mind, seeds of doubt had already been firmly planted into his brain.

After doing all that he could think of to shake those amalgamated thoughts from his mind, he looked at his watch and realized that it was nearly three p.m. Immediately, his doubts were once again attempting to convince him of the unsupported assumptions that were there. It was getting easier and easier to think that his old snitch had asked him to meet at this gas station, just so that he could set him up one more time. Chevy, after all, had never been late before.

Maxwell stood quietly beside the front door of the building and attempted to refocus his mind. No indication had been there that this meeting was going to be something other than what it was supposed to be, what these have always been. If he were to allow any unwanted possibilities to invade his thoughts, what he had come here to get, might slip though his fingers — he just couldn't waste the opportunity he now had.

At five minutes past the hour, Maxwell's head snapped around; his ears had locked onto something out in the back alley. Promptly, he made his way across the room and positioned himself just off to the opening side of the alleyway doorjamb.

"Psst! Max? Are you in here? Hello? Max?"

Even though Maxwell had previously grilled Chevy on the phone, being in the same room with him was going to be much different. And with him only moments away from being face to face with his old snitch, an anxiousness that normally never consumed him, had — probably because Maxwell knew that he fully intended on using the interrogation skills he had, until the doubts that were there were satisfactorily put to rest.

Without any sort of restraint, he grabbed Chevy and in one motion, pulled him from the back door's threshold, straight across the floor to the opposite wall — it was there that he slammed his old snitch's back up against it. Maxwell then placed his left forearm up against Chevy's throat and used his obvious height and weight advantage to pin him in place.

Although Maxwell's intention wasn't to hurt Chevy, he did want to instill some fear into him — and it worked because the man looked as if he was scared shitless. Yes, time had changed the both of them. Maxwell had never been the kind of person to let his anger or emotions dictate his actions, yet at that moment, it was doing just that.

Since the last time Maxwell had seen him, Chevy had completely changed his appearance. No longer was he scrawny and scraggly looking, he had cut his hair short and he put on about at least thirty pounds. It also appeared to Maxwell that he had spent some time in a gym because his body was noticeably toned. Even the way he dressed now, made him look more normal: he wore new denim jeans, a Cardigan golf shirt, and the latest brand of Nike shoes. His piercings, all but one in his ear were gone, and the emperor's name tattoo across his neck had been expertly removed with a laser. But even with all the changes in his appearance, there was no mistaking him for someone other than the man that Maxwell had known for all those years.

With only a few inches of space in between them, Maxwell gave Chevy a look so intense that it was easy to tell he was all business. "How are ya doing, old buddy?" Maxwell said, while staying fixated on Chevy's scared face.

The closer he inched to his old friend, the more panic that he could see in him. Chevy attempted to reply to Maxwell's question, but was unable to do so due to the pressure that was being placed upon his throat. After a few minutes of intense silence, Maxwell backed off his forearm a little and gave Chevy a chance to breathe — but that lasted for only three seconds.

Without diverting his eyes, Maxwell again put pressure on Chevy's throat — this was done so Chevy would realize that if he wanted to, he could easily end his life. "I'm a really pissed off man... old friend."

Since he could not speak, Chevy simply nodded his head in acknowledgement.

With that now understood, Maxwell completely released his forearm from up against Chevy's throat. But the reprieve was brief, as he promptly grabbed his old friend's throat with his left hand and pulled Chevy away from the wall. He then dragged him over to an old burned out service counter where Maxwell then forced his upper torso to bend backwards over the top of the counter. Using his weight, he then pinned Chevy uncomfortably into place.

He didn't speak; he just stared wrathfully at his old friend. Slowly, Maxwell backed off on some of the pressure, pulling back just enough so that he could point a small flashlight directly in Chevy's now glazed over eyes; the tears that were there, combined with the beam of light, temporarily blinded him. "I don't think we've ever had a heartfelt chat like this before? Have we, old pal?"

Chevy desperately struggled for air as he strained to speak. "What's with all this (Cough)... physical shit?"

"Time and anger when left unaddressed can have a very negative effect on someone. So... as you have probably figured out by now, I no longer believe that you were ever truly on my side."

Chevy continued to struggle to breathe. He gurgled and gasped before being able to find enough air to respond. "It's kind of hard for me to... to convince you that I was always... on your side; that our friendship meant a lot to me."

Feeling that he had finally proven his point, Maxwell pulled Chevy away from the counter and in one fluid motion, shoved him into a broken chair that had been just to the side of it. "If that is actually the case, then I want the truth from you. Did you set us up?"

Chevy rubbed at his throat. Slowly, he began to regain his speaking voice, now that he was no longer oxygen deprived. "Hell no! Why would I set up the only true friend that I have ever had?"

Silence filled the air as Maxwell took a few steps back away from Chevy, contemplating whether or not to believe him.

Taking this as a good sign, Chevy began to relax — although his heart was still pounding as he looked unsurely at the man who had obviously changed a lot over the years. After a few tense seconds, Chevy started to think that Maxwell had finally come to his senses; that his old friend had come to the conclusion that he had not done what he was being accused of. But that assumption of Chevy's had been wrong, as Maxwell suddenly removed his gun from its holster and fired it at Chevy's right leg — he missed. "Tell me something, Chevy. Did that just bring back some horrible memories for you? Or should I re-enact that horrendous experience of yours from which you had once barely survived."

"Please don't!" Chevy begged, as he instinctively got out of his chair, put his hands out in a futile stop gesture, and backed as far away from Maxwell as the building allowed. "I don't wish to ever go through that again."

Maxwell could easily see how rattled Chevy had gotten. His plan had been to push Chevy to the point of almost soiling himself. And once that had been accomplished, Maxwell felt that he would know without a shadow of a doubt whether or not his old friend was telling him the truth. Bad cop, very bad cop — that was the only angle that Maxwell felt he could play to get the results that he came here looking for.

He cocked his gun again. This time, he aimed it at Chevy's left leg; the same leg that bore the scars from being shot by those bikers thirty years ago. "Did you have any kind of prior knowledge that we were being set up that night?"

"I just told you no! I swear the information that I gave you was reliable. You know that I always double-check the legitimacy of my sources. I'm really, really sorry that the info I gave you was bad."

Although Maxwell was nowhere near yet convinced that Chevy was telling him the truth, he did feel some twisted satisfaction that his plan seemed to be working — just as he had hoped it would. However, he had yet to get even one of his questions answered, so he purposely kept his gun in Chevy's line of sight. He then asked him, in a more normal, friendlier tone of voice. "Who gave you the bad information?"

"What do you want to know that for?"

"Because I do, Chevy!" Maxwell had hoped that his interrogation wouldn't last too long — but it certainly looked as if that was not going to be the case. Chevy wasn't freely giving him the answers that he sought — he instead, was being very reticent. Many times, Maxwell had to interrogate individuals who refused to cooperate, but this was the first time that his usually patient self, was nowhere to be found. The lack of forthcoming information was easily frustrating him. All that he wanted was the honest truth — but Maxwell wasn't getting it.

At that moment, he felt that he had no other choice — his bad cop persona had to continue for a little while longer. He again fired off his gun — this time, it caused Chevy to close his eyes and cower.

After also intentionally missing his second shot, Maxwell sternly looked at his old snitch and said, "It would be in your best interest to simply tell me what I want to know. Who gave you the bad info?"

Chevy paused for a moment, took a few calming deep breaths, and then, with as much confidence as he could portray, approached Maxwell. Although his nerves were now completely shot, he knew that he had to find a way to get his old friend to see that he was not the enemy. At three paces away from being nose to nose with Maxwell, he stopped — that left him with just enough distance between the two that if it became necessary, Chevy would be able to grab somewhat of a head start if he felt that he had to bolt for the back alley door. He didn't care in that moment if the percentages of out running a bullet were slim to none as that, he believed, was the only option he had if his old friend didn't soon come to his senses.

As calm as he could make himself, Chevy began the task of explaining to Maxwell everything that he knew and remembered. He told him that he had heard on the streets that the person who passed him the bad information was no longer alive; that one of Antonio Marcone's men had killed him off the day after the set up had taken place, because the D.U.O. wanted to make sure that the informant they used to pass along the bad information wouldn't run scared and go to the police. He then said that after he had learned of his source's fate, he immediately crossed the border into Canada because he feared that his death would soon follow. That was also his reasoning as to why he had never tried to contact Maxwell over the years for fear of his own whereabouts possibly being discovered.

Even with this now being revealed, Maxwell was still uncertain if he believed Chevy — although he could certainly understand why his old snitch would disappear across the border if what he said was actually true. But he suddenly became curious at that moment as to why Chevy had decided to return to Detroit with Antonio Marcone now being out of jail — so he asked him that question, seeing that the risk to his life would be much greater now. His reply was simple. Once the American / Canadian borders were opened up and both countries decided to become one and form the Ameri-Can Union (although they still remained separate countries, the

207

amalgamation of both nations was done so that the political, economical, and military situations in each country, would become stronger and much more stable), he was all but certain that the D.U.O. would come looking for him. But they didn't. So, after four years of there being an open border and no imminent threat against his life was present, Chevy had to conclude that his involvement in what had happened that night had long since been forgotten. Yes, there was still a chance that he was a wanted man, but he decided that it was finally safe enough for him to return home to Detroit.

With a sympathetic look that no one could refuse, Chevy then apologized for every mistake that he had made and being somewhat responsible that his old friend's life had gotten ruined — all because of some bad information that he had passed along to him.

Maxwell took a moment and let everything sink in that Chevy had just told him. Once it had, he looked his old friend in the eyes and could see the desperate want for forgiveness. Immediately, Maxwell felt like a total jerk — it was he who needed to be asking for forgiveness. By letting his years of accumulative frustration and anger dictate this meeting, his bad cop interrogation technique only resulted in an old friendship being torn up and thrown out the window. What he had done had not gotten him the answers that he thought he was going to get. He knew that Chevy was the only hope that he ever had of finding out the truth; a different sort of truth that came at a price he didn't expect to have to pay. He was disappointed with himself that he had let this happen. And now, after threatening Chevy like he did, Maxwell himself had become the 'real' bad guy. He should have trusted his gut and not listened to all of the emotions that had continuously enveloped his mind for so long, because that was what had caused him to cross over that same line he swore all those years ago that he would never traverse.

He turned away from Chevy, walked over to the other side of the room, and parked his ass up against a scorched tool crib. Maxwell faced away from Chevy and he gazed meaninglessly through a charcoal-camouflaged window; reflecting in shame on what he had just done. "I'm so sorry. I wouldn't blame you one bit right now if you hated me for what I just did to you. I'm... I'm just so furious at Antonio Marcone; not just for what he has done to me and my family, but because of all of the suffering and heartache that he has caused everyone else. I should not have accused you of being associated with his crimes."

Chevy went over to Maxwell and put his hand upon his shoulder. He then said, "I vid-phoned you yesterday because I wanted you to return to Detroit so that I could tell you in person what I have found out. I knew that you would instantly jump at this chance that I'm about to give you; a chance that I hope will help to make everything right."

Maxwell stepped away from the tool crib and paced the room for a few moments, unintentionally kicking up some dust and soot residue as he walked. With a small tear beginning to trickle down his face, he turned and finally looked at Chevy. "I can't believe that you are still willing to help me after what I just did to you."

"To be honest, I've never thought you had that kind of evilness in you. And as scared as you made me, I can understand where it came from — I just wish that you would have gone about all of this differently."

"So do I."

"It's too late now. But as far as I'm concerned, Max, what you did here today is now forgotten." Chevy reached out his hand in a peace offering. "Forgiving you though... I'm not sure?"

Maxwell could not fault the man if he never did.

With a genuine smile on his face, Chevy stood there patiently waiting, hand extended, for Maxwell to shake it.

Maxwell was reluctant to accept the offer because of how shitty he was feeling. However, he knew that unwarranted, spitefully inflicted wounds could never truly begin to heal unless he took responsibility for his actions — it was up to him to take that first step. So with a heavy heart, and an immense amount of embarrassment, Maxwell accepted Chevy's overly kind gesture.

"Now... Do you want to hear what I know, or not?"

"Well, of course I do."

With the hatchet now seemingly buried, Chevy proceeded to inform his old friend about everything that he knew. He told Maxwell he had learned that the D.U.O. was going to start expanding their already large arms smuggling operation, and that they were planning on going into the high end, high tech aspect of dealing. He then explained to Maxwell that the D.U.O. had just recently intercepted a shipment of military 'S.M.A.R.T.' microchips (**S**elf **M**anipulating, **A**uto-**R**eprogramming **T**echnology). A programmable microchip that can be attached to any object that has its own computer system — such as: a rocket, a drone, an airplane, a helicopter, or any kind of motorized vehicle: a car, a boat, a motorcycle, or a train.

Once it has been installed into the intended object, it releases a 'Trojan' like program that takes over the entire operating system, converting the object into a programmable remote controlled device. No matter how simple or complex the objects programming is, the S.M.A.R.T. technology will hijack the object by rewriting the existing program or by installing its own. Once that is done, any man made vehicle with a computer in it, essentially becomes a bullet with your name on it.

"Son of a bitch!" Maxwell could not believe what Chevy had just told him — his anger immediately returned and he, without thinking, kicked the melted filing cabinet that was on the floor next to where he had been standing. Unlike the pail in his office, the filing cabinet did not move — he nearly broke his foot. After taking a few seconds to allow the pain in his foot to subside, Maxwell said, "Marcone has truly lost his mind. Do you happen to know what his plans are?"

"Yup... I do." Chevy then proceeded to inform his old friend that a truck was supposed to arrive at eight p.m. this evening at the Sturgeon Fishery Warehouse at the end of the new Trafalgar Avenue docks, and that Antonio Marcone was planning on using those shipping facilities to send the S.M.A.R.T. microchips by boat out to Serbia.

This was something that Maxwell would have never expected from Antonio Marcone — but then again, the man was known to do just about anything so long as he made a profit. Profit — that was probably the only reason he needed to take such a large risk and once again, strike a deal with an individual from an eastern bloc country. "Ok. So who in Serbia are they for?"

Chevy answered Maxwell's question, simply by explaining to him what was currently going on in that country. He informed him that a political group named the C.R.A.P. (**C**ommunist **R**evolutionary **A**ssembly **P**arty), which consists of members from the countries of: Romania, Bulgaria, Hungary, Montenegro, Croatia, Bosnia, Albania, Kosovo and Serbia, have begun to lay the foundation to establish a separate eastern bloc union so that they can create a modern day, communist type of superpower. With the S.M.A.R.T. technology in their possession, they would then be able to take the first step needed for the C.R.A.P. to begin their outrageous plan to overthrow all of their own governments. And once that was done, they would be able to use their collective strength and put pressure on the world financially and militarily.

This was news to him; this supposed potential formation of a new superpower was something that he should have been well aware of. Unfortunately, he had been content to stay in his own bubble and ignore the world around him. *'Marcone is fuckin' crazy!'* he thought. *'There is no way that I'm going to let him get away with this. I have to stop the bastard!'* Although he knew that he should bring this information straight to the police, Maxwell decided against it. The moment that he involved the authorities, he would be kept so far away from it all that he would have to find his own computer hacker to hack into the C-4 network so that he could at least watch what was going on.

This was his fight. Jail for Antonio Marcone this time was not going to be an option; only his death would be acceptable — it was something that Maxwell had decided upon a long time ago. He was not going to chicken out either. This trip he had taken, all along had been one way — and he was going to ride it all the way to the end.

With his mind made up, Maxwell looked at his old friend and said, "I truly am sorry for ever doubting you, Chevy."

"That's ok, Maxwell. I can understand where you were coming from. Especially considering how much you have been through. But did you have to scare me with that gun of yours? You know how much I really hate guns."

"Yeah, I know," Maxwell, stated. "That's why I used it. Although you'll be happy to know that I had no intention of actually shooting you." Maxwell removed the clip from his gun, and showed the ammunition that was inside of it to Chevy. "I used simu-nition — training ammo."

It was a few minutes shy of eight p.m. and Maxwell Banks was sitting in his rented vehicle just down from the Sturgeon Fishery Warehouse. Again, his conscience was telling him that he should have taken what he had learned from Chevy and passed it along to the police — but he just didn't want to deal with all the bullshit that he knew would surely be thrown back in his face. He did however, call Christopher White and brief him on what he now knew — because of the history that was there, and friendship they had, Maxwell felt he owed him at least that much. However, there were aspects of what was going on that he just didn't want his old friend to know about — like, where he actually was or what he was planning on doing. And although Christopher had given him his word that he would stay out of it and keep the law off of his back, Maxwell couldn't risk the possibility of having a posse of police officers sent to the docks. That would screw up his plans.

Yes, his plan was severely flawed. More than likely, this was going to be his last day on Earth — but he was all right with that, as he had no reservations about his decision. And even if there was a possibility of finding his missing son once he took out Antonio and his lackeys, Maxwell wasn't really sure that he could slip right back into a normal life or even be a part of his son's — he hadn't known what a normal life was like since Sabastian was born.

Tonight was the night — he was going to completely cross that line. Maxwell was going to try his damndest to attain his long awaited revenge. He was either going to claim ultimate victory, or go down in flames. One way or another, the many years of pain that he had been forced to live with was finally going to come to an end. His mission was going to be executed in the name of all of those whom Antonio Marcone had victimized.

For once, the arms shipment was on time. No sooner had the cargo truck disembarked, a brand new metallic gray, Presidential Edition, Lincoln Continental limousine, arrived carrying Antonio, Louie, and Sal. Maxwell couldn't have asked for more. All three of the bastards were here at once. *'Well now, I guess that I won't have to waste my time searching the entire city in order to eliminate all three of them. One unexpected surprise by me; three diseased rats exterminated at once.'* Everything inside of him urged him to go do this now, but Maxwell recognized that he needed to take a step back, survey the area more closely, and wait until the right moment came before he made his move. That way, he would be certain that he would catch all three of them with their hands in the proverbial cookie jar.

After only a few minutes had passed, his eagerness began to overwhelm him. He couldn't resist any longer, so Maxwell went for it. He promptly abandoned his rental car and made his way over to the warehouse. Once he arrived and was able to determine that the coast was clear, he cautiously maneuvered his way to the front entrance of the building and quietly entered it with his trusted Smith & Wesson nine millimeter positioned out in front of him — it was the same gun that he had been using since he began his private investigator's career.

Once he was inside the place, Maxwell immediately noticed the same truck that he had seen entering earlier — it was now parked over at the other side of the building. Carefully, Maxwell moved a little closer; stopping abruptly once he had realized that the truck was not sitting there alone — four men were hastily unloading small corrugated boxes from inside of it.

Unsure as to what exactly was going on, Maxwell hid behind the corner of a protruding wall — from there, he stood and observed these four men for a few moments. And although he did not know for sure, what he suspected was inside those boxes couldn't be, in his opinion, anything other than what Chevy had said was being smuggled — the S.M.A.R.T. chips.

Maxwell's conscience was making its way to the surface — this wasn't what he wanted. Who he had always been, had taken over. It hadn't been his first priority when he entered the warehouse, but the opportunity was now there to hit the D.U.O. where it hurt the most — right in the pocketbook. Kill two birds with one stone — that was what he was now going to do.

With the decision made to add one last good deed to his legacy, Maxwell made an unwise move. He took two steps out into the open to get a better look — Salvadore Batiste had unexpectedly emerged from out of a nearby room at the exact same moment,

213

promptly placing him only a short distance away from where the truck was.

Realizing his mistake, and hoping that he had not yet been seen, he quickly leapt back in the direction from which he came, and then tucked himself even further back behind the same corner wall. *'Whoa... That was close,'* Maxwell thought to himself. He then took a few seconds and gathered his thoughts. Where he was and where he wanted to go; the truck seemed to be a fair distance away. And unfortunately, there was nothing for him to use between where he was and where it was that would allow him to stealthily work his way over there. He needed an opening — and he needed everyone to leave the area of the truck so that he could see for himself if those S.M.A.R.T. chips were actually inside those boxes.

Cautiously, Maxwell stuck his head around the corner and watched as Sal barked out orders to his four workers. To his pleasant surprise, the four men immediately dropped what they had been doing and headed towards the room, which Sal was standing just outside of. Once the four men had made it to where Sal was, he ordered them inside and then followed, shutting the solid wood door behind him.

This was the opening that Maxwell needed — but he also clearly remembered what had happened the last time he was inside a warehouse with an abandoned truck. The potential was certainly there for history to repeat itself. Still, his past training and instincts refused to abandon him; his curiosity refused to leave him as well. He had to find out for sure if those S.M.A.R.T. chips were actually inside the truck.

He took a moment and let the conflict that was in his mind sort itself out. Maybe his willingness to originally walk into this with it being a one-way mission didn't need to be that after all. His strong desire for revenge had been what had convinced him that was what it should be. Yet, his beliefs right from the beginning of his career in law enforcement had suddenly reappeared to remind him exactly why he had chosen such a profession. And although he hadn't been an active police officer for twenty-five years, he still lived by those beliefs whenever he was out investigating someone or something. What was right was right, and what was wrong was wrong. This shipment of technology could not end up in the hands of the Serbians — Maxwell knew that would be the beginning of something that could eventually change the whole landscape of the world. In good conscience, he could not let that happen. His mission, he officially changed. No longer was this about him and his desire to make things right; the elimination of the three main players of the D.U.O., had now taken a back seat to what was clearly more important.

In that moment, Maxwell wished that he had brought with him his vid-cell so that he could call the police. Unfortunately, he did not, as it would have been easy for someone with a limited amount of electronics knowledge to track him by it. He was on his own now, and it was up to him to get the evidence he needed.

He cautiously stuck his head around the corner to make sure that the warehouse was still empty — it was, so he proceeded forward. Once he arrived at the truck, he wanted to make sure that this wasn't another trap, so he knelt down and quickly scanned the underside of the vehicle. He didn't have with him a portable electronic bomb sniffer, so his eyes would have to suffice. He didn't see anything unusual; the undercarriage appeared to be clear of any foreign objects — but that didn't mean that there wasn't an explosive device of some kind strapped somewhere else on the vehicle.

Having no choice but to assume that the truck was bomb-free, Maxwell righted himself and then climbed up inside the back of it. *'I really hope that I don't have to dig through everything back here to find the evidence that I need.'*

Once Maxwell's eyes adjusted to the dimly lit interior of the back of the truck, the first thing that he had noticed was that there weren't many boxes left that were identical to the ones that the four workers had been removing. Those that were, were haphazardly scattered throughout the floor at the back near the left side wall — some were even open. Maxwell took a quick glance inside those open boxes and disappointment immediately consumed him — the boxes were empty.

That feeling however, promptly dissipated when Maxwell's eyes locked onto a rather large item that was still left in the truck. Right against the back wall was a mound of something that had a nylon tarp draped over it. He hoped that there were more boxes underneath, so he walked over to it and curiously removed the tarp. What Maxwell saw wasn't a stack of unopened boxes — before him instead, was a large, haphazardly welded together steel box that roughly measured the size of a standard coffin, and it had several small holes drilled out on its sides.

This of course nudged Maxwell's curiosity even further — and although he couldn't even begin to speculate what might be inside this makeshift 'crate', he had to assume that there might be something of value inside it, which Chevy may not have known about that the D.U.O. was also planning to sell.

Before Maxwell did anything, he turned and took a quick look behind him, as he wanted to make sure that no one was around. Once he was satisfied that the coast was still clear, he returned his attention to the steel box. Maxwell stood there for a moment a bit perplexed. This steel box didn't have any kind of locking mechanism on it — it was wide open. Many reasons why this steel box was like this taunted Maxwell's curiosity, but he just did not have time to speculate — all that matter was what might actually be inside it.

There wasn't a sign of any kind on it warning people to stay out; in Maxwell's mind, he had just been given an open invitation to look inside. But he wasn't stupid; a surprise could be waiting for him within. Therefore, before he opened up the unlocked box, Maxwell stepped off to the side as far as the space inside the back of the truck allowed, and cautiously lifted the metal lid. Nothing happened. He looked inside the 'crate' and perplexity immediately consumed him. There was nothing of value inside; nothing that the Serbians would want. What he saw instead, were everyday items you could find at your neighborhood building supply store: a dozen bags of concrete mix, half a dozen bags of sand, and some half inch thick steel chain.

Maxwell stood there, scratching his head. *'This just doesn't make any sense?'*

***

Desperation was clearly there as she called out to him. But for some reason, he was not able to move, nor was he able to answer her pleas. As impossible as it should be, invisible bindings seemed to be attached to every one of his extremities; his mouth also appeared to be muzzled. Wherever it was that they were, this strange place caused him to feel a bit disoriented — and because of that, he wasn't even sure if he was standing upright or was horizontally suspended.

He felt helpless as he looked at his ever-pleading wife. The more he struggled to try to get over to save her, the faster she seemed to fade away. Nevertheless, he kept on fighting. Finally, he began to find some success. His everlasting love for her was the driving force behind his determination to get free and save her before it was too late. However, he soon realized that came with a price, as pain shot right through his entire body. But no matter how excruciating it became, he was not going to use that as an excuse for his failure — he was not going to stop until she was safe in his arms.

His struggle had only been for a few minutes, but it seemed like an eternity. So much so, that his wife was now merely an apparition — if he did not soon get free of his manacles, he feared that any chance there was to bring his wife back to him, would forever be lost.

With every ounce of strength that he could find from within, he finally broke free and took a desperate lunge forward. But it was too late. She was now gone — and in essence, so was his own existence.

"Uuuuuhhh..! Ooooohhh..! Where in the..?" Reaching up, Maxwell grabbed the back of his head and felt a rather large goose egg firmly planted there. "Oh, my fuckin' head!" he said, as he tried to regain his bearings.

"Well... look who finally regained consciousness," Sal said.

"He wouldn't have been out as long as he has if you had used some restraint," Louie pointed out.

Sal knew that he was right, but he just could not resist cracking Maxwell on the back of his head as hard as he could. Thankfully, he hadn't killed the man, as Antonio would have probably done that to him as punishment.

With their guest in the capable hands of Louie to watch over, Sal left to go and inform Antonio of the news. Once he was out of sight, Louie snared Maxwell's ashen face with his oversized left hand — it covered Maxwell's mouth and nose and made it difficult for him to breath. "That lump on your head is nothing compared to what is going to happen to you, Banks. Antonio gave you an opportunity to

217

live out the remainder of your life without us ever being a part of it again. Yet, you chose for that not to happen. Your decision to pursue us after all these years, validates the objection I had then that your elimination should have happened right along with your partner's. But for some reason that I'll never understand, Antonio decided to grant you a pardon from the death sentence you so deserved. This here," Louie extended his left hand out to the side, showcasing the warehouse for Maxwell in case he was unsure where he was exactly, "proves that his decision was a mistake. However, the past is the past and you are now here. I know you remember that night like it was yesterday — but your appearance here just proves to me that you didn't learn a damn thing from the lesson my boss wanted to teach you. Therefore, a much needed refresher course seems to be in order." Louie removed his left hand from Maxwell's face and promptly belted him right across the chops with his right.

That woke him up completely. After running his tongue across the top and bottom of his teeth in order to feel whether or not they were still there, Maxwell looked up at Louie and said, "How long have I been out?"

"I'd say oh, about an hour and a half — but that doesn't matter, because time is what you have very little of."

"Well... Well... Well... Look who decided to drop in for a visit?"

Maxwell couldn't turn his body to see to whom that voice had belonged to, for his hands and feet were bound tightly to an old rickety wooden chair — but he really didn't need to see who owned it, for he knew right away who was now behind him.

Antonio Marcone strolled up to Maxwell, a cane in his hand (which he now was forced to use on occasion when he had to stand for long periods of time), and made his way directly in front of him. He then said, with intended insolence in his words, "I see that the time has done you no favors at all, my dear old friend."

"And I see unfortunately, that jail was way too kind with you," Maxwell replied in turn.

Sal gave Maxwell an unexpected backhand that landed against the left side of his face. He hit him so hard that Maxwell's bound body

218

would have slammed onto the ground if it weren't for Louie grabbing his shoulder as he had begun to fall.

Louie righted Maxwell; Sal then maneuvered himself behind and took his rather large, abrasive hands, and covered Maxwell's mouth.

"I do believe that I sense a little hostility from you, Max." Antonio took his cane and then pressed it firmly up against Maxwell's groin. "That's no way to talk to someone that right now, has you literally by the balls."

Intense pain shot through Maxwell's body. He let out a scream, but it was barely heard because of Sal's meat hooks wrapped around his mouth. The discomfort of that cane continually pressed against his manhood was extremely difficult to disregard. Yet Maxwell knew that the pain he was feeling was nothing compared to what he knew was about to come his way.

Right from the very start, he knew that the odds of his success were going to be pretty slim — he also knew that his chances of being killed were pretty good. That was why he had initially approached this mission of his with the mindset that he was not going to survive it. However, if for some reason the enemy was to give him even the slightest window of opportunity to escape, then Maxwell needed to take it — the D.U.O. had apparently become way too big for their britches.

The bigger picture had finally become clear to him. Why this had not happened to him before now, he did not know? This wasn't just his war. The bully on the block, threatened everyone — they needed to be dealt with accordingly. Because he had more firsthand knowledge of the enemy than anyone else, it meant that he was the most valuable asset there was. But in all honesty, Maxwell had to admit that the odds of him living to fight another day were now rather slim.

Antonio instructed Sal to remove his hand from Maxwell's mouth and ordered him to step aside. As soon as this took place, Maxwell looked right into the eyes of a man who had no scruples. He then knew at that moment, he had reached the end of the road — this warehouse was where he was going to die.

He had never denied that he, at times, was a child stuck in an adult's body. That was why Maxwell on occasion, enjoyed having some harmless fun at other people's expense. He had done so to his brother, to Joshua, to his captain, and to many other officers whom he had worked with. He even had done it once before to his wife on their wedding day — but Sylvia had not been impressed at all that her bouquet of flowers had been switched at the church from red and white to black and blue.

Maxwell had thought it was funny, a symbolic representation of their future first fight. Little did he expect that came close to happening on that very day, as his ill-timed brand of humor had put the happiest moment of his life at risk of not even happening. Still, that admitted slight bit of misjudgment on his part did not deter him from ever having his fun again — which is exactly what he was going to do today, as he was going to go out with a bang and annoy the piss out off his enemy.

With a slight devilish grin plastered on his face, Maxwell said to Antonio, "You know... If you really feel the need to play with my balls like that, old man, the least you could do is use your hands."

With a flick of his wrist, Antonio maneuvered his cane from Maxwell's groin, straight upwards; it connected solidly under his enemy's chin and caused him to bite his lip. "Do you not realize that the future of your pathetic life will be decided by me? You better watch your tongue or I will have it cut out." He had waited twenty-five years for this day to come and Antonio wasn't about to let an insolent man ruin his moment.

Maxwell wished that he still had his gun in his possession, because the man deserved a retaliatory strike for what he had just done to him. It was a cold-hearted thought on his part, but at that moment, he had no qualms about putting a slug in one of Antonio's legs so that his cane became a necessary item he would use, from this moment forward, in order to get around. Unfortunately, it was tucked in the front of Sal's pants — Maxwell was certain that the man had put it there for the sole purpose of taunting him. Therefore, the only thing that he could do was fire off another insult. "I should take that cane of yours, turn that sucker sideways, shine it up real nice, and then shove it up..."

Not wanting to hear any more of the crap that was coming out of his enemy's mouth, Antonio took his cane, placed the end of it up against Maxwell's chest and then pushed him backwards. The rickety old chair tipped over easily, Maxwell's restrained body fell straight back. Instant pain shot right through him. It wasn't so much the concrete floor that caused that to happen, it was the strategically placed clay brick that had been on the ground — that item, had cracked the back of his skull wide open. "You need to start showing me some respect, Banks!"

Maxwell looked up from his bound and contorted position on the floor, completely oblivious to what had just happened to him. His thoughts were now a conglomerate of illegible words. The only thing he knew for sure was that he probably had another concussion. "I, uh... no have... for low-life... scum-sucking... piece of fuck... trash like you!" It took Maxwell a few moments after he mumbled those words for the cloud in his head to somewhat clear. Once it had, he formed what he wanted to say in his mind and then made sure that Antonio heard a carefully chosen phrase, mixed with colorful words that he felt perfectly described the man. He then said, "You murdered my wife and took my son away. You have destroyed what has meant the most to me. You are nothing but a heartless piece of shit!"

"Your opinion of me is irrelevant. And need I remind you that you are in no position to back up your accusations. You are, after all, currently fucked."

Having no other choice but to agree with Antonio, Maxwell decided to follow up his enemy's statement with an unfounded declaration — one that would only come to fruition if all the stars miraculously aligned. "At this moment, I may not be able to do anything. But just like that day in the courtroom before they hauled your ass away, I promise you that a day will come when you will get what is coming to you. Karma is a bitch and I believe that she is going to take a big chunk out of your ass."

All that Antonio could do was laugh at Maxwell's baseless prophecy. He didn't believe that Karma really existed. To him, stupid mistakes were the only things in this world that could cost you — and Antonio wasn't making one right now. As far as he was concerned, the end of Maxwell Bank's life was supposed to happen tonight, and there was nothing that anyone could do to stop it. "My ass is always guarded."

"Trust me! Kismet is one day, going to show up on your doorstep. And when 'He' does, you'll have wished that the decisions you had made long ago were much different."

He could have stayed there and exchanged threats and so-called prophecies with his enemy until the sun went down, but Antonio just didn't want to waste too much more of his valuable time. He only wanted to get the last word in before he finally put an end to what had been a very long delay in the ending of this running game between the two. Antonio had patiently waited the majority of his life in a prison cell for this moment, and now he was ready to put that preverbal knife in Maxwell's back; a moment that he could no longer wait to have happen.

As ordered, Sal picked Maxwell up off the floor, sat him upright, and then stood back out of the way; Antonio then promptly leaned in close to his enemy and whispered a few parting words into his ear, "Goodbye, Maxwell. It's been long, but it's also been fun." He then took a step past Maxwell and in one motion, swung his cane at the back of Maxwell's already concussed and bloody head, knocking him and his chair forward. Both Louie and Sal mockingly laughed as Maxwell's unprotected face slammed into the concrete floor.

Antonio then nodded at his associate, signaling that it was time. Sal, who was just as eager to get this over with as Antonio was, nodded back his acknowledgement. He had waited a very long time for this day, and was thankful that Antonio had entrusted him to be the one to terminate the pathetic life of Maxwell Bank.

Sal propped Maxwell back upright once again. He then pulled out of his jacket pocket a pair of brass knuckles that he had custom made for this occasion. Across the top of the knuckles were numerous small stud-like shaped spikes that were made out of dia-metal (A fusion of fine diamond particles and carbon steel alloy — the hardest form of hybrid steel that was currently known to exist) that were equally spread across the entire thing. He also had these knuckles personalized in order to document the occasion — engraved in Italian were the words 'Addio, mio nemico' (Goodbye, my enemy), and the date of July thirty-first, two-thousand and thirty-five.

Savoring the moment, Sal moved in close to Maxwell, raised his left hand in an open fashion in Maxwell's line of sight, and mockingly, waved goodbye to him — Louie stood behind Maxwell and held him in place.

Sal then began his vicious assault, maliciously lacing him, over and over and over again. For five continuous minutes, Sal verbally taunted, then beat Maxwell — he literally re-arranged his entire face. There probably wasn't a plastic surgeon in the entire world who was talented enough to put Maxwell back together again, as that's how mangled his face now was.

Tapping his cane on the ground to get Sal's attention, Antonio gave him the signal to end his barrage. He acknowledged his cue from his boss to stop, but not before he hauled off and gave Maxwell one more shot for good measure, right between his eyes.

"That's enough, Sal! Do you want me to also crack you across your head with my cane?"

"I'm sorry, boss. It's not too often that I have a chance to have this much fun in one day."

As he turned his head and tried to wipe off the crimson mask that now covered nearly all of his face onto his shirtsleeve, Maxwell began to cough. Yes, his face was now nowhere near recognizable, but that didn't stop the childishness he was famous for from appearing once again. "Oh... I don't feel so good. I could really use a comforting hug from someone."

Maxwell didn't even get a chance to see what kind of reaction he'd gotten as his face promptly met the concrete floor once again; Louie had given him a shot across the back in between his shoulder blades. "There! Hug the ground if you need one so bad."

After a few seconds of lying there in a pool of his own blood, Louie grabbed the chair and hauled Maxwell back up. Antonio then maneuvered himself back in front of his bloodied enemy and said, "You know Maxwell, I really felt crushed when you didn't come to visit me while I was in prison. It's obvious to me that you never ever wanted to see your favorite 'Uncle' Antonio again."

"You're not even close to being..." Maxwell paused momentarily as he spat some of the blood that had drained into his mouth and aimed it at Antonio's new alligator shoes — he hit his target. "…blood to me."

"Let me correct you, Maxwell. You can deny it all you want, but we are 'blood'." Antonio took the bottom end of his cane and wedged it up against Maxwell's bloody throat. "You see my friend; our family trees had long ago been grafted together. I ordered the murder of both your wife and son, and now it's time for that family reunion to happen that you so desperately want. I'm going to be a nice uncle and arrange for you to once again be together with both of them."

"You killed my son too?" Maxwell struggled to talk as Antonio's cane was still rammed up against his throat. "I… I thought that he was still alive?"

"Get real, Maxwell. I only led you on so that you would believe that your son was alive. That way, you would spend the rest of your sorry ass life trying to find him. I knew that the hope you had that your son was still alive would mess with your mind and drive you as insane as I already am."

"You're a fucking asshole! You won't get away with this you son-of-a-bitch!"

Antonio took a step back, removing his cane from Maxwell's throat in the process. He then whacked him with it across that same area as hard as he could — he hoped that his strike would do enough damage so that not another word would be spoken between now and what little time the man had left to live. "I do believe that the time has come, Sal, to remove this useless heap of trash — it's making me real sick to my stomach the longer it stays sitting there." Antonio dispassionately walked away from Maxwell toward his awaiting limousine at the far side of the warehouse; finally feeling free now of the burden that had been weighing him down ever since the day he became a convicted criminal.

Maxwell would have probably said something insulting at that moment as a final send off, except he had no strength or voice left to get in that one last parting shot.

Two of the four unknown men who Maxwell had earlier seen around the truck, brought over that same nylon tarp that had been draped over the steel box in the back of it. Sal then promptly ordered them to spread the tarp on the ground in front of Maxwell's chair. As they were doing that, Louie injected a fast acting tranquilizer into the back of his neck. Within a few seconds, Maxwell's body went limp. Louie then removed a Swiss army knife from his front pocket and cut away the bindings that had kept him tied to the chair — he unceremoniously poured forward from it onto the tarp. Then, those same two men, without having to be told, proceeded to wrap Maxwell's lifeless body up inside it like a fajita.

With the use of a forklift, the other two unknown men unloaded the steel box from the back of the truck, and then brought it over to where the others were. The four of them then picked up Maxwell's unconscious and cocooned body, and then dropped it unceremoniously inside the steel box.

The D.U.O. didn't really care that there was a considerable amount of evidence left behind in the warehouse: Maxwell's blood on the chair, on the concrete floor, on Antonio's cane (which he left behind on the ground because it had broken pretty much in half after he cracked Maxwell across the throat), and his DNA on the bindings that held him in the chair. After all, it had been well documented that the D.U.O. had a personal vendetta against Maxwell Banks, and it didn't really matter that another murder would be tied to them.

This, one time Detroit police officer's murder, was something that they not only felt had to be done, but firmly believed that his coldhearted death would clearly send the world a message that could not be ignored. The D.U.O. was back, stronger than ever, and is an organization that should be feared by all — including those who not only made the laws, but enforced them as well.

12

From the moment Maxwell hastily departed for Detroit, Savanna began to worry. She had known him since her early teens, and it was one of those 'in the right place at the right time' situations that had forever changed her life. Maxwell had become as close to a real father as she could have ever wanted. And whenever he had to leave the state because of a case, Maxwell had always checked in with her at least a few times each day. This time however, he hadn't. That was why she knew in her heart that something had happened to him.

Sydney, on the other hand wasn't so sure that his big brother had fallen off the grid just yet. Maxwell's pure survival ability, and his past experience of being a decorated police officer, was enough for Sydney to feel at ease with his brother's lack of communication. He honestly believed that his brother was fine — although he understood why Savanna was feeling the way she was. Therefore, he tried everything that he could think of to reassure his brother's secretary that Maxwell was just fine.

Savanna truly wanted to believe what Sydney was trying to convey to her, but her emotions just would not allow her too — it was the not knowing part that was interfering with her sanity. She needed to find something to keep herself busy, something to distract her thoughts from continually being negative. So Savanna decided to go into Maxwell's office, gather up, and then reorganize all of the files on Antonio Marcone that had been left scattered all over her boss's office for the past three days.

One box at a time, she returned the files to where they belonged; in order and probably more organized than they had ever been before. This task she had taken on had helped her a bit. But every once in a while, something that was written in one of the files would catch her eyes and cause her volatile emotions to surface, forcing Savanna to stop what she was doing and take some time to compose herself before she could continue. Gathering up and putting away those documents, she knew had to be done — but the task was turning out to be more arduous than what Savanna had thought it would be. Each time she read a passage or scanned a note pertaining to Antonio Marcone, her perception of how evil of a man he was grew exponentially — the documented truth about him was all that was needed for Savanna's worry to become even more validated.

By the time she had completed what she had set out to do, she was convinced of one thing — the man she loved as a father, was not coming back. And although she felt like locking herself in Maxwell's office so that her tears could flow freely in private, she knew that she had to stay strong. She could not let her own belief ruin Sydney's, as he still firmly believed that his brother was going to come home. And until they knew for certain what, if anything had indeed happened, Savanna was going to do her best to keep her emotions in check, and what she honestly felt in her heart, to herself.

By the next morning, those same seeds of doubt had finally begun to appear in Sydney. In fact, he no longer felt that he could just stand on the sidelines and wait around in his condo for any sort of news about his brother. So, shortly around noon on that fourth day, he left his place and went to the agency. Going there, he was certain, would not help to alleviate his worry — but he knew that Savanna did not need to be left alone there any longer. "Have you heard from my brother, Savanna?"

"You know that if I had heard something, Sydney, that I would have vid-phoned you right away."

"You sure you haven't heard anything at all?" Sydney realized immediately after that question had escaped his mouth that he should not have asked Savanna again. But it was his own desire to know what was going on with his brother that had allowed those uncalled-for words to come out.

Savanna's head promptly snapped towards Maxwell's brother, as if to tell him that today was just not a good day to test her. Her eyes were severely bloodshot and her hair was so messy that it made a rat's nest look like a suite at the Ritz Carlton. "Can't you see that I've lost what little sanity I had left worrying about Max? I've had very little, if any sleep over the past four days — along with the fact that I've drunk enough sim-caf to keep my system regular for the rest of my life."

"You're not going to do yourself any good staying up all night worrying like that, Savanna. Pardon my French, but you look like a fucking piece of shit. I know it's difficult not knowing what's going on, but I think that you should just go home and take an extra long hot bath and try to get yourself some rest — it's obvious that you need it. I'll stay here and make a few calls. I do know a few people in Detroit that know people who once knew Maxwell. It's been years since I've made contact with them, but maybe they can find out something for us?" Sydney knew that his words hadn't helped to put Savanna at ease, but he was uncertain of what else to say. "I know that I'm grabbing at straws here, but it's all that I can think of right now. Until then, we just have to be patient and wait for Maxwell to call us."

Savanna really wasn't at all happy that Sydney was essentially kicking her to the curb — but she knew that he was right. If she didn't get some sleep and allow her mind to return to a normal state, she'd turn into a useless zombie. She had to recharge her batteries; especially if word got back to them that Maxwell was alive but needed their help.

"If I haven't heard anything by eight o'clock tonight, then I'll hop on the computer and book us on the next available flight to Detroit."

That promise from Sydney seemed to help. He then picked up Savanna's purse and displayed it in front of her eyes; an obvious hint that it was time for her to go home and get some rest. Savanna really hated to be told what to do, but she could not deny that Sydney was right. So she got up from her desk, accepted her purse, and started toward the front door. For some strange reason though, she stopped just before she got to it. She then turned and looked in the direction of Maxwell's office. It was at that moment when she finally realized something that she should have thought about doing a lot sooner, *'I'm so stupid sometimes.'*

"Are you ok, Savanna?"

She didn't answer Sydney. She set her purse back down onto her desk and then walked right past him towards Maxwell's office. Once she entered the room, she sat down in Maxwell's chair and fired up her boss's computer. "I can't believe that I didn't think of doing this sooner."

"Doing what?" Sydney asked, as he entered his brother's office.

She didn't answer him. She wasn't trying to ignore Sydney; she was merely trying to focus on what she wanted to do — make an attempt at accessing Maxwell's password protected computer. "I really hope that this isn't going to be as difficult a challenge as I think it is going to be," she mumbled.

After a few moments of awkward silence, Savanna glanced over top of the computer's monitor and could see the puzzled look that was plastered on Sydney's face. With a slight glimmer of hope in her eyes, she smiled for the first time in days. Her smile was nice to see, but for Sydney, it still didn't give him any sort of clue as to what she was doing.

For as long as Savanna had known and had worked for Maxwell Banks, there were still a few things that he had kept secret from her — his passwords were one of them. She wasn't sure what the reasons were for that, because she knew that he had always fully trusted her with everything else. She just assumed that he felt it necessary to kept parts of his life a secret; things from his past she was certain that he kept documented on his computer. Although she did not know this for sure, it was what she believed.

"Are you going to tell me what you are doing?"

"I'm trying to get into Max's computer so that I can call the Governor of Michigan on his private personal line."

"You know… it would be much simpler just to access the Michigan vid-com directory?"

"It would, Sydney. But not just anyone can make an unsolicited vid-call to any government official. The only government numbers that are accessible to the public are for general information and services. Think about it, Sydney? This is a state governor that we are talking about here, not a local hick-town mayor. You just can't go and call the Governor of Michigan whenever you damn well please. His number is not readily available to the general public, which is why I have to make that call through Maxwell's computer and not the public vid-lines. Besides, even if you somehow found out the number to the governor's office, there is no way that they would put you through to him. You are not anyone who is of any importance to him."

For fifteen disappointing minutes, Savanna continued to try and figure out Maxwell's password — one full cup of sim-caf down, and she had gotten nowhere. "Shit! Why does this have to be so damn difficult?" She continued to stare at Maxwell's computer monitor while the words on its screen '*Invalid password*' kept reminding her of her continuing failure.

"Maybe you should just leave this till tomorrow? You'll probably figure this out after a good night's sleep."

"I'm not going anywhere, Sydney!" Savanna slammed her fist down onto the top of Maxwell's desk; her empty sim-caf cup rattled. "I've tried everything that I can think of, but I still can't figure out what Maxwell's password is."

"Here, let me try it." Sydney walked over to the computer side of the desk; Savanna got up from behind it. Sydney didn't sit down in the vacated chair; he instead, stayed standing and typed in the word '**SABASTIAN**' — he immediately gained access to Maxwell's computer.

Savanna just stared at Sydney. She wasn't sure if she should be impressed or pissed off. The password seemed so easy to her now. She really wasn't having a good day — sleep deprivation had certainly caused her to miss what now seemed so obvious.

She spent a few moments looking at the computer screen before she located the link she needed. She then sat back down in the chair and clicked on it, believing that it would connect her directly to the Governor's office. However, what popped up onto the screen was enough for her to want to throw her empty sim-caf cup at the monitor. '*Why can't things be easy?*' she thought.

If the past four days haven't been frustrating enough for Savanna, Sydney would have just laughed at the difficulties that his brother's secretary was having. But where he was at that moment, standing right beside her, put him in a very vulnerable position for a reactionary retaliation from her — inflicted pain from a tired and pissed of woman wasn't what Sydney wanted to experience firsthand.

On the computer screen, the words '*Security Access Code required*' were there, big and bold. In Savanna's eyes, it was an encouragement from whatever Gremlins that might live inside Maxwell's computer to just give up. But after a few minutes of feeling like she was once again defeated, she knew that she could not give up so easily. "Do you have any idea what this security code is, Sydney?"

"No. I don't know this one." Whether or not he did this intentionally, Sydney took a few steps further off to the side and back, just in case Savanna's frustrations inadvertently caused her to lash out.

She covered her face with her hands and took a few moments to try and clear her thoughts. This was an important task that she just could not fail at. Not only for her own sanity, but she needed to succeed to ensure that they had a chance at finding where Maxwell was — and she just didn't care if her boss was going to be pissed off that she had broken into his secured computer because she just had to know for certain if he was all right or not.

After a few seconds, the smell of fresh sim-caf invaded her senses. While her hands had covered her face, Sydney had left Maxwell's office to go and get her another cup; he set it down in front of her on the desk.

Four straight days of that stuff continually touching her lips was enough. However, she didn't want to be rude to Sydney, knowing that his heart had been in the right place with the gesture. So she graciously took a sip and then gave Sydney a thankful smile. She then returned to the task at hand and began to search through her memory of all the repetitive phrases, words, and sayings that Maxwell would use, hoping that one of them would be the correct code she needed.

She tried a few different words and combination of words, but she kept getting *'Invalid Access Code'* appearing on the screen. After her fifth failed attempt, she got a different message on the screen — one that she did not expect. It read *'One more failed attempt to enter the correct access code will permanently terminate the link that this program is associated with'*. "Shit! Do you have any idea, Sydney, what the access code is? It's only giving me one more chance."

"I honestly don't know?" Sydney didn't dare tell Savanna that he had previously known what Maxwell's password was. It was mean on his part, but he admittedly enjoyed watching her try to figure it out. "His password was obvious, so I would be a betting man that his access code would also be."

"Well, I figured that much, Sydney. But I still have no clue as to what the access code would be." Savanna took a moment and looked around Maxwell's office, hoping for some inspiration. She was at a total loss. She didn't want to make a wrong guess, because then her one and only chance of possibly getting the information that she was looking for would end.

After a few panic filled moments, she was ready to go for broke and typed in '**ANTONIO MARCONE**' as the access code. But just before she hit enter on the keyboard, something caused her to glimpse at Maxwell's family photo that was still sitting in the cracked frame that she had yet to get replaced — then it hit her. "Hang on… I think that I may know what it could be. Cross your fingers, Sydney, otherwise we'll be screwed." Savanna removed what she had entered and typed in Maxwell's wife's name '**SYLVIA**'; she immediately gained access to the communication's directory at the Michigan State Capitol Building — relief promptly consumed her. *'Good! Now I just hope that there are no more roadblocks in my way.'*

After scanning the directory list, she found the Governor's name and selected his extension. A non-personable computerized voice then startled Savanna as it told her that she had thirty seconds to 'Enter your authorized identification or the secured access line would be traced, the authorities notified, and then the line severed'. "Damn! Not again. Think obvious. This better be it or we are in deep shit." She quickly entered the words '**MAXWELL BANKS**' and then prayed — a moment later, that same computer voice returned.

"Hello, Mr. Banks. Please hold and your call will be forwarded to the Governor's office."

"How did you know to type in Maxwell's name?" Sydney asked.

"That was easy," Savanna answered. "It was obvious."

"Good afternoon; Sylvia Winslow speaking. I'm sorry, but the Governor is in a meeting right now and is not taking any calls. Would you like to leave a message?"

"Hello. My name is Savanna Rivard. "I'd rather not leave a message. I really need to speak to the Governor, please."

"As I said, the Governor is busy right now," Sylvia repeated before a feeling came over her that something was not quite right.

The video feed suddenly went black; only the words '**PLEASE HOLD**' showed on Maxwell's computer screen —

Savanna's heart started to race. Her immediate thoughts were negative. She hadn't even had a chance to speak with the governor, and she honestly believed in that moment that she was going to get into some serious legal trouble for using a private and secured line to contact a government official. "Um.., I think we are in shit, Sydney."

"We? I'm not the one who hacked into Maxwell's computer."

Before Savanna could accuse Sydney of being just as guilty as she was, the governor's secretary re-appeared. She did not look at all impressed. "We have a problem here," stated Sylvia. She had placed Savanna on hold so that she could bring up the governor's personal contact list on her computer of all of the authorized names that had permission to call his office directly — the name of Savanna Rivard was not on it. "You, Miss, are not authorized to contact the governor via his private secure vid-com line. Do you know that it is illegal to hack into a private governmental line?"

The governor's secretary did not give Savanna any time to respond to her abrasive question. She instead, advised her to disconnect her call and refrain from ever calling the governor's office again. Sylvia then made a point of informing Savanna that her name has now been logged and if she failed to comply, the proper authorities would be notified."

"Wait! You have to listen to me. This is an emergency. I really must speak with the governor. I'm Maxwell Bank's secretary and I just wanted to find out if he has..."

"Oh?" Sylvia responded. "Hang on a minute."

The computer screen on Maxwell's desk went black again and the words '**PLEASE HOLD**' reappeared. This time, Savanna didn't even try to speculate on what was to come next. She just did not have enough time to be able to accurately assume what Governor White's secretary was going to do. Was she going to come back on the line and grant her request, or was she going to inform her that the authorities have been contacted — essentially solidifying that she had broken the law.

This time, Sylvia had placed Savanna on hold so that she could confirm the woman's claim. She did not want to dismiss it, strictly because she had contacted the governor's office through unconventional channels. If she was indeed who she claimed to be, then Sylvia had a responsibility to confirm it before she permanently disconnected the call.

She quickly pulled up on her computer the governor's personal file on Maxwell Banks; a file that included old and current pictures of him, his brother and secretary. Sylvia had never felt that it was necessary to familiarize herself with all of the governor's friends, as none of them ever bothered in the past to contact him here at the State Capitol Building — which explained why she had never recognized Maxwell Banks when he had first showed up here a few days earlier.

Once Sylvia was satisfied that Savanna was whom she claimed to be, she took her off of hold and said, "I must apologize, Ms. Rivard, for coming across like such an anal bitch a moment ago."

Savanna exhaled in relief, then turned and projected a smile of success at Sydney. For the third time, she was put on hold. This time, the impersonal words did not appear on the monitor; piano renditions of Elton John played instead, while a digital slide show of beautiful landscapes from all around the world materialize every few seconds on the screen.

About three minutes after she had been placed on hold, a distinctive, slightly raspy voice, said hello. Savanna immediately felt compelled to apologize to the governor for hacking into Maxwell's computer so that she could contact him directly. His response was one of reassurance; apologizing himself afterwards for not giving her access to his office long before now, as he honestly never thought that a need would arise for which he would have to speak with his old friend's secretary.

Once he finished listening to what Savanna was requesting of him, Christopher sunk back in his chair, disheartened that he would be unable to satisfy her wishes. However, he knew that she deserved to know what little he did, so he proceeded to inform her that Maxwell had briefly dropped by to pay him a visit when he had first arrived in Michigan and that they had a lengthy conversation concerning why her boss had decided to return after all these years.

Almost immediately, Savanna could hear the regret in the governor's voice. What he was sorry for, she could only speculate. She did however, understand that the underlying emotion he had was probably because his hands had been tied. By the end of their conversation, the governor had all but confirmed what she had feared — Maxwell had gone back to Detroit, not to get information concerning his son's whereabouts, but for the sole purpose of obtaining his personal vengeance. In Savanna's mind, it became all but solidified that both she and Sydney were never going to see Maxwell again, as he had apparently made a conscience decision that his return trip home was going to be one way.

Sydney personally found it difficult to accept what the governor had said. He never wanted to believe that his brother would ever consider throwing away the remainder of his life in exchange for revenge. To hold onto a grudge like that and let it eat away at your soul was understandable, yet Sydney never thought that Maxwell was the type of person to let something affect him in a way in which his mental stability would eventually break. His brother had always been strong willed and had an overly large heart, which allowed him to care about everyone and everything. It was why he had stepped up and became a surrogate father to Savanna — he loved her as if she was his own flesh and blood.

It took Savanna a few moments to control her negative emotions before she was able to ask the governor for a favor that she was uncertain he could agree to doing. And as she suspected, his answer was no.

Regretfully, the governor apologized to Savanna, and then explained that his reasons for denying her request were; political, personal, and based upon sheer respect for his old friend. "I've known Max for a very long time, Ms. Rivard. And I can tell you that he has always been more than willing to pay a very high price if it ever became necessary to do so. One way or another, Max was going to carry out this vendetta of his... no matter what the cost might end up being."

Savanna's heart continued to break into more pieces the longer she spoke to Christopher White. Before she had made this call, she had feared the worst. Now, only a dead body was needed to confirm what her heart was telling her — Maxwell was not coming back home.

After wiping away the single tear that she could feel had escaped the corner of her left eye, she mustered up all the strength that she could and focused on the moment. "I don't want to put you on the spot but... Maxwell has always considered you a close friend. I am begging for you to please find out for me whether or not he is still alive. I need to know. His brother needs to know."

Christopher conceded — though technically he would still be involving himself in an unsanctioned affair. But at that moment, he realized that he didn't care. As much as Savanna needed to know, so did the governor. A definitive answer to an unknown was required so that an end of some kind could take place — Christopher just hoped that the end was a positive one.

After thanking the governor for his time, information, and willingness to find out where Maxwell was, Savanna disconnected her call, placed her elbows on top of Maxwell's desk, and rubbed her aching head with her left hand. She was mentally wiped and emotionally drained.

Unable to hold back her feelings any longer, the four days of stress forced the floodgates to finally open up. At first, Sydney felt that he should pull up a chair next to Savanna and console her. But then he thought it best to just leave her alone, so he quietly vacated his brother's office, shut the door, and gave Savanna all the privacy and time that she needed.

It was Union Day, August 1st, the fifth anniversary of the day that the United States of America & Canada officially amalgamated into one great nation. Shortly after the merger had taken place, most northern and some residents of the upper Midwestern States of this new 'Country' had adopted a slang term in reference to themselves; the word 'Canusa', which had been affectionately used for generations by many Canadians when referring to an American who was married to a Canadian, or to who had just chosen to migrate and live in the Great White North.

Although the Union's intent was only to strengthen their long standing alliance, it also created a rift among many other non-democratic countries and political groups. And because it had, the Ameri-Can Union's government decided that there was a need to establish the first A.C.U. military base in Houston, Texas.

This base's construction was completed at the end of two-thousand and thirty with its sole purpose being a training facility for military personnel for homeland security, border security, and national defense. Calling this base home was also a specialized group known as S.N.A.F.U. (the **S**pecial **N**orth **A**merican **F**reedom **U**nit), a military platoon where its soldiers' skills rivaled that of a Navy Seal, but also included the proficiency of a highly trained assassin.

The Ameri-Can Union's government determined that the increased threat by Marxist Militant Leaders, Radical Religious Groups, and International and Domestic Terrorists, was more than enough of a reason to create such an elite fraternity of highly trained individuals whose sole purpose was to protect the Union at all cost against every possible threat there may be out there so that freedom and democracy could be preserved.

So with today being a National holiday, and in recognition of their impeccable record, all of the S.N.A.F.U. personnel had been given a weekend pass so that they could go out and celebrate; no restrictions and no surreptitious monitoring would be there — just the usual code of conduct was expected to be followed by each.

With their time off, a half a dozen high-ranking command officers had decided to gather at one of the dozen of military residences that was on the base for an evening of fraternizing and socializing (gambling, booze, women) — even though they knew that what they planned on doing was generally frowned upon. However, these residences were treated in much the same way, as an Indian reservation would be. For that reason, none one of them feared that any such consequences would come their way, because unless something egregious was going on, a blind eye was generally turned so long as it stayed behind closed doors.

Major Terrance Burelli's personal vid-cell had rung roughly an hour after their fun had begun. He glanced down at the display on his vid-cell, but the incoming number had been blocked. He looked one more time at his hand and confirmed that the cards he had were useless. He folded, got up from the table, and walked into the next room before he answered his unknown call — it wasn't something that he normally did, but he wanted to stretch his legs anyway.

"Hello, Terrance," said the caller. "How's it going? Do you have any idea who this is?"

"No I don't know who the hell this is since you are refusing to show me your damn face? This is a private vid-cell number. How did you get it?"

"Well now... I see you still have that short temper, even after all these years, Terrance. Come on now, I can't believe that you don't recognize my voice? I'll give you a clue. I spared your life."

Terrance didn't have to search his memory for long to figure out who was calling him — and he was not at all happy that a ghost from his not-too-proud past had picked this moment to resurface and uninvitingly haunt him. Immediately, Terrance thought about disconnecting his call. But he knew that doing so would not prevent his ghost from trying to make contact with him again. He had no choice in that moment but to deal with this call and hope that when it was over, the man on the other end would understand and abide by his desire to be left alone — forever.

The same image that was implanted in Terrance's mind, a few seconds later, appeared on his vid-cell screen — and although this one was much older looking than what he remembered, there was no denying that it was Salvadore Batiste staring at him with a genuine egocentric look. Never in a million years did Terrance ever expect to see him again. He prayed almost every night that part of his life would never, ever become known. He had done everything he could, and then some, to keep his past hidden from everyone — especially the military. Now, that one mistake he made from his impetuous youth had resurfaced to haunt him. "What reason would there be, Sal, for you to contact me?"

"Well... It's been a long time since we spoke last and I was beginning to feel like you forgot about me. So I just thought that I'd give you a quick buzz."

Terrance never forgot about Sal or the others. In fact, he remembered vividly that one specific day, all those years ago, when Sal had told him that he had been ordered by Louie to dispose of him — and he never forgot that he owed Sal his life for not following through with that order. All Terrance had to do for Sal was to complete one last task and he would let him disappear. He never understood why Sal had done this? Maybe it was because he had remembered hearing that Sal and Louie never really liked each other and he did this in spite of the man. Or maybe, this was just Sal's way of silently flipping off Antonio for something that he did not agree with. Whatever his reason was, Terrance wasn't about to question it after all this time. "When you told me to disappear, I assumed that I'd never hear from the D.U.O. again. My nose has been squeaky clean ever since I did what you asked of me, and I plan on keeping it that way. My involvement with the D.U.O. was the biggest mistake of my life. I'm sorry, Sal, but I can't risk having anyone overhearing this conversation. From now on, if it is that important that you feel the need to contact me, please just send a text or V-mail and I'll return your message when I'm in a more private setting. With all due respect, please don't call me on my vid-cell again."

"No problem, Terrance. I do understand the position you are in. I won't call you ever again. However, there will come a day where your skills will be needed and I will expect your co-operation when I contact you."

Terrance did not immediately respond to Sal's statement. He knew that he had a favor to repay — he just hoped that day would never come. "I'd honestly prefer that you never ask me for anything... ever."

"No guarantees on that request. Remember, you agreed to work for us. And because you had, you became a part of our world for life. Even though Antonio and Louie believe that you are dead, that doesn't excuse you from paying back your debt. The statue of limitations does not apply here. Just because I have not asked anything of you over the last twenty-five years, does not mean that I won't in the future."

Terrance was not happy that Sal had just laid down his hand. Unfortunately, he knew that the man still held one more trump card — that damn favor that Terrance owed him. He had tried his best over the years to conceal his whereabouts, but he obviously failed — Sal had somehow found him. And even if Terrance were to try again: maybe change his name, leave the military and disappear to some remote island, he was sure that Sal could find him again with relative ease. As much as it ate away at his soul, for as long as Terrance stayed alive, he knew that he was bound to Sal's beck and call.

"I know that you want to hang up on me right now, but don't. I didn't call you today to cash in that favor. Instead, I just felt that it was important that I, as your only friend within the D.U.O., pass along some pertinent information of which I think you just might be interested in."

Terrance kept looking over his shoulder through the doorway into the room that everyone was gambling in, afraid that someone was listening to his unwanted conversation. Although Sal had asked him not to hang up, he wanted to do just that — especially since he wasn't being asked today to pay back that favor. But Terrance didn't. His curiosity was beginning to push aside his sensibility.

After a few seconds of thought, influenced by his ever growing paranoia, Terrance said to his one-time associate, "I don't think that I want to know whatever it is that you think I should. The less that I know about anything tied to your organization, the better off I will be. I am sorry, Sal. I don't wish to be rude, but I have to go now. Goodbye." Terrance disconnected his call; shut his vid-cell completely off, and then spent a few moments trying to calm his nerves. The only thing he knew for sure at that moment was that he needed to get himself a new vid-cell number.

Paranoid that someone did, but still hoping that no one had overheard his conversation, Terrance placed his vid-cell back into his pocket, and wandered unsurely back into the room where his fellow officers were not only feeling just a bit buzzed, but the 'company' that they had ordered had arrived. Terrance quickly scanned those who were in the room; he did not notice any signs that anyone had heard his conversation — but that didn't mean that someone didn't, nor did it mean that he could allow himself to feel relieved.

Terrance took his chair, smiled at those who were in the room, and then apologized for missing a few hands. He sat back down in his chair, fully expecting that someone was going to say something — they didn't, so he poured himself a stiff shot of Forty Creek whiskey, and exhaled a breath that surprisingly, unleashed some of his built up tension.

Right after he had taken his first sip, he felt a hand on his shoulder. The first thing that went through his mind was that one of his military brethren was about to inquire about his call. But then

Terrance realized that the hand touching his shoulder was too dainty to belong to one of his senior brethren — it had instead, belonged to one of the ladies who had been invited to join them.

Terrance took a hold of the young woman's hand; she invited herself to take up a seat on his lap. His card playing luck had been pretty shitty up until his call — maybe that had been a sign that this evening was going to be one that he wanted to forget. Then again, there was a way for him to salvage some of it, so after playing a few more losing hands, he excused himself from the game and led his consort to the stairs. One look at her walk as she made her way up to the second floor and Terrance knew that his troubles were going to be taken care of. By morning, Terrance was certain that he was going to wake up with a smile on his face. Unfortunately, it would not be enough to make him completely forget about the unwanted revisiting of his not-too-proud past.

Life around Maxwell's office had ceased to exist ever since he had decided to go to Detroit. The more time that went by without any confirmation, the more time Sydney and Savanna had spent stressing over the unknown. As each day passed by, the chances increased that insanity would take full control over them.

Day ten had come and gone; a record number of cups of sim-caf, and even some Red Bull, had been consumed. By the next morning, there still hadn't been any news. The waiting around for that call was the most helpless feeling that a person could have — and that is why both Sydney and Savanna decided that they had waited long enough. Even though Governor White had told them to just stay at home and let the police do what they were paid to do, neither one of them liked feeling useless. Being kept in the dark was no longer going to be accepted. They wanted answers, so they booked themselves on the first available flight to Detroit.

Upon arriving in Michigan, Sydney and Savanna immediately went to the State Capitol Building in Lansing, as all that they wanted was a chance to speak to the governor and offer him their help. Of course, gaining entrance to the governor's office would involve more than just hacking a secure access number on a computer — that was something they'd just have to figure out once they got there.

"Hello, there. Your name is Sylvia, right?"

"Yes it is. Do we know each other?"

"My name is Savanna Rivard. I spoke..."

"Oh, I'm sorry, I didn't recognize you. Your hair is styled completely different than when we last spoke on the vid-phone. I mean, I like the haphazard look and all, but I..." Sylvia paused. She felt a bit embarrassed once she realized that she had just put her foot into her mouth. Her genuine attempt at being friendly with Savanna had probably insulted her instead. "...Anyway, it's nice to finally meet you in person." Sylvia stood up and reached across her desk to shake Savanna's hand — even though she didn't honestly think that Maxwell's secretary was going to accept it.

Savanna did; Sylvia smiled, happy that her unintentional insult had not been taken to heart. She then took a puzzled pause, noticing that both Savanna and the gentleman that was standing next to her, were wearing state capitol tour guide badges which read, '*Dawn and Garrison*' respectively. It was then that Sylvia realized how the two of them had managed to make it all the way up to the governor's office without first being escorted by the building's security. *'I think the Governor needs to be made aware of the possibility that our security might have a few issues that need to be addressed,'* she thought.

Savanna just stood there with a somewhat guilty smile on her face once she realized that the governor's secretary had noticed the tour guide badges that they had swiped. She immediately removed her state capitol badge and placed it on Sylvia's desk. "Uh... I'm sorry about that. It's just that... we couldn't stand waiting around any longer for some news about Maxwell, so we flew into Detroit this morning, hoping that we could offer our help with locating him. I may only be Maxwell's secretary, but I've learned a lot from him over the years when it comes to finding people."

Sylvia could not begin to fathom what they were going through. She could however, definitely understand how desperate they both were for answers. "I really don't blame you for coming. I'd probably do the same thing if I were in your situation." Sylvia then looked over at Sydney and addressed him somewhat cynically. "I assume that your name really isn't Garrison, is it?"

"No, it's not. My name is Sydney, and I am Maxwell's younger brother."

"It's a pleasure to meet you, Mr. Banks." Sylvia extended her hand for Sydney to shake.

Sydney accepted it, but he didn't shake it. He instead, decided that he would greet her with a gesture that some might consider inappropriate, while some might consider it to be a touch romantic — he placed a gentle kiss on the backside of her hand. "If you wish, you may call me Garrison. It is, after all, a much more exotic name than my given one," Sydney declared, while sporting a somewhat impish smile.

"Well I can definitely tell that you and Maxwell are brothers. You, Mr. Banks, are without a doubt, a tarnished heirloom that will by no means shine no matter how much effort you put into polishing it." Sylvia glanced over at Savanna and noticed her trying desperately to hold back her laughter.

"That may be so, my dear," Sydney replied, but I do have the ability to make anyone's wish come true, no matter how unattainable it may seem to be."

Savanna's jaw dropped. She found it very hard in that moment not to reach out and slap Sydney for his chauvinistic comment. He had, after all, just made himself look like an old pervert — whether or not it was intentional.

After taking a sip of water from her mug, Sylvia invited Savanna and Sydney to take up a seat in the lobby area. She then explained to them that the governor was currently in an important meeting with some state officials, and that she would go and find out how much longer his meeting was going to be.

Sylvia then excused herself, left her desk, and walked on down the short hallway to the conference room off to the left at the end. Once there, she placed her palm up against the infrared identi-scanner, entered her access code, and walked into the room.

With the governor's secretary now out of sight, Savanna promptly kicked Sydney's shin.

Sydney reacted with a sharp cry of pain, as Savanna's kick had connected solidly. "What the hell was that for?"

"That was for being a dirty old man," Savanna answered. "Give it a rest. You're more than twice her damn age."

"I'm way passed my prime dear. So whenever the opportunity presents itself, I shall do everything that I can in order to continue feeling young."

Savanna didn't have a rebuttal for that last comment. She just sat there quiet, looking away from Sydney, and wondering why all of a sudden he was acting like he was. She had never in all the years that she had known him seen him act so juvenile-like. She knew that Maxwell could regress and that 'inner child' of his would surface on occasion, but never had she seen Sydney do it. *'This must be some kind of genetic, family flaw,'* she thought.

A few moments later, Sylvia stepped out of the conference room and motioned for the two of them to join her. Once they had, she led Savanna and Sydney down another short hallway off to the right of the conference room and directed them into the governor's office. As she was leaving, she encouraged them to make themselves comfortable and made them aware that the governor would meet with them very shortly.

After first admiring the artwork, police accommodations, and other eclectic artifacts displayed throughout the office, Sydney took up a position in front of the large picture window, standing almost lifeless, and staring out at the city below. He then began observing the pedestrians as they waited across the street for the bus. For his own amusement, Sydney began to describe some of the pedestrians he saw using extreme colorful comparisons to lower life forms — others, he commented on by using non-flattering, derogatory remarks about their appearances.

Savanna's tolerance towards Sydney's unusual behavior this day was quickly beginning to disappear; however she continued to do her best to ignore it. This was a difficult time for the both of them and Savanna was certain that Sydney's antics were just his way of coping with everything so that he would not have to acknowledge the uncertainty of his brother's well being.

Irritated as she was, she humored him by pretending to listen, cracking the occasional smile, or even expending the odd chortle of noise. And while she did her best to block out the occasional remarks of his that had clearly crossed the line, her own train of thought had begun to wander off track. Without realizing it, she had begun to nonchalantly snoop through the governor's top desk drawer.

"Sorry that I took so long," Christopher said, as he entered his office.

Savanna had been unprepared for the governor's sudden appearance. She recovered well though, as she quickly sprung up from behind the governor's desk, and in one indiscrete motion, quietly shut the drawer that she had been sifting through. "I'm sorry for sitting behind your desk, Governor. The chair looked really comfortable and I just wanted to get off my feet for a bit and relax, as it's been a long and stressful week and a half." Savanna's lie sounded pretty convincing, considering that in the process of closing the desk drawer, she had inadvertently broken off one of her nails, causing her mind to fight to control her instant rush of pain.

"That's all right, don't worry about it. Being that it's a hybrid tempur-pedic, synth-leather office chair, it's easy to fall asleep in it — especially if you are even remotely tired, as I tend to get after one of those three hour meetings like the one I just finished." The governor then reached out and shook Savanna's hand, noticing but not acknowledging that she was missing one of her nails. "Please feel free to call me Chris."

Sydney then walked up to the governor and shook his hand. "I'm Maxwell's brother, Sydney."

"I figured as much," the governor said as he walked around behind his desk. "I can definitely see the resemblance between you and him." As Christopher sat down in his office chair, he encouraged both Savanna and Sydney to do the same in the two chairs that were in front of his desk. "I can only assume that the reason you both are here is because neither one of you felt that you could wait around any longer back in San Antonio for word on Maxwell's whereabouts."

"Exactly. We decided to come to here and offer you our services to help find him."

That was the expected response to the assumption that the governor already had before he entered his office. Immediately, he held up his right hand; a universal sign that he knew they would understand. "I know that this is very difficult for the both of you right now, but I'm asking that you just please let the authorities who are working on this, handle it. Ok?"

"Obviously, they're not doing a good enough job! My brother is still missing!"

"Calm down, Sydney... please." Savanna leaned over and placed her hand on the side of his right arm. "I'm sorry, Chris. It's just that we feel so damn helpless waiting around for some sort of news. We feel that we need to do something since we still know nothing."

As Christopher was listening to Savanna speak, he opened up the top drawer of his desk — once a police officer, always a police officer. He was aware that Savanna had been harmlessly sifting through his desk drawer, and now he was curious to see if he could figure out what had drawn her interest. He knew what he kept inside that drawer; which wasn't very much — that was why he was able to easily spot Savanna's missing nail right away, lying inside the front left hand corner. "That's not entirely true. The police that have been assigned to locate Maxwell's whereabouts received an anonymous voice mail shortly before I went into my meeting an hour ago. That message was brief, but it did supply us with an approximate location. Then, just before my meeting ended, I was informed that the police had located Maxwell's rental car."

The governor could immediately see a glimmer of hope appear in Savanna's eyes; Sydney's expression did not change. He seemed to not take the news of the rental car's discovery as a good sign. He was right. All that meant was that they finally had a starting point to begin their search. "Don't get your hopes up. It has been so long since Maxwell's disappearance, that the chances of him still being in that area are not that good. But this does give the police that first solid lead they've been looking for"

"Well, any news is good news as far as I'm concerned," Savanna stated.

The governor's vid-phone beeped and startled Savanna. It was Sylvia calling to let him know that he had an important incoming call from Captain Stratton. Immediately, Christopher excused himself, got up from behind his desk, and walked over to Savanna; he was sporting a 'you've just been busted' kind of smirk on his face. He then handed her missing nail back to her, and left his office to take his awaiting call in private in the conference room.

Less than five minutes later, the governor returned to his office; he had a look on his face that was easy to read. In that moment, Savanna and Sydney didn't need to hear what the governor's call was all about, as they both knew that what he had just learned was not good news.

"Um… that call was about Maxwell, wasn't it?"

"Yes. After searching the area where Maxwell's car was found, the police were able to find the clues they needed to locate him…"

Sydney knew exactly what it was that the governor was going to say next — and he didn't want to hear it. Because once he did, then he knew that there would be that finality to what he and Savanna feared. So he got up from his chair and walked over to the lone office window where he aimlessly looked out it.

The governor followed his old friend's brother and joined him at the window. He then placed his hand on Sydney's shoulder and looked apologetically at him. "I'm so sorry… but your brother is dead. His body was found a short time ago in the Detroit River."

A few tears had already started to fall before the governor had made it official what she knew in her heart to be. Savanna's world immediately came crashing down. In disbelief, she just sat there and covered her face with her hands. "This can't be?"

"What the hell happened to him?" Sydney asked.

"I don't think that I should tell you what I know," the governor said. "I think it's best that the two of you just check into a hotel and get some rest. I'll get in touch with you when I get some more details."

"I want to know what you know," Sydney requested; his eyes still locked onto what he could see on the other side of the office window.

After briefly organizing his thoughts, Christopher returned to his desk chair; he invited Sydney to return to his seat. Several seconds of unnerving silence then passed before Christopher felt ready enough to begin the dreadful task at hand; a task that seemed at that moment to be much more difficult than any other unpleasant one he previously had back when he was a captain or the chief of police.

He warned Savanna and Sydney that the few details he had were gruesome; hoping that they would be able to somewhat prepare themselves for the truth. Once he was certain they were as ready as they were ever going to be, the governor explained that Maxwell's body had been found inside of a custom made steel box that had been filled with cement, and then sunken into one of the deepest parts of the Detroit River. If it weren't for the fact that the coast guard had access to the latest in sonar imagery, they probably would have never been able to locate where Maxwell's body had been dumped.

"Oh my God," Savanna responded in horror. "Why in God's name would someone do such a heinous thing to Maxwell?"

"I don't know why?" Christopher then folded his arms across his chest. Guilt was flowing throughout his body, but he knew that his hands had been tied and there was nothing that he could have done to prevent what had happened to Maxwell. "I'm so sorry, but your brother insisted that I not get involved."

There was no hate, and there was no anger. Sydney instead, looked the governor directly into his eyes and said, "It's not your fault. I fully understand the position that you were in… and I know how stubborn my brother is." Sydney paused for a moment so that he could try to keep his emotions in check. "I remember Maxwell telling me once before that your relationship with him for the most part, contained more animosity than it did admiration. And that was why you eventually realized that your only option was to become one of his very close friends in order to try and understand him better."

Even in this somber moment, Christopher could not help but smile. Only Maxwell would explain his friendship with him in that manner. "In all honesty, as many times as we found ourselves at odds with each other, especially when I became his boss, there was always a lot of respect there. That is the real reason why we became good friends."

That was something that Sydney believed. Just by looking into Christopher's eyes, he could tell that the man was very distraught about Maxwell's unfortunate passing. Therefore, he hoped that with what was to come next, the governor would graciously be willing to help them.

There were two things that Sydney needed from Christopher White. First, he asked him if he could have his secretary find them a decent hotel in Detroit, as Maxwell's funeral would need to be planned. The second thing he hoped to get from the governor was a 'yes', as he wanted him to be the one to give his brother's eulogy.

It was a request that Christopher did not expect, nor was it one that he could refuse — it was also a request that he admittedly, felt uncomfortable with. He hadn't seen Maxwell for twenty-five years and was uncertain that he could properly explain the life of a man whom he had only really known for about five years. But from what he had remembered, to what he had been reminded of when Maxwell had re-appeared in his office, the man had not changed. Other than his reason for living, Maxwell Banks had been the same man that Christopher had known all those years ago. Therefore, the governor's hesitancy had quickly disappeared and he felt honored that this responsibility had been bestowed upon him.

Epilogue

August tenth, two-thousand and thirty-five will forevermore be remembered as the day in which Detroit's Law Enforcement lost one of its well respected past heroes; a loss that has left a sour taste in the mouth of those who protect and serve. Although there are very few police officers that are still around now who were serving when Maxwell Banks was, this heinous crime committed against a man who once fought for justice, has caused an unsightly black mark to permanently scar this once stately union of respected members.

Because of what had occurred, there are questions that now needed to be answered. Could the citizens of this great city continue to feel safe? They would like to believe so. But with such an uncertainty being there, what assurances do the people of Detroit have that they will be protected? None! The only thing they have left is their hope; hope that the way things are will not be the way things will continue to be.

And what about the city's law enforcement? Do they even feel safe? The answer to that question is — probably not. But it's their job nevertheless to continually enforce the law to the best of their ability and help to work on a way to neutralize the city's biggest threat.

For years, too many years, law enforcement officials have been baffled. The Detroit Underworld Organization has somehow found a way to continually do whatever it has wanted to do, whenever they wanted. The city wide C-4 network was supposed to give law enforcement a major advantage when it came to fighting crime. But ever since it went on-line, the D.U.O. has somehow found a way to maneuver itself around it. Is Detroit better off with the C-4 network? Yes, it is. Has the C-4 network done what it was supposed to do? No, it has only acted as a deterrent to those who commit petty crimes; it has done nothing to prevent any well-organized groups or individuals from breaking the law. To those who agreed to let Detroit become one of the first cities to use this network, a consensus feeling of failure was there — a very expensive failure it appears to be.

Many of Detroit's citizens, some political officials, and some officers of the law, are actually close to giving up hope. They honestly believe that it is only a matter of time before the city is no longer theirs. The evidence is easy to see. Even a blind person can see just how hopeless it will become if this city can't find a way to remove the poison that is running through its veins. It doesn't matter that the poison is, in a very twisted way, responsible for the complete revitalization of its downtown core. It has to be neutralized. Unfortunately, there are those in city counsel who truly feel that things are going to get much worse before a solution is found — especially if the D.U.O. continues to add at will to its already massive conglomerate.

To give up and say that the city is now beyond repair would be considered premature. There are still many who feel that it can be salvaged and returned to a city that those who choose to live in, can be proud of. But for that to even begin to happen, an aggressive plan immediately needs to be put into place, and someone needs to step up and execute it. The problem is that no one has any idea who would have the wherewithal to take on such a task.

Could all of this have been prevented? Certainly it could have. Who is to blame for allowing this to occur? Some say that those who were in political power when the D.U.O. first became more than just a gang of thugs were responsible for allowing that to happen. Some say that city cutbacks to necessary services and limiting resources available to the police had a lot to do with it. Others believe that this was allowed to happen because there were those who just did not care and willingly allowed their own palms to be greased. And then there were those who were in a position of power that just did not believe that the D.U.O. ever had the potential to grow and become a viable threat.

Neither one individual, nor one organization or group is to blame for this. Ignorance is to blame for what the city of Detroit now has to suffer through — a problem that just may already be too big to ever solve.

———————————————————— ◯◯ ————————————————————

Death is inevitable. We unfortunately, do not have the luxury of knowing when that will occur. We do, however control our own lives. Some of us end up making a decision pertaining to it, which others will never understand — but to us, it makes perfect sense. Every once in a while, our existence on this earth will come to a premature end: because someone has chosen to take their own life, because someone was in the wrong place at the wrong time, because someone had chosen to make the ultimate sacrifice to protect those whom they love, because someone was unfortunately stricken with an incurable disease, or because someone's decisive courage allowed them to take on an insurmountable task against an evil entity that just had to be stopped.

The latter is what Maxwell Banks had attempted to do. Although he had still been healthy enough to continue on living for many more years, he knew in his heart that his existence on the earth had to end — and he was content with that inevitably happening. Still, his sacrifice just did not make any sense to those who knew him; loved him. It seemed unwarranted; without merit — as if he had just given up so that he no longer had to carry around with him the burden of the unknown.

On a day of great sadness, the sun stayed away. The clouds were low, thick, and grey. The wind was somewhat strong and it was thankfully, far from cold. Still, this rather gloomy early spring day seemed to negatively influence the grieving individuals that gathered at the Holy Cross Cemetery.

Surrounding the hole in the ground where Maxwell's casket was suspended over, right beside the final resting place of his late wife, Sylvia Banks, were those who knew him well. Besides his brother Sydney, Savanna, and Governor Christopher White, former chief of police, Jacob Winslow was there along with his wife and daughter. Colin Ramirez and his wife, Olivia, were also in attendance, as well as several other officers from Maxwell's past — they included three recently retired officers who had been there with him that awful night and survived the explosion: Sharna Williams, Denny James and Samuel Everett. Also who had been there and survived that night, Abdul Hassam, the man who had succeeded Christopher White as captain, and who now just recently accepted the position of chief. Additionally, there were two R.C.M.P. officers in attendance, both of whom Maxwell had worked with when he first became an officer of the law back in Ottawa — his first partner and his first commanding officer.

Maxwell's death seemed to hit everyone hard. No one seemed to know how to deal with, or fully understood how this tragedy could have occurred. The emotions that encompassed the man's final resting place seemed more intense than what there would normally be at someone's funeral. Yes, Maxwell had been a very well respected officer during his day, but it wasn't until his death that people who knew him finally realized just how much of an impact he had made in their lives.

Being there today brought back all the guilt that Colin Ramirez had worked so hard to suppress. It had taken him nearly five years after the warehouse explosion before he had been able to do just that. Today, it all came back to him. Once again, he felt as if he was to blame for all of this; this moment, Maxwell's funeral, was all because he had become complacent — and that was also what had put him in a wheel chair. Because he had failed to do what was necessary to gather the needed evidence to shut down the D.U.O. when it was still a 'fly by night' organization, four good men had lost their lives. Aaron Thompson, Charles Blake, Joshua Brampton and now, Maxwell Banks were dead, all because of his self-assurance. Colin Ramirez had failed as a police officer. If he had paid more attention to his job and not simply rested on his laurels, Lenora Lexington would not have stabbed him in the back, he would not be paralyzed, and four of his brethren would probably still be alive.

Unfortunately, there was nothing that Colin could do to change the past. He had made his choice: Aaron, Charles, Joshua & Maxwell had made their choices. They each knew what it meant to be a police officer and what risks came along with being one. Still, what had happened to them was something that Colin knew in his heart, whether legitimate or not, he was partially responsible for — he just wished that there was something that he could do so that their deaths would not be in vain.

Sydney and Savanna stood beside Governor White at the head of Maxwell's casket; each trying their best to keep it together. This was a sad moment for not just them, but for everyone. Maxwell had touched a lot of lives and had inspired many. For that reason, Savanna knew that she would forever be proud of the man who had stepped into the role of father, mentor, and had influenced her life more than she had ever expected he would.

For Sydney, his life had forever changed. As much as he loved to rip on his brother for being 'old', there was a love for him that he did not know was as strong as it had been. Not until his brother had been taken from him, did he even realize the kind of bond he had with Maxwell. Now, Sydney was alone. He was the last of his family; a bloodline that had been traced back hundreds of years to Marseille, France.

He had never had any children of his own. Now, Sydney had wished that he had not been so scared of fatherhood; of commitment. He had just been content to let the years go by and hope that his soul mate would one day appear at his doorstep. It was a very foolish belief on his part for someone who would never hesitate to give of himself to others who needed it. So in that moment, he made a promise to himself — to Maxwell. He was too old to start his own family, but he wasn't too old to find it. Sabastian was still out there, and until proof was had that he was not alive, Sydney was going to spend the remainder of his life trying to find his nephew.

Savanna and Sydney parted and allowed Governor White to step in between them. Once there, he asked the crowd to all join hands; the clouds, almost on cue, separated directly above them and allowed the day's first bit of sun to peak through. The rays shone directly over Maxwell's casket, encasing it like a natural spotlight.

"We are gathered here today to honor the memory of a man who not only touched our lives, but fought to make a difference; not just here in this great city of ours, but wherever he chose to live. Although he had spent many years away from here, his influence on those whose serve and defend this city is still felt to this day. Maxwell Banks was dedicated, determined, and relentless; that was what had made him one of the most respected individuals to ever wear a police uniform.

After his wife had died," Governor White pointed with his opened hand at Sylvia's grave, "he continued to fight. Though his pain had taken him away from here, he still lived by the same convictions he always had. He always stood up for what was right, helped those

who were in trouble, and rescued those who needed to be."
Christopher glanced over at Savanna; she smiled back at him knowing
that he was referencing her.

"Maxwell was sent to us for a reason. For those of us gathered
here today who knew him, it was to make each of us a better person.
For those who didn't know him, his purpose was simple — to leave a
lasting impression in hopes that by crossing his path, their path would
change. And I can honestly declare, as we all stand here this day and
say goodbye to Maxwell, we are all better off because we knew him...
because he became our friend."

Governor White then stepped back, removed his old police
revolver from his inside jacket pocket; former officers' Williams,
James, Everett, Colin Ramirez, Chief Hassam, and Jacob Winslow did
the same. They each stood side by side, aimed their police revolvers
up into the sky, and fired twenty-one shots; saluting a man who
deserved more than the cards he had been dealt.

A few seconds after that observance was complete, those who
had gathered to pay their respects began to disperse. Savanna and
Sydney had stayed beside Maxwell's casket, waiting for one final bit
of alone time so that they could privately say their goodbyes.
Governor White returned to their side and had planned on
participating, but then Colin Ramirez quickly garnered his attention.
All that Colin had to do was point with his eyes and Christopher
immediately became aware that they had spectators off in the distance.

Although there were plenty of cars parked along the roadway
that led into the cemetery grounds; near the front entrance by Dix
Drive, there was a parked jet black Cadillac Escalade IV. Standing
along the backside of the vehicle were three people. Yes, their faces
were just too far away to positively identify, but both Colin and
Christopher knew who they were — and neither were at all happy that
they had come to essentially gloat.

In that instant, Christopher wanted to take his gun and fire off
the remaining three shots he had, but he knew that would be a waste of
time and an irresponsible thing for him to do. As much as he was
certain that those who were here and were formally under his
command would follow suit, Christopher knew that this was not the

time or place to enact their revenge. That day would come soon enough when the D.U.O. finally got what they deserved.

Colin was pissed that Antonio, Louie, and Sal, had the nerve to show their faces here at Maxwell's funeral. Like Christopher, he wanted to empty his gun at them — but he was too far away. Unless he knew a way to ensure that his shots would cleanly take out all three targets, he thought it best that he refrain from acting on his impulses. Yes, he owed these three bastards more than just the fact that he was wheelchair bound — in the name of his brethren who lost their lives, he wanted revenge. But his confinement; his disability all but assured that he would probably never get a chance to even the score. Still, if the opportunity ever came his way, he would not think twice about putting a bullet in any one of their backs. To him, an eye for an eye was the only thing that would even the score.

Former officers Sharna Williams, Samuel Everett, and Denny James, along with Chief Hassam, all clued into what was suddenly going on. Although three of them were no longer active police officers, each followed suit and aimed their police revolvers. Combined, the five of them had fifteen shots left. But Christopher quickly made sure that none of them did what he knew they all wanted to do — this just was not the time or the place.

After he was certain that his instructions would be adhered to, the governor started to walk toward the Cadillac. His intent was only to send a message to Antonio and his men; a message that he unfortunately, did not get a chance to verbally communicate.

They were the enemy, but they were not stupid. They knew that their presence was not welcomed. Still, Antonio felt it was necessary for them to see firsthand if the man, who had been one of the biggest thorns in the organizations side, was indeed dead. This service had officially ended the existence of Maxwell Banks — to him, this was the icing on the cake that he had waited twenty-five years to taste.

Recognizing that it was time to leave, Antonio, Louie and Sal got into their vehicle and promptly drove off. He knew that the graveyard was no place to get into a confrontation with the law — or what was once the law. Their appearance here had been strictly for personal satisfaction. However, he didn't expect that a message of any kind would come his way — and it was one that Antonio could not dismiss. This was far from over. One day, when he least expected it, someone was going to be coming for him and his organization. Who that was, Antonio had not a clue. But he was certain that he could no longer take for granted that he was going to easily win this war and control the city. Whether he liked it or not, his organization was now a target — no longer was it just an awaiting threat.

Christopher knew that the only reason those three bastards had showed up here on this day was to rub salt in their wounds. However, the moment he started to walk toward them, Christopher saw an acknowledgement on Antonio's face. The game had changed. The man now clearly understood that the written law was no longer going to apply, that the rulebook was going to be torn up, and that he was now public enemy number one.

"When one door closes another door opens; but we so often look so long and so regretfully upon the closed door, that we do not see the ones which open for us." (Quote from Alexander Graham Bell)

He knew that he was standing, but he had no idea where he was. All that he saw was white. If this was heaven, then God certainly needed to hire an interior decorator — vivid white upon white upon white was very hard on the eyes.

Maxwell took a few steps forward, hoping that he would not fall. He could not see the floor, any walls, the ceiling, what was ahead, or even behind him. There seemed to be no sense of perception where he was nor did he even have a clue just how big of a room he was in — if he was even in a room at all. He knew that he was walking on a solid surface, as he could hear the heels of his shoes make contact with each step he took. The funny thing was though, as he walked, the noise his heels made did not echo at all.

After a few moments of aimlessly walking, the intense white began to soften somewhat. It didn't dull down any, but he was finally able to register just how vast the wide-open space that was around him appeared to be. Even though proof was not yet there, Maxwell believed he was in an actual room — and not just because he saw up ahead of him, two oversized white leather chairs that faced each other.

Both chairs were spaced about ten feet apart; one of them was already occupied by a man whom Maxwell could easily see radiated of importance. At that moment, he had a pretty good idea who this man may be — but until he knew for sure, Maxwell wasn't about to assume anything. What Maxwell was certain of though, was that a one on one meeting was waiting for him.

Although this individual was sitting down, he could easily tell that the man probably stood no shorter than six foot eight. He was wearing only a pair of off-white colored jeans, had straight golden brown hair that hung down just past his shoulders, and was clean-shaven. And although a man's body was not something that Maxwell would ever take the time to check out, this individual's upper torso was hard to ignore. There was just no disputing the facts that this ethereal man had muscles upon muscles; washboard-like abs that one could actually do laundry on. Yes, this man belonged on the cover of a Harlequin romance novel, and he also could easily steal your wife and there would be absolutely nothing that you could do about it. He was what every out of shape male wished they looked like. "Mr. Banks. Please take a seat." Even the tone of the man's voice had a romantic vibrato to it.

Maxwell did what was asked of him and briefly scanned the man's sculptured features as he sat — his eyes even briefly wandered where a straight man's should not. He did this only because he just wanted to confirm his suspicions that the man was blessed with everything. *'Lucky bastard,'* he thought. But just because this man was the embodiment of perfection, didn't mean that Maxwell was willing to switch teams — he was content to stay on team hetero for all of eternity. "This isn't heaven, is it?"

"That is very perceptive of you."

"I was a cop and a private eye. My observation skills were pretty good."

"Yes. That fact, I am aware of, Mr. Banks."

"So then… where exactly am I?"

The man chose not answer him. He didn't see a reason to tell him that he was in a special area of his Netherworld.

Maxwell didn't like the lack of an answer he got — and just because he was dead, didn't mean that he had a lot of time on his hands to meaninglessly waste. He had no problem playing the waiting game for a while, but only because he was in the visitor's stadium and he had no idea what the ground rules were for this place. For that reason, he decided not to push for an answer that this man might not readily be willing to give. However, when the fourth quarter came to an end, he no longer would be willing to be left on the sidelines. "Ok then… why have I not gone to heaven? I don't think that I have done anything to warrant not going there."

"You were intercepted. And yes, you have done nothing to warrant going anywhere other than there.

"Then why was I… intercepted?"

"Because, Mr. Banks. You have unfinished business. The Fates have agreed with me that you are not yet finished walking the path that you were put on."

He hadn't intended to ask the man, but this was much different than what he had expected the afterlife to be like — apparently, specific decisions need to be made on occasion other than who goes where once they die. Maxwell wasn't too sure at that moment if he liked being a 'special case'; he just wanted his eternal existence to begin, not be delayed — his heart ached to be reunited with his wife. "So… am I correct in assuming then that you are not the Almighty Lord?"

"You are. I am not he."

"Then… who are you? And what gives you the right to do what you have. Only God has the right to determine whether or not I should be standing in front of the pearly gates in anticipation of admittance."

"I am a fallen. And as you can see, you are nowhere near the pearly gates because you failed to fulfill the true purpose of your existence on earth."

"My purpose?"

"Yes. You were born with a specific purpose. In fact, very few people are handpicked by the Fates to complete such an important task."

"Sorry… but if you had to live with the pain that I did, you'd understand why I chose to alter my so-called destiny."

"Giving up like you did is grounds enough for you to spend eternity in Purgatory. You blatantly turned a blind eye to your destiny and chose to walk away from it instead of doing what you were born to do."

"I was not born to live twenty-five years of my life in pain."

"You let your emotions fuel your pain instead of letting them fuel your motivation."

Maxwell was beginning to not like this fallen angel. If his memory served him correctly, a fallen angel is one of God's servants who have been banished from the heavens for committing an unforgivable sin. And if this individual was indeed a fallen, then Maxwell had certainly found himself in front of someone whom he needed to tread lightly.

This angel looked harmless, but he was certain that he had an agenda of some kind. Maxwell needed to gather some more information — but before he could understand what it was that he had to do to earn his ticket out of this place and go to where he was supposed to, Maxwell had to indulge this angel's reasons for intercepting him and bringing him here. "I think that you are mistaken. I was more motivated than a forty-year-old virgin would be who had deep pockets and was locked inside of a whorehouse. I spent twenty-five years of my life looking for my son with no viable leads whatsoever to go on. When that one lead finally came my way, I had to go after it with everything that I had."

The fallen leaned back in his chair and actually wanted to laugh at Maxwell's justification. Instead, he leaned forward and threw the crap right back in his face. "You never followed a lead pertaining to your son. You were finally given the excuse you were looking for in order to enact your revenge. You purposely leaped forward without a net and placed yourself in a position in which you knew full well you were going to fail. And don't tell me that you changed your mind once you assessed the situation. Even after realizing the difference you could have made, you chose to give up."

Ok, so this Angel did his homework. It now meant that Maxwell could not do what he was famous for; bullshit apparently was not going to work where he was. Here, only the truth was what mattered; it was something that he no longer could deny. He knew right from the beginning that his mission was doomed to fail and he had voluntarily walked right into his own execution. He had failed without trying or caring. But at the time, Maxwell just could not see any other option. In his mind, there was no way for him to ever come out the victor. His life had essentially been over since he had lost everything that had mattered to him. He thought that it was best he just concede defeat to his enemy and let his painful life be over with. "I made a decision to..."

"...To give up. You allowed your enemy to get inside your head, and instead of using the talents that God gave you to find your missing son and make those pay who were responsible for your wife's and fellow officer's deaths, you accepted the unproven facts that came your way and bowed to your enemy's wishes."

Again, this angel was right. Maxwell had easily been played and had not used his intelligence to change the game. Instead, he just quit. But that wasn't the only thing that was suddenly bothering him. This conversation with the angel had allowed his mind to open up, a mind that had been slammed shut by doubt.

When he had been bound to that chair in the warehouse, Antonio had declared that he had actually killed Sabastian — but the angel's words all but contradicted that statement. Maxwell suddenly felt ashamed. He had let years of uncertainty and failures dictate his decision. And because he had, not only had he thrown in the towel way too early, he had essentially turned his back on his own son. "There is nothing that I can do now to change what I've done. I am just thankful to know that Sabastian is indeed still alive."

"Ah… but there is something you can do. That is why you were intercepted."

A coffee table appeared between them both. On the table were two cups of fresh coffee, not sim-caf, but real coffee. The angel reached forward, picked up a cup, and then took a sip. He smiled, "Drink up."

Maxwell was hesitant. His first instinct was to leave the coffee on the table, assuming that there might be poison or a drug of some kind in it. But after a moment, he remembered one important thing — he was already dead. So Maxwell reached forward, picked up the other cup and took a healthy sip. He exhaled; the enjoyment of tasting real coffee for the first time in nearly a decade, instantly brought back memories of his early adulthood.

"I hope this will help you to relax and allow you to clear your mind because I am about to make you an offer that I believe you cannot refuse."

"Ok. But I first have a question."

"I know what it is that you want to ask of me. As a fallen angel, how is it that I am able to make you an offer… seeing that I no longer work for the Almighty Lord."

"You are in my head, aren't you?"

"No. But you're very easy to read, Mr. Banks."

Maxwell didn't reply to the angel. He had never been told by anyone that he was easy to read — he had always assumed that he had a pretty good poker face. How this fallen angel had known what he was thinking was irrelevant. What interested him more was what this offer was going to be.

"For the record, my boss is the one who is making you the offer. I am just the one who was asked to present it."

So, this angel was nothing but a puppet. That little bit of knowledge however, wasn't enough to put Maxwell in a position to challenge him. This ethereal being would probably kick his dead ass for even considering it. Instead, Maxwell kept his thoughts to himself and allowed the angel to continue.

"If you refuse his offer, you will leave here immediately and go to the realm that you were destined to spend eternity."

"Heaven?"

"Purgatory."

"What! Why?"

"Do you not remember what I said to you earlier?"

He did. At that moment, no convincing words came to Maxwell to help him to dispute the facts. He realized then that he was in no position to barter. Purgatory wasn't Hell, but it wasn't Heaven either. If what was being asked of him was the only way for him to have a chance of spending eternity in Heaven, then he had to do it. He only hoped that this angel would keep his word. "So… if I agree to your offer, once I have fulfilled my obligation, you will allow me to spend eternity in Heaven?"

"No. Unfortunately, I cannot send anyone to Heaven. Remember, I am a fallen angel. Let's just say that God has a rather large chip on his shoulder when it comes to me."

"If you can't send me to heaven, then why should I do what your boss, whoever that is, wants me to do?"

"Because my boss will revoke your one-way ticket to Purgatory and bring you right into his domain where you will then, spend the rest of eternity."

Maxwell didn't even need to ask what that domain was. And he also knew right then and there whom this angel's boss was and that he was someone whom he never wanted to meet in person. "Ok. But before I make my decision, I have another question. What happens to me after I complete this task that your boss wants done?"

"I do not know. It will be up to the Fates at that point to decide where your eternal resting place is. They were the ones who allowed me to intercept you and bring you here."

"I am getting a second chance?"

"Yes. It was you who decided to change the path that they put you on in the first place. It would be in your best interest to take this offer and make it right, because the Fates do not normally give anyone an opportunity like this."

"And if I accept this offer, when does my task begin?"

"Soon. Until then, this will be your home." The angel motioned with his arms, encircling the domain.

"The place is a little sterile, don't you think?"

"It is... but this will only be your home for as long as you are working for my boss."

"And... who exactly might that be? Lucifer?"

Again, the angel said nothing. No confirmation as to where he actually was, and no confirmation as to who the angel's boss was. Due to the lack of co-operation, Maxwell instantly threw up a guarded wall of his own. Whatever this offer was, Maxwell had to be certain that it would not cost him an eternal stay in some place where he did not want to be. "This here place where I will be staying," Maxwell put both of his hands out to the side and cynically looked around with his eyes. "What exactly is it?"

"Think of it as a 'Holodeck'. This is a place that will allow you to mindscape, invade someone's thoughts, or bring someone's unguarded soul to.

"As fun as that sounds, I don't think it is right to violate someone's thoughts for my own entertainment purposes."

The angel could not help but chuckle. Up until this point, Maxwell Banks had followed along pretty well — now, he seemed a bit lost. "If you accept the offer, this space will become an essential tool for you to use. The offer is basically another opportunity to get your revenge, as well as you having the ability to guide your son onto the path that he was meant to walk."

"The same path as mine?"

"Yes."

That sweetened the pot. But it also sounded way too good to be true. Maxwell knew that there had to be a catch of some kind — he just could not figure out what that might be. But before he officially accepted this outrageous offer, Maxwell decided to try again and get at least one of his questions answered. "Why is your boss giving me another crack at the D.U.O.?"

"Because he wants their souls; souls that he should have had possession of long before now."

That all but verified who the angel's boss was — The Prince of Darkness. Maxwell now had a decision to make. Refuse and essentially punch his own ticket to Hell, or accept a contracted position working for the Devil. The decision was now easy. "How am I supposed to accomplish this task?"

The fallen angel waved his left hand slightly and an object appeared on the edge of the coffee table nearest to Maxwell. "That is an Apollo's Stone. It is generally used to grant one last wish for a chosen soul that is condemned to an eternity in hell. Because that chosen soul is black however, the Apollo's Stone limits what the owner of that soul can do. But with your soul being near pure, you will have the ability to do things that are unimaginable."

"Like what?"

"That is something that you will have to figure out as you go."

"So... this stone is like a magic lamp?"

"Somewhat. But it will not grant unattainable thoughts and desires."

"I take it the reason for that is so those who are in possession of it don't use it for the wrong reasons?"

"Yes. And before you even ask, this stone will not grant you a second chance at life. Your life is over, Mr. Banks. This offer, if you agree to it, will bring you as close to being alive again as can be allowed."

Maxwell took a moment and absorbed what luck had just fallen into his lap. He had made a hasty decision that ultimately ended his life. Now, he had an opportunity to go back to earth in some kind of unknown form and make right what is still wrong — he might even get a chance to see his son for the first time in twenty-five years. This was an offer that he just could not refuse — even if it came from the devil himself. And then once this task was completed, Maxwell's soul would be in the hands of the Fates. Then hopefully, they would send it where it was always destined to be for all eternity. "This offer is very tempting."

"It is. Not many people get a second chance at fixing a huge mistake."

"That is true. But if I do agree to this, how am I supposed to complete my mission if I can't use the Apollo's Stone to become a living, breathing, human being again."

"It will not be easy, but it will be up to you to find a way to manipulate your enemies and lead them to their own demise without actually physically doing it yourself."

That small detail caused Maxwell to temporarily reassess what his decision was going to be. He was going to say yes, but now he wasn't sure that he would be able to do what was being asked of him. He got up from his chair and walked away. He could walk all day in this place, he speculated, and never find a wall or a window. The irony in that was, all of the walls that Maxwell had encountered when he was alive, were erected by his own doing. It was time for him to tear them all down so that nothing stood in his way — it was time for him to finish what had been handed to him all those years ago.

He stopped his walk, turned around and looked at the fallen angel. No longer was he in an infinite white space, he was now standing in his own living room — the angel was sitting on his sofa. "Why have you made this place look like my apartment?"

"I haven't, you have."

Maxwell looked in the palm of his left hand and for the first time, saw the swirl of incredible colors dancing within the Apollo's Stone. It was then that he realized the stone had replicated his thoughts. This was his apartment; this was where he wanted to be. This realm that he was in had been transformed by his thoughts. This is what the angel meant by 'Holodeck'. Now he understood why this place was going to be of use to him. Instantly, he began to conjure up several satisfying ways of fuckin' with his old enemies. Head games were the best form of mental warfare, and he was salivating at a chance to play again and use this space to control his own game for once.

The opportunity, which Maxwell was now being given, was one that he could have never foreseen. He'd be stupid to say no. And even though he knew that this was going to be a rather big challenge, it was one that Maxwell was now willing to take on. It no longer mattered to him that Lucifer was the one giving him this opportunity. Nor did it matter if he failed and ended up spending eternity in hell. The chance to use such a place to his advantage for one more shot at revenge would be worth the end result. "I accept."

"Good." The angel got up from Maxwell's couch, turned, and walked towards the apartment door. He didn't look back; a wall of white light replaced the door. The angel walked into it and slowly began to fade into the white nothingness.

Before he was completely gone however, Maxwell remembered that there was one other question that he was itching to know. "Hey! You never did tell me your name."

"It's Nefieti."

The fallen angel was gone, leaving Maxwell alone in this manifestation of his own apartment. He no longer cared where his eternal stay was going to eventually be. The only thing that he cared about now, was not squandering his second chance.

Maxwell took up a seat right where Nefieti had been and placed the Apollo's Stone on the glass coffee table in front of him. He curiously stared at it. He had never seen anything like this before, nor did he think that something like this even existed in the real world.

But then again, he wasn't in the real world. He was in a place that gave him a distinct home field advantage.

His mind had recreated his apartment; it only made sense that his mind was what controlled this Apollo's Stone. But Maxwell wasn't sure that he was ready to try and use his thoughts to control it; he only wanted to look at it right now and try to understand it. That, he was sure, would take some time — the Apollo's Stone was most certainly a magnificent and mysterious object that Maxwell was definitely looking forward to learning all about.

The neon-like colors of blue, yellow, purple, white, and green, harmoniously swirled together. It was incredible to watch. It looked almost as if the stone was alive. Maybe it was; maybe it wasn't. The only thing that Maxwell knew for certain was that his curiosity was locked onto it; more like, it was locked onto him — a connection had been established.

The longer that Maxwell stared at the stone, the happier he felt. For the first time in a long time, he felt joy. He also began to understand how it worked. It wasn't just his mind that controlled the stone — his emotions affected it as well. Now, all that he had to do was learn how to use both at the same time. Then once he was able to do that, he would begin to understand what the stone could do, how it could help him right what was still wrong, and how it could help him to get his revenge.

This stone was amazing. In time, he was certain that he would figure it all out. Until then, Maxwell was content to stay in his manifested apartment — not because he felt like he was home, but because he now had company. No, Nefieti had not returned.

Although he hadn't really tried, his emotions had unlocked one of the stone's abilities — it had allowed him to bring his wife to where he was. And as happy as that should have made him, he quickly learned that his desire wasn't what had brought her to him. In his thoughts, the reason suddenly appeared. The stone had the capability of summoning souls from other realms of the afterlife — but only whenever an aperture that led between them, was open.

The smile he had abruptly got much bigger. He had done it. He had controlled his emotions and for the first time ever, felt at peace. His wife was now with him — although he was certain that it was only temporary. And for the first time in twenty-five years, he could see his son.

Together, hand in hand, Maxwell and Sylvia looked into the Apollo's Stone at Sabastian, all grown up. He was a mirror image of who Maxwell once was; a young man who without a doubt, was going to continue on with the legacy that he had left behind — a young man who most certainly was going to make both of his parents proud.

To be continued...

*** Other releases ***

www.ingramcontent.com/pod-product-compliance
Lightning Source LLC
Chambersburg PA
CBHW031259170626
46807CB00001B/214